Pr

"Wildly delightful! With *Earl Crush*, Alexandra Vasti has crafted a marvelously funny and sexy read featuring a brawny Scottish earl, zebras, and a feminist heroine ahead of her time. This belongs on every romance reader's keeper shelf!"

—Joanna Shupe, *USA Today* bestselling author of *The Duke Gets Even*

"I dare anyone to read this book and walk away without a crush on this earl! Arthur Baird is the new definition of a pining, besotted hero, and his deep love and appreciation for Lydia Hope-Wallace's mind and courage had me swooning. Both a rollicking romp and the most tender of love stories, *Earl Crush* is sexy, kind, and full of adventure! Alexandra Vasti is an immense talent, and I look forward to reading everything she writes until the end of time!"

—Naina Kumar, *USA Today* bestselling author of *Say You'll Be Mine*

"With witty banter, endearing characters, and smoking-hot chemistry, Alexandra Vasti's *Earl Crush* will enchant readers and establish her as a breakout star of historical romance!"

—Liana De la Rosa, *USA Today* bestselling
author of *Isabel and The Rogue*

Praise for *Ne'er Duke Well*

"As hot as it is heartfelt, this will have historical romance fans hooked."   —*Publishers Weekly* (starred review)

"The kind of romance you want to wrap around yourself like a blanket."   —NPR

"*Ne'er Duke Well* is a delightful, quicksilver romp with unforgettable characters that readers will be rooting for from start to finish."

—Deanna Raybourn, *New York Times* bestselling author of the Veronica Speedwell series

"An irresistible delight from a remarkable new talent . . . Vasti has quickly earned her place on my list of favorite writers."

—India Holton, *USA Today* bestselling author of *The Ornithologist's Field Guide to Love*

"A witty page-turner with two adorable leads whose funny banter and chemistry is off the charts! I didn't want their antics to end."

—Virginia Heath, author of *Never Fall for Your Fiancée*

"Utterly delicious and undeniably clever, Alexandra Vasti's *Ne'er Duke Well* was unputdownable. . . . Regency romance fans everywhere will love this warm, wonderfully witty, and oh-so-sexy novel just as much as I did. What a spectacular debut!"

—Amy Rose Bennett, author of *Up All Night with a Good Duke*

Praise for the Halifax Hellions Series

"These stories are hot, smart, funny, and charming as hell—much like the Hellions themselves. I've read them each twice."

—Alix E. Harrow, *New York Times* bestselling author of *Starling House*

"Emotional and sexy and full of thrilling hijinks with jaw-dropping prose that transports you in every possible way. Each sibling and their partner has a unique journey, but there's an undeniable thread of finding radical acceptance in love that ties the three together beautifully. Alexandra Vasti has easily secured her place as a superstar in the genre."

—Jessica Joyce, *USA Today* bestselling
author of *You, with a View*

"Alexandra's plots are so zany and so fun but also earnestly explored and impeccably executed! Perfect for anyone who loves Tessa Dare but with a fresh voice wholly her own. I will pick up anything Alexandra writes."

—Rosie Danan, *USA Today* bestselling
author of *Do Your Worst*

"Delightful, truly scrumptious—like if Lisa Kleypas and Tessa Dare had a sexy baby. Alexandra Vasti is my favorite writer, full stop." —Mazey Eddings, *USA Today* bestselling author of *Late Bloomer*

"Filled to the brim with heart and heat, these absolutely delicious stories are not only ideal comfort reads but master classes in novella writing. I'm forever in awe of Alexandra Vasti's talent."

—Sarah Adler, *USA Today* bestselling author of *Happy Medium*

ALSO BY ALEXANDRA VASTI

Ne'er Duke Well

HALIFAX HELLIONS NOVELLAS

In Which Margo Halifax Earns Her Shocking Reputation

In Which Matilda Halifax Learns the Value of Restraint

In Which Winnie Halifax Is Utterly Ruined

Earl Crush

A NOVEL

ALEXANDRA VASTI

ST. MARTIN'S
GRIFFIN
NEW YORK

First published in the United States by St. Martin's Griffin, an imprint of St. Martin's Publishing Group

EARL CRUSH. Copyright © 2024 by Alexandra Vasti. All rights reserved. Printed in the United States of America. For information, address St. Martin's Publishing Group, 120 Broadway, New York, NY 10271.

www.stmartins.com

Designed by Omar Chapa

Library of Congress Cataloging-in-Publication Data

Names: Vasti, Alexandra, author.
Title: Earl crush : a novel / Alexandra Vasti.
Description: First edition. | New York : St. Martin's Griffin, 2025.
Identifiers: LCCN 2024034256 | ISBN 9781250910967 (trade paperback) | ISBN 9781250910974 (ebook)
Subjects: LCGFT: Romance fiction. | Novels.
Classification: LCC PS3622.A8584 E27 2025 | DDC 813/.6—dc23/eng/20240726
LC record available at https://lccn.loc.gov/2024034256

Our books may be purchased in bulk for promotional, educational, or business use. Please contact your local bookseller or the Macmillan Corporate and Premium Sales Department at 1-800-221-7945, extension 5442, or by email at MacmillanSpecialMarkets@macmillan.com.

First Edition: 2025

10 9 8 7 6 5 4 3 2 1

For the romance-reading Vasti women before me, who taught me that the genre is meaningful, joyful, and empowering. (And especially in memory of Grammy Vasti, who would have loved this book, even though I could not get a sexy shirtless man on the cover per her request.)

And for Matt, with love in abundance.

Earl Crush

Chapter 1

I am, undoubtedly, an idiot. Also an arse.

—*from the 1818 papers of Arthur Baird,*
Fifth Earl of Strathrannoch, unsent draft

"Based upon our respective financial situations, our mutually agreeable political interests, and the general compatibility of our persons," Lydia Hope-Wallace said, "it seems to both our advantages that we unite in holy matrimony."

Her voice shook only a trifle, which was a notable improvement.

Her friend Georgiana Cleeve gazed at her from across the post-chaise, expression impassive. Bacon, Georgiana's dog, gave Lydia a sympathetic moan from his position on Georgiana's lap.

Lydia winced. "Too wordy?" She fiddled with her sheaf of papers, trying not to look at her notes. Again. "I was afraid of that. Perhaps there is some way I can compress the language of the third clause—"

"I am not certain the *language* is the problem."

"Perhaps not." Lydia chewed on her lower lip and stared

blearily down at the papers in her lap, draft after penciled draft of marriage proposals in her own hand.

Marriage proposals. To a man she had never met.

It turned out it was rather difficult to get such a thing right.

She pulled out the pencil she'd stuffed into her coiffure and scratched out a hasty revision. "How about this: *Based upon the mutual benefits conferred by a legal union—*"

"*Mutual benefits?* Lydia, you are the third-richest unmarried heiress in London. The benefits are all Strathrannoch's."

"Second-richest, I think." Lydia frowned and drew a line through *compatibility of our persons*, which suddenly struck her as a bit indecent. "Hannah Harvey got engaged last week to that fellow in tin from Birmingham."

She drew a line through *mutual benefits* as well, for the sake of caution.

Georgiana cleared her throat, and Lydia redirected her gaze to her friend's finely drawn, deceptively innocent face.

"Perhaps," Georgiana said—as though she had not said it half a dozen times in the last week—"we might consider a social call on Lord Strathrannoch first. You might discuss your 'mutual interests.'"

Lydia clenched her teeth. Her heart beat harder in her chest, as it did every time Georgiana proposed an alteration in their plan. "No."

"I can ask for a tour of his castle. You can take tea in his parlor. And then we can return to Dunkeld for the evening."

They had left the posting inn in Dunkeld that morning to set off for Strathrannoch Castle. It had taken quite a bit of coin to persuade the postilion to take them *away* from Perth and Dundee, rather than *toward* those centers of civilization—a fact that had given Lydia a moment of pause—but the farther afield they traveled, the more the view out the hazed glass soothed something inside her. Softened the spiked edges of panic in her chest.

They'd spent nearly an hour winding along the river before they'd passed into a forest of thick-branched oaks and clustered fir trees. When they'd emerged, it had been to a wide soft vista of green—all hills and sun-spangled water and no other humans as far as the eye could see.

Lydia had loved every moment she'd spent peering out the coach window. It was only when she looked down into her lap, at the rumpled papers and scratched-out notations in her own neat hand, that panic resettled itself somewhere above her breastbone.

"You needn't propose to the man immediately upon meeting him," Georgiana went on. Also not for the first time. "Perhaps you might consider making him earn the privilege of your hand. Men perform better when they are required to rise to the occasion."

"No," Lydia said again.

Her blood had begun pounding in her ears. Her stomach churned.

She could not recall a time—even in the furthest reaches of her memory—when she had been comfortable with basic social congress.

In her own home, within the comfortable knot of her friends and family, she was perfectly capable of human interaction. Outside that circle, however, she tended to fade silently into the background—or, alternatively, become so flustered and dizzy that she fainted in the middle of a drawing room and had to be carried out by a footman.

She knew herself. There was no possible way that she could sit down with the Earl of Strathrannoch and make polite conversation for several days before revealing the truth of why she had come to his castle. She had to get it over with as quickly as possible before she made an utter cake of herself.

"We've come this far," Lydia said. She looked down at the papers in her lap—some in her own hand and some in Strathrannoch's, dozens of his clever, charming letters—and tried to force the tremble out of her voice. "I'm not going to give up now."

She could not. She had hidden her whereabouts from her mother and brothers, revealed the truth of her plot only to her closest friends, and set out for Scotland armed with nothing but a trunk and a fresh pencil.

This is your chance, she had thought to herself. *This is your chance to change your life.*

Three years ago, Lydia had begun writing radical political tracts, distributed anonymously by the scandalous circulating library Belvoir's. Lydia's first pamphlet had called for universal suffrage for both men and women. Her second had argued for the complete abolition of the aristocracy in England.

It had been that second pamphlet that had prompted the Earl of Strathrannoch's response, delivered care of the library.

Dear H, he had written. *I admire your fighting spirit and wonder when you mean to write on the question of Scotland.*

(Lydia had, of necessity, employed a simple pseudonym for her pamphlets. *H* for *Hope-Wallace*. *H* for *heart* and *hardihood*. *H* for *Holy hell, what have I done?* and *Hope I don't end up in prison!*)

Dear Strathrannoch, she had written back. *What Scotland question do you have in mind? I assure you, I have numerous opinions, most of which you probably will not appreciate. Your lordship.*

Two weeks later, she'd had his reply: *Dear H, I suppose you mean because the Strathrannochs have for five generations allied them-*

selves with your monarchy instead of our own people? Aye, I can see why
you'd think I'd oppose your incendiary ideas. You'd be wrong, however.
Tell me what you think about the Scots fighting for your English king
against Napoleon and don't hold back. I'd like for my eyebrows to burn
off when I read your next letter.

She'd written back. And in the months and years that had
followed, she and the Earl of Strathrannoch had developed a
peculiar friendship.

He did not know her true identity. He did not know she was
an absurdly rich spinster. He had no idea that she was so terrified
of interacting with other humans that, despite her fortune, she'd
been a disaster during her seven unbearable Seasons.

But he knew her, in a way. He knew the heart of her—at least,
the political part—and the shape of her ideas. And he agreed with
them all, even the most outrageous.

When Strathrannoch had confessed in his last letter that his
ancestral home in the Scottish Lowlands could scarcely support
itself financially, that he was struggling to keep the place running,
an idea had crystallized in her mind.

She could marry him.

Strathrannoch needed money, and Lydia had coin in abundance.

And Lydia needed—

Her chest felt tight. She rubbed her fingers at the ache there
and stared down at the papers in her lap.

In the years since her ignominious debut, she had folded in
on herself. She'd hidden behind the protective wall of her older
brothers and let herself become smaller and smaller. More and
more invisible.

Her anonymous pamphlets had felt almost miraculous at first.

Suddenly, she had a voice—a way to make herself heard even when she could not manage to speak aloud.

But the rich, honeyed taste of independence that her writing had given her only made her crave more of the same. Her pamphlets were secret, hidden; she had no real autonomy. Almost no one in her life knew of her work—to everyone else, she was only silent, mousy, helpless Lydia Hope-Wallace.

Except to Strathrannoch. He did not know her for an awkward wallflower. He saw only her radical spirit, the bright ferocity of her writing.

And if she had her way, he would never know the way the *beau monde* perceived her. If she marched into his house and proposed a marriage of convenience—if he said yes—

She could *be* the woman from the pamphlets, strong and independent. She could be proud of who she was.

"This is my chance," she murmured to the letters. "I will not waste it."

"I beg your pardon?"

She blinked and met Georgiana's gaze. "I am not going home in disgrace. I can do this. It's going to work out."

"Your abilities are not my primary concern," Georgiana said. Her lovely face had gone slightly peevish. "I don't doubt that you *can* persuade this stranger to marry you. I wonder whether you are certain that you want to."

Lydia set her teeth. "I'm certain."

The coach shuddered and slowed down. Bacon made an excited circle in Georgiana's lap, leaving a trail of white hairs.

Georgiana pressed her lips together firmly, and Lydia knew her friend would not speak of her hesitations again. She might doubt Lydia's plan, but if anyone could understand a desperate desire for independence, it was Georgiana.

"Time to pluck up, then," Georgiana said, "because we seem to have arrived."

• • •

Lydia had known what to expect from the castle itself. She'd found a picture of it in advance, in an illustrated guide to the great estates of Scotland. She'd blinked at the page in shock, wondering if it was romanticized, so closely did it match the drawings of a fantasy castle one might find in a children's storybook.

But no. The impression of a fairy-tale castle was, if anything, stronger in person. Though she could see from the outside the signs of disrepair that Strathrannoch had told her about in his letters, she was still boggled by the place, white and turreted, crenellations notched against the sharp blue of the early-autumn sky.

She had expected the fairy-tale castle. She had anticipated the missing glass on the upper-floor windows and the tumbledown ruin of the gate lodge, overgrown with mosses.

She had not anticipated the zebra.

The black-and-white equine moved placidly past them as they approached the castle's front door, wending its way down the drive and toward the postilion.

The postboy swore in a Scots so thick and broad that Lydia could not quite make it out. "What in hell—"

"Not to worry!" Georgiana called out. "'Tis only a zebra!" She turned to Lydia and the expression of blithe unconcern fell off her face. "Why is there a *zebra*?" she hissed.

"I—I don't—"

"Your earl did not mention a penchant for acquiring African mammals?"

Lydia felt a familiar panic swell in her chest, the kind that always rose when she was forced into unpredictable social situations. "I—no, he didn't mention any—any animals—"

Georgiana appeared to notice the blood draining slowly from Lydia's face and heaved a sigh. She gave Lydia a gentle shove toward the front door. "Never mind. I'm sure there's a perfectly reasonable explanation." Under her breath, she muttered, "For a *zebra*."

The front door to the castle was tall and arched, positioned between two dainty towers. Lydia lifted her eyes higher, straining to see the crest of the ramparts above her.

Her heart fluttered. Her throat tightened.

Strathrannoch, she reminded herself. *This is Strathrannoch's home.*

She knew him. He knew her. He was not a stranger. She did not need to be afraid.

She tried to make her unruly body believe it. She bit down hard on her lower lip and knocked on the door.

It was flung open almost instantaneously, and Lydia promptly dropped her reticule in shock. Papers exploded outward at her feet, but she did not look down.

She stared instead at the man who had opened the door.

He was an enormous fellow, tall—considerably taller even than Jasper, the tallest of her brothers—and probably twice as broad about the shoulder as Jasper as well. His hair was a goldish sort of brown, curly and rumpled, and his face was obscured by a haphazard growth of whiskers. He wore some kind of boiled-leather smock over his clothing, and Lydia wondered, half hysterically, where they had found a pot big enough to boil the leather for a man of these titanic proportions.

He was scowling.

Lydia swallowed. Was this the . . . butler? She racked her

brain and found to her horror that she could not recall Strath-rannoch mentioning, in any of his letters, the name of his butler.

Georgiana gave her another, slightly more discreet shove. Bacon whimpered.

"Good afternoon," Lydia said. Oh hell and damnation, her voice was trembling so hard, he mightn't be able to make out her words. She felt her face flame but forced herself to keep talking despite her embarrassment. "I am here to see the—the Earl of Strathrannoch."

This is your chance, she repeated in her head. *This is your only chance.*

The words felt suddenly less inspiring and rather more ominous.

"Aye," the man said, "you're looking at him."

It was a measure of her rapidly increasing terror that she looked from side to side in desperate hope of some other hidden fellow before returning her gaze to the bearded giant.

"Oh," she whispered. "You are—you are—"

"Aye," he said again, "I'm Strathrannoch."

She stared up at the man's stern face, the hazel eyes boring into her from beneath the fierce line of his dark-gold brows.

This was Strathrannoch. *This* was Strathrannoch? This glower belonged to the man who had teased her about her politics and confessed his most private vulnerabilities over the last three years?

"Oh," she said again. "I see your eyebrows are none the worse for wear."

The aforementioned brows shot toward his hairline, and beside her, Georgiana made a stifled sound of despair.

Oh hell, oh damn, she was mucking this up. She tried again. "That is, I—I—I should like to make your acquaintance. Um. In the flesh."

She instantly regretted the word *flesh*, which seemed distressingly . . . fleshly.

This is Strathrannoch, she told herself. *He knows you. You know him. He just doesn't know it yet.*

"I am H," she managed to say.

That wasn't quite how she'd imagined it coming out. Truly, when she'd imagined this part of the scenario, they had simply *recognized* each other and then fallen into the habit of conversation built by three years' correspondence.

Her imagination, Lydia was coming to realize, was thoroughly fuddled.

"H," Strathrannoch repeated.

Did his eyes sharpen upon her—in recognition, perhaps? She could not tell.

"H," she said again. "From the letters."

His gaze flickered down to the papers strewn about her feet, and then up, up her body and back to her face. "And what are you doing here?"

She sucked in a lungful of air and tried with all her not inconsiderable brainpower to recollect what she had written in her notes for this precise moment.

Mutually . . . persons . . . union . . .

The words swam. In fact, the whole world seemed to be swimming slightly before her eyes, with Strathrannoch framed in the doorway and her head tilted up to look at his face.

"I am here," she said, "to marry you."

No, that wasn't how she'd written it out. Strathrannoch made a faint choking sound, and, at her side, Georgiana did as well.

"I have money," Lydia said desperately.

Your only chance, shouted her brain. *Your only chance!*

She tried again, attempting to tamp down her panic. "I know

that you—that you need money—from what you said in your let-ters. And I have plenty—and I know that we—that we get on—"

"Lass," Strathrannoch said. Lydia's words died in her throat. "Should I have some idea who you are?"

"I am H," she said again. Surely the man could not have multi-ple correspondents by that pseudonym. "From the letters. From all the letters we exchanged these last three years."

He met her eyes straight on. His were brown and green and blue, all the colors of the landscape they'd passed through on the ride from Dunkeld. She had loved the sight. She had been so hopeful.

"Lass," he said, "I've not written you any letters."

There was a buzzing sound in her ears. "Not to—to me as *me*. But you wrote to me as H, in reply to my political tracts. Dozens of letters about Scotland and revolution and Napoleon and—"

He gave his head a short, sharp shake. "No," he said. "I didn't. I don't care a fig for politics and I've no time for correspondence."

Lydia couldn't feel her fingers. Her heart bolted forward like a rabbit, crashing against her ribs, and it hurt, and she couldn't catch her breath.

He did not know her? Her head seemed to whirl, and she blinked dizzily at the letters at her feet. "You did not write those?"

Strathrannoch's gaze was steady on her face. "No. Not a one."

"Oh," she said.

And then, to her very great relief, everything around her went cold and black and senseless. She toppled forward through the door-way, out of conscious awareness and into Strathrannoch Castle.

Chapter 2

I have made many mistakes in my life born of fear or desperation or the desire for safety, but the greatest error I have ever made was letting you go. I should never have let you go.

—*from the papers of Arthur Baird, written upon the back of an envelope, never posted*

Arthur Baird, Fifth Earl of Strathrannoch, caught the madwoman in his arms when she fell.

Great bloody bollocking hell.

He did not have time for a mad English ginger on his doorstep. He had to go catch a bloody *zebra*.

This, evidently, was to be his fate: no fortune, no prospects, but rich in exotic equines and insensible ladies.

The unconscious woman's companion—blond, frowning, and half a head taller than her short, unhinged friend—leapt forward across the threshold. "She's perfectly well, I assure you. Give her some air."

"Oh aye," he said drily. "I'll just lay her down on the stone floor and leave her there. Very hospitable."

Instead he turned on his heel, leaving the stern blonde and her small white dog in his wake, and made for the drawing room. He was at least fifty percent certain there was a chaise longue in the drawing room.

He hoped.

He hitched the madwoman higher in his arms as he strode forward. Christ, she was an armful, all softness and curves everywhere, the sunset-colored sweep of her hair spilling over his shoulder, and—

He coughed and nearly tripped over his own feet.

Surely to God he had not just entertained a brief stab of attraction toward an *unconscious mad Englishwoman*.

He shook himself, causing the woman's head to jostle about alarmingly. Her eyelids fluttered. Her eyelashes were long and thick and—he had no name for the color of them. The darkest, warmest, rosiest copper.

He kicked a child's puzzle-box out of his way, swept three leather-bound books off the faded chintz chaise, and plopped the woman on it in some relief.

Orange. The color of her eyelashes was *orange*.

The other woman had gathered up the loose letters and trailed him into the room. When he deposited her companion onto the chaise, she knelt immediately before the still faintly fluttering redhead. The dog leapt up onto the chaise, and the woman picked up her friend's wrists and chafed them briskly.

"Lydia," she said, her tone crisp. "Wake up. This is no time for hysterics."

The ginger on the chaise cracked open one blue eye. She flicked her gaze around the room, landed on Arthur, hesitated briefly, and then closed the eye once more.

"No," she rasped. "I have chosen the abyss."

Despite himself, Arthur laughed.

Her eyes flew open, both of them this time, and she pushed herself upright, disarranging the dog. A bit of color came back into her milk-pale cheeks. "No," she said. "Never mind. I don't want the abyss. I—I want an explanation. For all of this."

The blond woman blinked at her companion, looking surprised and ever so slightly impressed.

"Aye," said Arthur. "As do I. Who are you? And why did you—" He paused, quite unable to find the proper turn of phrase for this situation.

Why did you just offer me your person and your fortune? seemed a bit unseemly.

And oh by the by, do you truly have a fortune, because I might be persuaded to accept you after all? seemed even worse.

He settled for, "Why did you seem to think we are acquainted?"

The redhead took a deep, fortifying breath. She opened her mouth, then closed it again, and attempted several more breaths.

Arthur waited. He did not look at the woman's bosom as she breathed, which was astonishingly difficult, given how she'd felt in his arms. He did not know whether to congratulate himself on his restraint or be alarmed that it was required.

"My name is Lydia Hope-Wallace," she said finally, "and this is my friend Lady Georgiana Cleeve." She looked down and gestured at the dog. "And this is Sir Francis Bacon."

Arthur did not know what to do with that information. He elected to nod.

"My eldest brother, Theodore Hope-Wallace, is an MP in London," Miss Hope-Wallace went on, "and our father was the third son of the Marquess of Vye."

She appeared to be waiting for some acknowledgment of the

name, but Arthur did not recognize it. His brother, Davis, had all the political ardor in the family—he would have recognized the names of Vye and Hope-Wallace and known straightaway who this woman was.

But thinking about Davis was like pressing his finger against the fine edge of a blade, and so he forced the thought back down.

"Right," Miss Hope-Wallace said, taking another deep breath. "I am a writer. I write, um—" She looked up at him, then down at the letters her companion had gathered up. She seemed to set her teeth before going on. "I write political pamphlets under the pseudonym H, distributed by Belvoir's Library in London. They are"—she licked her lips—"radical pamphlets. Hence the pseudonym."

She looked up at him again, her cheeks going pale once more, but he only nodded at her to go on.

"Nearly three years ago, I received a letter from the Earl of Strathrannoch, inviting me to discuss the role of Scottish soldiers in the fight against Napoleon. We have corresponded regularly since. Our letters passed only through Belvoir's—I never wrote to Strathrannoch directly, and he never wrote to me. You—." She tightened her hands around the bundle of letters and locked her gaze with Arthur's. Her eyes were dark blue, a velvety midnight blue, and just now close to spilling over with tears. "Did you truly mean what you said? You *are* Lord Strathrannoch? And yet you did not write these letters?"

He had the sudden and insane desire to tell her that he *had* written them, simply so she would stop looking so wounded, but he shook his head. "I'm Strathrannoch. And I've never written to a political pamphleteer in my life, I can promise you that."

She looked down at the letters, her thick rosy lashes—*orange*, damn it—veiling her eyes. Arthur felt a discomfiting tension rise between his shoulder blades at the sight. She was going to cry, and then he was going to do what he always did when someone dissolved in front of him—act a complete nodcock.

But she didn't cry. She lifted her lashes and those great dark-blue eyes were hard with outrage.

"Then who," she said precisely, "has written these letters? Before you answer"—she appeared to notice his mouth opening in refutation—"keep in mind that this individual has been impersonating you, your lordship, for nigh on three years. It may be in your best interest to figure out who would do such a thing."

Arthur ran a hand through his hair in exasperation before answering her. "I've no bloody idea. Probably someone pulled my name out of Debrett's—Strathrannoch Castle is far away enough from London that you'd never know the difference."

Miss Hope-Wallace shook her head. "That's impossible. We spoke of Scotland often—the letters were certainly written by a Scot. And more than that, it's someone who knew this place intimately. I could tell you the number of windows that need replacing on each floor of the castle."

Arthur felt heat start in the tops of his ears. He knew well enough how many windows in the damned castle needed replacing, and where each was located, and he didn't very well require a reminder from—

His thoughts ground suddenly to a halt. "Knew this place?" he repeated. "Knew Strathrannoch Castle?"

"Yes," she said. "From the gate lodge to the stables to the tops of the ramparts."

The tension between his shoulder blades redoubled, and he had to force his muscles to unlock so he could stride over to the chaise and pluck the topmost letter from Miss Hope-Wallace's lap.

She let out an outraged squawk, but Arthur barely heard her.

He sank down atop the desk in the corner of the room and stared at the letter.

At the handwriting he knew almost as well as he knew his own.

"Oh Christ," he said quietly. "Oh *fuck*."

There was a squeaking sound from the chaise, and Arthur was abruptly recalled to the present moment.

The friend, Lady Georgiana, seemed to have been the one who'd made the sound. He could not quite discern if her fingers pressed to her mouth were holding back horror or laughter.

Miss Hope-Wallace, on the other hand, was staring at him, her full lips pressed tightly together. "You know," she said. "You know who authored the letters."

His voice came out low and furious. "Aye. I know who wrote this."

It should not have been a surprise. He'd had a lifetime of such surprises, a thousand cuts that were always just a bit too fresh to heal.

What was this new betrayal after the last one, the greatest one?

And yet—stupidly—he was still surprised. It still hurt.

"Who?" Miss Hope-Wallace demanded. Her cheeks were pink again, flushed and rosy, and her chin was set. "Who wrote them?"

"Davis Baird," Arthur said. "My brother."

The words were still ringing in the silence when two of his employees burst into the drawing room.

"Strathrannoch!" Huw Trefor, the Welshman in charge of the Strathrannoch stables, was out of breath, his cheeks ruddy over his white beard. "Get the bloody hell out of your books, man, and help me with the damn zebras! They're all over the estate—I think one's made it down to the forest, and I—"

At the sight of the two women on the chaise, Huw stopped speaking abruptly.

Bertie Palmer—Arthur's estate manager and secretary, as well as the love of Huw's life—peered curiously around his much-taller partner.

An expression of utter delight stole across Bertie's face, and he adjusted his spectacles with one finger. "Well," he said, in his gentle voice, "what have we here?"

Bloody *hell*.

"These are—" Arthur began, and then paused. "This is—"

He had no idea how to finish his sentence. What had Davis told the woman? What had he promised?

Davis could charm the wool off a goddamned sheep. He could convince anyone of anything—no one knew that better than Arthur himself. If Davis wanted something from this woman, he'd have promised her the bloody world. He must have promised her something, because somehow she had turned up here believing herself the next Countess of Strathrannoch.

Davis had always been the same. Handsome, clever, charming, perfect—a winning smile that deflected punishment, always the right words to persuade people to bend to his will. A natural leader, a charmer of women, the second son who ought to have been the first.

Who *wished* he had been the first. Who never saw an obstacle he couldn't manipulate his way around. Who let nothing—neither wisdom nor morals nor compassion—stop him from getting what he wanted. It was no surprise that his charming, traitorous, contemptible *arse* of a brother had persuaded this woman to fall in love with him. Arthur had seen it plenty of times before.

He cursed Davis to the depths of hell—again—for leaving him alone with this catastrophe. How the devil was he meant to introduce her? *This is my brother's affianced bride?*

Or, worse—*mine?*

No. There would be no mention of weddings or troths in front of his staff.

Huw was the more practical and forthright of the pair. Bertie, on the other hand, was crafty. Cunning. Almost Machiavellian.

On the faintest suggestion of a potential Lady Strathrannoch, Bertie would have Arthur's mother's silver ring polished and presented on a platter. Bertie would have a special license procured and Arthur and Lydia's first five children named—*not* that Arthur was thinking about procreating with Miss Hope-Wallace.

The tops of his ears burned again. "Nothing," he declared. "No one."

He paused. That hadn't come out right.

But Miss Hope-Wallace was nodding her agreement. "Nothing," she said. Her voice was shaking again, her pupils bigger than Arthur felt they ought to be, her eyes glassy. "No one. We were never here."

And then she leaned forward, her flame-colored hair tumbling over one shoulder, and vomited on her own shoes.

Chapter 3

. . . We arrive at Strathrannoch tomorrow. Do you recollect the bit in the Vindication *in which Wollstonecraft claims that the only way for women to achieve spiritual vigor is for them to first run wild? Well—let us hope she was not wrong.*

—*from Lydia Hope-Wallace to Selina Kent, Duchess of Stanhope and patroness of Belvoir's Library, posted from Dunkeld*

Lydia was not certain she had ever, in her entire life, so longed for oblivion.

It was not the first time she had vomited in public. It was also not the second, nor even, lamentably, the third. (The third had been a rather unfortunate incident involving her next-oldest brother Ned and a not-very-grief-stricken widow whom Ned had been attempting to charm. At her own husband's funeral.)

It was, however, the first time Lydia had vomited in front of a man to whom she had recently offered her hand in marriage.

She had *liked* these slippers. They were pale green and pointed, with huge floppy bows on top. She'd thought, when she put them on that morning, that they would give her a burst of courage when she looked down and glimpsed their optimistic adornments.

They were now a horrifying, ruined, utterly unmentionable metaphor for the outcome of her fondest hopes and dreams.

Independence. A life of her own devising. A partner who did not see her as an object of pity.

Everything she'd imagined—all of it as insubstantial as smoke.

Her total humiliation had been made worse by the fact that rather than permitting her to lapse into another swoon, they had instead all very decorously introduced themselves. Strathrannoch's estate manager, Mr. Palmer—a bespectacled older man with deep brown skin—had been the very picture of soothing comfort. In between words of consolation, he'd fetched her a warm blue-and-green plaid and a wet cloth. Lydia was not sure whether to use it on her face or her slippers.

Mr. Trefor, the stable master, had been tasked with securing chairs for the room, which was mostly empty, aside from scattered books and a few incongruous children's toys. The state of the castle's interior did not surprise her, from what she knew of the Strath-rannoch earldom's finances. She supposed that the furniture and candlesticks and anything else that might fetch some coin had been carted off and sold.

Eventually, Lord Strathrannoch himself returned from a long absence, bearing a pot of tea and a hefty bottle of whisky. He added a hearty splash of the whisky to her teacup and then rather grimly filled his own cup nearly to the brim. She could not discern if he looked worried or furious, and when she caught herself staring at his face, she lifted her teacup to her mouth, abandoned decorum, and gulped.

The alcohol-laced concoction brought some feeling back into her fingers, and after a moment, she lifted her gaze to the men arrayed across from her. Mr. Palmer was the first to speak. "Are you feeling better, my dear?"

She was not feeling especially better. But she nodded anyway.

"She's here because Davis tricked her," said Lord Strathrannoch bluntly. "Meant to take her fortune, no doubt. If I was not already of a mind to kill the bastard when we find him, I'd be plotting murder now, damn it."

"When you find him?" Lydia asked in surprise.

At the same time, Mr. Palmer's brows rose over his wire-rimmed spectacles. "Take her fortune? However did he mean to do that?"

A roomful of eyes swung in her direction. She made a small, involuntary whimper. There was nothing—*nothing*—more calculated to discompose her than a vista of interested strangers peering into her face.

She directed a pathos-filled glance at Georgiana, who gave a delicate shrug.

Lord Strathrannoch reached over and poured some more whisky into her teacup. Mr. Palmer coughed meaningfully, and Strathrannoch added a splash of tea as well.

Lydia drank again, grateful for brothers, secret liquor stashes, and Ned in particular, whose commitment to the proper behavior of society ladies was negligible. She did not even cough at the whisky's endless burn.

And when she felt herself capable of it, she stared down into the teacup and, as quickly as possible, explained her marital intentions toward the Earl of Strathrannoch.

Her *former* marital intentions, back when she'd thought she'd known the man. This whisky-pouring giant was a stranger who had seen her faint and vomit in close succession. A wedding did not seem imminent.

"I'd meant to propose a mutually beneficial arrangement," she informed the teacup. "I am an heiress—"

"Very rich," put in Georgiana helpfully.

Lydia shot her friend a brief glare. Georgiana did not look repentant.

"I would not have come empty-handed into the agreement," Lydia went on. "It was not purely self-interested. I had something to offer."

She felt absurd saying the words. She had *money*. That was what she meant. That had been her enticement: The Strathrannoch estate needed money, and she could provide it.

She knew she had other good qualities. She was clever and well-read. She had a head for figures. She'd had a hand in the elections of at least half of the decade's most progressive Whigs and had personally organized the downfall of a corrupt MP who'd championed the death penalty for political protestors.

She was an excellent sister, recent deceptions notwithstanding. She tried to be a good friend.

It was just that, in her plan to propose marriage, her inheritance had seemed by far the most appealing part of her person, and she'd intended to capitalize upon that.

It felt surprisingly painful to say so aloud.

"I don't understand," said Mr. Trefor. "Why would Davis pretend to be Strathrannoch? What could he have hoped to gain?"

"For God's sake," said Strathrannoch, "he wanted her blasted fortune. Thought to play her like a fiddle, get her money for himself somehow." His ears had gone rather red again; he looked furious.

Lydia shook her head, compelled to set him straight despite her instincts urging her to hide underneath the plaid. "I don't think so. I don't see how he could have known of my fortune. My identity is closely guarded by Belvoir's—I would trust the patroness with my life. In fact, I *do* trust her with my life. I could be charged with sedition and imprisoned for those pamphlets."

Mr. Palmer nudged his spectacles up his nose. "If not for money, then perhaps for information. You said you spoke of politics?"

"Yes," Lydia said slowly. "It's possible. I assume he was a radical, looking for more information about radical causes?"

The three men all made various noises of scorn and disbelief, and she blinked.

"There was a time when he was," Lord Strathrannoch explained, "but that time is long since passed. A few years ago, he became a great pet of some of the Scottish peers—always entertaining, always the merry charming flirt."

Lydia felt ill. "It's impossible. He disparaged them in his letters. He was never more scathing than when he spoke of the Duchess of Sutherland—"

"One of his fastest friends," Strathrannoch said.

Her mind reeled, and she licked her lips. "I had expected that a Scottish earl would be horrified by my more radical beliefs—the abolition of the aristocracy, for one. But he was never horrified. In every possible way we seemed to be in agreement. Even my most outrageous ideas, he . . . he . . ."

She looked up at Strathrannoch. The *real* Strathrannoch, plainspoken and disheveled and casually exploding everything she'd thought she'd known.

"Your brother lied," she said. "Didn't he? He lied about that too. He agreed with whatever it was that I said, not because he felt the same but because—because he wanted something from me. If not my money, then the information I provided him in all those letters."

It had been a fantasy, all of it, from start to finish. Her friendship with Strathrannoch. Her carefully embroidered dreams.

She could never be the woman from the pamphlets. Her family—her loving, absurd, wildly protective family—had been right to shield and cosset her.

She had been wrong to believe that she could stand on her own.

Strathrannoch looked furious, his big hands opening and closing on his teacup. "I'm sorry, lass."

Tears pricked at the backs of her eyes, and she absolutely *refused* to let them fall. "Don't be."

"Not just because of Davis's actions," he said. "But because I must ask something of you, and I fear that doing so makes me not so very different from my brother."

She looked up at him, his tight jaw, his grim mouth. "What do you mean?"

"I need you to help me find him."

At this pronouncement, there was a small but decided clamor.

Mr. Trefor looked outraged. "You cannot mean to ask this poor girl, after all she's been through—"

Mr. Palmer, meanwhile, appeared delighted. "What an excellent idea! Strathrannoch, I do not give you enough credit for cleverness."

"I—" Lydia said. "I—I'm not certain—"

Strathrannoch quieted them all with a slight lift of his deep voice. "I would not ask if it were not urgent." He hesitated, then seemed to steel himself to go on. "A month ago, Davis came to stay with us at Strathrannoch Castle. He had not spent so much time here in years. I thought perhaps things had changed between us. He seemed so interested in the estate, in the tenants and my work." He laughed, and it was a brief, bitter sound that clutched at Lydia's insides. "He was, in a way. He stole something from me. A prototype I had built—an object of my own design."

"Your design?" She did not know what he meant. Was the man not an earl? What sort of designing did he do? She glanced again at the boiled-leather smock he wore. Was he a *painter*?

"A rifle scope," Strathrannoch said.

"I don't know what that is."

"Imagine a telescope," Mr. Palmer put in, "mounted to the top of a rifle. Imagine how far and how clearly you could see through it—and how precisely you could aim your weapon in that case."

"I don't understand. You design weaponry? Are you an especially avid hunter?"

Strathrannoch made a sort of growling noise. "For God's sake, no. I'm a farmer. I make plows. Reaping machines. Sometimes I mess about with engines. I'd thought"—he rubbed at the back of his neck—"I'd thought to make the rifle shot more accurate, if I could. Sometimes shots go wild and the tenants are injured, you see."

She stared at him in astonishment. "You are an inventor?"

He looked as uncomfortable as Lydia herself. His throat had gone pink, and his hands—she could see now that they were flecked with small burn scars—rotated his teacup rather madly. "I make things, that's all. For the tenants and the villagers. Little things to ease their way."

"And you invented this—this rifle telescope? And your brother *stole* it?"

"Aye. He asked plenty of questions. How the device worked. How far away you could be from your target and aim true." She could see the muscles of his jaw work. "A hundred leagues. Do you *know* the kind of damage that could be done with a weapon like that? When the Duchess of Sutherland cleared her lands of the farmers who'd been there for generations, she had them driven out, their homes burned. But not all of them wanted to leave. Had her men a weapon of this kind, there could have been a massacre."

"You think he means to use this weapon of yours—and the information I gave him—to do violence?"

"Aye. I can think of no other reason that he would have stolen the rifle scope."

She could feel her heart beat hard, doubling, tripling in pace. Her brain tried to keep up, to take in the facts. The man she'd corresponded with these last three years had deceived her, had lied to her for information and meant to use what she'd told him to work *against* everything she believed in.

"I think you can help us," Strathrannoch went on. "Write to this Belvoir's. Find out what they know. And while we wait for their response—let me look at your letters and see what information Davis might have let slip." He looked at her, his multihued eyes hard and direct on her face. "Please, lass. I need your help."

Her heart clenched. Her throat constricted. Speech seemed suddenly beyond her, as absurd and impossible as flight.

She leapt to her feet. "No," she got out. Her voice sounded strangled. "I'm sorry. No."

Georgiana stood as well. "Lydia?"

She felt humiliation crawling across her skin as she looked at the three men who'd been so kind to her. Mr. Palmer, Mr. Trefor. Lord Strathrannoch.

She was going to let all of them down.

She could not change her life. This was what she was—a foolish spinster. A woman who wrote pamphlets instead of living. Who blushed and cried and fainted too easily, whose emotions swam through her body like physical things.

"I can't," she said. She felt almost frantic to get away. She wrestled with the blue-and-green plaid Mr. Palmer had given her, trying to pull it off her body while Bacon turned bemused circles at her feet. "I'm sorry. You don't want me here. I'll write to Belvoir's. I promise I'll write to them. I'll tell them to send you whatever they know. But I cannot—I cannot—"

She couldn't stay here.

She had imagined Strathrannoch Castle so many times—had pictured herself here, *living* here—a marriage of practicality and convenience, to be sure, but nonetheless a marriage. Her own off-kilter happily ever after.

Had she really thought she could change her life? Upon what basis would such a mad fancy have seemed possible?

She knew herself. She could scarcely manage the trials of a routine dinner party. Why had she thought she could succeed at something as outrageous as this?

She finally managed to get the plaid off her body, letting it fall onto the chaise behind her. "I'm sorry," she said again.

There was no sense in trying to control the shaking of her hands or her voice, but she picked her way carefully across the floor, her letters clutched in her hands. At least this time she would not swoon.

"Miss Hope-Wallace," Mr. Palmer said gently.

And at the same time, Strathrannoch's voice rasped out from behind her: "Wait. Wait a moment."

But she couldn't wait. She couldn't even turn back to look at him, or the burn at the backs of her eyes would turn into hot flooding tears of embarrassment.

That, Lydia felt, would be too far. The full cornucopia of indignity.

She could faint. She could vomit. She could make a perfect ninny of herself by *proposing* to a complete stranger.

But she would not cry in front of all of them, in front of their gentle sympathy and fresh-brewed tea.

Instead, she hiked up her skirts in one hand and ran.

Chapter 4

. . . The censures which may ensue from striking into a path of literature rarely trodden by my sex will not cause me to keep silent in the cause of liberty.

—*from Lydia's private copy of Catharine Macaulay's* THE HISTORY OF ENGLAND FROM THE ACCESSION OF JAMES I, *underlined thrice*

Lydia could recall clearly the first time she'd seen one of her pamphlets in the hands of readers.

It had been 1816—a late July afternoon, hot and blue. Her lace petticoats had clung to her legs, and her heart had nearly stopped in her chest when she'd recognized the crisp printing. Two matrons, seated beside each other on a bench, had bent their heads together over Lydia's words.

One of the women had looked around as if uncertain of her audience, and had cupped her hand protectively over the pamphlet. The other had hesitated, then folded the tract and tucked it away in her reticule, her expression caught somewhere between reticence and desperate, brilliant-edged hope.

That piece had argued for the expansion of the rights of women to sue for divorce. In Lydia's lifetime, only *two* women had been successful in their divorce suits in England—a breathtaking double standard that Lydia had become determined to change. She'd worked the language over with Selina Kent, the duchess who ran Belvoir's Library, again and again, and then Selina had commissioned a satirical print mocking the opponents of reform and their many paramours.

It had sold like wildfire. Her words, Selina's incisive cartoon—the piece had been daring and honest and *right*. Lydia had been so proud of that pamphlet. When she'd seen the two matrons in the park—had sensed the hope her words had engendered—she'd felt strong and certain and bright with resolve. She'd felt as though she could do anything.

She tried very hard to recall that confidence as she looked between Strathrannoch's groom and the two bay horses that had drawn their carriage all the way up to the castle from Dunkeld.

"Where did you say Angus went?" Angus, she had learned that morning, was the postboy.

The groom ran his hand through his thinning sandy hair and looked apologetically at her. "The sheep walk, lass."

"Perhaps you might point me in the direction of—"

The groom coughed. "With his wife, you ken."

Lydia did not precisely ken.

"Yon Angus has been away these last two weeks, you see." The groom's ears had gone quite red, and he seemed unable to meet Lydia's gaze. "I suspect it may be some time before they're back. Perhaps dusk. Perhaps—er—tomorrow morning."

Ah. That was—ah. She felt her own face heat.

And then the rest of the groom's words registered. *Tomorrow morning.*

Tomorrow.

No. No. She could not do it. She would not. She *refused* to go back to Strathrannoch Castle with her tail between her legs and beg the earl—to whom she had first proposed and then run from like her frock was on fire—for his leave to remain there overnight.

She looked from the groom to the post-chaise, which was currently devoid of horses. "Can you reattach them?"

"What's that?"

She gestured, a little wildly. "The horses. Reattach them. Harness them back to the carriage."

"Aye," he said slowly. "But how do you mean to get back to Dunkeld?"

Lydia thought very hard about her pamphlets and the way she'd felt that day in the park. Resolute. Capable. Intrepid.

Oh God. Oh hell. She licked her lips and forced herself to say the words.

"I will do it," she said. "I will drive the carriage."

• • •

Roughly a quarter of an hour later, Lydia found herself perched atop a large bay horse, pondering the nature of her life's choices. At what point, precisely, had this journey gone from "bold and daring" to "utterly, disastrously doomed"?

She had brought a riding habit in her trunk, a fact she was grateful for because a post-chaise was steered not by a seated driver but by a postilion on horseback. There was no driver's seat.

She was *in* the driver's seat, and it was on the back of a horse.

There was also no sidesaddle—of course there was not—and though she'd occasionally ridden astride, she was not especially proficient at it. The saddle between her thighs felt huge and un-wieldy, the post-chaise behind her back a looming threat.

She did not care. She was getting herself out of this bloody castle, even if she had to abandon her belongings and walk back to Dunkeld.

She hoped she did not have to walk. Georgiana, she was quite certain, would not be enthused about walking.

Georgiana wouldn't be terribly enthused about *crashing*, either, but Lydia tried not to think about it.

She guided the horses and carriage back to the front of the castle. Georgiana—bless her—was waiting just outside, Bacon at her feet and her expression inscrutable. Beside her stood the Earl of Strathrannoch, looking large and imposing and utterly fearsome.

Georgiana arched one elegant brow at the sight of Lydia on horseback. "Well. I presume Angus was otherwise occupied."

"Get in," Lydia said, her words coming out a jumbled rush. "The luggage is still loaded. We're going to Dunkeld."

"Have you *murdered* Angus? Because otherwise I cannot fathom why we are not simply waiting for his return—"

"Georgiana," she said through gritted teeth, "get in."

"Bloody hell," said the earl over her, "get down from there. I'll drive you back to Dunkeld if you're in such a great tearing hurry—"

"No," she said, "no, that's not necessary. I am perfectly capable—"

"I didn't say you weren't capable, I said I can bloody well take care of it—"

"Georgiana!"

Her horse danced uneasily beneath her—probably alarmed by the shrill undertone her voice had begun to take on—so she tightened her grip on the reins and clenched her thighs around the animal's back.

Don't fall, she told herself fiercely. *Don't fall, don't fall.*

Georgiana gave Lydia one more incredulous look and then gathered her skirts in one hand. She lifted Bacon up into the post-chaise, then leapt up after him, and Lydia did not even turn to look at Strathrannoch or his beautiful, ramshackle castle before she kicked the horse into motion so fast its mate nearly tripped as it tried to keep up.

Don't fall, don't fall, don't fall.

She didn't. She steered the horses down the long drive, past the ruined gatehouse that she'd looked at with such fondness earlier in the day, and headed back down the road toward Dunkeld.

For all of ten minutes or so, until she heard hooves thundering up the road behind her.

The horses shifted. The one beneath her made to break into a trot, and she tried to pretend she was riding sidesaddle, tried to pretend she was comfortable and competent, tried to pretend she was a woman capable of changing her own life.

But she was only Lydia Hope-Wallace, after all. She was not that other woman.

She twisted her head after she'd calmed the horses to locate the source of the sound.

Strathrannoch. It was Strathrannoch, riding hell-for-leather behind them, mounted on a black horse. He'd shed his smock, and he wore only trousers and shirtsleeves rolled to the elbow. His mount had a long feathery black mane, which fluttered as horse and rider charged down the road. From a distance they were so well-matched a set that Lydia almost forgot the size of the man, but as he approached, she fairly goggled.

Of course. Of course the man would have a giant horse as well. She suspected that were she to stand beside the horse, its shoulder would top her head by several inches.

But the animal was not half so impressive as the man. His shoulders were huge and broad; she could see the muscles rippling straight through the threadbare linen of his shirt. His thighs strained his trousers as he controlled his enormous mount. It was almost indecent, for heaven's sake, and Lydia could not tear her eyes from him.

Truly, not even the bravest, boldest, most fantastical version of herself would have ridden up to Perthshire and offered her hand if she'd known the man looked like *that*.

She forced herself to stop ogling the earl and stared fixedly at the road stretching in front of her.

"I told you," she said when he was close enough to slow and hear her, "I will look through the letters. I promise you, I will send along any information that you need to know."

"For Christ's sake, you wee bampot, I'm not worried about the letters. I'm worried you're going to kill yourself halfway to Dunkeld."

"I can ride a horse perfectly well, thank you."

"You couldn't even make it across a room without needing me to catch you!"

She was taken aback by his blunt words, and yet strangely she did not feel intimidated. She felt a tiny frisson of outrage, a hot desire to defend herself.

So often, Lydia's mother and brothers sheltered her from her fears, safeguarded her from harm. If they could, her brothers would wrap her in cotton wool and set her upon a shelf like a doll: just as safe and just as lifeless.

It was peculiar—good—to face this man's challenge head-on.

"Stop your mount," Strathrannoch said. "Let me take over."

Her blood went hotter at his words. Outrage felt nothing like panic and humiliation, Lydia realized. It felt *wonderful*.

"I do not need you," she said, and for once her voice wasn't thin or shaky. It came out strong and carrying, and if she was a little breathless, it was only because she was perched atop a thousand pounds of poorly controlled horseflesh.

"*I* came to offer my fortune to *you*," she went on, her voice rising. "I came to help you fix *your* ancestral home. I have ridden horses since I was six years old and my brother placed me atop his pony and set it loose on Rotten Row. I do not need your help!"

"I don't give a damn whether you think you need it or no," he snapped. "You're getting it. I will not have you try to cross two hours of unfamiliar terrain by yourself, with no one to help you if you get stuck or overturn—"

"The terrain is perfectly familiar! I crossed it this very morning."

"You were inside the carriage!"

"It has windows! I have eyes!"

She was so busy shouting nonsense at the earl that she failed to notice the zebras.

But the horses did. The horse beneath her caught up short, pulling the one beside it back, and Lydia squeaked and grabbed for her mount's black mane.

Her fingers caught hold, and she squeezed her thighs into the horse's flanks. As she did, she looked for what had made the horse startle.

Her mouth came open. Nothing but a soft wheeze emerged.

This morning she and Georgiana had seen a single zebra, wandering down the lane in front of the castle. Now they numbered more than a dozen. They were distant, probably several minutes away, but it was easy enough to make out the churning mass of stripes and hooves.

And they were running.

A stampede. It was a stampede of African zebras, coming toward her at top speed down a poorly maintained dirt track in Perthshire, Scotland.

Lydia whispered an oath.

Beside her, the earl cursed quite a lot louder. "Bloody hell, I forgot about the zebras!"

"You *forgot* about your *zebras*—"

Her mind whirled at the inexplicable nature of this man, her circumstances, and the existence of a stampede of zebras in her general vicinity. She ground her teeth and regained the horse's reins, trying to force her brain to function properly, for all it wanted to freeze in panic and let the zebras trample her into the ground.

"All right," she said. "You and your horse stay back. I need to get the carriage off the path so we aren't run down."

"Do it," Strathrannoch ordered.

"I *am*," she muttered under her breath.

Strathrannoch's reply was a decidedly unfamiliar Scots word, which she chose not to attempt to interpret.

She urged the horse beneath her into motion again, nudging it with knees and reins toward the side of the road. The horses looked at the approaching herd nervously, their ears flicking back and forth between Lydia's instructions and the hoofbeats and churning dust ahead. Lydia's mount was the worst, stepping more quickly than she liked and arching its neck.

Georgiana, meanwhile, stuck her head out the window. "Is everything all right? I heard a peculiar noise and then we . . ."

Lydia shot her friend a quick glance when her voice trailed off. Georgiana was staring at the approaching stampede, her pale blue eyes roughly the size and shape of robins' nests. "I . . . see," Georgiana choked out. "Carry on, then."

Georgiana's head vanished back into the carriage. Lydia kept her gaze on her horse and her fingers locked around the reins.

At her side, she heard Strathrannoch begin to speak, his voice a low, rough-yet-soothing murmur. "You're doing fine. All's well. Just a bit more, my bonny one."

Lydia's mouth nearly fell open before she realized he was talking to her horse.

They had almost eased the post-chaise off the road when catastrophe introduced itself in the form of a fat little black-and-white bird. As the carriage's outer wheels tipped from the packed-dirt road into the softer loam near the forest, the bird burst up from the ground directly in front of Lydia's horse. The bird gave a short, sharp cry at having been disturbed, fluttering its wings wildly.

And Lydia's mount promptly panicked. She had just enough time to wrap her fingers in its mane as she felt it gather itself beneath her.

Then it leapt forward and dragged the other horse and the carriage behind them into a mad, frantic flight.

Chapter 5

. . . I know it pains you not to oversee the proceedings personally. But you needn't fret. She's stout of heart, our Lydia.

—from Lady Georgiana Cleeve to Selina Kent,
Duchess of Stanhope, posted from Dunkeld

Oh God, Lydia thought, *oh God* and *oh damn* and *I'm sorry* and also *please don't let me kill Georgiana*.

She had no idea if the horse had the bit in its teeth—she'd dropped the reins. But it certainly felt that way, because her horse was hurling itself forward, seeming not to notice the fact that every step brought them closer to the fast-approaching zebras. The post-chaise was still half off the road, which slowed their progress as the wheels dragged through the mud—but the weight of the carriage seemed only to further alarm the animal, which was breathing hard and dancing wildly as it tried to tow its terrified mate and the carriage as well.

"Slow down," she said, her voice breathless and frantic, "oh please, we're all going to die, *please* slow down!"

And then Strathrannoch, the great enormous idiot, was beside her.

"Turn back!" she shrieked at him, chancing a glance away from her horse's churning front hooves.

"You have to cut yourself free!" he bellowed back.

"What?"

"Cut yourself free! I'll stay with the other horse and the carriage. Cut the straps and then get out of the way!"

"With *what*?"

Strathrannoch rode a little closer, his black horse eating up the ground with its long strides. "Take my dirk."

She chanced another look at him. He had the reins in one hand and a small knife in his other, brandishing it hilt-first. The blade must have been wrapped in his palm.

"Oh God," she said. "I can't. I can't do that."

"For Christ's sake, take the damn dirk or we're all going to meet the wrong end of sixty-four hooves!"

She squelched a brief flare of astonished admiration for his ability to do arithmetic at such a moment.

She looked at the dirk. She looked at the stampeding zebras, looming larger as they approached. And then she squeezed her eyes closed and thrust out her hand in the general direction of the earl.

She felt the hilt land, warm and solid, in her palm. She pulled it into her chest, her other hand still wrapped in the horse's mane, her boots sliding about in her stirrups.

"Now," he said. "Do it now. Cut yourself free. There are two leathers behind you that you'll need to cut. I'll hold the reins, and then hand them back to you when you're done."

"I can't," she whispered. Her fingers flexed convulsively around the dirk's hilt.

"I can't do it for you, lass. I can't reach that far."

Terror squeezed at her lungs. The horse rocked beneath her, and her fingers were wrapped so tightly in its mane that she feared what would happen if she let go. She could fall. She could be trampled.

But Georgiana was in the carriage behind her. She could not simply sit atop this beast and wait for death. She had to do what Strathrannoch had said. She *had* to. Her fear meant nothing in the face of Georgiana's endangerment.

She took one shaky inhale. Armed with the dirk, she turned, her thighs squeezing the horse's sides for dear life. She had to bend to reach the leathers that attached the horse to the carriage. She leaned, the horse's mane in one hand and the dirk in the other, extending her body, her chest clamped down tight with anxiety. The horse's hindquarters were dark with sweat and mud, bunching as its legs churned up the ground.

She stretched out the dirk and sawed it along the leather strap.

"Good lass," said Strathrannoch.

She did not spare a glance to determine if he meant her or the bloody horse.

The dirk was razor-sharp, and it was the work of a moment to slice through the first harness strap. Carefully, so that she did not cut the horse, she moved the blade to the second strap.

"Wait," said Strathrannoch, and she froze. "When you cut the strap, the horse is going to break free. I'll ride alongside you long enough for you to turn around and grab the reins, and then I'll go back for your friend in the carriage. Do you understand?"

"Yes," she rasped.

"Hold on like hell," he said. "Cut fast and don't let go."

"On three," she said.

"Aye."

She waited. The horses thundered on. No one spoke. Finally she realized—

"I meant for *you* to count!"

"For Christ's sake, woman! One—two—thr—"

Lydia cut the strap.

As Strathrannoch had predicted, her horse shot forward, outstripping the earl and his mount. Her fingers ached from clutching the horse's mane, and her throat burned from—

Oh. She was screaming.

She made herself stop. She wrenched herself forward and dropped the dirk, trying not to fall, trying to get herself turned back around and able to ride. Georgiana was safe. She would be fine. She just needed to grab the bloody reins and—

She had them—she almost had them. She was half turned, the stirrups slapping against her feet and her hair whipping around her eyes, when the horse realized it was free and plunged sideways, toward the center of the road.

She felt herself slip to one side. Her hand scrabbled for the saddle, the reins, *anything*—

And then Strathrannoch was there at her side, heedless of her horse's erratic flight. He was well above her on his enormous black, and he reached down toward her and wrapped one powerful arm about her waist.

"Are you caught in the stirrups?" he shouted.

"I—no—"

Before the word was fully out of her mouth, Strathrannoch flexed his arm at the elbow and dragged her up and into his chest.

Her face smashed against thin linen and, beneath it, a rock-solid pectoral muscle. She felt his arms rippling as he clutched her close and sawed at the reins with his other hand, urging his horse to slow, pulling them off the road and into the trees that flanked it.

"For God's sake, woman!" Strathrannoch bellowed in her ear. "I have you! Stop screaming!"

Oh. She hadn't realized she'd started again.

She forced the screams back down and turned her head just in time to see the zebras blow past them in a blur of black and white. She smelled the mud from the road and animal sweat, and also the scent of the man who held her: smoke and earth and burnt honey.

"Georgiana," she mumbled into his shirt. "The carriage."

"Aye, aye, dinna fash—"

Dinna fash? Had the man not realized she was composed primarily of worry? She clutched his shirt in one hand and dragged herself up to look over his shoulder as his mount finally came to a halt beneath the canopy of oaks.

Good heavens, her horse had covered a lot of ground. Georgiana was yards back, the carriage halted just off the road and well out of range of the passing zebras. She was, as far as Lydia could tell, already on her feet and busily attempting to detach the remaining horse from its harness. Bacon was on the ground, charging alternately at the zebras and a tall stalk of grass.

Lydia's horse, meanwhile, had spun about and was making its way back toward Strathrannoch Castle. Rather than running from the oncoming zebras, it appeared to have *joined* them.

"Traitor," she mumbled.

"What?"

"Nothing," she said, and then she looked up into Strathrannoch's face.

He was looking down at her. His face was set in a scowl, and though the goldish stubble might have disguised it when she was on the ground and he was looming a full head above her, she could see now that the line of his jaw was hard and sharp and precise.

Nothing about his face was soft. Even his eyes—gold around the pupil, surrounded by blue and green—were hard as they bore down upon her.

Her lips parted. His gaze dropped to her mouth.

And Lydia became suddenly aware of a number of physical sensations.

She was pulled across his lap, her chest crushed against his, one of her knees tangled in her skirts and pressed into his hip. Her other leg was stretched across his opposite thigh. Her hand was wrapped in his shirt, holding their bodies pressed together. His arm encircled her waist.

They were as closely entwined as two people could be. She could feel his heat straight through the layers of their clothes. He was hot as a forge and hard as iron, and the burnt-honey smell of him went straight to her belly and then lower.

She felt a sudden, dizzy unfurling in her body as she looked at him looking at her mouth.

She licked her lips. His arm flexed, as if involuntarily, but she could not come closer to him. She was already pressed as tightly as she could be, her curves molded to the contours of his chest.

He made a quick, rasping sound in the back of his throat, and she—

She liked that sound. She liked it quite a lot. Her indrawn breath was almost a gasp.

His eyes flew back up to hers.

"I beg your pardon," he said hoarsely. "You're—are you—can you get down?"

"Oh," she said.

"The crisis has passed—'tis perfectly natural to—that is, I—"

She had no idea what he was talking about. "I'm not entirely certain I can, er, use my legs."

"Bloody hell." He dropped the reins and shifted his grip on her, scooping her legs up with one arm.

The musculature on the man's limbs was absurd, really. She was not a tall woman, but certainly no one would describe her as petite. She had plump thighs and generous hips and breasts that regularly threatened the wide, low necklines currently à la mode. But the man lifted her up against him as though she were a delicate little waif.

Perhaps she shouldn't have liked it quite so much. But as he flung his leg over the horse's side and brought them both to the ground, she was forced to admit to herself that she found all that leashed physical power rather alarmingly appealing.

"I'm going to set you down," he informed her once he had his feet. "Can you stand on your own?"

"We'll find out."

He muttered something under his breath and then let her slide down his body until her feet touched the ground.

Lydia felt every slow, hot inch of that slide. Her riding habit was made of sensible cotton twill, but it might as well have been made of gossamer for all it seemed to separate her body from his. She felt the press of his chest, and the buttons of his falls. She felt the cool brush of air on the backs of her calves as her feet met the ground.

And when he released her, she promptly crumpled back into him.

"Good Christ," he muttered, and wrapped his arms around her again. "Take a moment to get your legs under you. I have you."

He continued to mumble under his breath, something about

devil and *lunatic*, and she decided it was best for her dignity if she did not try to discern any further words.

When she could finally stand on her own, she tugged herself out of Strathrannoch's grip, and he dropped his arms so fast that a flare of embarrassment lit inside her.

He had rescued her, yes. But surely he had not anticipated that such a rescue would end with an extended embrace. Perhaps she had imagined that heated glance at her mouth.

"We ought to go back to Georgiana," she said. "Make certain she's all right."

"Aye," he said.

"Can we, er"—she shot a glance at his horse—"walk? I am not entirely confident I can get back up on a horse. Ever."

He gave a raspy laugh. "Aye, lass. We can walk. Had you ever ridden astride like that before?"

They made for the road, and Lydia glanced up. Strathrannoch's fancifully colored eyes were fixed on his horse, lipping at grasses near the road's edge.

"Of course," she said primly. "At least . . . four or five times."

"Christ." He ran his fingers through his curls, which were a little sweaty and standing out in all directions. "That was good work. Brave and deft."

Her face warmed at the praise. "I screamed the whole time."

"Aye. I might be deaf in my left ear now."

She lifted her gaze to his face. He was not smiling, but she thought there might be a hint of amusement at the corner of his mouth.

"But that doesn't make it any less brave," he said. "More, I think. Not less."

She looked down at her slippers and did not respond.

She'd experienced a pure animal terror on the horse's back,

with Strathrannoch's dirk clutched in her fist. But fear was not a new emotion for her. She felt it when she had to enter a ballroom and a hundred pairs of eyes fixed upon her as she was announced.

She'd felt it—cold and paralyzing—the first time she'd delivered a manuscript to Selina at Belvoir's. She'd passed the argument for universal suffrage across Selina's desk and looked down at her own neat handwriting, the product of eleven painstaking drafts.

Selina's wide mouth had been tilted crookedly up, half a familiar smile. "Are you certain?"

Lydia's hands had trembled, and so she'd locked them behind her back.

What hope could there be for change without universal suffrage? Why would anything ever improve in the British Empire if a handful of terrible men controlled its fate and answered to no one?

How could she expect to make a difference if she let herself be ruled by her fears?

"I'm certain," she'd said. "Print it."

With every manuscript she'd delivered to Belvoir's—her arguments for divorce reform, the anti-royalist tracts that could very well land her in prison—she'd known that same throat-tightening terror. But she went on anyway, just as she had cut the leathers and saved Georgiana and the carriage from disaster.

Because some things were worth the panic and the potential for humiliation. Some things mattered more than her own personal dread.

They were almost back to the post-chaise. She licked her dusty, salt-grimed lips and thought about Strathrannoch and the invention his brother had stolen. She thought about the farmers dragged from their homes in the Clearances and the aristocrats who believed the land they lived upon was owed to them by right of nothing more than being born.

She thought about her fears and her humiliations, and then she put them aside.

"I will do it," she told him.

He looked down. His shirt was wrinkled, and she could see the golden column of his throat. "Do what?"

"I will write to Belvoir's and stay here until they reply. We can examine the letters together. I should not have tried to flee."

His eyes flickered over her face, but he did not say anything. He nodded once, a quick and stark acceptance.

"By the by," she said, "why do you possess a herd of wild zebras?"

Chapter 6

~~Entrap in gatehouse.~~ ~~Entrap in barbican.~~ Entrap in bedchamber—enlist Fern?

*—from the private notes of Bertie Palmer, hastily
concealed upon the arrival of his employer*

Arthur was not entirely certain what had changed in Miss Hope-Wallace between when she'd lit out from his castle like her slippers were afire and when they'd returned, perspiring and dusty and dragging two trunks between them.

Actually, he could identify several things that had changed. Her attire, for one—somehow she'd gone from something filmy and pale green to a riding habit now splotched with dirt from hem to shoulder. Her hair too—in the morning, her vivid hair had been caught in a neat coil at the base of her neck, but now it was free and straggling loose down her back, sticking in her mouth, where she swiped at it absentmindedly with a hand.

Everything about her physical person had gone disheveled and unruly, and he—

Bleeding Christ if he didn't like it all much too much.

He'd lost his head for a moment when he'd had her in his lap on Luath's back. He'd been half-mad with relief that he'd gotten to her in time. When he'd seen her clutching her horse's black mane, her face white with terror, his mind had been evacuated of everything but fierce, ravaging purpose. *Get to her. Keep her safe.*

He had not calmed until he'd had her in his arms. He'd held her there, soft and lovely and close to his chest, and for the second time that day, he'd felt a little wild at the sensation. When he'd hauled her up against him, she'd dragged herself closer like she wanted to be there.

Dolt, he told himself. *She was trying not to fall off.*

But his mind had been full of pent-up terror, and his arms had been full of the sweetest, roundest curves he'd ever encountered, and when he'd looked down at her mouth, he'd thought of—

A great many things, most of which weren't achievable on horseback. He prayed—an actual, carefully worded prayer to the divine—that she had not recognized his abrupt and violent erection.

He supposed she probably had not, given that she suddenly seemed *less* afraid of him, rather than more.

Something, to be sure, had changed though. They'd walked along the road, side by side and silent as the grave, until Miss Hope-Wallace had shaken her hair back from her face with a decisive jerk of her chin. "I will do it," she'd said.

And that, it seemed, was that.

He tried not to think about Miss Hope-Wallace after he left her at the castle door under Bertie's alarming glinty-eyed supervision. He made a serious attempt to redirect his thoughts from her person, from the bewitching combination of timidity and raw courage that seemed to coexist within her.

From the color of her eyelashes, which he couldn't stop trying to name. From the way she'd felt in his arms.

He helped Huw recapture the horses and the zebras, and then spent some time hacking away at the rotted section of fence that had permitted the mass zebra exodus in the first place. Eventually Huw bluntly informed him that bashing down the fence—without repairing it—was not as helpful as it might have been.

So he took himself off to his barbican and continued to think—that is, *not* think—about Lydia Hope-Wallace. The barbican was his respite. He'd fashioned the structure—originally a fortification near the castle's entrance—into a kind of forge-courtyard-laboratory for his mucking about with coal and metal. These days, it was the place where his mind went clear. The place where fire and beeswax smoke burned through his constant worry over his brother and the earldom and the state of his finances.

And yet his work did not seem to take his mind off of Miss Hope-Wallace. How could it, when the iron he was turning glowed the precise color of her hair? When a spark landed on his shirt and burned a hole straight through to his chest, right where she'd been pressed against him?

Soft. Lush. Clinging.

Thinking about her was as useless as it was distracting. He burned himself twice whilst pondering the shape of her lower lip, plump and deeply curved.

Which he had no business thinking about. She had come here to marry his *brother*.

The very thought of Miss Hope-Wallace and Davis was a rough scrape against an unhealed wound. Arthur had been so happy when Davis had come back to Strathrannoch Castle a month ago. He'd been entirely taken in by Davis's questions, his brother's interest in Arthur's work.

He'd wanted to believe it. A lifetime could not quite dull that unguarded edge of want.

More fool he.

Davis had lied to him, just as he'd lied to Miss Hope-Wallace. She had been nothing more than a tool to Davis, a pawn manipulated to achieve his own purposes.

And even as fury rose in him—how could Davis have exploited her, her earnest bravery, her toughness and her strength?—Arthur felt uneasiness as well.

Was he the same? Was he not taking advantage of her as Davis had done? He meant to have her help, to use her letters and her connections. True, his motives were not selfish. He wanted to protect those who might be hurt by his own ill-considered invention.

But his motives were not entirely unselfish, either. He still wanted to shake some sense into his brother, to bring Davis back to the fold. He still wanted Davis to change.

Arthur had never had an easy time asking for help. He would do almost anything to avoid it—would grind the glass himself in his barbican to fix the broken windows of Strathrannoch Castle. He would travel for hours astride Luath, to town and back again, before asking one of his tenants to borrow their mill.

But he'd asked Lydia Hope-Wallace. He did not know any other way to find his brother.

He would *make* himself stop thinking about her mouth, he resolved as he left the barbican. He had no other choice.

• • •

He was still thinking about her mouth when the heavy oak door of the bedchamber beside his own opened with a thud directly into his face.

"Ouch—Jesus—fuck—" His voice came out garbled around the hand he'd clapped to his nose.

What the devil? That chamber was *empty*—Fern, his maid,

rarely entered it to clean, since the countess's chamber had not been occupied for well over a decade—

A gingery head peeked around the door. Her dark blue eyes were wide above the hand she had pressed to her mouth.

"Oh goodness," Lydia Hope-Wallace croaked. "I'm so sorry."

He swiped his hand across his nose and checked it for blood. Seeing none, he turned his gaze onto Lydia.

She looked back up at him. Or—sort of at him. Her gaze seemed to be arrested somewhere at the level of his nipples.

He absolutely refused to think about nipples in her presence.

"What," he said, trying to make his voice even, "are you doing here?"

Her mouth opened and then closed again. She turned redder than ever—it made a startling contrast with her orange hair—and addressed his shirtfront. "This is—ah—my chamber? Mr. Palmer told me to sleep in here?"

Bertie. He was going to *kill* Bertie.

He'd thought the revelation of Davis's misdeeds had extinguished Bertie's machinations involving a future Lady Strathrannoch and a half dozen tiny Strathrannoch heirs, but it seemed the man had only been temporarily put off. He had been, evidently, lying in wait for Arthur's moment of vulnerability.

Bertie had installed Lydia in the *countess's* bedchamber. The room currently reserved for Arthur's nonexistent *wife*.

It was a bloody miracle that Bertie had not shackled them together to Arthur's headboard until their wills gave out.

That was another highly vivid image he was not prepared to entertain, and it was all Bertie's fault.

Arthur locked his hand around her elbow and prepared to drag her down the hall. The castle had a dozen bedchambers, and he meant to relocate Miss Hope-Wallace and the innumerable temptations of her person as far from his own as was possible. But before he made it half a dozen steps, Bertie himself came round the corner, followed closely behind by Huw, whose damp white beard suggested he'd bathed since fetching up the zebras.

Bertie's bright brown eyes saw everything, up to and including Arthur's fingers clutching the soft right angle of Lydia's arm.

Arthur let go as though her elbow had sprung red-hot from his forge.

"Ah," Bertie said, "I see you've settled in, Miss Hope-Wallace. I trust Strathrannoch has welcomed you to the castle to the best of his abilities?"

Arthur pinned Bertie with a glare, which Bertie did not acknowledge.

Lydia looked doubtfully between them. "Is there something wrong?"

"Nothing at all, my dear," Bertie said warmly. He flicked a slightly cooler glance at Arthur. "Do you see aught amiss, Strathrannoch?"

The message was clear. Arthur was not meant to insult Miss Hope-Wallace by implying that she was unwelcome.

Which he wouldn't have done in any case, for God's sake. He was not entirely insensitive.

He rubbed at the back of his neck and then promptly dropped his hand. His shirt had a hole beneath the arm, which he normally did not worry about when he was in his own blasted wing of the castle. *Alone.*

"No," he declared. "Everything's grand. Cozy, really. Snug." He peered around Lydia into the countess's bedchamber. "Have you even got any furniture in there?"

"I turned over the mattress," said Huw helpfully.

Arthur sent him a baleful look. "You're part of this conspiracy?"

"What conspiracy?" Lydia was looking between the three of them rather more vigorously.

"It's easier on Fern," Bertie said, as though this were a rational explanation. "She needn't walk so far between rooms to do her cleaning."

Arthur ground his teeth together. "Aye, to be sure. This is all for *Fern*." He turned back to Lydia. "You have furniture, then? You have whatever you need?"

She appeared to give up on the mystery of their conversation. "Yes, it's all perfectly well, except . . ." She trailed off, her cheeks going pink. "There's a small creature in the wardrobe. It appears to have made itself a little burrow of stockings and shredded correspondence."

"Ah," Huw said happily, "that would be the degu. I had no idea she had nested in the countess's chamber!"

"Of course," Lydia repeated. "The degu. In the countess's chamber."

Arthur felt as though he was beginning to lose his grip on sanity. "The creature's part of the menagerie," he said. "The one I told you about. With the zebras."

"Actually," Huw intervened, "Annabelle came from an entirely different menagerie than the zebras."

"Annabelle?" Lydia inquired. Her voice had grown slightly faint.

Arthur pinched the bridge of his nose. "Annabelle is the degu."

Typically he did not regret letting Huw build a small menagerie in his castle. But these were not typical times.

Huw's rock-solid system of ethics protested the mistreatment of any living creature, but neglected animals were his particular weakness. As stable master, he'd taken in several horses from the village that would have been put down for their health or temperament—Arthur's own gelding among them.

Outside of his job at Strathrannoch Castle, Huw had developed a predilection for rescuing abused animals from traveling menageries. Abetted by the ever-crafty Bertie—whose Jamaican solicitor father had bequeathed to him a capacious knowledge of English legal codes—Huw had embarked upon several philanthropic (and slightly felonious) trips across Great Britain to rescue exotic creatures. All of which explained why Strathrannoch Castle was now home to sixteen zebras, two flying squirrels, six macaws, and the small and fuzzy Annabelle.

Arthur took a single despairing breath and then shoved Huw in the direction of Lydia's door. "Relocate Annabelle," he ordered, and then grabbed Bertie and dragged him down to the end of the hall.

"You needn't be quite so peremptory, Strathrannoch," Bertie said when Arthur released him. The older man straightened his cuffs, which looked as pristine as they always did, particularly in comparison to Arthur's general dishevelment.

"I am not marrying this woman," he hissed at Bertie. His voice was barely above a whisper, but he still looked nervously back in the direction of the countess's—Lydia's—hang it, *Miss Hope-Wallace's* chamber. She'd gone inside with Huw, presumably for the degu rousting.

"No one said you were." Bertie had moved on to the neat fold of his cravat. He wore an air of beleaguered innocence, his London accent particularly crisp.

"I can see right through you," Arthur growled. "You've the

same expression on your face as you did when you made me hire young Widow Campbell as castle cook—"

Bertie polished his spectacles on his handkerchief. "I could not possibly have anticipated that she would set the kitchen afire."

"And when you trapped Polly Murray and me in the cold cellar together for twelve hours—"

"An unfortunate accident—"

"She nearly lost a toe to frostbite, Bertie!"

Bertie replaced his spectacles. "An exaggeration, surely."

"When I hired you and Huw a decade ago," Arthur snapped, "it was to help me run this damned estate and keep my people fed and housed, not ensure the continuation of the Strathrannoch line."

Bertie's eyebrows rose. He did not say anything for a long moment.

And Arthur, ludicrously, felt chastened.

He had been twenty-two when he'd hired Bertie and Huw. His brother had been away at school—he'd been sick with dread every time the bills arrived and too ashamed to tell Davis that he had to come home. He'd wanted to peel off his skin when he'd shown his account books to Bertie—terrified the older man would mock or pity him.

Instead Bertie had rubbed his hands together and nodded briskly. "Let's get to work," he'd said. "First, tell me what you possess that you cannot part with. And then I propose that we sell everything else and start fresh."

Bertie and Huw had been at his side ever since, with the notable exception of occasional animal rescue jaunts about the island of Great Britain. Arthur had no right to question their dedication or their years of service.

"I am not especially concerned with the continuation of the

Strathrannoch line," Bertie said mildly. "Nor, I can say with some certainty, is Huw."

Arthur blew out a breath.

It had been his father who had been obsessed with the Strathrannoch line, of course. He had never let Arthur forget what a disappointment he was as heir, and how infinitely preferable Davis would have been.

Arthur was dreamy, distracted, clumsy with his strength. He spoke too familiarly to the tenants. Was forever late to dinner after losing himself in piles of engineering books.

Davis was never late for dinner. Davis was easy and charming; he never had a black curl out of place, never addressed anyone too bluntly and accidentally caused offense.

"It is only that we would like for you to be happy," Bertie said, interrupting the decades-old direction of Arthur's thoughts.

"I am happy."

Bertie's mouth crimped at the corner, a tiny movement that Arthur was not certain how to interpret.

"I am," he said, more forcefully this time. "Just because you found the love of your life nigh on thirty years ago does not mean that everyone wants the same for themselves."

"I know that you need more for yourself than"—Bertie gestured at the stone walls of Strathrannoch Castle around them—"this. That you want love and family."

Arthur thought about his brother—the serrated twist of disappointment and grief he'd felt when he'd realized it had all been a ruse. That Davis had taken the rifle scope and fled in the night.

He thought about the small part of himself that still wished—somehow—that it had all been a misunderstanding. The same part of him that had greeted Davis with a spark of idiotic hope.

The part of himself that he quenched, ruthless as hot metal plunged into cold water.

He did not need more than he had. He would not ask for it.

"No," he said flatly. "I don't need love or family. And I do not want them either."

Chapter 7

. . . I can no longer satisfy myself with the common phrase "Ladies have nothing to do with politics." Female influence must, will, and ought to exist on political subjects as on all others.

—from H to the Earl of Strathrannoch,
received and read by Davis Baird

The next day, Lydia allowed Arthur to lead her up onto the ramparts. Her legs had to work twice as fast as his to keep up on the stairs, and she was panting slightly by the time they reached the top.

He, of course, did not appear to be breathing hard. He had an insultingly well-muscled bum and robust thighs to carry him up three flights of stairs, and brawny shoulders to match from his work at his forge.

She realized she had grown *more* breathless, rather than less, as she stood next to the earl beneath the blue bowl of the sky, and forced herself to stop thinking about the musculature attached to his physical person.

He held a drawing of the rifle scope in his large, burn-stippled hands, but rather than show it to her again, he let it flutter to the ground.

He pointed out into the middle distance, in the direction of the road that she and Georgiana had taken up from Dunkeld. "Do you see the pine tree there? The tallest one, scraggly near the top?"

She blinked. "I see dozens of pine trees."

He caught her chin between thumb and forefinger and angled her face up, out past the guardhouse where she had been looking and farther still.

She shivered. He dropped his hand.

"There," he said roughly. "Do you see now?"

She nodded. She seemed to have forgotten the connection between speech and the relevant parts of her mouth.

"When we first made the rifle scope, Huw tested it out. He shot a red grouse out of that tree, so distant I could not see the bird at all without the lens. I didn't believe him until we rode down there and found it, a cluster of red feathers, dead at the foot of the tree."

She swallowed hard and looked up at him.

"This is no game," he said. "We must find Davis. The damned scope is too dangerous, and I—" His hand tightened into a fist. "I need to get it back."

"I understand," she said. "I promise. I will do everything that I can to help you."

He picked up the sketch that had fallen to his side and shoved it in his trouser pocket. "Thank you," he said gruffly. He did not look at her. "This would not be possible without you."

She felt heat rise in her cheeks, but he did not turn his face to see. They were both silent as he led her back down into the heart of the castle.

She took his terrifying demonstration seriously. She had written to Belvoir's the previous evening to request any information they had about Davis. Barring disaster, the mail coach would take five days to deliver the letter; they could expect another week for a reply.

But there was more she could do in the interim. She was convinced of it.

Over the next week, Lydia reviewed Davis's letters and Georgiana elected to interview the staff at Strathrannoch Castle. Georgiana was a Gothic novelist and a skilled researcher, possessed of a consummate ability to ensorcell others. Before she had revealed herself as a scandalous writer, she'd pretended to be an empty-headed debutante in order to avoid detection, a ruse which had fooled Lydia completely. Now, three years later, Georgiana used her unique talents to procure information about the sensational and the supernatural, gathering anecdotes to incorporate into her writing. She seemed delighted by the prospect of a mysterious investigation at Strathrannoch.

Research had, in fact, been her purported reason for accompanying Lydia to the castle. Back in London, she'd made a very convincing case for why her newest novel required a personal tour of a derelict Scottish estate—something about ghosts and portraits and decaying ruins.

In truth, Lydia suspected that her friend had wanted to protect her. Georgiana had not wanted Lydia to journey alone, and she'd known precisely how to convince Lydia that she was not motivated by pity or doubt.

The staff at Strathrannoch Castle, however, turned out to number rather fewer than Lydia might have guessed, even with her knowledge of Strathrannoch's dubious finances. After conversing with Mr. Palmer and Mr. Trefor, Georgiana had found only Willie, the groom; Fern, the lone chambermaid; and Rupert, Fern's seven-year-old son. Evidently, the Earl of Strathrannoch had been the only one in the vicinity willing to hire seventeen-year-old Fern, who had turned up in the village with a two-month-old baby and no husband to speak of.

Georgiana's reports were consistent: Davis Baird was a charming fellow, easy on the eyes and possessed of a great talent for winning adoration and affection. Rupert seemed the only one who had not been taken in by Davis's most recent performance—Rupert's hero worship, it seemed, extended only to the earl and not to his brother. The boy seemed generally convinced that Strathrannoch had slain giants, wrestled crocodiles, and placed the moon in its orbit about the earth.

Given the presence of zebras on the estate, Lydia supposed the crocodile tale might have some basis in fact.

While Georgiana deployed her information-gathering talents amongst the staff, Lydia found herself in close proximity—again—with Strathrannoch himself.

He wanted to examine all of Davis's letters, a desire which flustered her. In fact, everything about the man flustered her, in a physical fashion altogether different from her normal anxiety around strangers.

In truth, after her first few days at the castle, Strathrannoch no longer seemed like a stranger. Somehow—between the zebras and the degu and the exasperated fond looks he sent toward young Rupert when the boy turned up in his office with a flying squirrel ensconced in his hair—Lydia no longer felt the painful reserve that marked her interactions with people she did not know. She'd become comfortable in his presence, at least comfortable enough to speak to him openly and without too much distress.

No, her physical reaction to the man was decidedly not anxiety.

When he entered the downstairs drawing room in the late afternoons to meet with her, he generally seemed to have come from some work with his tenants. He always looked rather fierce, and once he shouted for Mr. Palmer's assistance—something about seeds and tomatoes and mad old Scots with no sense of agricultural timing. He wore his shirt open about the neck—always, except at dinner—and his sleeves rolled up to reveal forearms taut with muscle and gleaming with curly golden hairs. His beard had thickened since her arrival, but it did not disguise the sulky shape of his mouth.

Lydia found it all immensely distracting, particularly when he pulled a chair up to the desk beside her and asked to examine whatever it was that she was reading.

He was interested in everything. He wanted to know about her pamphlets, her politics, her exchanges with his brother. She perused his office one evening before dinner while he sorted through her correspondence and discovered that he was extensively well-read and possessed of notes and papers upon nearly every subject she could think of. Evidently much of the Strathrannoch library had been sold in an effort to raise funds, but he had made his own careful notes on hundreds of scientific texts. He informed her—the tops of his ears slightly red—that he was a member of a circulating library in Edinburgh, which he visited monthly to keep up with advancements in agricultural technology.

"Did you go to university there?" she asked curiously, resuming her place at the desk by his side. "One of my brothers graduated a few years ago from the Royal College of Physicians. Your scientific curiosity reminds me of his—I think you would get on."

But when she looked at him, he was frowning again, his fingers tense on the quill that he held over one of Davis's letters. "No," he said shortly. "Neither of us went to university, though Davis was schooled at Eton."

She blinked. "Was he? Why, he never spoke of it, not once, in all his letters."

"Aye, well, he couldn't have done, could he? Or else you might have known it wasn't me writing the letters."

"What do you mean?"

"He went." Arthur hitched one shoulder in a shrug. "I didn't. So he could not mention it."

She did not know what to make of that. It was not unheard-of— the heir being kept at home to learn the estate and its husbandry, the younger son sent off to school.

But it was not so very common, either. And from what little she had gleaned of the previous earl these last days, she did not imagine he had been a particularly good teacher.

"Davis spoke only of Scotland," she told Arthur. "I would not have guessed he had lived in England. Here—he mentions Argyll and Buccleuch. In this one, Glencoe—"

Arthur looked up sharply. "Glencoe?"

"Yes, I think that was it. He said you had a house there—he remembered it most fondly."

She could see the tension rise between Arthur's shoulder blades, could feel it in waves from his large form. Her body was always attuned to such things, ready to predict catastrophe from the stiffness in someone else's tone or the harsh line of their mouth.

But she did not think Arthur was upset with her. He looked back down at the letters, his curling lashes falling over his eyes. "Aye, we had a summer house in Glencoe. Our father sold it when Davis went to school. I would not have thought he remembered."

But Davis had remembered. The stories had been drawn in such vivid colors, his scene-setting sharp and precise. She'd laughed aloud at his anecdotes of tumbling into the water while fishing for trout with his bare hands, of stealing apples from a tree he'd later learned belonged to his own father.

It occurred to her now, as she watched Arthur compel his fist to uncurl, that Davis had never, in any of his letters, mentioned having a brother.

Had it been a fear of accidentally revealing himself? A wariness about referencing himself in the third person?

Or was it something altogether darker? A desire to pretend that he was the Earl of Strathrannoch—and that the brother who currently held the role had never existed?

Lydia did not know what to think. And she wondered—a strange ache rising in her throat—if Arthur had noticed. If it had hurt him to read the letters.

But he shook his head, rejecting the very notion of the house in Glencoe. "Argyll, Buccleuch: Those two are not a surprise. Those are the homes of his great friends these last years—the aristocrats who favor him."

Yes, Arthur had mentioned this—that Davis had not been a critic of the Scottish aristocrats whom they'd discussed but rather a friend to them. It was almost impossible for her to accept.

She withdrew a writing-covered sheet from the stack of correspondence, one she'd read so many times that the ink had worn down where the page was folded. "I find it difficult to believe that Davis supports Argyll and Buccleuch and Sutherland. It must be an act. Did you not read this letter?"

She found the lines she wanted quickly enough. "'Sutherland is beginning to wear a depopulated and ruinous aspect. The duchess sends a posse of men to eject the Highlanders from their dwellings—homes in which they have gone through all the stages of their lives, homes endeared to them by a thousand ties and circumstances—'"

"*Homes which are then burned before their very eyes.* Aye. I recall the words."

She raised her eyes from the letter to find Arthur's face. "You can read this and truly believe that he supports what Sutherland and the others are doing in the Highlands?"

She had admired this letter—its plainspoken sympathy, the care it evinced for the Highlanders whose homes had been ruthlessly destroyed.

"Aye," Arthur said. "Because Davis did not write those words. I did."

Her lips parted, and the moment stretched as she sought speech. "I beg your pardon?"

She could see, even beneath the beard, that his jaw was tight. His hand opened and closed on the desk. "I wrote down the stories the crofters told us. The ones who came here from the Highlands. We tried to find a place for them on our lands or, failing that, the means to move them to the Americas. I wrote their stories and then I sent them to the newspapers, and some of them were printed. That's where Davis got the words, I suppose. From my own damned pen."

She blinked several times in quick succession and reminded herself to close her mouth. *Arthur* had written these words? Had been the author of the sentiment she had so admired?

She scarcely knew what to feel. A bizarre twist of betrayal—though why this revelation should disturb her almost more than everything else Davis had done, she did not know. She felt unsettled, almost unmoored.

She had not truly known Davis. Of course she had not; she perceived that perfectly well by now. He had wanted something from her—information, political gossip that she was privy to. His letters had been filled with lies.

But perhaps in some small way, she had known the man he'd pretended to be. She had known the Earl of Strathrannoch.

Her fingers on the desk were inches from Arthur's, she realized. It would be easy to slide her hand over to his. To soothe the unhappy tension there. To ease her palm along the muscular line of his forearm and—

She coughed, then cleared her throat, then finally transferred her fingers to her lap. "I thought you did not care for politics. When I first arrived with the letters, you said that you could not have written them because you were not interested in political causes."

"The Clearances, the crofters—'tis not politics, lass. 'Tis people's lives."

She shook her head in automatic negation of his words. "All politics are about people's lives. Our experiences are what drive our politics—our experiences and our sympathy for the lives of others."

"Is that so?"

"Of course. I told you about my pamphlet on debt reform, did I not?"

"Aye."

"My maid, Nora, came to work in our home at fifteen because her father was sent to the Marshalsea." She pressed her lips together in remembered outrage. "The whole family was forced to either live with him in debtor's prison or else work off his debt—*his* debt, not their own." She made herself unclench her fingers, which had locked together in her lap. "It's *wrong*. And what's more wrong is that our own father came from debt—my grandfather, the Marquess of Vye, was deeply mired in generations of it—and yet his treatment was entirely different because he was a member of peerage. The whole system ought to be burned down and built anew."

Strathrannoch had a peculiar expression on his face as he looked down at her. "Aye," he said slowly, "perhaps you're right. I have always . . ." He hesitated, as if searching for the words. "It has always seemed to me best to do what I can for my own land—my own people."

Yes. She had seen that in him from the first.

Her sex, her unmarried state, her natural reticence—all of it had led her to come at politics in the shadows, always working just out of sight. But this man—blunt and softhearted by turns, somehow rough and gentle at the same time—tackled the problems of his world differently, with his sleeves rolled up and his hands set to a plow.

She admired that. She admired him.

"I'm sorry," she said impulsively. "I'm sorry Davis took your rifle telescope. I'm sorry I don't know where he might be."

There was a short, cautious pause as he took her in, his face close to hers. She could feel the weight of his gaze, the peculiar gravitational pull of his body beside her own.

"Yet," he said finally. "We don't know where he is yet. I'll find him."

She glanced back down at the letters they'd been examining, and her mind, which had been a trifle hazed by the combination of his eyes and voice and general proximity, suddenly sharpened. She slipped one of the letters free, and then another, lining them up on the desk.

"We should plot these sites on a map," she said. "Both of us, together. Some of them I'll know how to find—the estates, the villages he mentions—but others I'll need you for. *The cleverest little dry-goods store*, he says here, or *the burn where I fished as a boy.* You would know those places—I would not. If we mark them all out, perhaps they'll give us some indication of his whereabouts when he wrote the letters or a sense of the location of his allies."

She realized as she turned to him that Arthur was gazing at her, surprise and something else on his face, a deeper curve to his bottom lip than she had seen before.

Admiration? Or—no, not precisely admiration.

Pleasure.

His hand flexed on the desk and his smallest finger somehow brushed hers. She wore no gloves when writing. His skin was warm against her own.

"Aye," he said roughly, "I'll do that."

His hand came away from hers and she clutched her quill, cool against her heated skin, as he rose to find a map.

Chapter 8

. . . He's just spent three-quarters of an hour stewing apples with his own hands. When I asked if Miss Hope-Wallace especially fancies apple pudding, he fled like the kitchen was afire. Promising!!!

*—from Fern Ferguson, maid, to Bertie Palmer,
estate manager at Strathrannoch*

The drawing room of Strathrannoch Castle was overlarge and not quite warm enough at night. The windows were poorly fitted and late-October drafts occasionally put out the candles or sent a letter winging its way down from Arthur's desk.

And yet he could not stop returning to the room.

In the near-fortnight since Lydia Hope-Wallace's arrival, he had joined her in the drawing room again and again, a moth drawn to her flame. Every morning he told himself to stop, to visit his people and their fields. To stay away from the room and its temptations. He knew enough now about her correspondence with Davis; there was nothing to be gained by asking her about her writing or her politics or her numerous beloved brothers.

But eventually the sun would start to dip. His tenants would begin hinting delicately about their dinner. And his feet would make their way unerringly back to where Lydia pored over maps and notes at his desk while they waited to hear back from her library. He could not seem to stop himself.

She was shy, he'd learned—she rarely spoke in groups, and only when directly addressed. But she was far from timid. She had opinions on every subject—he knew, because he'd asked her about all of them. She opposed the Seditious Meetings Act and became nearly irate on the subject of rotten boroughs. She had thoughts on the Luddites, on the Corn Laws—when she learned of Huw's devotion to animal welfare, she engaged the elated stable master in a lengthy conversation on the philosophical work of Jeremy Bentham.

In some ways, she would have made a perfect wife for Davis— the old Davis, before he'd fallen into the clutches of the powerful and corrupt. Davis had loved to talk of politics and people; Davis would have known how to soothe her anxieties and draw her out of her shell in company.

But Arthur was content to watch her, bright-eyed, pink about the cheeks, just a bit flustered.

And in the evenings, after supper, he found himself returning to the drawing room, even though she was not there. The drawing room was where she worked during the day, and when he sat at the desk at night, he found that he could still catch her scent. It was soft—warm—edible, like cream on scones. The room whispered echoes of Lydia, and he was helpless to resist, no matter how much he knew he ought to stop.

A few more days. He would let himself linger in the pleasures of her clever mind and the sweet curve of her mouth for a few more days, until they received a return letter from her library. And then she would go back to London, and he would be alone again at Strathrannoch.

And alone was far safer. He'd learned that lesson well from his brother.

As he'd read Davis's letters to Lydia, he'd become increasingly convinced that he had been right about his brother's motivations. It seemed clear that Davis was subtly probing for information in the letters. He'd asked Lydia who in London was on her side, who she suspected would be willing to speak out against the Clearances or against Scottish involvement in the Napoleonic Wars. He had claimed to be looking for allies in England.

When Lydia had gone scarlet before handing the packet over to Arthur to examine, it had occurred to him with no small discomfort that some of the letters must contain his brother's attempts at lovemaking. He found that he did not—under any circumstances—want to read such a thing.

But the letters were not overtly flirtatious. In retrospect, Arthur supposed she had removed the more romantic missives before turning the letters over to him. But even without an obvious confession of his feelings, Davis did what he always did when he fixed his attention upon someone—made the recipient of his regard feel special. Feel as though their words mattered to him more than anyone else's.

It was a powerful talent, that. And one that made you feel quite the fool when you worked out that you'd been deceived.

Arthur was musing upon his brother's talent directed toward Lydia Hope-Wallace and fuming to himself so vigorously that he did not at first notice when the woman herself slipped into the drawing room in the middle of the night.

He did notice, however, when she kicked a stack of books, knocked several to the floor, and cursed under her breath.

His head went up. "Lydia?"

She jumped into the air like a startled doe. Or a zebra.

"Oh," she gasped, her dark blue gaze finding his. "Oh, I'm so sorry! I did not see you!"

Indeed, he could imagine that she had not thought to meet him down here in the drawing room at—he checked his decrepit pocket watch—two o'clock in the morning. She wore a night rail—he could see the edge of it peeking out above her toes, a silky-looking cotton—and over it a thick wool dressing gown, which fastened down the front with a row of fabric-covered buttons.

All the way down, from her chin to her ankles.

It must take her ages to get the thing on. Or off. He imagined it—one at a time, each slow slide of button through buttonhole. Each one falling free with a careful manipulation of her fingers, each revealing a new inch of that fragile garment beneath.

Oh Jesus, he had to stop thinking about her like that. He'd undressed her only to the level of plain white cotton, and he was finding even that mental picture terrifyingly arousing.

"Are you looking for something?" he managed to rasp. What *was* she doing downstairs in the wee hours? Should she not be tucked up into her bed in the chamber beside his own?

That too was something he tried very hard not to think about, with only middling success.

"Oh no," she said, as if by reflex.

He blinked. "No?"

"Oh," she said—this was, perhaps, the fourth time she'd uttered the syllable—and then laughed a little. She had the loveliest laugh—warm and soft, her fingers on her throat as though the very sound surprised her. "Yes, I suppose I am. I could not sleep—I often cannot. I paced my bedroom and looked through all the letters I have left to me, and I imagined for a moment that I could see the beginnings of a pattern—and then it all unraveled in my mind. I thought perhaps if I looked at my notes again . . ."

Her notes—yes. She was here for her *notes*.

She's not here for you, he informed his suddenly very alert body.

"By all means." He pushed back from the desk, his boots scraping the threadbare wool rug beneath his feet. "Do you keep the notes here in the desk?"

"Yes." She came toward the desk cautiously, and he noted the ridiculous things she had on her feet. Bed slippers, he supposed, with enormous tassels bobbing near the front in a rainbow-hued explosion of yarn.

He backed away from her with an unholy celerity as she approached. Lydia Hope-Wallace—with her sunset hair and her thousands of buttons and her ridiculous footwear—was altogether too much for his self-possession at two o'clock in the morning.

She was reaching for the drawers at the right-hand side of the desk when she paused, frozen, to stare at the map spread across the desk's age-spotted surface.

Her lips parted. He waited for her to speak; it was, he'd learned, not entirely unusual for her to pause to gather herself before voicing her thoughts.

But the silence stretched, a moment and then another, and then she said his name, in a whisper that slid down his spine like a delicate fingertip.

"Arthur. You did it."

It took him too damned long to recover from the effect of his name on her lips. God, the woman did his head in.

"I—what? I didn't—"

She clapped a hand down on the map and looked up at him, her blue eyes lit from behind as though her emotions produced candlelight. "You discovered where Davis has been living! How did you do it? How long have you known?"

"Lass, I didn't discover anything." But he found himself drawn back to the desk toward her, toward the map she was busily caressing.

Had he, somehow, ascertained Davis's location and then simply forgotten he'd done so? Perhaps the sudden descent of blood from his brain southward had impaired his memory. Hell, perhaps he was hallucinating all of this, and Lydia Hope-Wallace was safe in her bed and not inches from him, her face aglow.

"Look," she said, her mobile fingers no longer caressing the map so much as jabbing at it. "All of these dots—all of the ones you've done in blue ink, rather than black. There must be fifteen of them, all within a dozen miles of one another."

He looked down. "These are naught but the places you wanted me to mark. The places that Davis referenced but did not name. The dry-goods store. The assembly where he learned to dance. The home of the widow known hereabouts for her, er, bountiful charms."

"Oh yes—of course!" Her hands spread flat against the desk, and she leaned forward, her braided hair slipping over one shoulder. "Of course. You were so clever to change the color of the ink, or we might not have noticed the pattern. But it makes sense. If he was trying to keep his whereabouts a secret, it would not be the places he named that gave him away. It would be the places that he did not put a name to at all."

He had not intended it as cleverness—it had been borne of necessity, to track the work she'd asked of him.

But she was right. He leaned toward her, bending his head into the light of the lamp to see the pattern she'd indicated.

Good God, she was canny. It seemed plain as day to him now.

The line of blue dots marched up and down the River Tay, clustered above and beneath the nearby town of Haddon Grange. It was as if the letters had been encoded in a message only he could read—only he could have made sense of Davis's offhand remarks. Only he had the stories and memories of nearly thirty years of brotherhood, pulled together and apart like magnets, attracted and repelled at the same time.

"Do you know this place?" Her fingers were long and tapered, longer than her stature properly justified. She slid the pad of her index finger along the River Tay, a few inches from Arthur's own hand.

"Aye, I know it. 'Tis a town called Haddon Grange. There's an estate nearby—a family we've known since childhood. A proper town—sometimes I go there for supplies when I don't want to travel all the way to Perth."

She was smiling now as she looked up at him, her expression incandescent. He had seen her smile before—could practically enumerate the instances. Several times at Georgiana and at Rupert in his presence. Once at him, when she'd caught him slipping a misbegotten cabbage dish to the degu.

But none of those smiles could match this one for sheer luminosity. Her lower lip, usually a deep, plump curve, was stretched wide, and her eyes crinkled a bit at the corners.

"That must be where he's been living!" Her voice was a study in quiet triumph. "Perhaps he's there even now—or perhaps someone will know where he's gone. Oh, Arthur! We needn't wait for Belvoir's now—"

He did not know why he did it. Perhaps it was his name, again, on her mouth, setting off a small explosion in the part of his brain that made sensible decisions.

Or perhaps it was the word after his name. The confident, unhesitating *we*.

Whatever the reason, he reached out and touched her cheek.

He felt a bright, fierce little shock as his fingers met her skin, powerful enough to jolt his hand back.

He had half a heartbeat to stare at her in utter bafflement. Had he gone mad? Had she felt it too? It was as if his life had become a sentimental novel—touching her sent electricity sparking through his body; the woman was the kindling to his conflagration—

And then she yelped and clapped a hand to her face.

Oh. He was an idiot. There was no mystical connection instantiated by the collision of their bodies. He had simply given her an electric shock, right there on the smooth skin of her cheek.

"Och, for the love of God," he said, "I'm sorry. The rug—it collects a charge that way—I shouldn't have done—"

He stretched his hand back out, placing his fingers over her own.

She made another sound, soft and startled, though he was not quite sure why—he was certain he had not shocked her this time.

"Let me see—"

"Oh, no—I assure you, I'm perfectly well—"

She wrenched her hand free from beneath his, and then suddenly there he was. Exactly as he'd intended moments ago, the tips of his fingers on her skin.

Only now her cheeks were stained with pink, and he bent his head down to take a look at her.

She seemed unmarred. Of course she would be—he had only shocked her, not damaged her in some way.

Yet he could not stop himself from checking.

He wanted to make sure she was all right, that was all. He needed to make sure.

He slid his thumb along her cheekbone. She was surprisingly unfreckled for an ivory-skinned little ginger. Perhaps it was all the ridiculous hats she liked to wear, frivolous and pretty, like her seemingly endless collection of slippers.

Beneath his thumb, her skin was smooth and warm. So delicate—the blood rushed to the place where he touched her, flushing beneath his hand.

Was she like that—everywhere?

He did not mean for his thumb to slip down, but it seemed to move of its own volition. He watched himself cup her jaw. He watched his thumb trace the arc of her lower lip, and then, when she took one trembling breath, he watched himself brush against the corner of her mouth.

He would have thought it was some other man's hand on her face, except he could feel everything. He could feel the feather-light brush of her quick unsteady breaths. The heat of her skin, the gentle rise of her lower lip. The softness of her body, where his other hand had come to rest at her waist.

He could kiss her. God, he wanted to kiss her. He wanted her mouth under his. He wanted to know if she tasted as sweet and warm as she smelled. He wanted to know if her skin would flush when he sucked at the place where her neck met her shoulder; he wanted to know if his teeth would leave a mark. He wanted her up on the desk, her legs locked around his waist, wanted to kiss her and loose her buttons and touch her and touch her and touch her.

He might have, if she hadn't taken half a step backward. The edge of her dressing gown brushed against the desk, and there was a faint whispering sound as a stack of Davis's letters slid to the floor at their feet.

It might as well have been the report of a pistol.

He dropped his hand and backed away, a half step and then a little farther for good measure.

Davis's letters. Bloody hell, the woman had come here for *Davis*. She'd been in love with his own damned brother.

Arthur felt suddenly dizzy, almost sick.

What had he thought to do with her? Tup her on the desk? Take her virtue and trap her into marrying him?

Christ, she would think him a fortune hunter. She would think him no better than Davis.

He would *be* no better than Davis, if he used her that way. Had they not taken enough from her already, he and his brother? He had seen the tears in her eyes upon the revelation of Davis's deception. He had already trapped her here in this godforsaken castle, waiting for news and trying to help track down his brother and the weapon. He would not be party to harming her further.

It did not matter how much he wanted her. It did not matter how she looked—glowing and vibrant, tempting and real—or the way she felt beneath his hands.

He could not touch her again.

"I beg your pardon," he said. "Your—er, are you well? Your cheek?"

Her fingers rose to caress the skin where his hand had been. He watched the movement, memorized it. Wished with foolish desperation it was his own hand.

"Yes, of course," she said. "I'm perfectly well."

There was something in her voice at odds with the crisp words. A kind of—wistfulness, perhaps? A ribbon of yearning that wound itself round and round inside his chest. That pulled tight with a tension that felt like heartache.

"Tomorrow," he said shortly, "we'll talk of Haddon Grange with the others."

And then he turned on his heel and fled from her—from her big blue eyes and the heady, high-proof softness of her skin, and from the longing that rose in him when he looked at her.

Chapter 9

... *Men being the Historians, they seldom condescend to record the great and good Actions of Women* ...

—*from Lydia's private copy of* THE CHRISTIAN
RELIGION, AS PROFESS'D BY A DAUGHTER OF THE
CHURCH OF ENGLAND, *annotated in her hand:* "*And
so we must take up our pens.*"

They gathered in the drawing room the following morning after breakfast. Huw and Bertie arrayed themselves around the desk. Georgiana and Lydia sat on the chaise longue, Bacon between them and Annabelle the degu at their feet. And Arthur—

Lydia tried not to look at Arthur, looming grumpily in the threshold like a bear roused from hibernation. Her eyes were gritty—she had not slept well. She had caught a glimpse of herself in the glass this morning and winced at the bruised-looking purple beneath her eyes. Her cursed skin was too revealing, her fears written out there on her face for the world to see.

No, she had not slept well. She had not been able to stop recalling their encounter in the drawing room, circling round and round the moment when Arthur's thumb had caught the corner of her mouth and his hand had grasped her waist.

She had never been kissed. There was, of course, nothing wrong with never having been kissed at six-and-twenty, or at any other advanced age. There was no reason to be embarrassed by it—except that she was the sort of woman who *wanted* to be kissed, hard and thoroughly, and the opportunity had not presented itself, not even once, in her entire life.

She had never been kissed and yet, in that moment, she had been quite certain that Arthur's mouth was going to descend upon hers. She had *wanted* it, with a yearning that had stolen her breath.

She'd waited, wishing, hoping. And nothing had transpired after all. The man had dropped his hands and flung himself backward like she was hot to the touch, and she'd had nothing to do but leave the way she had come in.

There was no rational reason to be embarrassed—she had not done anything wrong. And yet she found she could not look at Arthur anyway, not at his eyes or his hands or the almost-pout of his mouth.

Especially not his mouth.

Arthur broke the silence that had descended upon the assembled group. "Miss Hope-Wallace has solved it."

She gaped at him, no longer pretending not to look in his direction. She had . . . what? She was not sure she had heard him correctly.

Behind the desk, Bertie took on a proud, almost avuncular smile. "Of course she did. I knew she would."

She felt heat rise in her cheeks. She hadn't . . . not really . . . "No," she protested, "I didn't do anything in particular. His lordship was the one who—"

"Aye, you did," said Arthur. "I merely did the labor. You saw the pattern in it. The whole project was your idea from the start."

She did not know what to say. She felt revealed, every eye in the room fixed upon her.

And yet, strangely, there was none of the squirming discomfort that usually filled her in such a moment. Somehow, she felt not pinned to a wall, examined like a trapped and wriggling thing, but *recognized*. Seen.

It was not an unpleasant sensation. Not at all.

"Well done, lass," said Huw. "What did you discover? Do you know where Davis has taken the rifle scope?"

Everyone waited for her to answer, and to her surprise, she found she could.

"I don't know precisely," she said. "I only know that when he was writing the majority of the letters, he seemed to be living in or near a town called Haddon Grange. His lordship says you are familiar with it?"

"Yes, of course." Bertie picked up a quill and spun it eagerly between his fingers, as though he meant to take notes on their conversation. "About three hours from here on horseback; we sell some of our grain to the milner there. A not insubstantial village—a few dozen houses and shops. The estate of Lord and Lady de Younge is not far."

"Could Davis have resided there?" Georgiana asked. "Perhaps under an assumed name? Would his face have been known to the people of Haddon Grange?"

"Aye," Arthur said. "We're both familiar enough to them—his face and mine as well. Most of the town, I think, would recognize him if they saw him there."

"He could be there now," said Huw, "practically right under our noses."

Lydia felt an unexpected ripple of pride.

Between her naive trust in Davis and her impulsive journey to Scotland, she'd marinated in her own foolishness since the moment she'd arrived at Strathrannoch Castle. But perhaps—if she helped Arthur find his brother, if she played a role in preventing violence—perhaps she would have turned a rash impulse into something worthwhile.

Perhaps she could do right in the end.

"You should go to Haddon Grange," Bertie said decisively, his gaze trained on Arthur in the threshold. "As soon as you can. Tomorrow, if you can manage it. See if you can find him—or, if he's no longer there, see if you can work out any clue as to where he might have gone."

"Aye," Arthur said. He levered himself up from where he had been leaning against the frame of the door. "Come up to your office with me, Bertie, and we'll make a plan for the estate in my absence. I trust you to know what's right, of course, but you'll understand if I want to speak of it anyway."

"Yes," said Bertie, drawing the word out as he slid the quill between his fingers. "Yes. But you ought not go alone. You should take Miss Hope-Wallace and Lady Georgiana."

Lydia felt slightly dizzy as the words registered. There was a faint buzzing sound in her ears that almost drowned out the rough sound of Arthur's next words.

Not quite though. His deep voice rumbled straight into her chest.

"Absolutely not."

"Only think upon it," Bertie said serenely. "If Davis is there, he may be more willing to meet with Lydia than with you. She may be able to entice him—"

"I will not use her as bait!"

"She need not involve herself beyond writing Davis a note, perhaps. He knows her hand."

"She is too bloody involved as it is!"

The words stung. They scraped at the soft parts of Lydia's heart.

She wanted to tell him he was right. She was far too involved; she should never have come in the first place. She wanted to say that she had no desire to accompany him in any case, that she only wanted to help him with the letters and then go home.

No. In truth, she wanted not to speak at all. She wanted to bury her face in her hands and let them argue above her head, to fade away until no one in the room could see her.

It would be so easy to disappear from the conversation. She was exquisitely accomplished at disappearing.

And what had it gotten her? That hiding, that lying in wait?

She had done some good these last three years as H. She knew that she had. She had helped rouse public sentiment in favor of universal suffrage and divorce reform. She'd been largely responsible for the failed campaign of a pro-slavery MP in Camelford. She had arranged alternate employment for all of the Marquess of Queensbury's female staff after she'd discovered that he'd impregnated three serving girls and then tossed them out on the street.

But she herself had not changed. Not yet.

"I want to go." Her voice came out small and strained, and though she was painfully embarrassed, she tried again. "I want to go with you to Haddon Grange. I'd like to see what we can find out about Davis."

Arthur turned toward her, shifting his glare from Bertie's face to hers. "And what will you do if Davis finds you there? If the first time he lays eyes on you is through my rifle scope, aimed at your heart from a hundred leagues away?"

"I don't know," she said. "Perhaps I'll propose."

There was a brief startled silence, broken by the squeak of Georgiana's hastily stifled laugh.

Arthur glowered. "For Christ's sake. I showed you on the ramparts what the scope can do. You could be hurt. I wouldn't . . . I would not have you hurt again by me or mine."

"I know," she said. "I understand. But I believe . . ."

She could not put it into words—what she thought, what she wanted. She struggled a moment, trying for speech, and Arthur—

Waited. He waited patiently for her, his hazel eyes resting upon her face.

This is your chance to change your life, she had told herself, and then lied to her family and set out for Scotland.

It had been an unqualified disaster. She'd proposed to a literal stranger, had been quite squarely rejected upon the basis that they were *literal strangers*, had nearly been run over by a herd of zebras, and had gotten herself involved in the theft of experimental weaponry. She had hoped, in her most optimistic fantasies, that this trip would end with her happily settled into a marriage of convenience with a man who respected her and her ideas, who appreciated the wealth and political connections she could bring to their marriage.

That happy outcome was, it went without saying, not to be.

And yet . . . and yet . . .

Was it not still possible for her to change? Was this not a chance for her to *do* something—to thrust herself into the world instead of hiding from it, to take action instead of waiting fruitlessly for a life that never quite seemed to begin?

"I believe I can help you," she said finally. "I cannot write to him from here—the postal mark will be unmistakable if it comes from the vicinity of Strathrannoch Castle. He will know I came here, know I spoke to you and discovered the truth of his identity. But I could leave a note for him at Haddon Grange. I can ask after him, in places that you cannot because your face would be known to all and sundry."

"'Tis not safe—"

"It is not more unsafe for me than it is for you. Perhaps less so—if Davis hears that you have come to Haddon Grange in search of him, he will either flee or fight. But he will not learn of my arrival except on *my* terms."

"I can help as well," put in Georgiana at her side. "I can speak to the villagers. I can gain their confidence and find out what they know or remember about Davis."

"She's very good," Lydia said. "You will want her along."

"'Tis not about wanting or no!" Arthur's voice was rough with frustration.

"You're right. It is not about what you want or what I want. It's about what is the most expedient—and right now, that is for all of us to travel together to Haddon Grange and locate Davis as quickly as possible."

"I can go with you," Huw said.

Lydia's gaze darted to the Welshman, whose normally booming voice was almost soft.

"If it eases your mind about the ladies' safety, lad, I'll go with you. Willie can mind the stables for a day or two without me to clout him regularly. It'll be good for him."

"And I will take charge of Sir Francis Bacon," said Bertie mildly, "whilst you are gone."

Arthur seemed to be gritting his teeth. "I don't need all of you to come to my aid. This is my brother—my damned responsibility. I've asked enough of Miss Hope-Wallace as it is."

Huw's mouth was quirked at one corner beneath his beard. "There is no particular honor in going it alone, lad. If Miss Hope-Wallace and Lady Georgiana want to help, then you are best served by letting them."

"And," Bertie put in, "there is no little urgency to the project of finding your brother."

Arthur rubbed one large hand across the back of his neck. His blue-green-gold eyes flickered to Lydia's for one brief moment and then away.

"All right," he said. "Fine. Let's go then, we four, to Haddon Grange."

Satisfaction flared in Lydia, bright and fervent, and alongside it—

Alongside it, a sudden horrible realization.

She had just committed herself to entering a town of strangers and *talking* to them. With no prior introduction or invitation—no, she would simply march up to a whole village's worth of people she had never met and demand to know the whereabouts of one Davis Baird.

She could picture herself, with a kind of hallucinatory clarity, fainting at their feet. Her mind offered up a banquet of horrifying possibilities. She would cry. She would speak out of turn and be pilloried. Somehow her identity as H would become known and she would accidentally kindle a resurgence of Jacobitism.

Dear God. She had run mad. She could not do this.

She opened her mouth to say something—*I take it back, I was merely jesting, ha ha ha, what a lark!*

And then she closed her mouth again.

She was going to help. She *could* help. She had ridden astride and cut her horse free before they were all trampled by zebras. She had helped Arthur solve the puzzle of Davis's whereabouts. She had gotten herself and Georgiana to *Scotland* without alerting her mother or brothers, for heaven's sake.

She could do this too.

She hoped.

Chapter 10

. . . I've decided to extend my stay with the Stanhopes a trifle. We are having such a pleasant visit!

—from Lydia to her eldest brother, enclosed in a letter to Selina along with a note: "Would you please post this from Sussex? No sense in alarming Theo just yet."

By the following morning, they were in a carriage together: Lydia, Georgiana, and Arthur, with Huw up front, holding the reins.

Lydia had been startled to discover that the Strathrannoch stables possessed a carriage at all—but when she saw the vehicle, it made rather more sense. The coach-and-four was a great, ugly thing that groaned and creaked as the horses pulled it into motion. Its style had been popular a generation ago, as the ancient hazed glass of the windows suggested. And it was decorated, all along both sides, with an enormous version of the Strathrannoch crest, inlaid in a little mosaic of multicolored wood. The crest appeared to be a giant boar, mouth agape, each of its tusks larger than Lydia's forearm.

"There was no way to sell it," Arthur explained when he

caught her staring at the coach in stupefaction. "The design could not be removed or scraped off without damaging the box. Both gaudy and impractical—a Baird family specialty."

Fern and Rupert had seen them off, the boy waving furiously whilst one of the rescued macaws tried to retain its purchase on his shoulder. Bertie had promised to pass along any information from Belvoir's the moment it arrived.

And though the carriage had seemed perfectly capacious when she, Georgiana, and Arthur had piled into it, after an hour's progress toward Haddon Grange, Lydia was starting to revise that impression.

It was just that the earl was so . . . substantial. She and Georgiana sat together on one bench, Arthur opposite them, and Lydia found that her eyes were drawn again and again to the man's thighs and shoulders, which seemed to take up nearly as much space on his side as she and Georgiana did together on theirs.

This was, obviously, the fault of his shoulders. Not her eyes. It was not *her* fault there was nowhere else in the carriage to look.

He had at least worn a coat and cravat for their journey, though he still had not shaved and his beard was growing thick with curls, like his hair. She wondered if it would be soft to the touch now—no longer a rasp of stubble but something she could put her fingers into.

She realized the direction of her thoughts with no small horror, and tried to make herself stop.

Of course, the man immediately made this resolution impossible by addressing her directly.

"Does your family know what you came here to do?" he asked. "Your brother—the one who's a politician?"

"Ah," she said. "Er. No. Not precisely."

Georgiana squeaked as she smothered her laugh. Lydia pretended not to hear her.

"I told my mother and brothers that I wanted to spend the month with my friend Selina Kent, the Duchess of Stanhope, and her husband at their country estate in Sussex. I chose a week when everyone was busy with their own affairs"—her mother parading debutantes in front of several recalcitrant sons; her eldest brother, Theo, deep in legislation; the next eldest, Jasper, away on holiday in Venice—"and met Georgiana at the Stanhope estate. And then we, er—"

"And then the duke and duchess pretended not to notice when we fled the country," Georgiana explained.

"I . . . see." Arthur looked slightly alarmed by her machinations.

"They did not know," Lydia said, torn between a desire to defend herself and the knowledge that her plan had, in fact, been a complete failure from top to bottom. "My family. They did not know about my correspondence with Davis, and I thought . . . I thought . . ."

She had thought to shock them with her triumph, she supposed. She loved her family, powerfully and without reservation, and yet they treated her like a fragile child half the time.

For God's sake, Theo, meet with your mates at the club, not at home. You know Lyd can't dine with strangers.

Mother, let Lyddie alone this Season, won't you? She doesn't have to marry; there's no sense torturing her.

She had envied her brothers—the way they seemed to move through the world so easily. And she'd wanted them to think her brave and strong. An equal, not a doll to be perpetually safeguarded.

"Were they not aware of your political writings, then?" asked Arthur.

Lydia felt the corner of her mouth lift. "Some of them. Two of my brothers."

"Two of how many again?"

"Four."

Arthur's brows rose.

Her mouth curled up further. "All older."

"I have heard Mrs. Hope-Wallace say that Lydia did not walk until she was two or speak until she was nearly four," Georgiana informed the earl.

Lydia laughed a little. "I had no need to. My brothers carried me everywhere and spoke my mind for me."

They still would, if she asked, and she felt the familiar tangle of emotions when she thought about her brothers.

Theo, Jasper, Gabe, Ned: All four of her brothers accepted her exactly as she was. They had never tried to force her into the mold of a perfect, outgoing debutante, nor had they tried to pressure her to marry one of the fortune hunters who had proposed in her first and second Seasons.

She was grateful to them—always and endlessly. But some part of her was resentful too, a creeping dissatisfaction that made her feel guilty and a little ashamed. It had always been the same: Lydia did not need to speak for herself because someone was always there to speak for her.

She had let them build a wall around her life, thinking it protection, and somehow that shield had become a cell.

Her journey to Scotland had never been about marriage, not really. It had been about choosing the person she believed she could be over the half life she'd let herself inhabit.

"And only two of your brothers know about your writings?" Arthur inquired.

"Yes, Ned—he's the closest to me in age, and he knew from the start. I lured him in as my accomplice. And Jasper."

Charming, rakish Jasper. He had come to her already knowing about her writings, somehow—she had not asked how. Jasper always seemed to find things out through the very force of his personality.

She'd begged Jasper not to tell Theo. Theo had become head of the family at fifteen when their father had died, and he had never stopped approaching his role with painful seriousness. She did not fear that Theo would try to stop her, precisely—no, she feared he would be sick with worry over her actions, and that was almost worse.

"All right, duckling," Jasper had said, nudging her with his shoulder. "Only let's not get thrown in jail, please? For me?"

They'd spoken of her writings exactly one more time, when Jasper had made a few offhand remarks about how she might keep her identity a secret. They had seemed like casual suggestions until Lydia had thought them through later and realized how perfectly each proposition solved an issue she had worried about.

Fun-loving, complicated Jasper. Sometimes she suspected she was not the only Hope-Wallace with secrets.

"And you mean to go back to them?" Arthur asked. "After all of this is done?"

"Yes. I suppose . . . I suppose I shall tell them we've been in Sussex this whole time." She would have to leave out the zebras. It was almost a pity—Ned would have loved the story, and Theo would have turned all sorts of interesting colors.

There was a pause, a brief tentative silence, and then Arthur said abruptly: "You're fortunate."

She blinked up at him. He looked chagrined by his own words, his lips pressed together in a harsh line.

"Me?" she asked. "Why?"

He did not seem at first to want to answer; he put her in mind once more of an ill-tempered bear. But finally he unbent enough to say, "To know you have them all to go home to, I suppose. To have someone in your life who grew up alongside you. Who can hold the memories of your childhood with you."

Her heart squeezed a little. "It must be difficult not to have such a thing."

"That's why 'twas so easy for Davis to get round me, I suppose. Because I wanted to believe him when he came back to Strathrannoch and called it home. It has always been home for me, even when he didn't see it that way."

"Were you happy there? Growing up at Strathrannoch?" She had not meant to ask it, not really, only—only she wanted to know.

"Happy?" He said the word as if it were unfamiliar in his mouth. "I suppose so, in many ways. I always loved the land and the people. I've never left Scotland, never wanted to. But . . . do you know how, sometimes, you love something more because it's so much damned trouble?"

"I don't know what you mean."

His laugh was soft and rough. "Luath, for example. My horse. He was gelded too late—a big mean thing who would sooner bite your hand than take an apple out of it. Took Huw and me years to gain his trust, years of petting and cosseting. But I would carve out my heart for the great beast now, and he for me. 'Twould not be the same if he had been easy to love."

"I understand." Her voice was almost a whisper, but he did not seem to mind.

"Strathrannoch as well. My father—he did not make the track smooth for me. I ought by rights to have hated the place, and yet I never could. When he died and the estate became mine, 'twas sunk so deep in a pit of debt and rot that I knew I could never bring it out on my own. And the land—even the damned land itself is hard at Strathrannoch. Hard to grow in, hard to till. Our people didn't trust me then. Some still don't."

He paused, seeming to realize the length of his speech. His gaze met hers, and his mouth tipped up, loosening from the slash it had been. "But I love it all anyway."

Lydia tried to smile back, tried to say something, but she could not manage it. She felt the press of tears at the backs of her eyes, and she looked blindly out the window until the feeling receded.

But it did not go away, not completely.

She wished she had not asked. She wished she did not keep learning more of this man, who coddled his horse and took in strangers when they had no other place to go. Who loved things more when they were hard to love.

When Lydia took risks in her life, they were calculated. Her anonymous pamphlets, for one—she trusted the discretion of Selina and Belvoir's completely, and the importance of her political work was worth more than the small chance of discovery.

This trip had been, in some ways, the largest gamble of her life. She had traveled across the country, proposed a sea change in her own life. The chance for independence, the chance to finally *live* instead of waiting for life to happen to her—the potential rewards had been vast.

And the danger inherent in her trip to Scotland had seemed not so very great. Aside from the serious but unlikely risk of brigands and highwaymen, there had been little that she feared. She'd had in mind a marriage of convenience, a financial and political partnership with a man she'd considered a friend.

Her heart had not been involved. Her pride would have been stung, to be sure, if her proposal had been rejected, but she also would have understood. She would have been disappointed. She would not have been crushed.

But now—as she sat across from Arthur, her gaze flickering to him and then away again as though the sight of him burned her eyes—she felt a new and present danger. A risk she had not anticipated. A consequence incalculably great.

She felt . . . something . . . toward him. She could feel his presence across from her even without looking at him, large and warm, stubborn and loving. She wanted to know him better. She wanted him to kiss her. No—*she* wanted to kiss *him*, to pull his head down toward hers and bring his mouth to her own.

She knew she was too emotional, her feelings boiling to the surface of her body and flinging themselves outward in blushes or tears. She was sensitive and prone to flights of fancy. She was easily bruised. Feeling something for Arthur would make her infinitely more vulnerable.

And as she thought of the crooked tilt of his mouth as he'd spoken of love, she was not certain that her calculations mattered in any case. She did not know if she could stop herself.

Chapter 11

Do you know when it started for me, love of mine? It was that first moment. The very first instant that I saw you on the doorstep, in your green dress and your green shoes and your hair the color Nature uses for things so sublime you cannot hold them in your hand. Autumn. Sunset. A flame.

—*from the papers of Arthur Baird, written upon the back of an envelope, never sent*

In Haddon Grange, they divided their forces.

Strathrannoch was tasked with remaining out of sight so as to avoid recognition. His afternoon activities seemed mostly to consist of lurking and attempting to look less conspicuous and strapping and earl-ish.

Lydia and Georgiana, meanwhile, wandered down the main thoroughfare in search of the boardinghouse Arthur and Huw had described to them. It had grown chilly in the fortnight since they had arrived in Scotland; Lydia held her embroidered pelisse close around her. Late-blooming cranesbill and lacy white hydrangea spilled from window boxes and pots set along doorways. Clematis in a dozen shades of blue and violet twined along thatched roofs.

Lydia's plan had been twofold. Georgiana—who'd dressed down for the occasion—would make her way to the boarding-house's kitchens and begin to work her magic upon the serving staff. Lydia, meanwhile, meant to delicately pump the owner for information about Davis Baird.

Like most of Lydia's recent plans, this one had been better in theory.

The owner was a brisk, bluff woman who had no time for mousy English spinsters. Every time Lydia attempted to speak, the woman finished her sentence with an impatient huff, and within the first several minutes, the four or five probing questions Lydia had prepared about Davis Baird had gone straight out of her head.

Things did not improve from there. By the time a quarter of an hour had passed, Lydia found herself back on the street outside the boardinghouse, having asked such useful questions as "Do you keep beds in your bedchambers?" and "Have you ever heard of, um, earls?"

She'd also apparently rented herself a room, which she scarcely remembered doing and certainly had not intended. But there was a key in her reticule in the place where several coins had formerly resided, so she supposed she'd somehow been talked into it.

Thankfully, Georgiana had been more effective.

"He's been there," Georgiana whispered under her breath as she caught up to Lydia in front of the milliner's shop halfway down the main road.

They reunited with Arthur and Huw behind the local inn's stables, where they'd temporarily boarded the horses. Arthur slouched against the wall. He'd once again lost his jacket and cravat, though if he'd thought to make himself *less* noticeable, showing a vee of muscular chest was certainly not the way to go about it.

Lydia was not, of course, looking at his chest.

"We've just missed Davis," Georgiana informed them. "He stayed in the boardinghouse as recently as last week. It seems he came back here after his stay with you at Strathrannoch Castle, though he mostly spent his time out of the village—the chambermaids I spoke to did not know where. He has his room rented for the remainder of the month, although I gather he meant to be away for some time, as the laundress said he'd left not a stitch of clothing behind."

"Well done, lass," said Huw, turning an astounded gaze upon Georgiana. "You can't have been in there half an hour, and yet you learned all that?"

Georgiana did not smile easily, but Lydia could see her gratification in the tiny tilt at the corner of her lips. "It was not the first time I have posed as a disgruntled servant, and I suspect it will not be the last." Her expression went abstracted—considering, Lydia suspected, how a mysterious missing boarder might feature in her next novel.

Arthur's jaw was tight. "I cannot understand it. Where would he have been spending his time? There are few aristocrats in these parts, and none of the people who usually put him up. And how in hell can he afford to rent these rooms for a month and yet live elsewhere?"

His brows were drawn together, his face set in lines of worry that had become familiar to Lydia in the last two weeks.

"I don't know," she said, "but we are closer now to finding out." She felt a sudden impulse to soothe him, to step closer and place her hand on his shoulder. To run her fingers over the rise of muscle there and learn its contours.

She didn't.

"And you, lass?" asked Huw, turning his white-bearded face to her. "What did you find out from the owner of the place?"

"Ah." She licked her lips. "I, er, rented us a room."

"Good," Georgiana said. "That will make it much easier for us to search Davis's chamber."

Lydia appreciated this generous interpretation of her efforts.

Huw's face, meanwhile, lit. "Excellent. We scarcely need Bertie and his craftiness with these two along, do we, Strathrannoch?" He gave Arthur a congenial sort of nudge.

"Indeed. They seem to have plenty of schemes of their own without any outside interference."

Huw nodded, as though this were the highest of compliments. Given his affection for Bertie, perhaps it was. "Whom do you mean to have search the rooms?" he asked Lydia.

She had just a moment to appreciate the stable master's willingness to allow two women to take the lead in planning the affair when Arthur interjected.

"I'll do it," he said firmly.

She lifted her chin to catch his gaze, which was irritatingly high up. "How can you? The owner, at least, will know you by sight."

"And the chambermaids and laundress too," put in Georgiana. "I asked them."

"Georgiana and I will do it," Lydia said. "I'll go up to the room I rented, and Georgiana can meet me there—we can get into Davis's room together—"

"For Christ's sake," said Arthur, "I cannot let you put yourself into danger for me."

"What danger? What do you anticipate is waiting for us in an empty room?"

Arthur glowered at her. "I don't know, but I will not let you face it alone."

Lydia scowled right back. "Fine. If you can come up with a way to get yourself into the upstairs hallway without being recognized, then feel free to come along."

• • •

"This is a terrible idea," Arthur muttered that evening.

Huw at his side nodded. "Probably."

"You're not supposed to agree with me, man!"

"Your solution to the dilemma of your familiarity in these parts involves homemade explosives. You expect me to tell you this is wise?"

"You tell Bertie his mad ideas are clever all the time."

Huw leveled a gaze at him. "You are no Bertie when it comes to scheming."

"A fair point, to be sure." Arthur rubbed a hand over the back of his neck and then finished wrapping the wick he'd fashioned from threads of his cravat. "All right. 'Tis done."

He handed Huw his tinderbox, the lengthy wick, and the small incendiary device he'd crafted from a pinch of black powder, strips of bark, pine needles, and padding from the remainder of his cravat. "Remember what I told you. Place it just beneath the window outside the dining room where everyone inside is busy with supper. It will flare up because of the pine needles and make a nice, loud boom. The building's brick, and there's no dry shrubbery about, so there should not be any danger of fire. But you'll keep an eye on it anyway?"

"Of course." Huw looked slightly injured. "I must say, Bertie's ideas usually involve less . . . arson."

"For Christ's sake, 'tis not *arson*—"

Huw was grinning beneath his beard. Arthur scowled at him.

In a few moments, the other man had the bundle placed and the wick lit, whilst Arthur lurked—there was really no other word for it—in the darkness behind a stand of trees. Huw stepped back hastily as the wick caught, and, within moments, the fire licked its way up to the device.

The volume of the subsequent explosive crack was startling even to Arthur, who was expecting it. At the same time, the pine needles caught fire and flared up in a bright yellow-white blaze, producing a thick column of noxious smoke.

It did not take long after that. The window was flung open, and people began to pour out the front of the building to investigate.

Arthur smothered a brief flash of glee at the success of his device and made for the servants' entrance.

It worked better than he had expected—O Huw of little faith!—for the stairs to the second-floor bedchambers were dark and empty, and he was up them in a trice.

Georgiana met him in the hall. "Can you pick the lock?" she whispered. She was frowning. "I'd thought the door would be open so that the maids could enter and clean, but evidently your brother's desire for privacy outweighed the demands of hygiene."

"Aye," he murmured back. "Pass me a few of your hairpins." He could make his way around a simple latch, to be sure—it was just a bit of metal. And if it were something more substantial, he could bloody well kick the door in and figure out how to pay for it later.

Fortunately, breaking the door down did not prove necessary. While he worked with dirk and pin, Georgiana fetched Lydia from the chamber she had rented, and by the time Lydia was at his side, he had the door open.

"Go," whispered Georgiana. "I'll keep watch from the other room and distract anyone who comes by. Be quiet and quick and go out the servants' entrance when you've finished."

Lydia did not speak, only flicked a dark blue glance at him before slipping past him into the room. Her skirts brushed his trousers, and her bare arm whispered against his sleeve. He caught her scent, warm and sweet and—what was it? Vanilla? Cream?

He gritted his teeth and put his mind to the task at hand.

Lydia dashed immediately to the small escritoire at the corner of the room, so he perforce made for the wardrobe. It had no latch or lock, and the inside was all but bare. A shelf of linens, a sachet of dried lavender within, and, on the ground, a leather satchel that had his heart racing before he discovered that it held only a few stale bannocks and a stoppered flask. He uncorked the flask and gave it a sniff. Water.

His heart lurched with disappointment, and he turned back to Lydia. "Have you found anything?"

She was bent at the waist as she rifled through the escritoire's drawers, leaning over the arm of the wooden chair. There was nothing overtly provocative about her pose; her dress, the fabric soft and striped in a pattern of blue and white, covered her nearly to her toes. He could make out her slippers—blue spangles today—and the hint of her stockinged heels as she stood almost on tiptoe.

No, there was nothing salacious about it, which meant there was no good reason for the direction his mind chose to take: Lydia bent over the chair, her skirts around her waist, her hair loose and wild and wrapped in his fist.

"Yes," she said, and he nearly lost his head entirely before he realized she was answering his question.

He came toward her. "What have you found?"

She stood, her heels sliding back into her slippers. Her eyes were bright. She liked this, he realized—the thrill of discovery, this exploration behind closed doors. "Invitations, mostly—five of them, all signed by Lady de Younge. Do you think there could be some kind of romantic entanglement between them?"

Arthur choked. "I don't suspect that, no. Lady de Younge was a close personal friend of our mother."

Lydia tipped her head to the side. "And you think a separation in age makes a tryst between them unlikely? Or do you think it improper? I understand some people quite prefer older women—"

"For Christ's sake." He put his hand over hers to take the invitations, rather effectively cutting off her flow of words. "I think it unlikely because she was our *mother's friend*. Give me those."

The tops of his ears felt rather hot, and her fingers were cool and delicate beneath his, and the excitement of the clandestine search sang in his veins as he touched her. He wanted to keep touching her.

He had not been so close to her since the moment in his drawing room when he had run his thumb along the line of her mouth.

He had not stopped thinking of it.

When she spoke, her voice was just a bit breathless. "They are dated within the last month—I imagine he was at Strathrannoch for most of that time, which is why they seem to have gone unanswered."

"Aye," he said, releasing her fingers with some effort so that he might flip through the cards. "But still, it gives us some idea of where to look next. If we cannot make out his direction, perhaps the de Younges will know more."

"Perhaps so." She returned to the drawers, bending again, and from his vantage above her, he could see the line of her bodice, the sweet swell—

Ah. No. He could remove his gaze from her person, resume looking at the letters, and at least pretend not to be wild with lust over the redheaded Englishwoman who had come to *propose marriage to his brother.*

Somehow that protestation had grown rather distant over time. He tried to call it back.

"The rest of the drawers seem to be empty," she said, "aside from some blank foolscap."

He dropped the cards on the corner of the escritoire, having assured himself that there was nothing more to be gleaned from them. "Have the paper out."

She did as he bade, though she directed a small frown in his direction. "You needn't be so high-handed, you know. And I already looked through them—the sheets are blank."

He made a small sound in his throat and then he picked up the paper and took it to the window, holding it at an angle in the dusky light.

"Oh," Lydia said, and the approval in her voice was clear. "I would never have thought—do you see anything? Any impressions in the paper?"

Of course she would grasp what he was about. He already knew she was clever as hell, on top of being openhearted, sympathetic, alarmingly organized, and so brave and loyal it made his chest ache.

He was so flustered by her nearness that for a moment he thought he'd imagined what he saw on the foolscap, pressed deep by the impression of a pen.

But no. He'd not imagined it. He lifted the paper, tilted it against the light.

Lydia, it said.

And then—again and again, scratched out and restarted

messily across the page: *I'm sorry. I don't know how to tell you. I'm sorry.*

The soft sounds of Lydia's breathing, the clatter belowstairs, the hum of a maid in the hall—all the sounds around him went dim as he looked down at the words.

He'd . . . known?

Davis had known who she was? Davis had regretted his actions?

Davis had meant to tell her the truth.

Arthur passed the paper wordlessly to Lydia. He felt—ah, hell, he could not stop himself from looking at her face. He was torn between the desire to give her privacy and the desire to burn the bloody thing before she read it. He didn't want Davis to hurt her again. He didn't want Davis to *talk* to her, damn it. He wanted—he wanted—

He watched, frozen, as she read the words.

She blinked rapidly, her lovely eyelashes fluttering. "I don't understand," she murmured. "That's Davis's hand. I recognize it. But how could he have known my name?"

"I don't know," he said roughly. If she started to cry, he was going to kill his brother.

But no. The thought struck him like a knife. He couldn't kill Davis, because—what if Lydia still wanted him?

Arthur had assumed that the revelation of Davis's misdeeds would have quashed Lydia's affection for his brother. Surely she would not still love the man who had meant to use her for his own gain.

But this paper showed something different. This paper showed a man who regretted what he'd done. A man—perhaps—whom a woman in love might be able to forgive.

He found himself doing some violence to the remaining blank sheets of paper in the tightening grip of his fist.

Lydia's gaze flickered to his hand, which now held a small snowball of crushed foolscap. "Goodness. Give me those. Have they anything you can discern?"

He had no idea. He hadn't bloody checked. He'd been too busy watching Lydia's face and trying to divine whether she seemed pleased or crushed or filled with longing.

But he could not make her out. She smoothed out the stack of papers and—did he imagine it? Did her fingers trace her name in his brother's messy scrawl? He did not know.

The remaining papers held faint impressions of numbers and sketches that looked rather like Arthur's own diagrams and designs. He had known—of course he had known that Davis too was handy with a drawing pencil. Only he had forgotten, somehow. It had been a long time since he'd seen that side of Davis.

Lydia flipped through the pages, holding them this way and that against the light. "They're measurements," she said finally, shaking her head. "I can see a mark for scale here—perhaps this is a building or a bridge." She looked up at him, eyes wide, face mystified. "Could this be some alteration to your rifle scope design?"

He shook his head. "I don't think so. I ground the lenses myself with a process of my own invention. I do not think he could create another scope, even with the benefit of my notes. But I . . . I don't like to think of Davis loose in a city with the prototype."

She blanched. "These numbers—could they reflect the rifle's range?"

"Perhaps. I can't say for sure."

She had drawn closer to him as they shared the papers, and now she placed a hand on his upper arm. He could feel her fingers, five light points of contact. His focus tightened onto the small square of connection between them, and his body tightened too. His head spun.

He wanted her. He craved her.

It was as though the revelation that Davis had known her name had shone a bright light into the shadowed corners of Arthur's heart. He did not want her to want Davis. He wanted her for himself, all to himself, and the hell with the rest of the world.

Christ, he was like a child with a toy! *Mine*, he wanted to say. *This one's mine.*

He needed to get out of this room. Proximity to Lydia Hope-Wallace seemed to cause his brain to behave in bizarre and unpredictable ways.

Unlike his brain's, his body's response was altogether too predictable, particularly south of his waist.

"Take the papers," he said. "The invitations as well. We'll take it all."

She looked up at him. In the dim light, with the sun slipping below the horizon, all the vivid colors of her were faded: an ember instead of a conflagration. But he knew each vibrant shade well enough that it did not matter. He could see the color of her hair with his eyes closed.

"Won't Davis suspect something?" she asked. "When he returns? If we've taken his papers?"

"He might," Arthur allowed, "but he won't know that we were responsible. These papers are the best we have to go on. I say we hold on to them."

She nodded and tucked the papers into a pocket concealed at her waist by a wide ribbon.

By mutual consent, they searched the remainder of the room.

She peered under the bed and washstand; he leaned the mirror away from the wall to look behind it. He ran his fingers along the backs of all the paintings, hoping fruitlessly for a hidden compartment—what he wouldn't give for a map! With a big X across it, ideally marked *Davis's Secret Hideout*.

There was nothing else. Davis had left the room almost Spartan in its cleanliness.

It was peculiar. The Davis that he knew was not slovenly, but he was a bit careless, always dropping things and leaving piles about left and right. Rather like Arthur himself.

Perhaps Davis had changed in this too. There were so many ways in which Arthur no longer knew his brother. He did not know what to make of their discoveries this evening, and his mind reeled with revelations and with Lydia's proximity.

When they were done, she peeked her head out the door, then whispered, "All seems clear." In the hallway, he followed closely behind her, and they crept to the servants' staircase without issue.

They were halfway down the stairs when disaster struck, in the form of a raucous male voice lustily singing "The Fair Maid of Islington."

Arthur froze, an instant of paralyzed panic. It might not be someone he knew—but if it was—and if they saw him coming out of Davis's chamber—with *Lydia*—

How safe would she be, if Davis learned that she'd discovered the truth?

Arthur did not know. But he knew he could not let her come to harm.

In the moment it took him to recover from his shock, Lydia leapt past him back up the stairs. "Come up!" she whispered frantically. "He'll see you!"

The voice was growing louder. "Hell," he said, "no time—"

And then he grabbed Lydia about the waist with one hand, yanked the pins out of her hair with the other, and pressed her to the wall, burying his face in the curve of her neck.

Chapter 12

. . . action was now a necessity to desires so much on edge as ours . . .

—*from Lydia's private copy of* FANNY HILL

Oh shite, he thought. *Oh hell*.

She seemed at once to understand what he was about. She tipped her head to the side with a gasp, making room for him to press his cheek against her skin. Her hair fell down around him, shielding his face.

And then she lifted one leg and hooked it around his waist, and he went ever so slightly mad.

Oh God, he thought. And *Lydia. Lydia*.

She was a step above him, but he was still taller, and her skirts fell back as she tightened her leg around him. He untangled his fingers from her hair and caught her leg beneath her knee. It was not layers of skirts and petticoats he felt there, but the thin silk of her stockings, and beneath that the warmth of her flesh.

Oh Jesus, she was soft and warm everywhere. His hand

slipped down the outside of her thigh, hitching her higher and tighter against him.

He felt the vibration of the sound she made as he did so, a breath that was not quite a moan. He could feel her breasts rising and falling unsteadily, and oh God, he wanted more. More of her. He wanted to slide his hand farther up that soft, lush thigh until he reached the bow of her garter and then past it. He wanted skin.

But ah yes, he already had skin—right here, where his mouth was pressed against her neck. His lips parted, and he tasted her, her sweet skin, her racing pulse. He dipped down, a little farther—her collarbone, God, *yes*, a perfect ridge for his teeth and tongue.

She gasped a little and tilted her head and then—ah, then she pushed her hips up into him. Like she wanted. Like she needed him too. He tightened his grip on her thigh and pressed her harder into the wall, and she whimpered and tangled one hand in his hair. God, it felt good—she felt so good, the almost-ache where she pulled his hair, the almost-surrender of her beneath him, her leg drawing him tighter, crushing his body to hers. He dragged his hand from her waist up—to her rib cage, to the side of her full breast, cursing the fabric between them. He wanted nothing between them, nothing but her breasts' heavy weight in his palms and his body rocking into—

"Aye, mate, wait till you have her in your room!"

Arthur froze.

It was the laughing, raucous voice that they'd heard from the bottom of the stairs.

It was the reason he had begun this charade in the first place, the reason Lydia stood beneath him, her leg wrapped around his body.

He was not trying to shag her on a staircase, for God's sake! He was trying to *hide*.

He kept his face pressed against Lydia's décolletage, his hand still clutching her thigh, and tried to control his breathing.

"Oh," Lydia said, and Christ, her voice was breathless. She laughed a little, that soft surprised laugh that he loved. "New-lyweds. Our"—Arthur's fingers tightened on her in surprise, pulling their bodies together, and she gave a little gasp—"our honeymoon."

Well, hell, it was as good of an excuse as any for why he'd been a hair's breadth from public copulation.

"The room's too damned far, my love," he rasped. He did not have to feign the desperate, lust-drunk sound of his voice, by God.

The unseen voice laughed again. "And the servants' stairs are awfully busy for your lady wife, but I'll not opine further. A happy marriage to you, indeed!"

The man's voice had faded as he spoke, the last words called down to them from above.

Arthur stood stock-still, his mouth an inch from the top of Lydia's breasts.

"Ah," she whispered finally. "He's—ah, he's gone."

"Aye," Arthur said. Her hair was around his face, strands of it tickling his mouth—God, he loved it all, her hair, her sweet-warm scent, her soft curves and softer skin—

"You can let me go."

"Aye." He exerted his will. He made himself lift his head and loose his fingers from her thigh. Slowly, slowly she uncurled her leg from around his waist and dropped it to the ground.

He looked down at her. Her eyes were brilliant in the dimly lit stairwell, her cheeks flushed, her lips parted. She looked—she looked—

Oh God, she looked like temptation. She looked the way he had not let himself imagine she would look: soft and roused and hungry. The way he had wanted her, every night and every morning, from the moment he'd first held her in his arms.

"We should go," she whispered.

Christ, she was right. He could not stand there in the stairwell, staring down at her and wondering if she felt anything like what he felt right now. Wondering if he'd imagined the gasp and whimper she'd made when his mouth had found her skin.

He wanted to ask. He wanted to know if she'd been pretending or if she'd been as lost and frantic as he.

He wanted to know how she'd felt when she saw her own name, pressed by Davis's hand into his papers. And he could not bring himself to say it.

In his and Davis's lives, Arthur had come first only once: in the order of their birth. He had been lucky in that, in the eyes of the world—his was the earldom, his the vote in the House of Lords. But their father's unforgiving expectations had also been his, and the responsibility of a failing estate and hundreds of tenants.

He had never lived up to those expectations. He had tried—God, for years and *years* he had tried—but it had been a useless project. He could recall with ice-edged clarity the day he'd come home after dark, damp and muddy, exultant over the afternoon he'd spent with one of the tenants. They'd built a small mill, powered by a waterwheel of Arthur's own design, and the man's wife had been beside herself with delight, crowing over the time she would save in pounding grain.

His father had taken one look at Arthur's disheveled state and cracked a laugh. "And now do you understand," he'd said, "why they will never take you seriously?"

The earl had left then—Davis in tow—for an evening out.

His father had made it clear, in a thousand large and small ways, that Davis, not Arthur, ought to have been the heir. Hell, everyone thought it. Davis was charming, easygoing—who wouldn't have preferred that to Arthur's awkward bluntness, his reclusiveness, his unrelenting intensity?

So he'd stopped trying to please them. He'd stopped trying to win approval when the outcome was always failure, the finish line ever further out of his reach.

Until now. God, now, with Lydia, he wanted to come first. Wanted it as he'd never wanted anything in his life. And he knew—he *knew* how setting himself up in competition with Davis would go. How it had always gone.

He could not ask her how she'd felt about Davis's papers. He couldn't bring himself to say the words.

"You're right," he said. "We should go."

He turned and made his way down the stairwell and out the back door. Lydia stayed close behind him.

Outside the building, Georgiana and Huw awaited them.

"What took you so long?" Georgiana demanded. "I was on the verge of a rear assault on the building—"

"We were waylaid," Lydia said quickly, "but all's well. He was not recognized."

"Good," said Huw, "now let's go. It's a long, dark ride back to Strathrannoch Castle, and the dining room is starting to empty."

It was true. Around the side of the building, Arthur could see people emerging from the front door, making their way to their homes or carriages.

"We'll keep to the shadows," he said. "Back here, amongst the trees, and find our way back to the coach-and-four before—"

It was a good plan. It would have been a good plan, at least, if the next voice he heard had not been one he was intimately familiar with.

"Strathrannoch? Good heavens, boy, is that you?"

And from around the corner of the building—my God, the woman must have the eyes of a hawk—came Lady de Younge.

She was tall and slim, her silver hair piled atop her head in a style faintly reminiscent of the previous century. She wore a white turban and white plumes, and a cloak over her severe purple evening gown.

"Ah, yes," he said. There was no help for it now. "Lady de Younge, a pleasure."

She came closer, and Arthur realized Lord de Younge was there as well, trailing his taller wife. Lord de Younge placed a hand on his wife's lower back and then raised his quizzing glass.

"I say, Maggie, you're right! Strathrannoch, m'boy! What brings you to Haddon Grange?"

"A bit of—a bit of—" He was an idiot. He had no idea what to say. A bit of arson followed by some casual groping in a stairwell?

He was saved from having to reply by the laughing voice he'd heard on the stairs, now pitched rather higher in tones of shock.

"Lord Strathrannoch!" The man stepped out the back door, his face flushed and his eyes trained upon Arthur's damned conspicuous form. "I'm so sorry I didn't recognize you at once, my lord—and—and—my lady!"

Arthur's mouth opened. Not a single word emerged. He watched the proceedings in a kind of silent daze, as of one watching a runaway carriage plunge toward the edge of a cliff.

The man from the stairwell—Arthur was fairly certain he was the third son of a former land steward—dropped into a bow at the waist.

Lord de Younge, meanwhile, pressed his quizzing glass closer to his face. "*My lady?*" he demanded. "Is there a Lady Strathrannoch now?"

"Aye," said the steward's third son, rising from his bow and looking even pinker about the cheeks. "Newlyweds they are— and celebrating here in Haddon Grange!"

Lady de Younge's smile went practically incandescent. "Lady Strathrannoch! Oh, Arthur! Where have you been keeping her? A new countess!"

"Ah," Arthur said again. "I—"

Lady de Younge pressed her hands to her bosom. "Your mother—oh, your mother would be so happy! Come here, child, let me have a look at you!"

And then she plucked Lydia from her place at Arthur's side and wrapped her in an embrace.

The carriage in his mind hit a rock, launched into the air, and sailed over the precipice.

• • •

The moon had barely risen by the time Huw halted the coach-and-four at the entrance to the de Younges' manor. The couple had, naturally, invited them to stay the night and celebrate their nuptials.

Bloody bollocking hell.

"This is a disaster," Arthur hissed.

"Not at all," said Georgiana. Her face was set with purpose and ever so slightly terrifying. "This is an opportunity!"

On the brief ride from Haddon Grange to the de Younges' residence, Kilbride House, he and Lydia had shown her Davis's papers, as well as the invitations from Lady de Younge to Davis that they'd stolen from Davis's chamber. She'd appeared absolutely delighted, muttering beneath her breath about *cryptography* and *investigative research*.

"Huw can go back to Strathrannoch Castle in the morning and gather your things," Georgiana went on gleefully. "If you can persuade them to host you for several days, I can pretend to be Lydia's lady's maid and sleep belowstairs with the servants, while you pry information from the de Younges themselves. Imagine what we can discover! You could not have planned this better if you'd tried."

"Except for the part where we have to pretend we are *married*!" said Lydia. Her voice was somewhere between a whisper and a despairing moan.

Despair. That was how she felt about the idea of being his wife. *Despair.* He might remind himself of that the next time he felt compelled to lick her collarbone.

Unfortunately, he also suspected that Georgiana was right. "'Tis not as though we'd be making it worse, I suppose, by keeping up the pretense—the de Younges already think we're wed. We can invent a story—tell them we met in Edinburgh, perhaps. There's no reason anyone need learn your true identity. No one from London knows you're here."

Lydia looked up at him, eyes an even darker blue in the moonlight. She reached out and grazed his knee with her fingers, then pulled her hand back as though she'd been burned. "Arthur—Lord Strathrannoch—I'm so sorry for saying that we were married. It was the first thing that came to mind when that fellow stumbled upon us—I never dreamed he would come back!"

"'Tis not your fault."

"Of course it is!" Her cheeks had gone pink again, and what he really wanted to do was put his mouth there and feel the heat of her skin.

Which was the *worst possible thing to be thinking about.* Christ, the woman addled him. One taste of her and he'd gone straight out of his head. She ought to be bottled and sold as a mind-altering substance.

Georgiana cocked her head. "And what exactly were you two doing that made the man think you were newlyweds?"

"Nothing," Arthur said, at the precise moment that Lydia burst out, "Kissing!"

Georgiana's eyebrows shot toward her hairline.

"Not—not really—that is, we were pretending to kiss—to hide Arthur's identity!"

"Naturally," Georgiana said.

Lydia buried her face in her hands and made another one of those despairing sounds.

"Dinna fash," he said, because the sight of her with her face hidden did something uncomfortable to his insides. "Perhaps we can, er, have the marriage annulled."

"We are not actually married!"

"Ah, no. I meant that's what we can tell people. When you disappear from Scotland, never to be seen or heard from again."

The words sent a queer, sharp pang through him, like a bell chiming in his bones.

Lydia emerged from her hands. "Surely that will be an embarrassment to you. Truly, I am so sorry."

He didn't think. He reached out and took her hands in both of his. "I told you. Dinna fash. I don't mind it. You were clever on the stairs, quick-thinking and brave. I wouldn't blame you for such a thing, not even if it hadn't worked at all. And it did work."

"It worked well beyond your expectations," said Georgiana, and Arthur recalled himself enough to drop Lydia's hands. "And now you have an opportunity to finish what you started and find out how the de Younges are connected to Davis."

Though he had not intended any of this, he had to admit that it did provide them with a clear path forward. And he meant what he'd told her. He did not mind.

Of course he did not, damn it. He would not mind pretending she was his, not when he wanted it to be real.

Lydia, meanwhile, was fighting with the tangled ribbon at her waist and looking miserable. When she had finally wrestled it into submission, she glanced up at him. "Yes, I suppose we cannot let this chance pass us by. Only—I shall embarrass you. Pretending to be your wife."

He blinked. "When you go, do you mean? Because I've been thrown over?"

She appeared slightly agonized. "No—well, yes, that too, come to think of it. I only meant—at a house party full of strangers, I shall be an utter disaster. I may well cast up my accounts into a potted palm. It would not be the first time, as you well know."

"For Christ's sake," he said, "I don't care about such things. What part of my ruined castle and rampaging rodents would lead you to believe I did?"

"Of course you care." She twisted her fingers together in her lap. "It will affect how everyone sees you. Their opinions of you."

This time, he considered Lady Georgiana's proximity, and decided it was worth it. He reached out and caught Lydia's chin in his hand. She sat frozen, staring at him, and her skin was so soft beneath his fingers that his grip gentled almost without his intending it.

"They'll think I'm a bloody lucky bastard for marrying a woman so bonny and fine. No doubt they'll wonder how I've managed it. But I don't give a fig for what they think. I've no need for their approval of me or my wife."

Her eyes were wide and blue, fixed on his, and God, she was so lovely, he almost could not think straight.

She took a few breaths before she spoke. He liked how she did that, how she calmed herself and considered her words at the same time. Her fingers worried the ribbon at her waist, a busy gesture, not quite a caress.

"All right," she said at last. "I'll do it."

Chapter 13

Evils of the Clearances.
Radical Parliamentary reform.
Abuses enabled by a corrupt aristocracy.
Novels?
Oh, hang this list!

—from Lydia's private journal, page titled
PROPOSED TOPICS FOR CONVERSATION AT KILBRIDE HOUSE

The following morning, Lydia found herself tucked under the comforting arm of Lady de Younge as she was led inexorably to the breakfast table.

Or, as she privately referred to it, hell.

Public dining was something Lydia did not enjoy, particularly when the table was arrayed with strangers and she was expected to speak to them. Strathrannoch Castle had not been so bad—she certainly had not needed to talk, what with the macaws and the degu and the constant patter between Rupert and the various adults. By the time they had left, she'd felt surprisingly comfortable.

But this was worse—this was the worst possible. She did not

know Lady de Younge, or the breakfast room, or any of the other people around the table. She was going to faint or cry or forget how to speak English. She was going to choke on a pastry and then drown in her teacup.

Arthur, her damned pretend husband, was not even there. She had not seen him since they had been ushered into separate bedchambers the night before—a sleeping arrangement which had caused a truly disconcerting wave of disappointment to wash through her.

No, Arthur was not at the breakfast table—there was only Lord de Younge, two other couples in their forties and fifties, and a blindingly handsome younger man in—

Lydia came to a dead stop, so abruptly that the much-taller Lady de Younge nearly knocked her over.

"Lady Strathrannoch?" she asked. "Is everything quite all right?"

Lydia did not know up from down. Everything had gone mad. *She* was Lady Strathrannoch, and the ludicrously attractive gentleman at the breakfast table was *Arthur*.

He had shaved. She would not have imagined a simple change in grooming habits could effect such a powerful transformation, but there it was, in the insultingly beautiful and virile flesh. His jaw, which had been camouflaged by his whiskers, was sharp and strong. His lips were beautifully, elegantly molded, and his cheekbones seemed higher and sharper now that the hollows of his cheeks were clear.

He looked like a statue. He looked like an *angel*.

Dear God, this was not going to work. Her heartbeat pounded in her ears. This man was a stranger, and she was going to make a hash of things, and she could not hear anything over the roaring of her pulse.

She was going to humiliate herself, and even worse—*far worse*—she was going to humiliate him. Damn it, she wanted to be worthy of him. She wanted, curse her foolish heart, to be a proper Lady Strathrannoch. Despite herself, she wanted him to see her that way, and yet she could not possibly pull it off.

She knew herself. She knew what she was and was not.

Arthur looked up and saw her. He came to his feet and then was at her side, and Lydia almost could not find it in herself to be embarrassed that he'd seen her encroaching panic, because he'd come to rescue her.

"Good morn to you, Lady de Younge," he said, and then he caught Lydia about the waist and drew her up to him. "And a good morn to you, my bonny wife."

Her head was spinning—or else the room had begun to revolve.

He leaned low and murmured into her ear, his voice a deep rumble that she felt all the way through her body. "Do you like kippers?"

She turned her head toward him, which brought her face into sudden, shocking proximity with his sharp, clean-shaven jaw. And his lips. She was in very close proximity to those. "I—what?"

"Kippers," he murmured again. "Come with me and let me show you how we make them here in the Lowlands."

She let him lead her like a doll over to the sideboard, whereupon there were, indeed, two large platters filled with breakfast meats and fishes.

"I have no opinion on kippers," she managed to get out.

"Forget the kippers."

"I beg your pardon?"

He nudged her around so that she faced the sideboard, and

then he arranged himself behind her. One of his hands came to rest on her shoulder; the other went to the handle of the serving fork, neatly bracketing her between his long, thickly muscled arms.

He was, she realized, almost hugging her.

He lowered his head to whisper into her ear. "What can I do? I know that you'd prefer to avoid this sort of thing. Shall we say you're ill? Or would that only make it worse later on?"

Oh. He had—oh. He had not wanted to speak of kippers.

It was a small kindness—this shielding her from view, allowing her a moment to catch her breath—but it was a small kindness that meant a great deal. He had not tried to do whatever he imagined best, or swept her out of the room, or attempted to solve her difficulties for her. He had *asked*.

"Give me a moment," she said. Her voice was shaking, but she knew he would not mind, and that mattered more to her than she wanted to admit. "Talk to me about—about kippers. Or whatever you like. And when we go back and sit down, try not to act as though there's something dreadfully wrong with me."

"'Twill be no hardship," he said. And then he did as he was bade.

By the time they returned to the table, Lydia had her wits about her enough to prepare herself for the introductions. She nodded, smiled, murmured a "How do you do?" while Arthur sat by her side, occasionally brushing his pinky finger against her own.

Once he nudged her slippered foot with his beneath the table, sending a frisson through her that was not quite the comforting sensation she'd imagined he'd intended.

No, the sensation that moved like a tendril of smoke through her body was something altogether more heated than comfort.

She tried not to think about fingers and limbs and the way his hand had gripped her thigh in the stairwell at Haddon Grange. Instead, she listened to the talk around the table, made her face smile pleasantly, and did not, in the end, need to speak after all.

Lord and Lady de Younge, who appeared to be in their sixties, were a decade or two older than their guests, all of whom were French émigrés who had come to England at the end of the eighteenth century.

Mr. and Mrs. Thibodeaux were the younger pair, both warm and smiling. Didier—as he'd introduced himself with a wink and grin—was a portly fellow of perhaps forty-five, whose bald head and thick spectacles did not mask the twinkle in his eye. Claudine, his buxom wife, was the less talkative of the pair—her English seemed not quite sufficient to keep up with the flow of conversation around the table. But she made lighthearted remarks to her husband in French, and generally appeared quite merry, if somewhat at sea.

The Marquis and Marquise de Valiquette—Lydia wondered if the marquisat in France was still intact after the nation's decades of strife—were a good ten years older. The marquise had a pinched expression, as though she'd smelled something unpleasant, and her remarks grew rather more acidulous whenever her glance fell on the cheerful Thibodeaux. Her husband—no first names were offered with *this* couple—looked upon his wife with a rather dour expression.

Lydia wondered how on earth the warm and welcoming de Younges had ended up hosting the Valiquettes. Perhaps the marquis and marquise had simply invited themselves prior to the Revolution, and the de Younges had not yet been able to work out how to make them go back.

Before they'd finished dining, Arthur turned the conversation to his brother.

"Ah, young Davis!" Lady de Younge took on an expression of indulgent concern. "That lad"—she shook her head—"always running up and down the country, visiting one estate or another. What I wouldn't give for a nice wife to settle him down."

The heat that went up Lydia's face and neck at this remark was palpable. She could actually feel it radiating from her skin. She could probably fry the kippers on her cheek.

"The young man who spent so much time with us last month—that was your brother, eh?" said Didier expansively. "But of course, I can see the resemblance quite plainly now!" He turned to his wife. "Monsieur Baird—the brother of the earl." He tilted his head in Arthur's direction.

Claudine perked up at this news, an impressive feat since she'd already been rather perked. "His brother! Ah, Monsieur Baird, so handsome!" She clasped her hands to her ample bosom. "To be ten years younger, zut alors!"

The Marquise de Valiquette gave Claudine a sour look. "Perhaps twenty."

Didier chuckled and ignored Madame de Valiquette. "We had many wonderful evenings with your brother, my lord Earl. You must have been quite bereft to have him leave your home and return to us."

"Indeed," said Arthur drily.

"But he did not even mention your marriage," remarked Lady de Younge. "I imagine you told him to keep your secret. What a lark you have had, hiding your wife from all and sundry. It will not do, Arthur—the countess must be introduced all over!"

Arthur, fortunately, saved Lydia from what must surely be Lady de Younge's next suggestion: an immediate tour of the countryside with Lydia in an open carriage. Also known as a fate worse than death.

"Davis was acting upon my request. My wife and I wanted to spend our first weeks of marriage together. Alone."

Good heavens. She felt the sensation of his words somewhere inside her lower belly. Had he meant to make the words sound so *suggestive*?

Lydia found that she was very suggestible indeed. She was brought back instantly to the stairwell, her leg wrapped around his hip. The sensation of his mouth on her skin, her hips pressed against his. Her thighs slackened beneath the table.

"Goodness, Arthur," observed Lady de Younge, "you've mortified your poor wife. Her cheeks have gone quite pink."

Lydia gulped and tried to pretend that the flush on her face was due to embarrassment and not the fact that Arthur's innocent words had set off a highly vivid erotic memory.

The man's voice was like a bloody aphrodisiac. It was absurd.

"Och," Arthur said, "I'm sorry, my love. 'Twas badly done of me." And then he set his hand to her shoulder again, his fingers warm and solid on the bare skin just above her puffed sleeve.

She licked her lips. "Not at all, my—my dear."

Mercifully, Lord de Younge turned the conversation from Lydia's face and the activities of newly married couples to an inquiry into how the young Strathrannochs had met. Arthur related the story they'd concocted about a mutual friend in Edinburgh and made absolutely no mention of London or the Hope-Wallace name. Lydia listened closely as the conversation meandered onward, trying to catch hints of people and places that Davis had mentioned in his letters. She had practically indexed them all in her mind by now, and it should not have been hard to listen for the names.

It would not ordinarily have been so. Only Arthur did not remove his hand from her shoulder but instead left it there, absently sliding a finger back and forth. She felt every delicate movement, each slow graze of his rough fingertip across her skin.

And that made it quite difficult to think clearly after all.

• • •

In the afternoon, Lydia was drawn into the ladies' activities while the men went shooting.

She found herself wondering what Arthur would do—she knew he did not enjoy hunting. Like as not, he would bluntly refuse to take a weapon and go on his way, unaffected by the judgment of the others. She envied that about him—his indifference to their opinions, his confidence in his own beliefs.

I don't give a fig for what they think. I've no need for their approval of me or my wife.

She could not imagine what that must feel like. She felt as though her entire life had been spent trying to force herself into the shape that would be most pleasing to others. And failing.

She listened intently as Lady de Younge, Claudine Thibodeaux, and the Marquise de Valiquette chattered over embroidery and correspondence. Mrs. Thibodeaux spoke in a French so rapid that Lydia's drawing room lessons could not quite keep up, but she was certain she understood references to Arthur and Davis both. Lady de Younge was the consummate hostess, ordering tea and small sandwiches, smoothing over the French ladies' apparent dislike of each other with ease and pretending as though Lydia were a participant in the conversation and not an awkward bystander.

And when Arthur returned from the outing with the gentlemen, Lydia made her excuses and followed him up the stairs.

Their bedchambers were across the hall from each other, and he was on the point of opening his door when she caught up to him.

"Wait," she said. She was a trifle breathless from following his long-legged stride up the staircase.

Her state of physical agitation did not resolve when Arthur took one look at her, cupped her elbow, and drew her into his chamber after him.

"Have you found something out?" he asked without preamble once the door was shut.

Goodness, he looked so *different* without his beard. Her fingers itched to stroke the line of his jaw.

She stifled the desire. "Not precisely. But I think it would be best if we searched some of the rooms today."

"Searched the rooms?"

"Yes. The de Younges' office, for one."

"Do you think they're involved in Davis's flight?"

"Perhaps." She brushed her lips with her fingers, thinking. "Lady de Younge does seem attached to Davis. And she mentioned in casual conversation eleven different people and places straight from his letters. There's a significant connection here—I'm certain of it."

"All right. Can you distract her for a time?" Arthur's serious face was set as he looked at her, as though the request were difficult for him to make. "I can search the office, perhaps even try her bedchamber, if you can keep her busy."

Could she do it?

She looked up at Arthur, hesitant, wishing. His eyes were a swirl of color, vibrant as the landscape, vivid as the sharp rush of desire that had unwound inside her body when he'd put his mouth on her skin in the stairwell.

"I can try," she said.

• • •

That evening, Arthur made his way carefully down the hallway past the sitting room in which the ladies had assembled after dinner. Gentlemen were meant to partake of port and cigars in one of the drawing rooms, but Arthur had excused himself with a vague reference to his wife.

Didier Thibodeaux had given him a rather ribald wink at that, but Arthur had ignored him.

Lydia had positioned herself facing the sitting room's door, and when he passed by, she looked up and gave him a brief, cautious nod.

God, he admired her. He could see from the pallor of her face and the tense set of her shoulders that she would rather be anywhere but there, exposed to the view of a roomful of strangers. And yet she did it anyway, because she believed it was the right thing to do.

He did not know if he'd ever been that brave—that willing to be vulnerable—in his life.

He made his way to the end of the hall, where Lord de Younge's office was situated. The room was neat and organized, and it was not especially difficult to suss out where de Younge kept his important papers. Arthur flipped through stacks of estate bills—the de Younges were looking a bit thin this year—and piles of correspondence, but found nothing that related to Davis.

He was on the point of sorting through the quills in the uppermost drawer when the door to the study came open, and he froze.

It was Lydia. She entered the room in a quiet whirl of white skirts and red hair, her face still turned back the way she'd come as though someone might be on her heels.

"What's happened?" Without waiting for a response, he began to stuff papers back into drawers, trying to replicate where they had been before his assault upon the desk.

"I could not hold her off!" She crossed the room and came to his side, her hands fluttering nervously. "Lady de Younge, I mean. She said something about going to seek out her husband—she wants to play a parlor game, for heaven's sake! I fear she will look for Lord de Younge in here if she does not find him promptly."

"Hell," he said succinctly. "Can you listen at the door while I put everything back?"

"Yes, of course." She hurried back to the door, which she'd shut behind her when she'd entered, then promptly whirled back to him. Her eyes were blue and enormous and terrified. "I hear someone!"

"Lock it," he ordered in a whisper. He flicked through papers, ensuring that he had not disarranged the chronological order.

"Wh-what?"

"Better they think we're trysting in here than that I'm searching through their things. If they toss us out of the house, we'll lose our best chance at finding Davis."

She threw the latch. "Can I help you somehow?"

"No, I'm almost—" There. He'd done it. Everything was back in the drawer.

He crossed the room in a handful of strides, coming up behind her to listen at the door as well. His palm went unthinkingly to the bolt that Lydia had thrown home.

Her hand, he realized, was still there. Where he had expected to encounter metal, he found her fingers instead. Those long fingers—capable as she grasped a quill, endlessly delicate as she held a crystal glass—

Beneath his own hand now.

He could not help himself. He meant to pull away from her and he *did*, he did pull away, only—

Slowly. He slid his fingers across the back of her hand, tracing the lines between her fingers, catching on her knuckles, then up, his thumb stroking the inside of her wrist.

The gasp she made was loud in the quiet room. He let go of her hand and placed his own on the solid wood of the door, trying to ground himself. Trying to remember who he was, and who she was, and what they were here to do.

And then she turned to face him. Her back was up against the door, and his hand was braced beside her head, and her eyes—those damned midnight eyes—were fixed upon him.

He did not move. He did not have to. She lifted her hand and placed it on his cheek. Her fingers coasted over his cheek-bone, then trailed down the line of his jaw. Her touch was no more than a breath across his skin, and it was madness how that delicate caress caught hold inside him and pulled his body taut with wanting.

He eased himself closer, her body a hair's breadth from his.

"You shaved," she whispered.

"Aye."

"I had been wondering how it would feel under my fingers."

Jesus Christ, it should not have been possible for the graze of her hand and the low murmur of her voice to make him so pain-fully hard. "The beard?" he rasped.

Her fingers went back to his cheek, dipping into the hollow beneath his cheekbone. "That," she murmured. "And now, too."

Her fingers found his mouth, and then stopped, as if uncer-tain. He caught her by the waist, and his lips parted on a sound—a harsh breath, a moan—at the heady sensation of her lush body under his hand.

His mouth had moved beneath her fingers, her hand slipping down. He wanted to grab her by the wrist and keep her there. He wanted to draw her fingers into his mouth and see if her eyes went black with pleasure. He wanted to put his fingers in *her* mouth, and he wanted her to suck hard.

But he didn't do any of those things, because she moved her hand from his lips to the back of his head. She gripped his hair and pulled him down toward her, and then he was kissing her.

Oh her *mouth*—God, how he had dreamed of her mouth. She tasted of tea; she tasted of heaven. He could feel the shape of her lips under his and the whisper of her breath, and by God, it wasn't enough.

A bit more, he told himself. *Just a bit more.*

He stroked up the curve of her ribs, his thumb grazing the underside of her breast, and she gasped against him, her lips parting.

His slide from reason to madness was slow. He licked her parted lips—*Gentle*, he said in his mind, *easy*—and she whimpered and tightened her grasp on his hair. Oh *fuck* it felt good, she felt so good, her body soft against his.

He pressed her back against the door, not too hard, and groaned a little at the feel of her. She made a sound too, a needy sound, and he wanted to please her. He wanted to give her what she needed.

He sucked at her lips, at her tongue—she liked that. He could tell by the way her breathing changed, erratic and wild, her full breasts pressing up into him. She made a tiny, almost whimpering sound, and then she came up on her toes, suddenly demanding.

He broke away, putting his mouth to her ear. "Whatever you need," he murmured. "Whatever you want. Ah God, Lydia."

He kissed her neck. He licked her collarbone and bit her there, and she made more of those little mewling sounds, her head falling back, her fingers tightening almost to pain in his hair.

"Christ," he growled, "Christ, I want to touch you. Can I—"

"Yes," she gasped. "Please."

He found the line of her bodice with his fingers and then with his mouth. He stroked the delicate skin there, then slid his hand around to the fabric-covered weight of her breast and dragged his thumb across one tightened nipple.

She gave a cry, bright and loud, and pleasure spiraled through his body. God, she was so responsive, it made his head spin. He needed her out of this dress. He needed her breasts bare in his hands. He needed her above him, riding him, while he pinched and rolled those nipples. He needed to find out if he could make her come just like that.

And then the door handle rattled.

He froze. They both froze, for a long moment, before he lifted his head.

Oh Jesus, she was so lovely like this, flushed and vivid. He'd somehow managed to tug down her bodice enough that her spectacular breasts were near to spilling free, and the sight was enough to inspire a bloody year's worth of erotic fantasies.

And oh *God*, this was a mistake. He could not touch her. He had to stay *away* from her.

He could not take advantage of her. Bleeding hell, if he compromised her—if he had her in truth the way he'd had her in his mind—they would be honor-bound to marry.

No one who knew her true identity was aware of their marital pretense; her reputation was not at stake. But if he lay with her—

She would think he had done it on purpose, for her fortune. She would think he had used her, far worse and far more ruthlessly than Davis had.

And he would never know if he could have done things the right way. He would never know if he could have won her properly, captured her heart and her affection for himself and not because he was her only choice. Her consolation prize.

"What on earth," came Lord de Younge's voice from outside the door. The knob rattled again.

"Och," Arthur said, pitching his voice loud enough for Lord de Younge to hear, "sorry, man. Needed a moment with my bride."

The words felt strange on his lips—sweet and astringent at the same time, desire and reality at war with each other.

Lord de Younge laughed. "The hysteria of young love! For God's sake, don't tell Didier, or you'll never hear the end of it. I'm only wanting my cigar case."

Lydia was frantically tugging at her bodice and patting her hair. "Do I look all right?" she said in an undervoice.

He took her in and, despite himself, memorized the sight. "You look as though you've been well ravished, but I suppose that's how you ought to look."

"Oh for heaven's sake," she mumbled. Then she turned back toward the door and—with no concern whatsoever for his still-exuberant erection—opened it.

Chapter 14

Having such a splendid time in Sussex that I've decided to stay on longer still. Please don't trouble yourself to visit!

—from Lydia to her brother Theo, enclosed in a
letter to Selina

That evening, Lydia shoved hairpins into her hair and tried not to look at Georgiana, cross-legged on Lydia's bed.

"I feel," Georgiana said blandly, "there is something you have neglected to share with me."

"No. Nothing. Truly, Georgiana, where *did* you find that dress? You have an unnatural talent for disguise."

Georgiana glanced down at the coarse serge frock she was wearing. It was slightly too big for her narrow form, which only added to the impression that she was, as she claimed to be, Lydia's lady's maid. When she ducked her head and put on the round tones of a South London accent, Lydia could quite forget that Georgiana was an earl's daughter who'd once been the most promising debutante of the Season.

When she arched one blond brow, as she was doing now, it was rather easier to remember who she was.

"I am not interested in discussing fashion," Georgiana said.

"Are you quite certain? Because I've brought these really lovely slippers with sort of a gold bit in the weave—"

Georgiana ignored her. "You're telling me that you broke into Lord de Younge's office, found absolutely nothing of note, and *nothing else happened*?"

"Correct."

"Then why are you avoiding my eyes and turning the color of a tomato?"

"I really think you would like these slippers."

Georgiana gave her a dubious look, which Lydia pretended not to notice by turning to examine her own face in the glass. She appeared much as she'd imagined she would: scarlet-faced and guilty as anything.

She needed to get hold of herself.

Yes, she had kissed Arthur. That was perfectly fine. The sky was not falling. Only—

Oh God, she had *kissed* Arthur. She'd wound her fingers into his hair and practically dragged his head down toward her mouth, which might have been embarrassing if Arthur hadn't responded as though she were a banquet and he a starving man.

It had started out so soft, so gentle—a girl's dream of a first kiss.

And then it had become something else entirely.

Lydia was no sheltered miss. Between her friends, her four older brothers, and the entire erotic catalogue of Belvoir's Library, she was perfectly well acquainted with the full range of what might happen in the bedchamber between consenting adults.

But she had not dreamed—

Well. She had not dreamed it would feel like that. His mouth all over her, licking and sucking and *biting*—oh God, she had especially liked the biting. She'd felt wild with wanting, her body unmoored, searching for pressure and touch and satisfaction. And then, when he *had* touched her, she'd felt hot, desperate shocks of bliss everywhere his fingers had passed.

Her body—so ungovernable, so bloody tuned to her emotions—had become not something that shamed her, but something wonderful, something that spilled pleasure by the handful. Her own pleasure—and his as well.

She wanted it again. She wanted *more*.

She was six-and-twenty years old. She had been on the Marriage Mart for seven Seasons; she had told herself she was content with a passionless life.

But she had not known what was possible. She had not known about this rough-tender blacksmith of an earl. She had not known that her heart could wrench when he said her name, or that his hands on her waist would feel like an anchor when the world spun free around her.

Now she knew. And she could no longer be satisfied with what she'd had before. It ought to have terrified her—it *did* terrify her.

But she felt strangely, stubbornly determined as well. She was tired of waiting for her life to change. Had she not resolved already that she would change things for herself?

So she would do it. She would grab on to him with both hands, and if it ended in her own heartache, damn it, she would at least go to her grave knowing the sharp, shocking pleasure of Arthur's skin touching her own.

"Are you ready to go down?" Georgiana asked. "I suspect it's time."

Lydia swallowed hard and shoved her feet into the aforementioned slippers. They made her several inches taller, and if she turned too fast, her silk-stockinged ankles were visible beneath her hem.

For luck, she told herself.

Heavens, she was going to need it.

She made her way down the stairs and to the drawing room, where the guests had gathered before dinner. She spotted Arthur immediately and was on the point of sauntering over to him when Lord de Younge caught her by the elbow.

"Lady Strathrannoch," he said happily, "what a beauty you are. I hope your rooms are to your liking. Come, I shall introduce you to one of your own people—a visitor we have from England who's just arrived."

He steered her to a small group of chattering guests. Lydia spotted Claudine Thibodeaux—who was showing vastly more bosom than she had been that morning at breakfast—and her bespectacled husband. Both were talking avidly to a tall man with a thick head of wavy blond hair, a man who looked remarkably like—

"This is Mr. Eagermont," said Lord de Younge, "newly arrived from a *fascinating* investment tour of the Midlands, is that not right?"

But Lydia was not listening. Her mouth opened, and nothing came out.

Mr. Eagermont?

"How do you do?" the man said in a rich, mellifluous voice. He bowed over Lydia's numb fingers, pressed a kiss to the back of her hand, and then looked to her face with an expression of graceful charisma.

And then the expression dropped right off his face as he recognized her.

"Lydia?" he demanded.

His regular voice was just the slightest bit different from the rich one he'd used a moment ago. Rougher, a little care-worn. A voice she knew almost as well as she knew the shape of his shoulders or the precise shade of his eyes.

Because the voice belonged to her brother Jasper.

She blinked. She swallowed. And then she managed, "I am not sure we've been introduced, *Mr. Eagermont.*"

Jasper, to his credit, did not blush—her other brothers certainly would have—only looked from Lydia to Lord de Younge and murmured, "I beg your pardon, my lord."

Then he bent to Lydia's ear and said, in a voice like ice, "The hallway. Now."

She had never in her life heard Jasper use that particular tone of voice. He excused himself from the group and, a minute or two later, she silently followed. No one appeared to notice her departure.

In the hall, Jasper caught her elbow and began to drag her rapidly away from the drawing room's open door. She squeaked and dug her nails into his arm, but he made no sound, only pressed his mouth into a grim line and piloted her all the way to the fabric-covered threshold that marked the servants' staircase. He yanked open the handle and put a hand on her lower back, meaning to thrust her up the stairs.

She widened her stance and put a hand on the doorjamb to brace herself. "Jasper," she hissed, "what in heaven's name is going on?"

"Why aren't you in Sussex?"

"Why aren't *you* in Venice?" She squeezed his forearm so hard she thought she might draw blood, but—infuriatingly—he did not appear moved, only nudged her harder through the door.

"I'm not going anywhere until you—eep!"

Jasper was gone. He was one moment beside her, his forearm being slowly mangled by her fingernails, and the next moment altogether vanished.

"In the future," said a familiar deep voice, "I trust you'll listen to my wife."

Good heavens, Lydia thought dreamily.

And then, a moment later, *Oh hell.*

Arthur swept her into his arms and held her against his broad chest for a long, luxurious moment. She caught his familiar scent of burnt honey. And then he pushed her back and began gently examining her for injury.

At least, she supposed that's what he was doing. It was rather hard to think clearly with his hands methodically exploring her person.

Jasper, meanwhile, got himself up from the floor. His hair was standing on end, which gave her normally dapper brother the appearance of an extremely large and disorderly rooster. "Your wife? Get your damned hands off her—that's not your wife!"

"Lydia," Arthur said in a low murmur, "is this fool someone you know, or should you prefer that I throw him out on his arse?"

"Ah," Lydia said, "both?"

"Aye, all right, then," Arthur said, and began stripping off his jacket.

"Try it," snapped Jasper, "just try it, you Scottish oaf, and we'll see how far height gets you when you've not the brains to back it up."

"'Tis not the height," said Arthur, and he reached out and caught Jasper's cravat, pushing him into the wall and holding him there by the throat. Jasper's toes just barely touched the ground. "'Tis the reach that matters."

Lydia stared, agape, at the sight of Arthur holding her brother against the wall like a rather forlorn quilt. She had been witness to a great deal—a very great deal—of male tussling in a house with four older brothers, but it had been a long time since she'd seen anyone get the best of Jasper. It had been years since she'd even seen anyone *try*.

Jasper's fair skin had begun to fade into a whitish-purple before it dawned on her that some action was required on her part.

She leapt forward and grabbed Arthur's arm. Dear *Lord*, the man had biceps muscles that could break—she did not know what. Things that were difficult to break. Stones. Bricks. Mid-sized country mansions.

"Best let him go," she said to Arthur, tugging at the immovable fixture that had once been living flesh. "That's my brother Jasper, and I'd hate to have to explain his demise to our mother."

Arthur dropped Jasper, who slid slowly down to sit upon the floor.

"Your brother?" Arthur was looking in bafflement from her to Jasper and back again. "Did I not hear Lord de Younge introduce him as Mr. Eagermont?"

Lydia nodded, then reconsidered and shook her head. "I cannot explain it."

"Did *I* not hear," Jasper rasped from the floor, "Lord de Younge introduce *you* as Lady Strathrannoch?"

Lydia looked at Arthur. He gazed back impassively, and then raised his eyebrows slightly, as if to say, *By all means, explain that one.*

And then Lydia made a very rash decision in a series of very rash decisions, the sum of which had landed her in Scotland, investigating a missing weapons thief with her fake husband.

She lied.

"Yes," she said, "I am Lady Strathrannoch. I left from Selina's country house in Sussex and came to Scotland in order to elope with the Earl of Strathrannoch."

It was, she supposed, only about half a lie, if one wanted to do the mathematics. Perhaps even only one-third, depending upon how one separated out her deceptions.

Jasper, who'd struggled to his feet, began wheezing and appeared to consider retiring to the floor once more.

"You went to Scotland?" he gasped. "On your own? To *elope*?"

Lydia was too afraid to discover whether Arthur's expression registered equanimity or horror at her words. "I wasn't entirely alone. I came with Lady Georgiana."

"Oh, well, that makes it all right then." Jasper scrubbed his hands over his face several times, then once through his hair, thus committing the rooster version of her brother to its mortal end. "Mother is going to go off her head."

"Ah," Lydia said. "Well. Perhaps you ought to let me tell her first. As the"—she was going to hell for this, surely—"the Countess of Strathrannoch. In the flesh. Mother will like that."

"If she doesn't bayonet you for marrying without her guiding hand."

"Don't be ridiculous," Lydia said. "Mother would use a rapier. More elegant. Far less blood."

"Lyd—"

To her surprise, Arthur interrupted Jasper's pointed questions with one of his own. His hand came warmly to her upper back, his thumb resting on the bare skin above the buttons that closed her gown. "I think my wife's satisfied your curiosity well enough, and you've not yet answered any questions of hers. Why are you here under false pretenses?"

"I am on business," Jasper said. He stood a little straighter as he faced Arthur, and his voice had taken on that mellifluous tone again. His Mr. Eagermont voice, evidently. "It is important that de Younge not know my true identity."

"On business?" Lydia stared at him in frank astonishment. "You do not even *like* business."

"I have been known to dabble—"

"You most certainly have not," she said. "What did Theo have to do to you to persuade you?"

"Theo?" Jasper blinked, and then, changing course, nodded. "Yes. Theo. He's involved himself in textile-factory reform. I've been tasked with gathering information for him."

"By . . . playacting?" It made a kind of sense, she supposed. Jasper was by far the best of the Hope-Wallace siblings at winning friends and mesmerizing innocent bystanders with his charm. If anyone could wheedle information from a roomful of strangers, it was certainly Jasper.

And yet—it also did not make sense. "Why here?" she asked. "Why Scotland, for heaven's sake? Is de Younge one of Theo's competitors?"

"He is."

"In politics or investments?"

"Yes," Jasper said decisively, and then he pushed himself off from the wall and angled his face toward Arthur. "Don't think this is over, Strathrannoch." His voice was icy, but Lydia noticed that this time he kept himself just out of Arthur's reach as he headed back toward the drawing room.

"'Twas over before it started," observed Arthur mildly.

It was remarkable. Even from behind, she could see Jasper's ears turning a rather virulent shade of puce.

"You needn't antagonize him," she whispered to Arthur.

"He tried to remove you to a place you didn't want to be. Brother or no, he deserves what he got and more."

She blinked up at him. His curls were slightly disheveled, his jacket off and his sleeves falling open at the cuffs. The appeal of him was boggling, really. She wanted to launch herself at him. She wanted to wrap her legs around his waist. She wanted to find out if their height difference would matter if he had her up against the wall and—

"Ah," she said. "Forget about Jasper. Put yourself back together or they'll think we're out here trysting again."

"Lady Strathrannoch"—her stomach did a neat somersault as he nudged a wayward lock of hair out of her mouth—"I suspect they already do."

• • •

Lydia encountered Georgiana at the top of the stairs, one long hall away from the precious respite of her bedchamber.

"Formidable evening?" Georgiana asked as she surveyed Lydia's general state of, presumably, pallid bedragglement.

It had not been so very awful at first. Over dinner, she had not needed to speak, and she'd rather enjoyed listening with one ear for the conversation of the Valiquettes and Thibodeaux and with the other for the increasingly less subtle barbs traded by her brother and her faux husband.

And then they'd all entered the drawing room for music, coffee, and general postprandial relaxation, and things had become—

"Worse than formidable. There were *parlor games*."

Georgiana's mouth quirked. "Did you have to sit on someone's lap and meow like a cat?"

Lydia blinked. "What kind of parlor games—no, never mind. I don't want to know. No, I merely had to propose a riddle, except Jas—" She stopped, arrested. "Oh! You'll never guess who arrived at Kilbride House today."

Georgiana's expression went slightly smug. "I already know. Mr. Joseph Eagermont, an investor—though no one seems to know quite in what."

"They wouldn't. Because Mr. Eagermont is *Jasper*."

Georgiana stopped in her tracks, still several feet short of the bedchamber door. "Is that so? Your brother Jasper?"

"The very one."

"Under an assumed name?"

"Indeed. I played charades with him as Mr. Eagermont for the last two hours. Fortunately, he will not reveal my true identity to anyone here, since he cannot admit our connection without compromising his own facade. However—ah, if you encounter him, you should know that he believes I am the actual Countess of Strathrannoch."

Georgiana's expression was unreadable. "Are you not?"

"I—what? Of course not."

But Georgiana was not attending. Her pale blue eyes had taken on a terrifying glint. "Secret identities. Unintelligible writings. You must realize this scenario is more Gothic than my last three novels."

"I suppose I had not considered it."

Georgiana turned on her heel back toward the hall, away from Lydia's chamber. "You don't need my assistance to retire, do you?"

"I've managed the last twenty-six years without you. You know you are not actually my maid?"

"Just so. I think—I think I should like to see what I can find out about this Mr. Eagermont." She appeared slightly glazed—dreaming, no doubt, of Scottish mystery novels with very large print runs.

Lydia waved a hand. "Go. Enjoy yourself."

Georgiana was already halfway down the hall. Lydia gazed after her friend until Georgiana vanished down the servant's staircase—truly, it was remarkable how she could *watch* Georgiana transform into her role, her hair tugged up into a hasty twist, her shoulders curving to hide her height—and then pushed open her door.

Whereupon she took one look at her bedchamber and emitted a single, quickly stifled scream.

Chapter 15

Dearest, I've no doubt you're acquitting yourself brilliantly in Scotland. By the by, did you intend to write "Lady Strathrannoch" four or five times at the bottom of your note, or was that merely a slip of the pen?

—from Selina to Lydia

It took Arthur nearly an hour to come upstairs after Lydia's abortive attempt to enter her own bedchamber. Luckily, his door across the hall had not been locked, and so, in an abundance of caution, she had elected to spend that window of time waiting cross-legged upon his bed.

When he finally deigned to return to his room, Lydia heard muffled Scottish swearing and the rattle of the handle from outside the door. She crossed the room, threw open the latch, and let him in.

His eyes widened at the sight of her. "Och," he said, "I've lost my head, it seems. I thought this was my chamber, but I suppose I've—"

He was backing swiftly out of the chamber, but she caught

his hand and dragged him inside. "This *is* your chamber. Hurry in. Good heavens, are you drunk? You smell like a whisky still."

He gazed down at her, looking stupefied but thankfully clear-headed. "I'm starting to think I must be. But no, 'twas only Thibodeaux, the right wee idiot, spilling his brandy all down my best shirt."

Indeed, she could see, at this proximity to his chest, a pungent and spreading brown stain beneath his cravat.

"What are you doing in here?" Arthur went on.

"Someone has ransacked my room, and I—"

"They've *what*?"

"—thought it best to wait here until you returned, and we—"

"Did you say *ransacked your room*?"

"—might examine the scene of the crime, as it were, together."

"Are you daft, woman?" He glared down at her from his impressive height and crossed his arms over his chest, a gesture which had a truly supernatural effect on both said arms and said chest. "Why did you not send for me? Or come down, damn it? You've been up here all alone, while I've been listening to Thibodeaux burble about 'The Lusty Smith of Tipperary'?"

"The what?"

"Never mind." He yanked off his cravat, which caused brandy fumes to waft into the air. "Why did you not find me?"

"I—" She almost did not know. It had not even occurred to her to do anything but wait. "I suppose I did not want to trouble you."

"Christ!" he exclaimed, and caught her chin for one rough, heart-stopping moment before he let go. "Next time, damn it, trouble me! You can always trouble me. God knows you already do."

Somehow, it sounded almost like a compliment.

"Stay here," he grated and made for the door.

She followed him.

"For God's sake," he said, glowering at her, "can you not stay put? Will you not let me look for a moment before throwing yourself headlong into danger?"

"I'm certain whoever perpetrated the deed has long since gone. Had they wanted to harm me, they could have done so the moment I opened the door."

"Then why did you wait for me to join you, if you were so bloody certain?"

She lifted her chin. "I am a prudent woman."

"Aye," he said, "and I'm the prince regent. Come on then."

Inside her bedroom, things were as disordered as she recalled. Her belongings were tossed from the trunk Huw had brought down from Strathrannoch Castle and strewn about the room. Her letters—Davis's letters—were spread across the floor. An inkstand on the escritoire had been overturned and was dripping steadily onto the green-and-white floral rug and—blast it!—one of her favorite hats.

Arthur was already in motion, searching beneath the bed, behind the draperies, and even inside the small wardrobe and her now-empty trunk.

"Are you quite satisfied there are no children or medium-sized dogs hidden about the room?" she asked when he finally halted.

He scowled at her. "I don't like this at all. Let's put your things back together, and we'll try to work out if they've stolen anything."

Together, they set the room to rights. A dozen pounds sterling had vanished from the bottom of her trunk, and a pair of lacy stockings, but she was not certain about the correspondence. Even with the letters stacked and reordered chronologically, she could not recall if any were missing.

She gave Arthur an apologetic glance. "I did not memorize

them, you know. Perhaps if I had my notes, I could work it out more precisely. I can cross-reference them when we return to Strathrannoch Castle."

To her surprise, he greeted this admission with a look of some buoyancy.

The look vanished, however, when she attempted to bid him good night.

"You cannot mean to sleep in here," he protested. "The bastards could return any time."

She pursed her lips. "Surely not. Whoever searched the room in the first place deliberately chose a time they knew I would be out—"

"Are you so certain of that? Certain enough to risk your life upon it?"

"I haven't anywhere else to sleep," she said in exasperation.

There was a short, tense silence. Now that Arthur's jaw was clean-shaven, she could see the muscles leap as he ground his teeth. It was astoundingly attractive. She prayed his whiskers grew quickly. Perhaps she could ask Georgiana to abscond with his razor.

"You can sleep in my chamber," he said finally. "I'll exchange with you."

"If it is safe for you, then surely it is safe for me as well—"

"I knew you were going to say that, damn it." He glowered at her. "Fine, then. I'll sleep outside the door in the hall."

"In the hall?" Her voice rose so precipitously that Arthur looked toward the door as though anticipating a sudden influx of concerned parties.

"'Twould not be the first time I've—"

"Slept in the hall?" She put her hands on her hips. "Everyone in the bloody house would hear of it by morning. No. It's out of the question."

He gave her another black look. "'Tis the hall in front of your door or of mine. Take your pick."

She threw up her hands in disgust. "Fine. Fine, then. I'll sleep in your chamber, but you mustn't sleep in the hall."

"I would not compromise your reputation if I can help it—"

She directed her most disbelieving stare in his direction. "Arthur. We are pretending to be married. If anyone discovers my true identity, whether we slept in the same bedroom or not will be immaterial, don't you think?"

"Christ, woman." He opened the door and crossed the hall to his own room, gesturing for her to follow. "I thought you were shy and retiring. Not too bloody clever and slippery for your own good."

She entered his chamber and heard him lock the door behind them both.

A little frisson of . . . something . . . went through her at the sound.

They were alone. They were alone, and the bedchamber was locked, and between them was a large, well-appointed, and entirely empty bed.

More. She had wanted more after their abbreviated kiss. And now they were together, and alone, and within sight of a bed. Her mind's eye went wild—a flame-bright staccato series of limbs intertwined, sweat beading on skin—

"Why did you tell your brother we were married?" Arthur asked.

She blinked up at him, startled out of her erotic haze.

His mouth compressed, his head tilted, and she could not read his expression. "Surely you did not . . ."

He trailed off, and she hastened to explain herself. "I don't mean to let him go on thinking it, of course. I would not take advantage of you in that way."

He coughed.

"Only I feared that if I told him the truth just then, he would be . . . vexed. There might have been a commotion. A mild fracas, if you will." She tried not to look too guilty as she peered into Arthur's face to judge how he was receiving her explanation. "I shall tell him the truth when I return home."

She had no idea what she would say, but that was a problem for Future Lydia to contend with.

"Grand," he said. "No doubt he'll be ecstatic."

"Ah—"

"When we're facing each other over pistols, I'll have to remember to aim low."

"To, er, wound him only?"

"Because he's short."

She laughed despite herself. Arthur's eyes caught on hers. The room was dim in the candlelight, but she could still make out the gold around his pupil, the spiral of green and blue around it. He almost smiled back before he caught himself and rubbed one hand across the back of his neck.

"Still and all," he said, "I find myself worried about much more than your brother. There's more to this situation than we know. I cannot think Davis is here, hiding somewhere and hunting for your letters. Yet there must be a reason someone broke into your room and searched your things. Someone is suspicious."

"Someone in league with Davis, perhaps."

"Aye," he said slowly. "And I've no notion whether it's our hosts or someone else." His face was set and earnest as he spoke. "Lady de Younge extended us an invitation to stay longer, just as we anticipated. Perhaps in the coming days, I can investigate their library—"

"And I can ask Georgiana to search the rooms of the French

couples. They are all familiar with Davis; they could perhaps have plotted with him."

"Aye—mayhap Monsieur and Madame de Valiquette harbor the same sympathies toward our own Scottish aristocrats that my brother does." He paused, his mouth turning down at the corner. "Speaking of brothers—I think yours is lying about what he's doing here."

Lydia stroked a finger over her lips, thinking of her brother's quick and far too facile explanation for his presence, his rapid acceptance of her supposed elopement. "I know he is. Only I cannot fathom why."

She looked up at Arthur to see if any insight was forthcoming from his quarter, only to find that he had frozen in place, his eyes fixed upon the place where her index finger rested upon her bottom lip.

She felt heat gather all through her body. Not only the familiar warmth of a blush in her face and chest, but—everywhere. A slow swirl of warmth in her belly, rising to throb along her skin.

Arthur did not seem to move, yet suddenly she felt as though he'd surrounded her. Her gaze caught on his chest, where his shirt gaped open to reveal a mouthwatering triangle of skin. Her nose filled with the scent of whisky, and it went straight to her head, potent, dizzying.

She wanted to dissolve under that heated look. She wanted to feel his touch again; she ached for it. Her fingers twitched, desperate to slide into the vee of his collar and see if his body was as hot and solid as she remembered.

"Disrobe," she commanded, and then could have bitten off her own tongue.

His gaze flew to her face. His lips parted; his pupils flared.

"The whisky," she choked out. "I meant because of the whisky aroma. On, er, your shirt. I'm finding it . . . I'm finding this all a trifle . . ."

Overwhelming? Arousing? Will-sapping in the extreme?

"Intoxicating," she managed, which wasn't all that much better. "With the window closed and the whisky saturating the air."

His deep voice was hoarse when he spoke. "I take your meaning. I'll put on a fresh shirt in the hall, then."

She swallowed hard and very nearly agreed with him. But no. That was absurd. She was a strong, independent woman. She would not be overcome by the sight of his bared chest.

But then again—

"That's not necessary," she said. "I shall close my eyes."

To prove it, she leaned back against the wall and clamped her lids closed. She felt him retreat—her traitorous body gave a rather mournful wail—and then heard a great deal of muttering and shuffling.

What sound precisely did fabric make as it slid over skin? She had never considered it with quite so much fervency before.

Was that rustle the sound of his shirt slipping over his head? Was he, even now, bared to the waist? What would he look like unclothed? And how dreadful—how very dreadful—would she be if she opened her eyes to find out?

"I'm done." Arthur's deep voice interrupted her guilty quandary, and she startled.

She cracked first one eye, then the other. He wore a fresh shirt—spotted with a few scorch marks from his forge, of course—with the collar open. She tried to keep her wits about her with some difficulty.

"I shall need my trunk," she said, "to change into my own night rail. We left it in my chamber."

"I'll get it." He made for the door and then, pausing, looked back at her. "Do you need me to"—she did not think she imagined the way his voice dropped into a lower register—"unlace your corset?"

Did she? Could she possibly ask him to—

Flustered panic overcame her. "No," she squeaked. "This one laces down the front. I can manage it myself."

He looked slightly glassy-eyed at that. "Right. I'll fetch your things and wait in the hall while you tend to yourself."

She opened her mouth, but he forestalled her. "Don't argue. And lock the damned door while I'm out there."

"Surely that's not necessary," she protested. "Are you concerned someone will break in upon me whilst I'm unclothed?"

"Aye," he said. "Someone."

Chapter 16

I understand Strathrannoch and his countess have begun sharing a bedchamber, and—cariad—you didn't contrive this, did you? (Please take this query in the spirit of compliment it was meant!)

—from Huw to Bertie, posted from Kilbride House

Five days of cohabitation later, Arthur had begun to fear that proximity to Lydia Hope-Wallace was slowly ravaging his intellect.

She had certainly eroded his willpower. Wrecked his composure. Caused significant and irreversible damage to his heart.

But no. His heart was not the issue at hand.

The problem was in his brain, and in the fact that even after nearly a week's concerted investigation, he had made no progress toward discovering who had ransacked Lydia's room.

He had searched the library and found nothing but Jasper Hope-Wallace asleep on a chaise longue, a book open upon his chest. Arthur had made a god-awful racket whilst searching, but the man hadn't moved an inch, which suggested he either had been knocked upon the head or was faking it. And why he would be feigning repose, Arthur could not imagine.

He briefly entertained a wild fantasy in which all the Hope-Wallace siblings were in league with his brother and Lydia had been sent ahead to seduce him into compliance. Then he recalled her flight among the zebras and discarded that notion.

Besides—he trusted her.

After Arthur's failure of reconnaissance in the library, Georgiana had been tasked with gaining access to the chambers of the Thibodeaux and Valiquette couples. Once that was accomplished, Arthur and Lydia had surreptitiously searched, but they'd found nothing of interest.

Lydia, meanwhile, spent her time gathering intelligence directly from the other guests. Despite her manifest discomfort when forced into the drawing room or sitting room or wherever else the company happened to gather en masse, she was adept at listening and at putting together scraps of information from various conversations. Every evening, she consulted the index of notes she'd made back at Strathrannoch Castle. She was machinelike in her precision, matching points of reference from comments he'd scarcely perceived.

But thus far, it was no use. The de Younges, the Thibodeaux, the Valiquettes—all, at various points, made statements that could somehow be connected to Davis. Even Lydia's brother Jasper—still in the guise of Joseph Eagermont—had once made an offhand remark about a grocer he'd encountered near the border who sold turnip paste molded into the shape of a cod's head. Later, Lydia had shown Arthur the exact same story written in Davis's hand.

That, at least, had not been something Davis had stolen from him. Arthur had never heard of such a thing in his life.

Lydia was dogged and persistent and clever as the devil. He could see that she hated the evenings of entertainment—he'd once caught her surreptitiously examining the pianoforte's wires as though searching for a way to destroy them—but she kept throwing herself at the general assembly anyway. Most nights, he tried to draw her away from the small crowd and into the hallway or out to the gardens for relief, but she rarely allowed it.

"I want to help," she'd said the previous night. "I know I can do this." Her face was still pale and a little greenish after Mrs. Thibodeaux had asked her in thickly accented English to *lift her angelic voice in song*.

He did not know how to explain to her that she was *already* helping. That she did not always need to make herself uncomfortable because she thought it was what others wanted from her.

And when he tried, she did not seem persuaded.

In addition to their decidedly poor information-gathering, they also had not yet heard back from Belvoir's, though Bertie had reiterated via letter his promise to forward any correspondence from London immediately.

At this point, Arthur had no clearer sense of Davis's motivations than he'd had before they'd arrived at Kilbride House. Every time he began to think he'd made some headway—when Lord de Younge began to speak of new rifle craft over a brace of pheasant, for example—his suspicions soon faltered, faded, and snagged upon someone else. To wit: Monsieur de Valiquette had replied to Lord de Younge's commentary on improved rifle design with a flurry of outraged French decrying the problem of poaching and the beneficence of aristocrats like himself and the Duchess of Sutherland, one of Davis's benefactors.

Either *everyone* in Kilbride House knew something about Davis's nefarious activities or no one did.

A third option presented itself: The solution to the mystery of Davis's accomplice was obvious. Arthur simply could not think of it because his brains had been plundered by Lydia Hope-Wallace.

Every night in their shared bedchamber was torture. She was an argumentative wee thing, but he was obstinate enough to hold off one ginger Englishwoman. She hadn't been able to talk him into sleeping in the bed.

At least, not the first evening. That night, he'd slept on a thin rug on the stone floor and woken to bollocks so chilled he feared they'd never be seen again. He had, in the cold—*very* cold—light of dawn, come to the conclusion that he was resolute enough to share the bed with her and still maintain some semblance of honor.

And he had. Sort of.

For the subsequent nights, he'd slept lengthwise across the foot of the bed, which meant everything from his calves down dangled off the edge. His personal discomfort was not nearly as much of a problem, however, as was the fact that he was obsessed with her.

He thought about her all day: her bravery and wit and fortitude, her nervous, busy fingers. And then he thought about her all night as well. He could sense her in the bed—God, he could not have been more aware of her if they were mid-coitus. He could feel every time she shifted or turned; he knew the weight of her body on the mattress. He could smell the warm vanilla scent that clung to her, and he wanted to taste it. Lick it. Lick *her*.

He knew that she had two night rails with her. He had not seen them; she wore her many-buttoned dressing gown to bed and then struggled out of it beneath the bedclothes and tossed it down onto the floor.

But he knew there were at least two. Some nights, he could see the spill of silky-soft cotton down by her feet. That was the first night rail: the one that went all the way to the floor.

Other nights, he could not see the edge of fabric, which meant she was wearing the second nightgown. The shorter one. He harbored a number of vivid and specific fantasies about where on her body the hem of the garment fell.

Her calves? Above her knees? Higher?

If he was not thinking about her legs or her smile or her bloody nightclothes, he was thinking about his brother, and *her* brother, and where the deceptions stopped and started. By the time the sun rose each morning, Arthur was an exhausted, aroused, deeply unpleasant shell of himself. Lydia now rang for tea before even greeting him.

All of which explained why, when he woke just before dawn on their sixth day at Kilbride House, it was with a fogged brain and a rampant erection.

"Arthur—wake up!"

Yes, it was Lydia's urgent whisper that had roused him. He flipped over in the bed, trying simultaneously to protect her with his body and arm himself against an intruder.

"What's wrong?" he murmured, pitching his voice as low as hers had been.

"I heard something. Not—*ouch*—not here in the bed, for heaven's sake! At the door. I think there's someone at the door."

She scrambled out of bed and launched herself in the direction of the room's entrance, the daft woman. He followed. She was small but quick, and in a moment she had herself pressed up against the crack between the door and the wooden jamb, evidently trying to peer through.

He came up behind her. "What—" he tried to hiss, but she gave him a forbidding glare and put her finger to her lips.

For Christ's sake. The woman did not attract trouble, as he'd previously believed. She flung herself at it. He glowered at her and then put his eye to the crack as well, his chin above the top of her head.

If she'd heard someone at their door, there was no one there now. But from the tiny gap where the door's iron hinge abutted the jamb, he could see someone across the hall, fiddling with the door to the room that had been Lydia's.

It was not an intruder. It was a chambermaid. As he watched, a buxom woman in the navy-and-gold livery of the Kilbride House staff shifted the copper coal scuttle on her hip and tugged harder at the door handle, easing the door open with a heavy creak before slipping into the room.

"Oh," Lydia whispered, "I'm so sorry. What an idiot I am."

"You're no idiot. Perhaps a reckless bampot for throwing yourself at the door when we didn't know whether there was a primed pistol on the other side. But not an idiot."

She shifted, still watching the empty hallway through the crack in the door, and Arthur was suddenly aware of her position: pressed against the surface of the door while he stood behind her, his hands braced on either side of her head.

He could smell the soft, sweet scent of her body. He would only have to bend his head to bury his face in the autumn-colored spill of her hair. He would barely have to move to be touching her.

Her voice, when she spoke, was still a whisper. "It's only

that—well, the chambermaid doesn't usually come for hours yet. I was not expecting to hear anything, and when I did—"

"You did the right thing." He hoped she attributed the sudden rasp in his voice to the remnants of sleep.

"Shall we wait until she comes back out? To be certain everything is as it should be?"

Say, "No," he thought. *Say, "Get back in bed. I'll keep the watch."*

But he'd lost his brains and his willpower and other things he was not thinking about, because instead he said, "Aye. Let's bide here a moment."

And as Lydia pressed her face to the crack in the door again, he let himself look down at her.

There was only a glint of dawn light in the room. He could just make out the brilliant copper of her braid. Little wisps of curls escaped all along the length of that thick braid; his gaze skimmed down to the tail, tied off with a scrap of lace. It rested along the back of her night rail, which was—

He barely restrained a rough, greedy sound.

She wore the shorter night rail, and it clung to her decadent curves, mapping the contours of her body in a whisper of—blue? lavender?—silk. It was too dark to tell the precise color. It was too dark to make out all of her, but he tried anyway, his eyes falling upon the taut silk across her buttocks, the pale slide of her calf.

He was desperately aroused. He could feel blood beating in his cock. He wanted to press into her body, spin her around, and push her up against the door. He wanted to see the blue of her eyes while he buried himself inside her.

He knew there was a reason he ought not do it, and yet he could not recall what it was.

"Arthur," she whispered. She started to shift, to turn toward him in between his arms. "Do you think—"

He caught one of her hands in his and pressed it to the surface of the door.

"Don't move," he gritted out. "Don't turn around."

She made a surprised little gasp and turned her head, exposing the curve of her ear, the tender line of her throat.

"I cannot think if you turn around. I can—Christ, I cannot think as it is. You cloud my mind."

Her breath was coming quickly. He could see the pulse beating hard at the base of her throat.

"I spend all day and night wanting to touch you," he said hoarsely. "Wanting to have my hands on you again. My mouth."

She swallowed and said nothing. He still held her hand pressed between his and the door, and she did not pull away, and he could not make himself stop talking.

"'Twould be so easy to slide my fingers under the fragile wee strap of this nightgown. Push it down. See you bare and lovely before me. Christ, when I think of you wearing this in the bed beside me, it makes me—"

He broke off. Her breasts rose and fell erratically as she breathed, and he thought of the sound she'd made, loud and wanting, when he'd touched her there.

"What?" she whispered. "It makes you what?"

In answer, he pressed into her, pushing his arousal into the generous swell of her buttocks, and groaned a little from the pleasure of it.

"Hard," he said. "Desperate. Maddened."

"Arthur," she gasped, and her hand twitched under his, and for one crushing instant he thought she was trying to pull away, until—

"Touch me," she said. "Please."

• • •

Her head swam with want. Her skin was hot and sensitive, her nipples tight points that brushed against the silk of her night rail and sent shudders through her every time she breathed.

Arthur was behind her, his big hand closed over hers, pressing her fingers into the smooth wood grain of the door.

That was the only place his fingers touched her, and yet it was enough to send arousal spilling through her, a leap and slide in her lower belly, a throb between her legs. His hand was large, much larger than her own, and the contrast between his restrained strength and the small bones of her wrist aroused her further.

The muscles of his arms flexed beside her head, as though all the power in his body was held in check by the barest thread of his control.

She had done that. Power of a different sort mounted inside her, and it made her dizzy and reckless.

When would she have this chance again? When would she have this man—this man, whom she wanted beyond anything she'd imagined possible—trembling with desire before her?

"Please," she said again. "I want your hands on me. On my skin." It was easier to say the words this way, facing away from him, his body warm and solid behind her, her gaze on their linked hands.

There was a long, frozen moment of indecision. She could feel his body go tense, his fingers tightening on hers.

And then his hand landed, hot and heavy, on the curve of her waist.

"Christ," he rasped. His hand was already moving, sliding forward to her lower belly, pulling her back against him with the barest pressure. She heard herself make a soft-voiced cry as her body came into firmer contact with his.

"Put your hands on the door," he said. "Both hands. Don't

turn around. I cannot—I cannot swear to the endurance of my honor if you turn around." His hand came higher on her body. His thumb traced the outer curve of her breast, and she whimpered, trying to press herself into his hand.

"Ah God," he murmured. His head came down, his lips against her ear. "Lydia. Lydia."

"I want you to do—what you said." It was all she could think of. Her breasts felt ripe and swollen, and the slide of his thumb along one heavy curve only made her crave more. "Pull down my night rail. Touch me that way."

"Aye," he said against her ear. She felt the tickle of his breath there, and she shivered. She had not known that part of her body could be so sensitive. She had not known any of this. And she wanted—God, she did not want him to stop.

His right hand—the one that had captured hers—slid slowly up her arm. She felt the scratch of his calloused fingers against her skin. At her shoulder, he paused. He slid one finger beneath the strap of her night rail and toyed with it. She pressed back against him impatiently, and he made a rough sound. A hungry sound.

He set his teeth against her ear. "Dinna rush."

"Don't *dally* then—"

His arms flexed, quick and powerful, and he split the lace-edged neckline of her night rail down the front.

She gasped. Her breasts were bared to the cool night air, and Arthur's hands were on her hips, and everything was spiky and uncertain until he cupped her breasts in his palms.

He groaned as he touched her. She made a sound too, a half-wild sound, and pressed her hands hard against the door.

He swore, soft and filthy, in her ear. His fingers found her nipples and rolled them, tugging slightly, and she felt an answering throb between her legs. The sensation was powerful, consuming, a wave that burst through her body and dragged her under.

He did it again, and again, and she felt her wits recede, the demands of her body taking over. She whimpered—desperate, almost feral—and squeezed her thighs together. She needed to soothe the ache there, but the ache fought back, rising with her frantic movements.

"Shh," he murmured. "Ah God, Lydia, I don't want you to stop making those sounds, but you have to be a little quieter."

She didn't know what he meant. His fingers did not stop their quick, sharp tugs and she felt herself being pulled higher, tighter, and tauter by the moment. Her hands flexed against the door, her hips bucking, seeking pressure, seeking *something*.

One of his hands was gone, suddenly, from her breast, and she felt dizzy with disappointment. Then it was back, large and hot on her hip, sliding up and down her silk-covered buttocks. The pressure felt lovely—so lovely, relief and pleasure in one—but it was not enough. Instinctively, she spread her legs, and then moaned as his tongue made a hot swipe down the side of her neck.

"Hush," he said. She felt his fingers bunched in her night rail, the silk pulling tight across her hips, and then one hand was beneath, sliding up her inner thigh. "Lydia, my love, you cannot be so loud—ah God you feel—ah *fuck*—"

His fingers had found her, and she was slippery with her arousal. He circled her entrance with one thick finger, then drew her wetness slowly up to the sensitive place at the top of her sex. He stroked her there, quick light movements that matched the rhythm of his other hand at her breast. Pleasure—all she could think was pleasure, the pleasure of his hands, the pleasure eddying through her body.

Oh God, she thought wildly, *oh yes, oh please*—

And then his hand was gone, and he was spinning her about and pushing her back to the door.

"For quiet," he said, and then kissed her.

It was a messy, frantic kiss, more raw and hectic than the first time. His tongue came hard into her mouth, and she found that she wanted it. She wanted everything he would give her. She wanted to *take*.

She could touch him now, and so she did. She licked and bit and sucked at his mouth, and her hands swept over all the parts of him she could reach. She wanted it all—his beautiful cheekbones, the back of his neck, his taut, powerful shoulders.

He caught her buttocks and pulled her up against him, pushing her body into the door and lifting her off the ground. Her legs went around him as though she'd done it a thousand times.

She could feel his erection through his trousers, shockingly large and hard, and he ground himself against her bare sex. He groaned helplessly into her mouth, and she tugged at his shoulders, trying to pull him against her even harder, even more.

She wanted him inside her body. She realized that with sudden clarity. She wanted to have all of him.

But the thought was swept away as he rocked against her. His cock thrust rhythmically against her clitoris, and in moments she was close to her peak again. She shuddered against him, digging her heels into his body. She did not ask—she *demanded*.

"What do you need?" he managed to say. His voice was fractured, and the rest of him was perfect, perfect—

"Don't stop. Don't stop."

Then his mouth was on hers again. He kissed her as he moved against her, urging her on with his tongue and teeth, with the rhythmic stroke of his cock. He held her as her body convulsed, as her legs tensed and trembled, as the dawn light in the room burst into shards and she went blind with pleasure.

"Aye," he was saying, kissing her mouth and her cheek and her neck, "aye, Lydia, my love, that's so good. You're so good. You feel—ah—"

He moved against her as she came, and as her climax began to recede, he did not stop. He rocked and thrust, his voice breaking, and she realized he too could find his release this way.

Yes—*yes*—God, she wanted that. She was desperate to see him undone with pleasure.

"Don't stop," she said again.

He swore and groaned and ground himself against her, and then she felt him shuddering. His fingers dug into her buttocks; his forehead pressed into her neck. He said her name, and jerked against her, once, twice, again.

And when he finally lifted his head, the room was bright enough to see his eyes. Gold and green and blue, circles in circles like the rings of a tree.

The sun was fully up. It was morning.

She waited. He held her still, his arms around her, her body pressed against the door. They did not move. She thought perhaps neither of them wanted to break the spell of this moment. His body fitted with hers, so close their edges blurred. His multihued eyes, serious and careful, on her face.

She reached up and touched the line of his jaw.

"Don't regret it," she said. "I don't want you to regret it."

He shifted at that, easing away from her. Slowly, he set her back on her feet, and she dropped her hand.

What a fool she was. She was softness and sentiment; her

emotions ran too high. She knew this about herself. Her heart was easily bruised, and this man—

In the unequivocal light of day, he could devastate her.

Then he reached out with both hands and cupped her face. "Ah, Lydia," he said. "Never."

Chapter 17

How I wanted you. I wanted to keep you in my bed forever,
give you words of milk and honey, pour out sweetness upon
you. Tell you to lay your head in my lap and rest awhile, for I
would keep you safe.

—from the papers of Arthur Baird, crossed out,
begun again

The only thing that Arthur regretted was the dawn. He would
have liked to haul Lydia into the bed, pull her delectable body up
against his, and go to sleep with his face in her hair. But it was
morning, so he had to watch her wrestle her dressing gown into
place and return to her own bedchamber to prepare for the day.

He regretted the sun. He regretted her thousand-buttoned
dressing gown. He supposed, as he washed and shaved and
changed his clothes, that he regretted the state of last night's
trousers.

But he could not regret the feel of Lydia against him, the
breathless pulsebeat of her desire—the demand of her thighs
around his waist and the cry at the back of her throat.

He had not compromised her. He had not done something irrevocable, something that might trap her into marriage with him. For all his faults, he had not lost that last portion of his wits.

He did not know if he could win her affection—after what Davis had done to her, he did not even know how to begin. But suddenly, somehow, it seemed possible. She had wanted him—desired him—told him in low heated words what she yearned for him to do. It seemed conceivable that, given time, she might be persuaded to say yes if he asked her to marry him in truth.

He held to hope with both hands and imagined how he might ask her to be his. He felt the shape of the words on his tongue with no small trepidation.

But she had done it. She had told him what she wished for. Could he not be brave enough to do the same?

He was still wondering when he pulled open his door and found Lydia there on the threshold, her hand poised to knock.

For all that he'd seen her day in and day out for the last three weeks, he was still knocked sideways by the sight of her. Her dress was green, her hair neatly coiled. She wore delicate lacy gloves that buttoned at the wrists, and he wanted to peel them off. With his teeth.

He entertained the brief fantasy of carrying her right back to the bed. He entertained a second, much longer fantasy that involved his head between her thighs and a prompt rectification of the fact that he had not yet tasted her.

But despite the erotic intrusions—which surely ought to be *better* after the morning's interlude, not *worse*—he still had eyes and ears for nothing but Lydia. Her expression was dismayed as she unfolded a sheet of paper.

"I've had a note from Jasper," she said. "He left it in my room—I'm not certain when. It's . . . troubling."

"Would you have me read it?"

She nodded and pressed the letter into his hands.

Lyd, it read in a deeply slanted scrawl, *I've been called back to London. I'll break the news of your marriage to Mother. Stay here in Scotland with Strathrannoch—in his castle or the summer house in Glencoe. I'll write you when she's calmed enough for you to come home.*

It was only initialed, not signed—a looping messy *J*.

He folded the paper and took her hand in his. He hated that she was upset—hated too that her brother would spread the word of their false marriage before Lydia had a chance to control the story.

But—God. He did not want to take advantage of her distress, and yet he wondered if this might be the opportune time to tell her that he wanted to make their deception real.

He felt a sort of comfort in the rationality of the notion. He could give her a reason to accept, some logical explanation for why she might choose to tie herself to him. If she married him, she would not have to tell her family anything beyond the truth.

He could appeal to her clever, methodical brain. He need not try to make inroads on her heart.

"Lydia," he began, clasping her fingers more tightly, "I'm certain that you must be worried about what your family will think of all this."

Her brows drew together for a moment, and then her face cleared. "Oh! No. It's not that. Jasper is being rather dramatic—I think Mother will be quite delighted, all in all."

He paused, somewhat taken aback. *Delighted* seemed an awfully rosy prediction even under the best of circumstances—and their reality could not, under any rational definition, be termed the best of circumstances.

"No," she said again, "it's not what he's said about our mother.

It's only . . . did you mention the summer house in Glencoe to him?"

"The summer house in Glencoe?" He glanced down at the note again, relinquishing Lydia's hand. He felt a prickling sensation along the back of his neck. "Never. It's nigh on two decades since we owned the house there. I thought you must have said something to him about it."

"I never mentioned it," she said.

"Perhaps the de Younges brought it up. They were friends with our parents."

"Perhaps," she said, "but if so, why would Jasper be under the mistaken belief that you still owned the property?"

The words on the paper had gone sharper, the black ink crisper, the small splotch near the bottom of the paper resolving into tight focus beneath his gaze. "Davis," he said. "You told me that Davis wrote to you about Glencoe."

"Yes." Her voice was very even as she waited for him to come to the same conclusions she had already drawn.

"Could your brother have been the one who searched your room? Could he have read the letters from Davis?"

Her mouth was tight as she too considered the page, and her eyes were dark when she looked up at him. "I think it possible. But I wonder . . ." She moistened her lips. "Do you recall when Jasper told the story of the turnip paste in the shape of a cod?"

"Aye."

"Davis told me that story," she said. "The exact same way. The exact same words. And Davis wrote to me of the summer house in Glencoe. I begin to suspect . . . I begin to suspect that Jasper has been reading my correspondence all along."

His mind reeled at the thought.

She was right—of course she was right. Her careful, precise brain had picked up the clues that Davis and Jasper had left and made sense of the connections that Arthur had not even divined. But—

"Why would your brother do that?" he asked, searching her face. "How would he even have had access to your letters? Did you not say that you picked them up directly from the library?"

His mind spun out further questions that he did not give voice to. Had Jasper known of Davis's nefarious intentions? If so, why wouldn't he have warned Lydia?

How could Jasper have let it go this far? And why?

"I don't know," she said. Her small gloved hand came out, catching his fingers in a tight grip. Her gaze locked with his, and he could not have pulled himself away even if he'd wished it. "I want to go after him. I want to travel to London and see if he's gone home as he said he would. And I want to ask him what the devil is going on."

Every part of him instantly, instinctively rebelled against the idea. He understood why she would want it—she must have a thousand more questions for her brother than he did. But he did not want to let her go—did not want to be parted from her. Not now. Not yet.

She seemed to misunderstand the reason for his hesitation. "I know it may seem like an interruption in our search for Davis. But think—if Jasper has been following my correspondence with Davis, he must have a reason for doing so. He may know more than we do. He may speed us along in our search for Davis and the rifle scope."

He had to clear his throat before he spoke, like a fool. "You mean . . . for me to go with you? To London?"

She blinked a few times. He could see the shadows cast by her rosy lashes on her cheeks. "Of course. That is, if you want to."

"I do," he said. Relief made his head light, made him tighten his grip on her hand. She did not want to part. There was still time. "I'll pack. We'll leave this afternoon. Together."

• • •

It did not take long to discharge themselves from Kilbride House, though their departure so immediately after Mr. Joseph Eagermont sent Lady de Younge into a state of fluttering dismay.

"Fortunately she still has the Valiquettes and Thibodeaux to occupy her," Arthur murmured to Lydia as Lady de Younge pressed a hamper of food into her arms.

"Fortunate indeed." Lydia's voice was a wry whisper, her gaze focused on the pinched face of Madame de Valiquette, whose dismal farewell had been quite French and portentous.

By the late morning, they were resettled into the creaking Strathrannoch coach, with Huw once again at the reins. Arthur hoped the carriage stood a better chance of surviving the trip to London than his arse, which absorbed every jostle and bump through the ancient flattened cushions.

He'd spent probably far too long on a letter to Bertie—the man knew perfectly well how to keep Strathrannoch Castle and its environs running in Arthur's absence. But the trip to London and back would be at least three weeks, if not longer. Arthur had never left Strathrannoch for so long—had never, in fact, left Scotland. So he wrote pages of idiotic anxious notes, as though Strathrannoch were his own newborn babe, and vowed to write again when they reached Edinburgh in case the first note did not arrive.

In the carriage, Lydia busied herself with papers: Davis's correspondence, the sheets they had taken from his room in Haddon Grange, and a compendium of notes she had recorded over the last week at Kilbride House. Her face was pink and her eyes were bright, and if Georgiana hadn't been in the coach with them, Arthur would've gotten on his knees before her to beg for her hand.

Well. He certainly would have gotten on his knees before her. He had a number of full-color engraved illustrations in his mind for what might happen after that.

But Georgiana *was* in the coach, which required some discretion. She spent the morning scowling so furiously that Lydia eventually looked up from her notes and blinked at her friend. "What on earth is the matter?"

"Nothing at all," Georgiana said.

"Is it—"

"I am worried about Bacon!" she burst out, all in a rush. "We have never been parted this long before!" And then she glowered at them so fiercely that neither Arthur nor Lydia dared to respond for some minutes.

He'd intended to steal a moment with Lydia alone at their first night's stoppage. He'd thought to pull her aside before she went into the bedchamber with Georgiana, perhaps, or maybe find a quiet corner of the inn. Only the bloody inn was packed to the rafters—why in *hell* was it so busy in late October? The dining room was so noisy that he had to shout to be heard, and the proprietress had only a single room available for sleeping.

He could not think of anything less romantic than a tiny, ale-scented chamber into which he, Lydia, Georgiana, and Huw all piled together in a tessellation of cots and bedrolls.

He didn't need starlight and orange blossoms, for Christ's

sake. He just needed not to have to bellow at the top of his lungs for her to hear his declaration.

But it was not to be.

He would propose to her on the morrow, he resolved to himself, and ignored the somersault in his belly at the thought. He turned on his side, nudged Huw's heel slightly farther from his nose, and tried quite fruitlessly to go to sleep.

• • •

It seemed to Lydia, as they stopped to dine in Edinburgh the next afternoon, that Arthur had been behaving rather oddly ever since—

Well. Ever since he'd torn open her night rail and brought her to sexual climax against a wall.

Which in itself could perhaps be termed "behaving oddly."

But she had *asked* him to do that—perhaps not the night rail shredding, but she certainly wasn't complaining—and he'd told her he did not regret it. And yet he appeared uneasy, a trifle distracted. Every time she looked up to meet his gaze in the coach, he was already looking at her and scowling quite ferociously. Part of her—the part that was always primed to see disaster around every corner—wondered if he was displeased with her. But he did not leave her side, not in the public rooms they dined in or the inn's bedchamber. Even today, in the coach, he had seated himself snugly on the bench beside her, his long muscled thigh pressed to her own.

At one point he grabbed her hand and then dropped it again as though it were hot to the touch.

During breakfast, he'd knelt beside her and then popped up so swiftly she'd inquired if he'd misplaced something.

He did not seem to have misplaced anything, except perhaps

the power of speech. He'd glowered silently at her and their companions and the bannocks and honey on the table.

Once they'd arrived in Edinburgh, though, he seemed to have quite lost his head. She was no more than three bites into the apple she'd acquired from a street vendor when he'd grabbed her elbow and dragged her down a narrow alley.

She, to her credit, dropped neither the apple nor her reticule, though she did stumble a bit on the small heel of her striped half boots.

Arthur's hand—large and solid—held her elbow steadily. He didn't let her fall.

"Is everything quite all right?" She peered up at him—his whiskers had begun to emerge once more, and his shirt, as usual, was open at the collar. He looked slightly overset and rather edible, in point of fact. Something about the open vee at his neck, the notch at his collarbone, called out to be explored. By her mouth.

"Lydia," he said, which was not precisely an answer. He nudged her a little deeper into the alley, which opened on the other side to a smaller, busier street of shops and stalls and marketgoers.

"Yes?"

He dropped her elbow. He ran his hands through his hair—he had a hole at the seam of his sleeve beneath his arm—and then picked up her hand, apple and all. "Lydia," he said again, and then hesitated.

"Yes," she said encouragingly. "That's correct."

He blew out an exasperated breath, and as he did, her attention snagged on something in the street at the other end of the alley. She narrowed her eyes, uncertain. Something—something in the bustling road beyond them struck her as out of place.

"I know these last weeks have been unsettling," he began.

She came up on her tiptoes, just a bit, peering over his shoulder into the crowd. "Unsettling," she agreed. "Indeed."

There was a couple in the middle of the street. Something about them had caught her eye, she was certain of it, only she could not say precisely why.

Arthur still held her hand, the apple cupped absurdly between their palms. "I know—that is to say, I believe—I *hope*, rather, that you are open to matrimony. To—to an earldom. To an *earl*, I mean."

She heard his words but did not register them, her gaze fixed on the couple in the street, haggling with a fellow leading a horse and cart.

The man was balding under his beaver hat. The woman was short, buxom, dressed in navy with gold embroidery.

Navy and gold. The livery of Kilbride House.

Her hand fell away from Arthur's. The apple hit the cobblestones with a wet thunk, and she gasped at the sound and shrank farther back into the shadows.

Arthur closed the distance between them in an instant. "What's wrong?"

"The Thibodeaux," she said. "They're in the street just before us. And Arthur"—she hesitated, but she knew, she *knew* she was not wrong in this—"they are the ones who ransacked my room. Claudine was the scullery maid we saw at my door, dressed just as she is now. I recognize her."

His body had insinuated itself between hers and the busy street, his solid form a wall of protection, his gaze following hers to the man in the hat, the woman in navy and gold.

It *was* the Thibodeaux. She could see that quite clearly now, and by the grim acknowledgment on Arthur's face, she knew he recognized them as well.

"They are the ones working with Davis," he said. "Not the de Younges. Not the Valiquettes."

"Yes," she said. "And we cannot let them get away. Not until we know what they are doing here in Edinburgh."

Chapter 18

G—if you should arrive in London before we do, please assure
my brothers I'm perfectly safe! Lie, if necessary.

—from Lydia to Georgiana, scrawled
upon the back of a bill of sale and thrust
into the hands of a porter

They crept out of the alley once the Thibodeaux finished their
haggling and began to move down the shop-lined street.

Lydia gritted her teeth. They were too recognizable, both of
them—she with her hair and Arthur with his height and looks and
general irresistibility. But they had to follow the Thibodeaux—had
to, if possible, get close enough to discern what they were about.

It could not be a coincidence that the Thibodeaux had searched
her room and now seemed to have followed them south. Perhaps
they knew where Davis was and meant to reunite with him.

Perhaps—for some reason—they were after Arthur. She had
to figure out why—had to get close enough to overhear their
words or ascertain their lodgings.

But if Didier or Claudine turned around and saw Lydia and

Arthur behind them, the game would, decidedly, be up. There would be no chance for the clandestine gathering of information if the Thibodeaux spotted them.

Arthur seemed to be thinking along the same lines. "I've a little gunpowder in my pocket," he murmured, his mouth close to her ear. "Perhaps I can distract them with a wee explosion and then we can creep nearer—"

An *explosion*? Surely there must be some less incendiary approach. Something covert, something they would not detect. She could—

A millinery just ahead provided a blaze of inspiration.

"This way," she hissed, and pulled Arthur bodily into the shop.

"What do you mean for us to do—"

She pushed him into the window display—dozens of silk roses and artificial fruits and tiny figural birds—and then down to his knees. He was staring at her in frank astonishment, and she caught his chin in her hand and turned it toward the aged rippled glass. "Don't look at me," she whispered. "Watch them. Stay out of sight."

And then she dashed farther into the shop to face the astonished proprietor.

Her usual anxiety at the notion of speaking to strangers rose up, as it always did, but the sheer urgency of the situation seemed to enable her to produce audible words.

"I beg your pardon," she said. Her voice had come out bizarrely sanguine, as though she shoved large earls beneath window displays on a regular basis. Her blood was pounding in her ears. "Don't mind us. The earl needs—a hat. We are"—she caught up her reticule and yanked at the strings, fishing out a ludicrous amount of coin—"in mourning."

She shoved the coins into the proprietor's hands. It was enough to buy a dozen hats, at least based on her knowledge of Bond Street. She presumed Scottish headgear operated on roughly the same sales-to-cost ratio.

The milliner blinked down at the coins. He had a jolly round face and a superlative conical Paris beau hat upon his head, and he must have been familiar with the bizarre whims of the aristocracy, because he nodded and gestured to the shop at large. "Indeed, my lady. Take your pick."

She gave him a grateful smile as she snatched up a black silk mourning bonnet. She thrust it onto her head, tucked the veil around her face, and made her way back to Arthur, vision only slightly obscured.

"Can you still see them?" she murmured.

"Aye," he said. He flicked a startled gaze in her direction before returning to the street. "But hurry, Lydia."

In answer, she snatched a straw hat from its place beneath the window, where it seemed to have been relegated as out of season. She ground it along the floor and then mashed it with her palm for good measure. The milliner behind her made an outraged sound, but she ignored him and shoved the hat down over Arthur's brow.

It wasn't enough. She turned frantically back to the window display and yanked at the wool draping. Roses flew everywhere in a shower of autumn-colored petals. A pear made of—she did not know what, something surprisingly springy—bounced off her boot. She pulled the draping free and wrapped it around Arthur's neck like an overlong scarf.

He looked . . . original, at best. But his face was almost completely obscured by hat and scarf.

The milliner made another, louder sound.

"I do beg your pardon," she squeaked. "Mourning! Quite

upsetting!" And then she grabbed Arthur by the arm and drew him out the open door.

"I'm a widow," she hissed when they regained the street. "You're my footman. Slump down a bit and walk two paces behind me, and—yes, that's it."

It was remarkable, how ruffled he managed to look with only his eyes and brows visible. He ducked his chin, pulled the hat further down, and—

Well, it wasn't perfect, and she'd obviously gone mad in the head, because her woolen pelisse was hunter green, not black, as anyone with eyes could see. But she thought their identities would be disguised, so long as the Thibodeaux did not look at them too closely.

Arthur's murmured words were quick. "They've turned just ahead. Two more streets and then to your left. Go as fast as you can without drawing attention."

She picked up her pace and then suddenly he was behind her, his hand on her shoulder.

"Wait," he said. "Your hair."

She felt his hand brush the back of her neck and, despite herself, she shivered. He nudged a loose lock up under the netting, then tucked the veil more securely about her shoulders.

And then they were off again, chasing the Thibodeaux. She walked quickly round the corner he had indicated and spotted the couple up ahead. Two more turns and then Didier and Claudine slowed, heading for a public house.

"The stables." Arthur's voice was low behind her, and she nodded and made for the whitewashed mews behind the inn. Arthur kept close behind, and they slipped inside without catching the attention of any roving groom or stable hand.

Once inside the stables, Arthur pushed open the door to an

empty stall and urged her into it, bringing his body to shelter hers in the shadows. She could smell the tang of horses and the sweet undercurrent of hay.

He lifted her veil, baring her face, and tucked the thin fabric past the brim of her bonnet. "Good Christ," he whispered, "I'm not sure whether that was cunning or mad."

She gave a strangled laugh, exhilaration like tiny bubbles bursting in her blood. "It worked," she managed, not entirely certain whether she was assuring him or herself.

It had worked. She had not fallen apart in a moment of crisis.

"Aye." His hand, which had come to rest on her shoulder, was a warm solid weight she could feel through her pelisse. "Aye, it worked. You're clever as the devil, Lydia Hope-Wallace, and twice as brave."

Brave. She had never considered herself so. But she could feel the earnest gravity of his gaze, the powerful pull of his perception of her.

Perhaps she had been brave. Perhaps she could believe it.

"We should search the carriages out back while they're inside the public room," he said.

She forced her brain to return to the situation at hand. "Yes," she breathed. "Of course. If they left Kilbride House after we did, they can't have been here long. Their luggage might still be in one of the hired hacks. Some letters, perhaps, or some other clue."

"Aye—or one of the drivers may know where they're headed next."

"Do it," she said. "I'm going to go find someone to carry a message back to Huw and Georgiana."

His eyes looked darker in the shadows, the green a forest, the blue a deep still pond. "A message?"

"Yes." She licked her lips and looked up at him. "To tell them to go on to London and speak to Jasper whilst you and I follow the Thibodeaux."

His grip on her shoulder tightened. His face had gone taut as well, his expression pained. "If we're right—if they're the ones who searched your room and are connected to Davis—then it's not safe for you to be here." He hesitated, his gaze flickering to the window that revealed the line of coaches for hire behind the mews. "I should not do this. I should take you back to Huw."

Some part of her felt cool relief at his words.

She could go back with Georgiana, back where it was safe. A small craven corner of her heart wanted desperately to retreat. Not because she was afraid—well, not *only* that—but because she did not know if she could manage whatever adventure was to come as they tracked the Thibodeaux.

Even to find a messenger and explain what she wanted seemed a near-insurmountable obstacle. She did not know precisely where she had left Georgiana, nor was she certain she could explain the turnings they'd taken to a stranger.

But—

Clever, she thought. *And brave.*

"This is important," she said. "We can do this together. I know we can."

His hand slipped into her hair. "You drive me out of my head," he rasped.

He leaned down and kissed her then, swift and hard and unexpected. A heartbeat later he pulled away, then nudged her in the direction of the inn's main building. "Send them a message and then make your way back here as quick as you can. I'll look about while you're gone and see what I can find."

She started to go, then dashed back into the stall. She wrapped her fingers in his shirt and pulled him down for another kiss. His mouth softened against hers. His lips parted as they fitted against her own, and his arms came around her—at once safe and stirring.

"I'll be as swift as I can manage," she murmured.

"I'll be here. I'm not going anywhere."

She relinquished his shirt, kept to the shadows, and hastened back out to the courtyard. It was easy to find a porter, idling beside the inn's front door, to carry a message to Georgiana. It was far harder to make him understand what she wanted, between her trembling voice and the anxious fog that seemed to suffuse her thoughts now that she was not in the middle of a crisis.

But through sheer force of will, she managed it. She scrawled a message upon a discarded bill of sale and pressed it into the porter's palm along with a handful of coins. And then he was off, his hat tipped toward her as he went.

She took a shaking breath, and then a second, and then a third. And then—oh Lord, she was drunk on her own successes, perhaps—instead of returning to the mews, she slipped the veil back over her face and crept toward the front door of the inn.

There was a public dining room. If the Thibodeaux were inside, perhaps she could seat herself close enough to listen in on their conversation. She patted at the back of her head, trying to make sure that her hair was fully obscured. With her hair covered and the veil in place, she did not think they would know her.

But inside the dining room, she did not see them. A sylphlike barmaid with hair even redder than Lydia's own sidled over to offer a table, but Lydia shook her head.

"I'm looking for my companions." Oh hell. She'd attempted a mumbling Scottish accent to try to disguise her voice in case the Thibodeaux were somewhere within earshot, but she'd quite missed the mark. She sounded Russian.

"A man and woman." Hang it, that wasn't any better. Now she sounded Welsh, perhaps by way of Newcastle. "They just came inside. She was wearing a dark blue frock with gold piping."

"Aye, I know the ones you mean," the barmaid said. "They went out the back a few minutes ago. Took their pasties for the road."

For the road.

The blood in Lydia's veins went to ice.

Arthur. The coaches.

She threw herself back out the way she'd come, heedless of her flapping veil and the bemused glances of the public room's patrons. She raced around the building and—barely sensible of what she was doing—ducked through the stable door and pressed herself to the wall.

Through the open shutters of the stable's window, she could see the line of hacks for hire. She flung back her veil for a clearer view.

At the end of the line stood Didier Thibodeaux, arguing in thickly accented English with the final vehicle's driver. Claudine had already mounted and sat on the high perch, her ankles crossed beneath her skirts and a paper-wrapped pasty in her hand.

At the coach's window, plain as day to Lydia's vantage, the leather curtain inside dropped suddenly, a quick unfurling that shielded the interior from view.

Lydia's heart clenched in terror. Someone was inside the coach. Someone who did not want to be seen.

Didier appeared to win his argument with the driver. He swung himself up onto the bench, and the driver stepped reluctantly away, shaking his head and muttering something Lydia could not hear.

The coach rocked into motion. As she watched, the door

cracked open, and a hand emerged, loosing something pale that fluttered to the ground.

The hand was Arthur's. She knew it even as he drew quickly back into the coach—she recognized the strong fingers, the freckled burns, the muscular turn of his forearm.

Had he intended this? Surely not—he had no way of knowing the Thibodeaux would take that particular coach at that particular moment. He must have been searching the vehicles' interiors, looking for the Thibodeaux's belongings, and been forced to hide himself when they arrived.

She stood frozen with fear and indecision as the coach rolled away. As she watched, she saw the pale shape that Arthur had dropped, which resolved into something that made sense to her eyes as the rear wheels of the carriage passed beyond it.

It was the straw hat from the milliner's. Half of his disguise. She supposed he'd meant it as a message to her: so she would know what had happened, grasp why he was not there when she returned.

He would want her to go back to Georgiana and Huw, she knew. To scurry off to safety like a mouse to a bolt-hole. But as she stared at the battered hat, some kind of insane courage rocked her. Set her back on her heels.

Arthur was in danger, and it did not matter if she was afraid.

To hell with mice and bolt-holes. She would not do it.

She ran back out to the courtyard. There was a reddish roan mare saddled and bridled near a mounting block, a man holding the reins while the horse placidly lipped at a bit of hay fallen between the cobblestones.

She plucked up her skirts, launched herself at the mounting block, and took the reins out of the man's flabbergasted grip.

"Och, what the devil—" he began, but she yanked open her reticule to forestall him.

"How much for the mare?" she said breathlessly. "Forty pounds?"

His mouth gaped open. He had enormous black eyebrows, between which a prominent nose declared itself.

"Fifty?" She shoved one foot into the near stirrup and flung herself into the saddle. Her reticule tilted perilously, and she spared a moment to wonder if a waterfall of fresh-minted sovereigns would make her appeal more persuasive or less. "I'm in a great tearing hurry and would rather not haggle."

His mouth snapped closed. His eyes fixed on the reticule. "Two hundred quid."

Oh for heaven's sake. It was an outrageous sum for the stocky mare. She ought not have said that bit about haggling.

"A hundred sovereigns," she said. "That's the whole purse." Slightly lighter, after the visit to the milliner, but close enough. She held the reticule out to the black-browed man, letting it dangle temptingly from her fingers.

He reached out his hand and took the purse. He nodded.

Relief made her limbs light, her fingers almost numb where they gripped the reins. She squeezed her knees into the horse's flanks, ducked her head, and urged the mare, as fast as she dared, down the street and after the Thibodeaux's coach.

Chapter 19

*. . . You cannot conceive with what joy I embraced the hopes
thus given me of seeing the delight of my heart again.*

—from FANNY HILL

Her rescue, as it turned out, did not take long.

There was no little congestion of vehicles on the Great North
Road, particularly here in the immediate environs of the Scottish
capital. The Thibodeaux could not travel too quickly, and Lydia
managed to stay far enough back that they did not mark her.

She was certainly remarked by everyone else who passed her,
a woman riding astride a red horse with a black silk bonnet upon
her head and a mourning veil trailing behind her like a very long
and diaphanous flag.

She was perhaps twenty yards behind the Thibodeaux, the
sun just beginning to tip toward the tree line, when she noticed
the first splinters of wood in the middle of the road.

The first few pieces were small, perhaps the size of her longest
finger. They were dark with age, almost black, their color the only

thing that distinguished them from the general brush and debris that found its way onto any well-traveled highway.

The next few pieces were larger. As she rode on, settling her mare in the lee of a mail coach, she noticed them every few feet: fragments of wood, like broken-off bits of planking, jet-black and roughly the size of her fist. Some were still and others were rolling, bouncing slightly in the wheel-worn channels of the road.

A sudden presentiment came to her mind. She brought the roan around the side of the mail coach, tugged her veil down over her face, and watched the Thibodeaux's carriage.

Within moments, another chunk of wood appeared between the rear wheels, tumbling and spinning along the road before coming to a rest just before her mare's hooves trampled it. A second emerged beneath the carriage as she watched, as if the vehicle had begun disgorging splintered wood fragments from its belly.

Which of course it had. Somehow, from inside the carriage, Arthur was slowly dismantling the vehicle's wooden floor.

She was torn between sheer delight at his cleverness and instantaneous terror.

What the devil did he mean to do when he created a big enough hole? Leap through? If the fall from the moving vehicle did not injure him, there were the two rear wheels to contend with—not to mention what would happen if the Thibodeaux happened to look behind them and observe a large and recognizable man rolling out from beneath their coach.

Perhaps he would wait until they stopped to rest or change out their horses. But no, that avenue was equally unsupportable. They might miss a bearded giant escaping from the coach while they drove, their eyes fixed on the road ahead, but they certainly would not overlook his emergence while they were stopped at a coaching inn.

Oh God. Oh hell. He would have to jump free while the carriage was moving. Surely he had come to the same conclusion she had. If only he could give her some sort of sign, so she might know when he meant to make his move—but he wouldn't, of course, because he had no bloody idea she was following him.

She muttered a prayer under her breath and kept as close to the Thibodeaux's coach as she dared.

She'd stopped seeing wood bits littering the road for at least a quarter of an hour when they came to a narrow stone bridge. All the vehicles on the road slowed, arranging themselves into a decorous queue. Lydia fitted herself in nervously behind the mail coach, her eyes darting from her roan to the Thibodeaux's conveyance.

And then she saw Arthur's legs emerge, a slow controlled descent, from the bottom of the carriage.

Oh bollocks, he'd chosen *now* to free himself, when the road was crowded with passersby? What was he thinking?

And then she knew, a brilliant electric revelation. She urged the mare out of the line, driving her toward the bank of the small swift river, where—yes—hell—

As she watched, Arthur lowered himself the rest of the way out of the carriage, landed on the stones beneath, and then rolled in one smooth motion off the side of the bridge and into the water.

She swore aloud and leaned over her horse's withers. They stopped hard at the bank, the roan pawing at the fronds. Arthur rose, sputtering, from the water and met her gaze.

Or—no. She was still veiled. He could not see her. She shoved the fabric to the side to behold his stupefied face more clearly. "Hurry," she hissed. "Get out of there and climb on."

"Lydia? How in *hell*—" But he was already obeying her instructions, water cascading from his body as he crushed several Scottish water plants beneath his boots. She loosed her foot from the stirrup just in time for him to replace it with his own and then swing up onto the horse's back behind her.

The mare had been worth the hundred sovereigns. She stood sturdily beneath the addition of Arthur's weight and the sudden slosh of frigid water down her speckled red flanks. Arthur's arms came around Lydia's body and he turned the horse quickly, carrying them both into the thicket of trees that lined the roadway.

"We have to get out of sight," he murmured. "As deep into the woods as we can go."

She nodded, and he transferred the reins to one hand, using the other to pull her against him.

"God," he murmured into her hair. "Oh Christ, it's good to see you." His voice had gone rough. His hand on the reins was trembling slightly, the physical manifestation of his relief.

He brought them deep into the shadows of the heavy-limbed oaks, where the late-afternoon sunlight made dappled patterns on the leaf-littered ground. When he finally halted and dismounted, she half fell into his arms, and he pulled her up against his dripping form. His arms were hard as iron bars, his chest a firm solid wall, and she let herself melt against him, let him take her weight. All the fear that had swamped her since the moment she had seen his hand emerge from the coach seemed to leak away as he held her, as her body pressed against his.

He was safe. They were both safe and together.

In one quick decisive movement, he yanked off her bonnet and kissed the top of her head. "God," he muttered. "God, I've been out of my head with worry. Oh *fuck*—" He stiffened and then pushed her back away from him, a trifle wild-eyed. "Your clothes. I'm soaking you with my wet things."

"It's all right. Everything I have on is wool. I'm perfectly dry. You, on the other hand—" She paused, noticing the raw scrape across the knuckles of his left hand. "Oh, Arthur! Is this from the floor of the coach?" She caught his hand between her palms and brought it up to her face. Her lips found the tips of his chilled fingers, and then she pressed them to her cheek, trying to warm him.

"Nay," he murmured. His fingers cupped her face. "Merely scraped myself with the striker from my tinderbox. I used it as a lever for the floorboards. Thought my gunpowder would be too noisy a way out of there."

"Oh for heaven's sake." She pulled his fingers gently away from her cheek to examine his knuckles once more, but he closed his hand over hers.

"I don't feel it, love."

"Of course you don't. You're frozen half to death."

"'Tis not so bad as all that." He looked down at his sodden garments. "Though I would not wish to ride together until I dry myself, I suppose."

His lips were pale. His hand covering hers was terribly cold.

She felt a hot rush of emotion, a tide of resolve and fierce tenderness. She had come to rescue him, had she not? He still needed her.

"Take off your wet clothes," she ordered.

He made a sound of protest, but she was already shoving at his jacket, urging him out of his shirt. When he was half-unclothed, she untied her own pelisse and curled herself around his chest, trying to share the warmth of her body with him. Her breasts crushed against him, and he took a slow, shuddering breath. His bare arms came around her, pulling her even closer, even tighter.

"For Christ's sake," he muttered. His fingers stroked her hair, the back of her head. Trailed down the nape of her neck and then wrapped around her waist. "Daft woman. Don't ever do that again."

She relished the ferocity of his embrace, curling herself tighter around him. She tried to make her voice light, but emotion—relief and pleasure and fast-fading terror—clogged her throat. "Do what, precisely? Watch as you are accidentally abducted?"

"Go away from me."

She swallowed against the ache in her throat.

She did not want to go. The truth of the thought struck her full force. She did not ever wish to be parted from him.

She wanted—God, what didn't she want? Her body bloomed under his in helpless yearning; his familiar scent filled her nose. She breathed him in and felt need spin up inside her, desire a spool wound tight and then tighter.

She tilted her head up to him. He moved at the same time, quick and almost desperate. His mouth found hers. One of his hands caught at her hair, tipping her head back. He made a low, harsh groan—an uncontrolled sound, the sound of something tearing free in his chest. Her lips parted, and he took the lower one between his teeth and sucked.

She gave as good as she got. She wrapped her hand around the nape of his neck, pressed up into him, and kissed him back, hard and rough and frantic.

"Please," she gasped when he started to draw away. "Arthur. Don't stop."

·   ·   ·

His mind had not been working properly since he'd lost sight of her that afternoon. Even when the Thibodeaux had come—when he'd been forced to hide in the coach—his only thoughts had been for her.

What would she imagine when she came back and found him gone? Was she safe, wandering the Old Town alone? His fevered brain had thrown up visions of cutpurses, her heavy reticule a glittering draw. With every splinter carefully prised from the floorboards by his steel striker, he'd thought himself one excruciating step closer to getting back to her.

But now she was here—*she* had come for *him*, a notion that caused his mind to reel—and still his faculties had not come back into order. He couldn't think—he could only see and hear and feel her.

Her sunset hair, her quick hot mouth—Jesus, the sweet little whimper at the back of her throat. She had wrapped herself around him, containing him with her body, her busy hands, the murmur of his name.

"Lydia," he gritted out. Her touch was light and devastating, her fingers skimming across his bared torso. With her jacket undone, he could see the frantic rise and fall of her breath, her breasts pressing against the neckline of her bodice. He cursed and lowered his mouth to her shoulder, his hands sliding down from her hair to grasp her waist.

She came up on her toes and her body dragged against his aching cock—a pleasure so charged he almost could not bear it. He pressed kisses along her collarbone, his mouth inches from her breasts. His hands slipped higher, his thumbs tracing the delicate unyielding bones of her ribs through her damp woolen dress.

He wanted her naked. He wanted to see every inch of her—to know her safe and well and his. God, how he wanted her to be his.

He did not know at what point his fear had transmuted into arousal. It was no rational thing, this wanting. He felt a terrible urgent need to care for her—to see to it that she was dry and warm, that no part of her was hurting. He wanted to touch her more gently than his large and clumsy hands were capable of.

And at the same time, he wanted to be inside her. He wanted

her writhing beneath him, sweat in her hair and a cry on her lips. He wanted—

Christ. He wanted to fuck her hard. Madly. Like an animal, mindless with desire and the feel of her.

He pulled back from her, staggered by the force of his desire. "Tell me to stop," he rasped.

"Never." Her voice shook with need, with all the courage and stubbornness inside her small form.

And, God help him, he listened. He cupped one breast, stroking his thumb across the stiffened peak. She whimpered—almost a whine—a sound that went straight to his bollocks.

He dragged his teeth along her skin and yanked her bodice down, baring her glorious breasts. "You've no idea the things I want to do to you."

"Do them," she gasped. "All of them. Don't stop."

Fuck, he thought, *oh fuck*, because her nipple was in his mouth and she was making those sounds again, eager and frantic as he flicked the taut nub with his tongue and then sucked.

Her nails bit into the skin of his back, and he heard himself make a desperate noise. His hips thrust forward without his conscious command, pressing his cock against her. His head spun at the sensation—at the heaven of that soft flesh. The word *generous* had been made for her body: the way it gave beneath him, the way it poured out pleasure for the both of them.

She was twisting, almost writhing, her face and chest flushed. Her pupils were large and dark, and the tips of her breasts were wet from where his mouth had been. The sight of her nipples, glistening in the dappled light, was the most dizzyingly erotic thing he'd ever seen.

Her fingers, he realized, were striving at his falls, where the damp cold fabric clung to his burning skin. She was not delicate—

she was almost frantic. His cock came free of his trousers, and her fingers—her—

Oh Christ. He closed his fingers over hers, unintentionally clamping her palm against his erection. Fireworks went off inside his brain, but he could not let her get her fingers around him, he *could not*—if she did, he would be inside her in half a minute, and he knew he could do no such thing.

So he dragged her hand away and bore them both down to the earth.

He took her weight onto him—the ground was cool and pebbled, and he did not spare one single second for regret as he rolled her over, pinning her beneath him. Her breasts shook as he did, and the sight was a lightning strike, sending demand arcing through him like a current.

He drew up one of her knees and wrapped her fingers around it, holding her skirts up and baring the auburn curls that shielded her sex. He moved deliberately between her thighs.

She made a tiny, plaintive whimper, her hips arching up into nothing, and then his mouth was there, licking up into her, his hands clamped on her thighs and spreading her wide. She was wet—Jesus God, she was so hot and wet. He could taste her arousal, feel it where his thumbs stroked the insides of her thighs, and everything shimmered out of existence except the feel of her body and the raw and begging sounds she made as he licked and sucked.

He circled her entrance with his thumb, then eased his first two fingers inside of her. Christ—the tight clench of her body, the squeeze of her channel around his fingers—his head spun. His cock throbbed, a desperate rush of blood he could feel in his belly, in the soles of his feet. He worked her clitoris with his tongue and felt her thighs tremble, her body close to release.

He wanted it. He wanted her to come on his fingers and on his mouth and on his prick. God, he wanted that last so badly he felt almost dazed.

But he wanted *her* more. He wanted her to be his—not just her body, but every part of her—her mind, her heart. He wanted to make her shatter around him not once but every day, a thousand thousand times, wanted to hear her voice go to pieces on his name for the rest of his natural life.

He would wait for her, for that. He had to.

He brought his free hand to her nipple, a slick caress, and that was enough. She gasped as she came, her body clenching around his fingers, an endless heady pleasure.

When her shudders stopped, she caught his arm and pulled him up her body, her legs locking around his waist. His cock slid against her slick folds—a sensation so intense, so intoxicating that he lost his breath. His vision went gray, then white, and something clicked in his brain like a latch sliding shut.

His. She was his. He would not go wrong in this.

He drew back, coming onto his knees and lifting her with him. He brought her hand to his length, a frantic gasp of *will you* and *please*, and then her fingers were around him, sliding against his erection. He groaned in helpless pleasure and thrust into the circle of her fingers, every part of his body taut and delirious with need.

Her face was flushed. Her lips were parted. Her hand was on him and her bodice was down, and his climax came upon him in a mad rush, his seed spilling on her bared breasts in time to the frantic beat of his heart.

As soon as he could manage it, he gathered her up into his arms. Her head fit neatly under his chin, their bodies interlocking as though they had been made for this moment, for this singular place and time. He stroked the nape of her neck, savoring the fine softness of her skin.

When he could speak again, the words on his lips were not a question, but a demand that was half a vow. "Promise me you will not go away from me again," he murmured. "Say the words."

She promised.

Some tightness in his chest eased.

He needed to get to his feet, to clean her skin with his discarded shirt. He needed to recapture the roan and find an inn and then figure out some way to get to London with her.

But he held on to her for a long time, lingering there, watching the patterns the shadows made on her hair. He marked the rise and fall of her chest with each breath, a slow and steadfast rhythm that matched his own.

Chapter 20

*This is what I ought to have said: You stagger me. Your wit,
your courage, your wide and tender heart.*

—*from the papers of Arthur Baird, rejected draft*

Naturally, things seemed worse in the morning.

After Arthur and Lydia had haphazardly restored themselves
in the woods the previous evening, they'd made their way to a
coaching inn—which, she'd informed him, she'd seen from the
road whilst chasing the Thibodeaux.

He'd clutched her to him reflexively at her words. The fear
of the day still clung to his bones, imprinted somewhere along
his spine. When they'd arrived at the inn, he'd requested a single
bedroom, a hot bath, and supper on a tray before recalling that
he'd left his meager funds in the trunk that had remained with
Huw and Georgiana.

Lydia's grin had been some recompense for the mortified heat
in his face. "I have some coins sewn into my hem," she'd confided,
"but we may have to sell the mare to afford the rest of the journey
to London."

God, he was mad for her, for her clever, practical brain and that impossible bravery. He'd kissed her, helpless to stop himself, right there on the stairs.

Over dinner, he'd told her what he'd been able to make out of the Thibodeaux's conversation—fragments only, as they'd spoken in French and he'd been on the other side of a carriage wall. "They spoke of Davis, to be sure. They mentioned London, and a duke, and a spy. And four or five times I made out the name Joseph Eagermont."

She'd paused and sat back in her scarlet brocade chair, her wineglass arrested halfway to her mouth. "Jasper?"

"Aye," he'd said. "I think we must find him now more than ever. And Lydia . . ." He'd hesitated, torn briefly between his need to protect her and his desire to tell her the truth. But she was strong, this woman—strong enough to hear it all. He'd swallowed hard and gone on. "They had weapons, several pistols on them. And they spoke of us. Of you and me, Lord and Lady Strathrannoch. I cannot help but fear that they've discovered our connections to Davis and Jasper both."

He was afraid—Christ, he was so afraid that he'd put her in danger.

She'd set the wine down untasted, her busy fingers sliding along the rim. "I wish we knew what they were after. We must find Jasper. And I begin to wonder . . ." She'd trailed off, her index finger tapping out a staccato rhythm on the glass.

"Yes?"

"I begin to wonder if there is not some connection to Belvoir's Library in all of this." She'd looked up at him then, chin set and midnight-blue eyes determined. "That is the only way I can conceive that Jasper might have known about my correspondence with Davis. And you said they mentioned a *spy*?"

"Aye." *Espion.* He knew the word—from *espionnage.*

The notion of espionage and the presence of the French couple in Edinburgh cast a troubling light over the situation. Could the Thibodeaux be French agents of some kind? And if so, what were they after?

If it had to do with Davis and the rifle scope, he did not think it could be good.

Lydia's expression had turned inward, a studied reverie that he knew well. She was thinking through the evidence, resolving the pattern in her mind.

"Belvoir's," she'd murmured. "And Jasper—and a spy." Her gaze, when she looked up, had been keen as a blade. "What better place for the Home Office to pass information than a library built upon the privacy of its members?"

"You think your brother works for the Home Office?"

"It's possible. I'd certainly like to go home and ask him about it."

He'd leaned forward and caught her fingers in his, then brought them to his lips. "Rest tonight. We'll go tomorrow on the mail coach."

From there the hot bath he'd ordered had come. The strings of her pelisse had dried into tight, tangled knots, and he'd worked them open for her. He'd slipped loose the buttons of her gown and taken down her stockings. He'd helped her wash her hair, and then—

Well. The floor had not stayed dry, nor had the scarlet brocade chair. He'd carried her to it, knelt between her heat-flushed thighs and watched her as he'd pleasured her. Her back had arched. Her feet had flexed and pointed, restless with demand, until he'd locked them around his neck. Her nails had pressed crescents into the upholstered arms of the chair, tiny imprints that had remained long after her deft fingers had brought him to culmination as well.

He loved that godforsaken chair. He wanted to take it home with him. He wanted to put it in a museum.

But now—in the morning—Lydia lay prone on the bed, her knees bent and her bare feet waving behind her, crossed at the ankles. She was propped up on her elbows, examining the hand-written bill that had come on the tea tray and counting the coins she'd removed from where they'd been sewn into her hem.

She wore only her chemise and stays. Her hem was unpicked and her dress was irremediably stained after their encounter in the forest from where he—from where he had—

Jesus. He had spilled himself on her breasts. He had *never*— had scarcely even *imagined*—

He was not sure what was more mortifying: the fact that he had done it in the first place, or the fact that right now, faced with the bounty of her half-bared bosom, he could not think about anything else.

Surely he could have planned this in some more strategic fashion. Did he really mean to declare himself to her—Lydia Hope-Wallace, the cleverest and most arousing woman in the world—less than twenty-four hours after he had despoiled her only frock?

What a way to convince her of his abiding respect and affection! *I worship the ground you walk upon, my darling, in case that was not apparent from the way I came on your tits. Would you like to be my wife?*

Good God.

From her place on the bed, she began to stack the coins. "These prices are absurd," she muttered. "They must have known you for a lord."

"Lydia," he managed. His voice was hoarse.

She peered up at him and grinned. "You shall have to be the

one to sell the horse. I fear I cannot manage haggling, even in extremity. It's most unfortunate. I quite liked that horse."

Her cheeks had gone pink. Her hair was in sweet flyaway tangles all around her face, and her smile curved right round his heart.

His stomach pitched. He had forgotten how to form words.

"Marry me," he choked out.

One gold sovereign rolled off the bed and landed on the floor. Her lips parted, and not a single sound emerged.

Oh Christ. Oh hell. "Marry me," he said again. "After London. After all of this is over. Come back to Strathrannoch with me."

"I beg your pardon?" she croaked.

He felt a desperate, rising panic at her apparent stupefaction. He had gone about this wrong, he knew he had. He ought to have found a more opportune moment, more persuasive words. He should have asked her over candlelight.

His hands seemed clumsy, his tongue thick. He felt—as ever—like the wrong Baird brother.

"You could still write your pamphlets," he got out, a haphazard stab at persuasion. "I would have my vote in the Lords. You could still do your political work. 'Twould be well—the two of us together."

But she did not seem to acknowledge his words. Her eyes were dark, dark blue, and when she spoke, her voice was shaking. "Is this—because of last night? Because we spent the night together? We did not do anything irrevocable, Arthur. You are not bound by guilt or honor to make such an offer. You are under no obligation."

"Bound by—" He could not bring her words into a sensible arrangement, could not imagine what she meant. Of everything in his heart as he looked down at her worried face, guilt was a pale whisper beside the chorus of admiration and yearning and—yes.

And love.

The deep bow of her lower lip trembled. He had touched her there, had put his mouth to that fragile curve. "I would not want a marriage that was not entered into freely," she murmured. "I should not want . . ."

Her voice trailed off, and he looked at her mouth, that sweet expressive arc, taut now with anxiety and hesitation. He had seen that look on her face before—had seen it over breakfast at Kilbride House and in drawing rooms when she was surrounded by strangers.

He knew she doubted herself. He could recall with painful clarity her words in the carriage. *I shall embarrass you—pretending to be your wife.*

Was it possible her hesitation was not about him, but about herself?

How could it be that she did not see herself the way that he saw her? The most desirable woman in the world—as glorious as a sunset—as brilliant—as impossible to look away from.

He took her hands and drew her up to sitting, then wrapped one arm about her waist. "You are not an obligation," he murmured. "I want you, Lydia Hope-Wallace. I want to bring you home with me. I want you to be my wife."

She searched his face. He lifted her hand and pressed a kiss to the inside of her wrist, felt his own pulse throb with hers.

The pattern of his heart was longing, was *please* and *mine.* "Marry me," he said again. "Say you will."

"Yes," she whispered. "Yes."

If there was uneasiness inside him at the soft rasp of her voice, at the trembling in her fingers, it was drowned out by the force of his relief. He bent his head and kissed her, and she kissed him back: in answer, in reciprocation, in promise.

She would be his, he thought as his arms came tighter around her body, as her cold fingers brushed the back of his neck. She *was* his. Nothing else mattered beyond that.

· · ·

By the time they arrived at her home in London, Lydia was fairly certain she had never been so bedraggled in her life, including when she'd nearly been run over by a herd of zebras. They'd slept on the mail coach in order to make their way to London faster, and they'd scarcely stopped to eat. She was in desperate need of a bath. She had not seen a mirror or the state of her own hair in nearly a week.

Arthur, for his part, only looked more handsome and appealing with his shirt open at the collar and his beard thick again with curls. Her body tipped toward his in sleep, and every time she jolted awake, it was with his arms around her and a distinct desire to put her mouth to his bare skin.

It was impossible on the mail coach—there were half a dozen other passengers and everyone was pressed nearly knee to knee. They'd had a few rushed private moments when the coach had stopped for food and drink, and every time she'd felt—

Wild and carnal desires. Irrational fears.

She wanted to peel his clothes off, the way she had in the forest. She wanted to slide her hands up his muscular chest and press every inch of her skin to his. She wanted to feel him over her again, his weight, his irresistible gravity.

She wanted to make things indelible between them. She did not want him to take it back.

Oh God, she was so tangled up inside she could not think clearly.

She'd been entirely caught off guard by his sudden proposal. She had scarcely dared hope that what had passed between them was something he might want to hold fast to. Her body's first reaction had been a familiar surge of anxiety—fear that his conscience had seized him, that his words were motivated by obligation, not by desire.

But he said it was not so. He had told her that he wanted her to be his wife, and she was trying to believe him.

She trusted him, knew him for a good and careful man. It was only her own lack of confidence, her tendency to fret and chafe, that had her in such a snarl. She did not doubt him. She would not let herself.

She forced her mind to the project of their return to London. She needed to send a note to Georgiana's house to ensure her friend had arrived safely; she suspected Georgiana was in a fever of worry over the precise mechanism by which Sir Francis Bacon would be returned to her from Scotland.

And she needed to go home. She wanted to find Jasper as quickly as she could. She would look for him first at the Hope-Wallace residence, and then—if he was not there—she intended to go to Selina at Belvoir's.

By the time they arrived at her own street, she'd almost managed to set aside her anxieties. Almost.

Just outside the residence, Arthur cleared his throat. His face had gone a delicate shade of pink. "Can I help you with your, ah—" He made an abortive gesture at her figure and then shoved his hand into his pocket.

Lydia glanced down. She'd bought a dress off one of the barmaids in the inn's public room, and though she'd tried to select a barmaid with a similar figure to her own, she'd not quite managed it. The frock dragged on the ground and did not in the slightest fashion contain her bosom.

Her hair hung in lank clumps over her shoulders. There was a smear of red currant jelly on her wrist. The handkerchief she'd tucked into her bodice in a vague attempt at decency had slid to the side, and if she took too deep a breath, she suspected her left breast might literally burst free.

Her mother would have an apoplexy.

"Ah," she said. "Hmm. Perhaps I can smuggle you into my bedchamber. I can, er, dress. And then we can sneak out again and pretend we've only just arrived."

She peered at Arthur doubtfully. He was scowling at the buff-colored brick facade of the house in a way that suggested it had done him some personal injury. He seemed unlikely to fit in her wardrobe.

"This way," she said, and led him in the direction of the servants' entrance at the rear of the residence. He followed her, wordlessly, all the way up the stairs. They encountered a handful of servants, all of whom were familiar with Lydia's propensity for sneaking about. If they had questions about her rather remarkable appearance and the bearded giant at her side, they did not ask them aloud.

When they reached the third floor, she pushed open the door and led Arthur out into the hallway, in the direction of her chamber. Halfway there, she paused and looked up at him.

She could not make him out. He looked distressed, his face almost a glower. He put one hand to the papered wall beside her head.

"Is everything all right?" she whispered.

He caught her about the waist with his other hand. "Aye. No. I don't—ah God, Lydia—"

His head dropped, his mouth nearly brushing hers, and desire for him outweighed caution. She went up on her toes, bringing her mouth to his. He groaned softly, helplessly, against her lips and kissed her hard.

One of the chamber doors flew open and crashed into the wall.

They broke hastily apart. Lydia peered underneath Arthur's arm and found herself staring directly into the stupefied face of her brother Ned.

"Ah," she said, "Ned. Good afternoon."

Was it afternoon? The days had started to run together.

Ned's mouth was open, working soundlessly as he tried to say something. His gaze took in her disheveled state, her slowly surrendering handkerchief, and then moved to Arthur beside her.

"Strathrannoch?" Ned said hoarsely.

Well. It appeared Jasper had been home long enough to inform the family of her supposed marriage.

"Aye," Arthur said. "I'm—"

He did not have time to finish his statement. To Lydia's astonishment, Ned sprang forward like an outraged jungle cat, launched himself at Arthur, and toppled both of them to the ground.

Chapter 21

. . . I've four separate letters from Lydia in Sussex assuring me that she is well. Does that strike you as . . . ominous?

—*from Theo Hope-Wallace to Jasper Hope-Wallace*

"Ouch—bloody—*fuck!*"

Arthur wrestled himself out from underneath the shortish blond fellow who was doubtless one of Lydia's ten thousand brothers. Despite his significant disadvantage in both height and reach, this particular Hope-Wallace fought like a deranged tiger. Arthur had felt *teeth*, for God's sake.

He planted his boot in the man's midsection and shoved. Something tore. He felt a draft on his shoulder.

"Ned!" Lydia seemed to be shouting, but only in a whisper. "Stop it! Calm down, you blockhead!"

Ned paused, panting from exertion. "Going to—murder him—for you—Lyddie—"

"For heaven's sake, *why?*"

Despite the fact that his arse was on the ground, Ned appeared to be gathering himself for another spring. "Look at you!

What has he done to you? You're *bleeding*, Lyddie! Your *husband*,
Jasper said—but Theo looked him up—he's a damned penniless
fortune hunter!"

"I'm not bleeding, you Bedlamite! Do you ever stop talking
and listen to something beyond the wind howling between your
ears?"

Arthur's eyes had flown toward her at Ned's words—she was
bleeding—*where*—how had he missed—

She wasn't bleeding, as it turned out, though she was scrub-
bing rather frantically at the jam on her arm. But the guilt that
had coursed through him like a torrent at her brother's words did
not falter.

A penniless fortune hunter. That's what Ned had called him.

He wanted to defend himself—he would never take advantage of her—he would *never* take from her—

But—God. He'd felt a great wash of shame and inadequacy as
they'd arrived at the Hope-Wallace residence. The town house—if
that was even the word for it—was palatial. She had been raised
here, on this elegant street with its neat foliage and carefully
trimmed shrubbery.

All he had to offer her was a half-ruined castle, and a name
and title he was not proud to own. Her fortune *would* be a help
to him—to the people of Strathrannoch and the villagers he supported. He could not pretend it wasn't so.

And he'd hated, too, to sneak her up the stairs, all travel-worn
and secretive. He wanted—

He scarcely knew what he wanted. Ridiculous things. He
wanted to march into her family home with her on his arm and
declare her his wife.

But he did not know how to speak to her now, here in this
beautiful house. He didn't know how to tell her that he'd gone

about everything backward, that his heart was hers to keep or trod upon, that he wanted her, in every possible way, forever.

A *fortune hunter.* How could he ever make her believe it wasn't true?

Lydia towed Ned into one of the chambers down the hall, a quick gesture of her head indicating that Arthur was to follow.

The three of them crowded into the room. Arthur supposed it was Lydia's bedchamber: He could see evidence of her everywhere. The political and historical tomes that spilled out from the bookcase, the escritoire nearly overflowing with pamphlets and notes. On top of the little desk's second shelf were three or four inexplicable decorative items that looked like the things she wore sometimes in her hair.

Beneath the bed lay a pair of floppy pink-and-orange slippers knitted to resemble clouds at sunrise.

Lydia shoved Ned down onto the bed, and despite his emotional tumult, Arthur found that he wanted to laugh. Her habitual reserve had altogether vanished with this young blond brother.

"Sit," she hissed. "Listen. This is Arthur Baird, the Earl of Strathrannoch—"

"Your husband?" Ned interjected. "You eloped?"

"I—we—" Her gaze flicked toward Arthur, her big blue eyes uncertain.

"Yes," Arthur said. "Lydia is Lady Strathrannoch."

If there was any chance—any chance at all—that she thought he would hesitate to make her his wife, he meant to disabuse her of the notion. If she needed certainty, he could give it to her. If she needed him to steady her, then by God, he would never leave her side.

Ned's face had gone somewhat red. He appeared to color as

freely as his sister. "And why in hell does she look like she's been run over by a cart, Strathrannoch?"

"I was," Lydia put in. "Er, that is, we had a carriage accident on the way here. And we were, ah, also robbed. By highwaymen. Arthur was quite heroic."

Arthur wanted very much to protest this description of events, but it did not seem the opportune moment.

"Jesus." Ned pressed his fingers briefly over his eyes. "Jesus, Lyddie. How did this all—and when—" He broke off in evident turmoil.

Lydia moistened her lips and looked at Arthur. "I . . . read something he wrote. About the Clearances. I . . . I traveled to his castle and met him there. We . . . determined that we suit."

Ned glanced at Arthur and then back to Lydia. "Trust you to fall in love with someone over their political beliefs. Good Lord."

Arthur felt a cold discomfort in the pit of his stomach at Ned's words.

She would. She had.

Only it had not been with him.

Lydia winced. "We can dissect my personal flaws at a later date, if that's all right. Is Jasper here? We need to speak to him immediately."

Ned shook his head. "He was here for a day and then off again. You know how he is—always flitting about between his friends and his ladybirds and his Venetian holidays and whatever else he does."

Lydia's voice when she replied was measured. "Indeed. I do know how he is."

"Mother's been off her head ever since he dropped in and told us about your elopement."

Lydia collapsed onto the bed beside her brother and groaned. "Of course."

"Have you heard that you're a *countess* now?" Ned's initial outrage seemed to have faded into a kind of irrepressible good humor. "Because I have. About a thousand times."

Lydia scrubbed her hands over her disheveled hair, an action which did remarkable things to her barely concealed breasts. Arthur tried desperately not to think about her breasts, here in her bedchamber with her *brother*.

"Do you think there's any chance that Jasper might turn up tonight?" she asked.

"I have no idea. I haven't been keeping his social calendar for him."

Lydia made a sound somewhere between a sigh and a snort. "Of course not. Well, we'll see if he does. If not, I have other ideas about how to track him down."

Ned's gaze sharpened upon her. "Why do you need Jasper so desperately? Is it something to do with your pamphlets?"

"Something, yes. I'll tell you everything after I talk to him."

Ned looked unconvinced by her words, but he nodded shortly.

Lydia glanced between Arthur and her brother and then turned back to Ned. "Listen, while I dress, can you take Arthur and"—she made a gesture that seemed to take in his whole person—"fix him up? Perhaps find him some clean clothing? We lost everything to the, ah, highwaymen."

Ned looked extremely put out by this suggestion. "I can't say as I've got anything that will fit a giant."

"Be resourceful," Lydia said and patted him on the cheek. "You're my favorite brother for a reason. And—Ned?"

He paused in his dubious appraisal of Arthur's person. "Yes?"

"Can you *try* not to trifle with my husband?"

Perhaps she had called him such before, but Arthur did not think so. His spirits shot upward so decisively that even the bloodthirsty look Ned shot him could not dampen them.

"I can't make any promises," Ned said darkly.

• • •

By the time dinner began, Arthur had met the rest of the Hope-Wallace brothers and concluded that they ought to be separated from one another for the general safety of the British Isles. Preferably via incarceration.

Once he had removed Arthur from Lydia's chamber, Ned had come out with the revelation that the only suitably sized clothing he could procure on short notice would have to come from a footman.

An hour later, Arthur was clean-shaven and more or less indistinguishable from the crimson-liveried male servants in the house, except that he'd refused the white wig and the tricorne hat. Ned had made an extremely cogent argument for the wig, but Arthur had glowered at him until he subsided.

Eventually Ned had hauled him downstairs to a spacious sitting room, which sported a tasteful wall-covering of fruits and birds, several old and no doubt priceless rugs, and a glassily polished pianoforte.

Lydia was there already, sitting beside another of the innumerable brothers at the piano and laughing—that sweet soft laugh he loved—with her elbows pressed to her knees.

His gaze fell on her and held there, like the point of a compass drawn to magnetic north. Somehow, quite without his realizing it, she had become the pole by which he was guided.

She looked so lovely, warm and comfortable beside her brother. She'd exchanged the precarious dress for one of her own, which was all white lace and miles of skirts. She looked pristine, exquisite, perfectly at home here in this expensive house with its matching servants.

He wanted to drag her upstairs and find her body beneath all those yards of snowy lace. He wanted to take down her hair, muss it, kiss her until she was flushed and tousled and dazed. He wanted—

Jesus, things he ought not want whilst dressed in silk knee breeches that were slightly too small.

He was introduced to the other brother at the piano—this one was Gabriel, the physician. He was as blond as the other brothers had been, though more sober-faced, and his grip on Arthur's hand was viselike.

Lydia, for her part, alternated between sympathetic grimaces in Arthur's direction and furious glances at Ned, who pretended not to see her. Presumably she had noticed Arthur's patently absurd costume, but was too decorous to point it out, in case he did not realize how ridiculous he looked.

He thanked God that he had not been talked into the wig.

"Gabe, you may be interested to know that Arthur is a great patron of the mechanical arts," Lydia said, with perhaps more loyalty than accuracy. "Perhaps you could tell him about your—"

Gabriel did not seem to be listening. "Do you vote your seat in the Lords, Strathrannoch?" he asked abruptly. "I have some legislation I want to introduce on the disposal of refuse in urban districts, and I—"

"Oh Jesus," said Ned. He threw himself down onto a settee and balanced his boots on the wooden arm. "It has been, quite literally, less than two minutes, and you've already brought up fecal matter."

Gabriel scowled. "It is an issue of public health, as you well know, and I will take support wherever I can get it."

"No one wants to bring out your shit bill, Gabe. It lacks a certain refinement."

"It is not a *shit bill*—"

"Lord Strathrannoch votes by proxy," Lydia cut in. She had the timing of one long-practiced in interruption.

Ned and Gabe fell silent and turned identical dismayed looks upon him.

"Oh bollocks," Ned said. He swung his feet down and sat up, which Arthur felt was not a good sign. "Don't tell Theo. He thinks proxy voting should be abolished. Enables corruption, something something, political cronies, and so forth."

"I prefer to remain in Scotland," Arthur said grimly.

In fact, he could not afford to travel to London and stay for the duration of the parliamentary session, but he would have rather chewed off his own arm than admit such a thing to Lydia's brothers.

"Do you?" inquired Ned curiously. "And Lyddie wants that too?"

He looked helplessly to Lydia. He thought she did. He *hoped* she did, as preposterous as it seemed here in this opulent sitting room.

"Yes," she said softly into the silence, and his heart leapt.

He wanted to pull her into his arms. He wanted to run his fingers through her hair. He wanted to ask if she was certain, if she could possibly be certain. He wanted—

To his mingled relief and dismay, their locked gaze was broken as two more Hope-Wallaces entered the sitting room. He turned reluctantly away from her.

The final brother was a buttoned-up sort of fellow, auburn-haired and of a height with Jasper and Gabriel. He looked to be a handful of years older than Arthur, and he had on his arm a tiny, fairylike woman in perhaps her midfifties with silvery-blond hair and familiar dark blue eyes.

Lydia was on her feet and in the arms of this eldest brother in an instant.

"Theo," she mumbled into his jacket, "I've missed you!"

After a moment, Theo set Lydia back away from him and gave her a thorough once-over. "I've missed you too," he said gravely, "Lady Strathrannoch."

Lydia went red to the roots of her hair and then slowly—like a woman facing the gallows—turned to the petite blonde at Theo's side. "Mother."

On a sob, Mrs. Hope-Wallace snatched her daughter into her arms and buried her face into Lydia's hair. "My baby! My little girl! I've been beside myself!"

The Hope-Wallace brothers emitted various scoffs and groans.

"Come off it, Mother," Ned said. "You thought she was in Sussex like the rest of us did."

"I knew," said Mrs. Hope-Wallace damply. "I felt it in my heart that she had left England. A mother always knows."

After submitting to her mother's attentions for longer than Arthur would have thought possible, Lydia wrestled herself free. "I'm fine, Mother." She half turned to Arthur, though she did not close the distance between them. "Ah—let me—that is, allow me to . . ."

She seemed slightly at a loss for words.

"The giant is her new husband," Ned put in. "Your baby out-ranks you, Mother."

Lydia visibly blanched.

"Despite his appearance," Gabe said blandly, "I have it on good authority he is not one of our footmen."

"Don't be ridiculous," said Ned. "He's not wearing a wig, is he?"

"Mother," Lydia tried again, "this is Arthur. The Earl of Strathrannoch, and my . . . husband."

Mrs. Hope-Wallace had one small hand pressed to her breastbone. She dropped it, stepped forward, and, to Arthur's absolute stupefaction, threw her arms about his waist. And hugged him.

"My dear boy," she said, "welcome to the family. You must call me Mother."

There was an instantaneous and vociferous round of heckling from the brothers.

And Arthur felt—

As though he were on precipice, balanced a thousand feet in the air. He did not know where to turn. He was afraid to take a step. Everywhere he looked seemed to augur a long and breathless fall.

How many times had he told himself that he did not want this very thing?

Family. Home. Love in all its forms, burdensome and overwhelming, generous and kind.

He had almost stopped wanting Davis back in his life. He had almost stopped wishing for things that were never to be. He had Strathrannoch Castle and his tenants and his barbican, and he had told himself it was enough.

But would it be enough for Lydia?

It seemed impossible, fantastical—she who had grown up in this wealthy, loving, boisterous family, the youngest, the most cherished. How could he ever give her anything like this?

How could he stop himself from wanting it too?

They lingered in the sitting room for quite a while, but Jasper did not arrive. Eventually Mrs. Hope-Wallace seemed to surrender, and they made their way into the dining room. Perfect identical footmen served perfect identical courses, one after another after another. Arthur scarcely knew what to make of them.

The brothers traded more and less clever remarks, Mrs. Hope-Wallace presided with affectionate absurdity, and no one ran too roughshod over Lydia. He had been prepared to pull her aside if she grew pale or anxious, as he had done at Kilbride House, but here, in the circle of her family, she did not need him.

Except once.

In the middle of a conversational odyssey between Gabe and Ned—which had meandered from gooseberry cream to something about Catullus that made Theo grow even more poker-stiff over his stewed celery—Mrs. Hope-Wallace broke in.

"Lydia, my love, won't you tell us about your wedding? My first child to marry—and I missed it. You did not even wear my lace shawl." She appeared to bravely fight back another round of tears. "Were you at least in blue? You know how fetching you look in blue. Tell me you didn't wear primrose. And, oh, my dear, did you have flowers? Did you have a bridal attendant?" A faint look of alarm crossed her face. "Are you . . . a Papist now?"

"This," muttered Gabe, "is why the rest of us are unmarried."

"Ah," said Lydia. She'd begun to blink furiously. "It was nice. Lovely. It was . . . in Scotland."

"That's specific," said Ned.

"In . . . October," Lydia managed. She was staring down at her stewed celery as if for inspiration. Every single inch of skin Arthur could see above the top of her bodice was carnation-pink.

"We were married at Strathrannoch Castle," he heard himself say.

The five Hope-Wallaces turned to look at him.

"In Scotland," he said, "there's no requirement of banns or license, only a bit of plaid and two witnesses. We had everything we needed."

He had not realized how clearly he'd pictured this—Lydia's hand in his, her elegant fingers and his scarred ones, wrapped together in a strip of his blue-and-green tartan.

"We stood on the ramparts under the sun," he said, "and Lydia wore a crown of meadowsweet in her hair."

He had seen her there. He had taken her to the top of the castle and wanted her—wanted it all—even then.

"Her dress was white"—it had been, that day on the ramparts; he remembered everything—"and her wee spangled slippers caught the reflection of the sun. She looked—she looked as though—"

But here his imagination faltered. How would she look at him, were she his bride?

His gaze caught on hers. She was staring at him, her face gone pale. Her fingers were locked on a piece of polished silver, clutching the stem of the fork like a lifeline.

"Lydia," he said.

She shoved her chair back from the table and stood. Her fine linen napkin fell to the floor.

"Excuse me," she said. "I—I beg your pardon, Mother, I have to—I must—"

She closed her mouth, turned on her heel, and fled.

Heedless of the Hope-Wallaces, of the rules of polite society, of the choked sound of amusement from one of the brothers, Arthur was on his feet after her in an instant.

Chapter 22

*You are the summer and the winter, the spring and the fall.
When you change, I want to change alongside you. I want
to discover you anew every morning. I want to forget what
dawn looks like except in your eyes.*

*—from the papers of Arthur Baird,
composed in pencil, copied out
in ink, unsent*

Lydia ran all the way to her bedchamber, which in retrospect was
not her cleverest play, since it was one of the only rooms in the
house that Arthur knew how to find.

His hand was on the door before she could close it. Before she
could shut him out.

She was panting from her rapid ascent up three flights of
stairs—at least, she wanted to believe it was from the stairs. But
in truth she'd felt as though she could not catch her breath from
the moment Arthur had started to speak of their wedding.

Her mother's delighted demand for the details of the ceremony had been—well, had been very like her mother, at once affectionate and shameless.

But Arthur's reply, the careful details in his low rough voice, had filled her with a longing so profound that she did not know how to guard against it.

She had felt ruthlessly exposed, there at the dinner table, with her family around her and Arthur's words conjuring her heart's desire in the candlelight.

Had he taken pity upon her—helpless in conversation, tangled in her own reserve—and thought to rescue her?

It had not felt like rescue. It had felt like a scalpel, paring away every bit of the armor she kept around her heart. He must have been able to see, when he'd looked at her, how much she wanted all of it to be real. All of them must have seen.

"Lydia," he said as he crossed the threshold, "I'm sorry. I did not mean to shame you in front of your family. I'd thought—I'd meant to help you." He closed the door behind him, shutting them together into her chamber.

She was hot, flushed and oversensitive, as though she could feel his gaze laying her open. She thought the faintest touch upon her skin might leave a bruise.

"It's not because of my family." Her voice sounded raw.

He had taken a handful of steps toward her, but at her words, he hesitated. "I'd thought perhaps I'd given you some embarrassment, with the attention of all of them upon you."

"They are my family—it's not the same—it's—"

How could she explain herself to him?

With his brother, she had imagined a marriage of convenience—precisely the exchange of political goals that Arthur had spoken of at the inn.

She had been willing to accept such a marriage once. But now that she knew Arthur Baird—his careful heart, his gentleness, his immense and quiet capacity for love—she did not want convenience alone. She wanted everything.

She wanted to know that without her impulsive words on a staircase in Haddon Grange, without the intervention of the de Younges and Jasper, he would still be here with her, asking her to be his wife. She wanted to believe it.

But she had been foolish once before, had built castles in the air, and she wasn't—she wasn't *good* at this, didn't know if she could trust what she wanted so desperately to be true.

If only he would speak first! If only she could be certain—if only there were no *risk*.

His face had gone stricken as he'd taken in her broken-off denial. "Is it regret then?"

She licked her lips. "I don't know what you mean."

"Do you regret what's passed between us?" The blue-green swirl of his eyes was a tide, a cataclysm. "Now that we've come back here, to your home and your family, do you wish to change your mind?"

Her lips parted in shock at his words. The blades of her shoulders brushed the wall behind her.

Of course she did not wish to change her mind.

She wanted everything—would take whatever he was willing to give her. She wanted decades at his side, a castle rebuilt, a village made plentiful together. She wanted to go home with him and never use the countess's chamber again because she slept every night at his side. She wanted children with eyes the color of Scotland.

But he did not appear to know it. He seemed uncertain—bruised, even, by her hesitation. Perhaps, somehow, her longing for him had not been as transparent as she'd believed. Perhaps he did not know how she yearned.

To speak first—to drop her armor—was terrifying. But— *Brave*, he'd called her.

If there was ever a time in her life when she had needed to summon courage, it was now. She would not hurt him, not by her apprehension nor by her cowardice.

"I will never regret it," she whispered. "Never, Arthur. I want everything you said—Strathrannoch Castle and the meadowsweet and your hands in mine. I want you. I care for you. I—"

He surged forward and pressed her up against the wall.

She gasped. His body was large and hard. His hands went to her waist, pulling her up, his knee sliding between her legs.

"Thank Christ," he rasped. "God forgive me, Lydia, but it would have killed me to let you go."

Her palms had come to rest on his chest. She reveled in his solid muscular warmth, and then she curled her fingers around the lapels of his jacket and pulled him closer.

"My Lydia." He trailed kisses along her neck, a lacework of wanting. "'Tis not because of the money. I don't know how to make you believe it, but I swear to you, I've not offered for you because of your fortune. I can't say truly that we don't need the funds at Strathrannoch. But I would have you penniless and barefoot."

She tipped her head back against the wall and shoved her fingers beneath his jacket, closer to his skin.

His voice was low and heated, his breath caressing her ear. "Do you know what I thought of when I saw you in this pretty white dress?"

"Tell me."

"Taking you in it." His hands came down to her buttocks,

gripping hard enough to pull her up against his arousal. "Like this. Up against the wall, your hair down and your legs around me."

"Arthur—"

He licked a hot path up her neck and rocked against her. His teeth closed around her earlobe, biting down softly, and she could not control the sound that slipped from between her lips.

She wanted. Oh God, she wanted him. Desire for him, always so close to the surface, raced along her skin and pooled between her thighs. She felt loose and liquid and not quite steady. Her toes were off the ground.

"'Tis not just the bedding," he said. "Christ Jesus, Lydia. It's everything—your heart and your brain and your laugh. You make me half-crazed. When you're gone I imagine the feel of you beneath my hands, and when you're with me, I think about how to make you smile. I want to—to read all your letters and your pamphlets. I want to listen to you talk until I fall asleep, and then I want to dream about your voice."

He kissed her. His mouth was a hungry entreaty, a desperate plea. Her head spun as she kissed him back, days of wanting distilled down to *take* and *now* and *please*. She let her anxieties drop away and allowed desire to pull her down, let it sweep her away like a current, inevitable and absolute.

She yanked at his jacket, pulling it off his shoulders, and when he lifted his hands from her backside to peel the garment off, she wrapped her legs around his waist.

His fingers found the buttons on the back of her dress. "Can I? I want to see you—I want—"

"Yes," she said. "Yes."

She had his absurd scarlet waistcoat off. Her hands were underneath his shirt. She could feel the ridges of muscle straining beneath her fingers, his heart pounding against her palms.

Somehow her dress was unfastened, her chemise around her waist. He cupped her breasts in his hands. His thumbs brushed across her tight nipples, and she cried out at the brilliant, shocking pleasure.

"I love that," he said hoarsely. "The way you sound when I touch you."

His fingers teased at her nipples, rolling the tips, pinching lightly. She felt her belly tighten, an ache redoubling between her thighs. She pressed helplessly into him, arching her back.

His mouth was on hers again. His tongue traced the outline of her lips, and she gasped and shuddered at the sensation. Everything in her felt constricted, pulling down and contracting—she felt the tightness in her abdomen, in her back, a hot and urgent need driven on and on by the firm torture of his fingers.

"God," he murmured. "How many times have I spent myself, imagining the noises you make when you come?"

She rocked into him, pressing her sex shamelessly to his arousal. She was a pinpoint, a clenched fist, a star. She needed—she needed—

He unwrapped her legs from his waist and set her down, a careful slide against his body.

"No," she said, and she did not care how she sounded, did not care if she had to beg. "Arthur, please—"

"Want this off you," he rasped, and shoved her dress and undergarments down to the ground. He spared an instant for his shirt, his shoes, hers. Then he picked her up and moved to the bed, bringing her to straddle his lap as he sat.

She might have been self-conscious—she was naked, after all, except for her stockings—had he not been so manifestly aroused. The skin of his neck was flushed pink. His hands searched her body, clinging to the places where she curved, the softest places, the most heated. He skimmed her thighs, her hips, the heavy weight of her breasts.

"I've dreamed of this," he said softly. "You bare before me, your eyes all dark and blurred with wanting."

He made one lazy revolution around her nipple, and she trembled.

"But to have you here," he went on, "to be able to touch you. To watch your face in the light. Christ, Lydia. No dream of mine could have come close to this."

The trembling in her went on and on, drawn up into her heart. She loved him. She would never regret that.

He passed the flat plane of his palm across her stiffened nipple. Her breath caught. He murmured soft and carnal words against her neck, his breath tickling her ear. She tangled her fingers in his curls, grown dusky in the twilight.

"Come here to me," he murmured, and pulled her atop him as he lay back in the bed.

Nothing felt impossible now. Putting her mouth to his was as easy as breathing. His lips parted beneath hers, and his hands moved along her waist, her hips, the back of her thighs. He groaned softly into her mouth, and it felt like a question against her lips.

"Yes," she answered. *Yes.*

He urged her body farther up, setting his mouth to her nipple, a firm suction that had her hips grinding down. He must have felt the wetness between her thighs as she straddled him, must have heard the sounds in the back of her throat—a whimper, almost a whine—but she felt no shame. Only pleasure, sweet and driving, pushing her down and bearing her away.

He released her nipple and pressed his head back against the mattress. His hands dug into her hips and brought her up his body. The muscles of his arms flexed as he lifted her, a quick weightless slide.

He pushed her past his shoulders and Lydia had a moment of confused hesitation. *What did he—*

He brought her knees to either side of his face.

"God, you're lovely," he said hoarsely. "Lean forward. Kneel over me. Hold the headboard."

She understood then, as she leaned forward, as he angled her hips so that her slick flesh was positioned above him. Her hands went to the back of her bed, the carved whorls pressing into her palms.

She could feel his breath between her legs. It was hot, unsteady. His hands were full of her thighs, and then he spread them wider and pulled her down into the wet heat of his mouth.

She cried out, an incoherent plea at the sensation. His tongue parted her, teased and toyed with her, and she felt herself jerk, writhing under his hands, above his mouth. Again—again—her hips made sharp pulses against him.

She gripped the carved headboard with all her strength. Tomorrow the curving pattern would be imprinted into her skin.

He made a soft, appreciative murmur. His fingers were inside her—first one and then another—and she felt the walls of her sex tighten around him, clutching as if to draw him in. His movements were steady and rhythmic: his fingers, the unrelenting friction of his tongue.

She squeezed her eyes shut and cried out as her climax took her. The force of it rocked her, a low shuddering that began at her sex and rippled through her body, throbbing through her abdomen, her limbs, the tips of her fingers.

She pressed her face down into her fisted hands and sobbed out her release.

When her thighs loosened, Arthur pulled her back against him, urging her body down toward his chest. Her hands were reluctant to part from the headboard; he reached up and slipped her fingers free.

Her mouth found his again. She could taste herself, her own arousal, on his lips. He kissed her—one long, hot, demanding kiss—and then pulled back.

"I want you," he said hoarsely. "I want you so much. But we needn't—I can wait. I can—"

Her palm was on his chest and she could feel the pounding of his heart, a match for her own.

"Yes," she murmured.

He froze, one hand in her hair and the other half-underneath her stocking.

"I mean, no," she said. "Don't wait. I don't want to wait."

He flipped her over in the bed. She laughed and gasped, and he pressed his face into the curve of her neck on a rough, pleading sound. She could feel his erection through his breeches, hot and hard against her.

"You won't regret it." She barely made out his hoarse promise, growled into her skin.

Somehow, she believed him. Her anxieties, her fears of wanting more than he could give—they were nowhere to be found in this soft dreamworld of twilight and bed linens. She did not let him go.

He came into her slowly, so slow and patient, as though desire were not a mad demand upon him. He fitted himself inside her, tiny shallow thrusts, and her hips arched to take more of him.

He made a desperate sound.

"It's all right," she murmured. "I'm all right."

"Oh Lydia." His voice had dropped, just above a groan. "Oh my love. I would not hurt you for the world."

It did hurt, a little—a stretch just past the point of comfort. But he brought one hand between their bodies and touched her. A soft caress, a gentle stroke. He whispered something in her ear, some small praise, and her hips pressed up again, seeking more.

His mouth was at her neck. His fingers moved over her, and she whimpered as need mounted in her, the ache rising as he thrust again, deeper this time. A little harder.

"Yes," she said, "oh please, yes."

She slid her knees up and the angle of their movements shifted—a sudden, dizzying pleasure. She cried out, her body tightening around him, her feet flexing against the bed. His hand caught hers, pressed her palm into the linens beside her head. There seemed no end to her culmination when it came—no end to his voice whispering endearments.

Beautiful, he said. *My love. My own.*

He was so careful with her. He moved slowly, languorously, almost until the moment of his crisis, until his rhythm grew erratic and his fingers held her fast. He trapped his cock between them and thrust hard, spilling himself on her belly as he clutched her hips. She welcomed his urgent grip, relished the way his hands recalled her to herself.

There was nothing in this moment as real as her body, and his, and the pleasure of their joining. In the gathering dark, his touch felt like a vow.

Chapter 23

Dearest, find enclosed an early copy of the library's newest pamphlet on condoms. If you do not find it personally useful, please assume I've sent it to you to assess the quality of the engravings. (They certainly are lifelike!)

—from Selina to Lydia

Lydia sat cross-legged in her dressing gown and surveyed the man in her bed.

He was still asleep, his curls mussed and one muscular arm flung across his face. After four nights on the mail coach, they had both slept long and deeply. If her mother had made up a separate chamber for Arthur, Lydia was not aware of it—no one had broken in upon them or knocked at the door.

She'd been awakened only by the dawn. In the soft light of the morning, she'd shrugged into her muslin wrap and pondered what she might find for Arthur to wear as well.

He certainly couldn't wear the scarlet footman's costume again. She intended to wreak some revenge upon Ned for that incident, once she stopped laughing whenever she thought of it.

Arthur's gold-tipped lashes fluttered slightly. He had the beginnings of golden stubble on his cheeks and jaw as well, and she
found she wanted to press her face there. Feel the rough scratch
against her lips.

Perhaps she could, now. Perhaps that would be permissible.

It seemed possible, this morning, that he would welcome it.
She felt a cautious and tentative hope unfurl itself, one petal at
a time, in her chest. She might have many mornings like this,
dawn-colored and sleep-warm beside him. She might have all of
them.

But her dream of the morning was not to be. She heard a
rustle at the door and then the quiet voice of Nora, her maid.
"May I enter?"

Arthur's eyes came open and went, instantly, to her face.
"Lydia?" he murmured. He lifted an arm, rolled to his side, and
caught her around the waist. He pulled her hard enough that her
body half fell into his and pressed his face against her muslin-
covered thigh.

Helplessly, she tangled her fingers in his hair. "Good morning." He did not move, only murmured something inaudible into
her lap. She breathed out a laugh. "Someone's at the door."

He turned his face just enough to blink reluctantly up at her.

Her lips curved as she looked at his face, almost boyish, all
curling lashes and sulky mouth. "You probably ought to fasten
your breeches." It was with no little regret that she pulled away.
"Hold on," she said to Nora. "I'm coming."

She crossed the room slowly, giving Arthur a moment to re-
store himself, and then tugged open the door.

Nora stood on the other side, looking fresh and crisp despite
the early hour. She held a bundle of clothing in her hands. "Welcome home," she said. "You look . . . rested."

Lydia's entire face went hot.

In retrospect, their behavior last night had been rather scandalous. She and Arthur had vanished halfway through supper and had not reappeared.

But—well—they were married.

After a fashion. If one did not put too fine a point on "were."

"Ned said you were looking for Jasper and for an appropriate suit of clothes," Nora announced. "I can't help you with your scoundrel of a brother, but I've managed the rest." She crossed the room to where Arthur had risen at her arrival and handed him the bundle of fabric. "Good morning, Lord Strathrannoch. This is the best I could do on short notice, but I've sent a request on to the tailor to have something ready for you by the afternoon."

"Ah," Arthur said. His voice was a trifle scratchy with sleep. "Thank you. A pleasure to make your acquaintance."

Lydia suspected she was as red as the footman's waistcoat that Arthur had worn to dinner. She supposed she would have to get used to Nora finding them together in the bed in the morning, if they were to be married in truth.

Good heavens.

She cleared her throat and tried to ignore the heat radiating from her skin. "Nora," she said, "I'd like to go over to the Stanhope residence this morning and speak to Selina. Can you—"

"To be sure." Nora, efficient as ever, had already begun to set out the appropriate underpinnings and day dress. "I'll go down and call for the carriage. Do you want breakfast?"

"No, thank you," she said, and then hesitated, turning to Arthur. "Unless—that is, do you want to remain here whilst I go out?"

His jaw was set, his expression rather grim, but when he

turned to look at her, his hazel eyes were soft. "No," he said. "I wouldn't have you go alone."

. . .

By late afternoon, their party had grown from two to five, and they found themselves not at the Stanhope residence, but at Belvoir's Library itself.

They'd called on the duke and duchess early enough that the couple were still at breakfast, along with the duke's adolescent brother and sister. Lydia had introduced Arthur—as her *husband*, dear God, would it ever stop feeling like a passing fancy?—and then ushered Selina into a sitting room for a whispered conference about Davis Baird, Jasper, and the stolen rifle scope.

Selina's dark brows, at odds with her honey-blond hair, had risen higher and higher as Lydia related the events of the past weeks.

"Good Lord," she said finally, when Lydia ran down. "You're certain that Strathrannoch's brother has this device—this rifle telescope? And you believe he means to sell it to . . . these French agents?"

"I'm not certain of anything," Lydia said. "But the Thibodeaux knew Davis well. And they were searching for Jasper. I cannot believe it's a coincidence. If there's anything you know— anything you have learned from the Home Office via Belvoir's— that might help us find them, we need your help."

Selina drummed her fingers along the arm of her chair. "I am not as involved with the Home Office as you seem to think. But—" She hesitated, straightening the seam of her glove before she spoke. "But you are right about your brother. He works for the Home Office. And I permit him to pass correspondence through the library. I could try to contact him."

"Yes," Lydia said. "Yes, please. If there's any way to find him—"

"There might be," Selina said slowly. "And I think . . ."

She trailed off. Her amber eyes had sharpened into an expression that Lydia recognized—an expression that occasionally terrified her, but in this particular instance sent a bloom of optimism through her instead.

Selina had a plan.

"You said you have Davis's notes?" Selina asked. "His papers?"

"I had some of them on my person when we were separated, yes. Georgiana has the rest in my trunk. They're not terribly clear though."

Selina made a dismissive gesture with one hand. "It doesn't matter. Meet me at Belvoir's this afternoon. I'll get Georgiana. Bring the papers, and we'll sort this out."

Lydia trusted Selina's cleverness enough to do exactly as she said.

And so, roughly six hours later, Arthur and Lydia were ushered by a Belvoir's staff member into Selina's top-floor office at the library.

Inside the office sat Selina, flanked by Georgiana and another one of their mutual friends, a dark-haired, curvaceous, perpetually abstracted antiquities scholar named Iris Duggleby.

"Er," Lydia said, "good afternoon."

"I know this may seem untoward," Selina said, "but I would like to bring Iris into our confidence. The five of us together have a far better chance of uncovering Davis Baird's intentions or whereabouts from his papers." She turned her gaze to Arthur. "I assure you, Lord Strathrannoch, you can rely upon the sanctity of what is discussed in this room. Lydia, Georgiana, and Iris have trusted me with their secrets for years now. Their cooperation in this endeavor will provide—"

"No," Arthur said flatly.

There was a brief, shocked silence.

"No," he said again. "I will not have my family's transgressions spread around more widely. I should like to avoid placing more innocent people in peril, for God's sake. 'Tis bad enough that you're involved already, Lydia."

Georgiana, seated behind the desk, arched one delicate eyebrow. "I am also involved, for what it's worth."

Lydia twisted her fingers together in front of her. "Arthur, I think Selina is right. Finding Davis and Jasper must take precedence over the vague possibility that someone might be endangered."

"The *vague possibility*—have you forgotten your room was ransacked? By people we now believe to be French agents?" Arthur's throat had gone pink.

"Her Grace is also involved," Georgiana put in. "One might observe that the majority of the women in this room are in fact already involved."

Lydia paid no mind to Georgiana's remarks. She untangled her fingers, gathered her courage, and touched Arthur's hand. "I know. I know you are concerned—"

"Christ, Lydia, *concerned* is not the word—"

"But the Thibodeaux could be hunting for Jasper as we speak, and he does not know it. We have to find him. And we have to find Davis. If Selina believes that this is our best hope of doing so, then I trust her judgment."

Arthur stared down at her. His thumb brushed across the back of her hand. "I don't like the idea of bringing more people along to help right my family's wrongs. I . . . very much misliked asking it of you."

"For what it's worth," put in Iris, "no one has asked us to do anything beyond appear at the appointed hour. I begin to wonder what I am doing here."

"Don't worry," Georgiana said. "Everyone else is invisible to Strathrannoch when Lydia is in the room. One becomes accustomed to it."

Lydia felt a flutter in her belly at Georgiana's words and chose to ignore it. Instead, she looked up and met Arthur's gaze.

"Please," she said. "I believe this is the right thing to do."

Arthur passed his free hand along the back of his neck as he stared down at her, his eyes a thousand shades of worried gold and green. "All right," he said finally. "So be it. You trust them. And I trust you, Lydia."

She squeezed his fingers, and he squeezed back.

And for the next several minutes, as she explained the situation to Iris while Georgiana produced Davis's letters and papers, neither of them let go.

"Well," Selina said when the recital was finished and the notes brought forward, "when you said that the papers were unclear, I did not think you meant that Davis's writing was *invisible*."

"It's not invisible," Lydia protested. "It's only . . . hard to read." She held one of the papers up to the light and tipped it, angling it so that the shadows fell into the impressions left by Davis's pen. "You can make it out, if you try."

"Actually," said Iris, "this is very exciting. I've been wanting to try out the Niebuhr-Savigny method of palimpsestic excavation! But I suppose on paper, not vellum, gallic acid may result in destruction, rather than excavation." She brushed her thumb across her lips. "Perhaps a wash of iron gall ink."

There was a small silence.

"Do you—" Arthur began.

Lydia shook her head. "I haven't the faintest idea."

Iris seemed not to hear them. The antiquities scholar shook her dark hair back from her face, twisted the heavy mass up abstractedly with an ink-drenched pen from Selina's desk, and began to spread out the papers. She made quick work of the inkwell and a small pitcher from a sideboard. She called for tea, and when it arrived, she chewed on her lower lip and appeared to perform some kind of chemical experiment within the pitcher.

When she'd finished, she tugged the quill out of her hair, grimaced as the shiny black weight flopped back down around her shoulders, and then dipped the feather end of the quill into the potion she'd hastily concocted.

With a steady hand, she swept the feather over the first sheet of foolscap, producing a thin wash of brownish liquid. As they watched, the pigment settled in the grooves left behind by Davis's pen. Iris blew carefully on the paper, but there was no need to wait for it to dry.

Every line set down by Davis's pen was now perfectly visible. Selina made a smothered sound behind her hand.

"Go on," Lydia said. "Say it."

"I can't."

"You said we needed Iris. You told us so."

"It would be smug of me to remind you."

"You've the look of a cat who's eaten the entire Christmas goose. You are already smug."

Selina laughed.

The rest of the group perused the letters Georgiana had retained as well as each of Davis's papers as Iris revealed the writing therein with careful tea-colored strokes. Their companions' speculations were similar to Lydia's and Arthur's—the figures were depictions of the rifle scope; the numbers might perhaps reflect the weapon's range.

Lydia ground her teeth as she angled her head over the letters that Selina had recently scrutinized. "Do you notice anything that I've missed? Here he asks about Piccadilly. I know there were more letters in which he mentioned London sites, but I fear I cannot recall them exactly."

Selina shook her head, frustration evident in the set of her jaw. She straightened the papers with quick, efficient movements. "I don't know. Based on his diagrams, it seems likely he meant to put the weapon to use, but we do not know where or when. He might not even be in London at all."

Georgiana, seated at the desk near where Iris worked with her quill, made a tiny, quickly stifled sound. Almost a gasp.

Lydia looked up. Her heart had clutched at the sound—fear and hope together. "What is it?"

Georgiana was staring down at one of the papers that Iris's ink wash had excavated. "I know this place," she said evenly. "I've been here."

Arthur made for the desk to look down at the papers.

Lydia felt herself frozen to her chair. "What is it? Where?"

"It's St. Saviour's Church," Georgiana said, still looking at the paper. "I set one of my novels there. It's fallen into disrepair inside—everything covered in cobwebs, most of the medieval furnishings rotted away. I went there last year for research purposes and had to sneak in past two separate padlocked doors."

Selina had risen as well. "They've started a renovation project there," she said. "They asked us to donate."

"Yes," Georgiana said. "I went back this year and could not

enter. The tower is in the process of being rebuilt from the ground up, and the chapel is to be demolished."

"Why would Davis have a drawing of a church?" Lydia asked.

Arthur had stopped behind Georgiana and was looking down at the papers. "This tower," he said slowly. "It looks out over the city?"

Selina pressed a hand to the base of her throat. "Somewhat. The tower overlooks the Thames and London Bridge."

"He would have excellent range to shoot from that tower," Arthur said. "Almost as far as from the ramparts at Strathrannoch Castle."

Lydia felt her blood run cold.

The rifle scope—the ramparts—the pine tree so distant she could scarcely make it out.

And now this drawing of St. Saviour's.

Somehow, she had never quite believed that Davis meant to do violence with the rifle scope. Part of her still did not believe it. It seemed impossible that the charming, irrepressible man who had corresponded with her for nearly three years could also be plotting some kind of attack.

But the church—the notes on the rifle's range—

The evidence, though circumstantial, was unnerving. She could not make it square with the person she'd thought she'd known.

"We have to tell Jasper," she said. "We must get in touch with him."

"Yes," Selina said, "we do. I have a signal that I use to alert him when he has correspondence here. A red leatherbound book I set in my office window, which can just barely be seen from the street. Within a day or two of placing the book there, I'll receive a note from him with a time to meet."

Relief washed through Lydia. "Meanwhile, I can wait for him at home. He may come there first, and if he does, I can alert him immediately."

Selina nodded briskly and turned to Arthur. "Strathrannoch, if you do not mind, I should like to take this information about the rifle scope and St. Saviour's directly to the Home Office in the meantime."

"Of course." He hesitated. His eyes, all the colors shadowed, flicked from Lydia to Selina and back again. "If you'll permit me to remain here in your library."

"In Belvoir's? Why?"

"If Jasper comes with a note, I might be able to intercept him. I should"—his voice hitched ever so slightly—"like to speak to him about my brother. Find out what he knows."

"Ah." Selina's face softened slightly. "I take your meaning. I assure you, Strathrannoch, I will do my very best to help you find your brother before he is able to make use of this weapon."

Arthur's jaw was as hard and ruthless as a blow. He looked down at the papers on the desk, nodded once, and did not speak.

Chapter 24

I want to say
I wish I could tell you
If you'll only come home

—*from Arthur Baird to Davis Baird, crumpled*
and thrown into the grate

In the shadowed office at Belvoir's Library, Arthur watched the rain paint streaks on the leaded-glass window. The duchess, who'd proven even more terrifyingly competent than Lydia had implied, had produced a folding military-style cot from her closet, which she laid out for Arthur to sleep upon. She'd also arranged for a cold supper, a decanter of brandy, and her husband's valet to attend to Arthur in the morning—a variety of luxuries which he was not used to and did not know how to account for.

He did not know how to account for any of this.

He'd pushed the cot to the far wall and arranged himself with his back against the plaster. From there he could see out the window to the alley where Selina had said Jasper might drop off a note.

Arthur suspected he could not stay awake for the next two days running, but he supposed it was worth a try.

Anything was worth a try. He felt off-balance, uncertain, almost desperate in his need.

He'd hated to be parted from Lydia. It had felt *wrong* to watch her walk out the back door of the library, to see her pale hesitant expression as she looked back at him.

But he'd had to do it. So many people—Lydia, Huw, Georgiana, now these new companions of Lydia's—had come to his aid, and their earnest eagerness had sharpened the fear inside him to a razor's edge.

He did not know what to do with all of their generosity. It had been hard—terribly, painfully difficult—to ask for Lydia's assistance, and she had been the one to come to him. To ask these strangers for their help was no easier.

Because of him, they could all be in danger. Because of him, Lydia had chased after the Thibodeaux's coach—and could, so easily, have been harmed by the weapons they'd carried.

Because he had not seen Davis for what he was. Because Arthur was not enough on his own to keep Davis from straying down an indefensible path.

The drawing of St. Saviour's Church, laid out in plain brownish lines, had felt like the scrape of glass against Arthur's skin. He had not realized until that moment how much he wanted it all to have been some kind of mistake. He'd thought he'd extinguished the last bit of hope inside him when it came to his brother, but it was still there, impossible to fully root out.

It was dangerous to hope. Hope made the potential for disappointment so much vaster—he knew it did. It was why, with Lydia, his fears seemed to rise in consonance with the desires of his heart. He wanted her—and he was afraid he could never be enough for her. The contrast between their families was all the more stark now: she with her boisterous and loving siblings, and he, frantic to prevent his brother from committing violence. From losing a piece of his soul.

But he could not stop himself. He wanted her anyway. He would do almost anything—

He came abruptly to his feet.

There was someone in the alley, a cloak pulled over their head against the rain.

He was across the office and down the stairs in an instant. He moved as quickly as he could to the rear of the building, found the back door, and pulled it open.

Standing at the door, her hand lifted as if to knock, was Lydia.

He did not think, only reacted. He caught her about the waist—Christ, she was soaked, and the November night was frigid—and dragged her into the building, then slammed the door behind her.

"Is everything all right?" he demanded.

Her hood fell back from her face. Water ran in streams down her hair, plastering her cloak to her body. "Goodness. Yes, everything's perfectly well. I asked Nora to keep watch for Jasper at the house."

He had both his hands on her waist now. "What are you doing here?"

"I came to see you. I . . . was worried about you. You seemed upset."

"You were *worried* about me?"

She flushed at his words, a sunrise of colors in her skin. "I do not think it so absurd."

"No," he said immediately. He would not have her feel embarrassed—not because of him. "'Tis not absurd. Only I . . ."

Only he had not expected it. He could not think of the last time someone had said those words to him. He shook his head against the maudlin thought and tried again. "'Tis only that it's the dead of night and teeming down out there. How did you come to be here?"

She lifted her chin. "I had a groom and footman bring me in the carriage. This is not the first time I've come to Belvoir's alone, nor even the tenth. I—" She hesitated. "I could not sleep."

"God." He pulled her against him, pressing his chin to the top of her head. "You're wet through."

She wriggled. His body, fool thing that it was, reacted instantly and vigorously.

"Let me go before we're both soaked, for heaven's sake," she said into his shirtfront. "Let's go up to the office. I thought . . . I thought perhaps I could help you keep the watch."

He had to force himself to release her. God, he did not know why her offers of assistance—so freely made, so generously given— should make his chest ache like a finger pressed to a bruise.

He let her lead him up the stairs, and when she entered the office, he followed and shut the door behind him.

"'Tis a proper Scots rain tonight," he said, and crossed to the sideboard to pour her a glass of brandy. "In truth I don't expect Jasper will come before the morning."

When he turned, her hands were beneath her skirts. She'd shed her cloak and boots, and as he watched, she stripped one damp stocking off.

He bobbled the glass.

She looked up, face a little pink. "I like the weather. Even if it did ruin these stockings."

"Aye," he said. Her hair was dark from the rain, and the curve of mouth was all sweetness. "I like it as well."

He took himself to the cot, cupping her glass of brandy in one palm. She laid her stockings across the grate and then crossed to him, passing the desk.

As she did, her gaze flickered across the paper-strewn surface and she paused, arrested. "You read my pamphlets?"

He followed her gaze. He'd found the pamphlets here in the office as he'd prowled—*Some Reflections upon Marriage*; *On the Equality of the Sexes*; *Remarks on the Incalculable Evils of Debtors' Imprisonment*—all attributed to H, the pseudonym he knew she'd used. He'd read every one.

He'd felt a hot flare of admiration as he'd read her words. Pride in her ability to make herself heard despite her own shyness, despite a society that pushed women's voices to the margins. He could hear her in every line, dogged and persistent and devoted to the causes she believed in.

But it had not all been pleasure. As he'd read, he'd seen echoes of the conversations she'd had with Davis in their years of correspondence. And he'd feared—

All sorts of things, familiar and foolish. That he was clumsy and untutored. That he was no fit match for her clever, capacious mind, her clarity of vision. That he could not give her what she needed.

But he forced the fear aside. "Aye, I read your pamphlets. You've not frightened me away with your radical ideas, so dinna fash."

The corner of her mouth came up as she met his gaze. "You've not yet read the worst of them. Some are unpublished yet."

"I expect I'll bear up somehow."

Her smile widened. She came the rest of the way to his side and sat next to him on the cot's thin mattress. He passed her the glass of brandy, and their fingers brushed as she took it.

"You may have to reconsider your desire to abolish the aristocracy," he mused, "now that you're to be a countess."

She tipped her chin up, a little queenly gesture. "If you suppose I will not seek to undermine the system from within, then you are quite mistaken."

He laughed, and so did she, burying her face in her glass as she drank.

And then, to his perhaps unreasonable surprise, she tucked her legs up under her and eased her body against his. His arm automatically went around her, and she sighed a little, leaning into him.

God. He'd not known anything could feel like this, easy and warm and close-fitting, as though she'd been made to curl up beneath his arm. He ran his fingers along her forearm, relishing her softness.

Could he have this? Night after night, Lydia in his arms, luminous and quick-witted and brave enough to break his heart.

He wanted it. He'd never wanted anything so fiercely, though he knew that wanting was a terrible risk.

She rolled her glass between her palms, slowly, before she spoke. "I'm so sorry about today. About . . . Davis."

His grip on her tightened before he made himself relax. "You're sorry? Why?"

"I know it must have been difficult for you to see those plans this afternoon. To believe that Davis would use the rifle scope for violence."

He drew a breath, chest tight. "Aye, 'twas not easy. Though in truth I blame myself as much as Davis. Had I not invented the rifle scope, none of this would have happened. If I'd seen him for what he truly was, I'd not have let him know about the device in the first place."

She tilted up her face, her mouth close to his. "But that's absurd. You did nothing wrong. You cannot blame yourself for your brother's sins, Arthur."

"I assure you, I *can* blame myself, and most heartily."

"Whatever for?"

He felt his lips twist a little, and he choked back the bitterness before he spoke. "I should have known better. I should not have been blinded by what I wanted to be true and failed to see what was perfectly plain."

"What do you mean?"

Her voice was quiet—so quiet in the shadowed room. The coals in the grate had burned low, but he did not get up to stoke them. He only held her—his Lydia, his love—and thought about her family, all that tangled-up protectiveness and misunderstanding and affection.

He thought she would understand.

"I was five years old when Davis was born," he said, "and I thought he was mine. Our mam said I was afraid of him those first few months, but I don't remember that. All I remember was carting his fat wee body around wherever I went—the nursery, the kitchen, the burn. He liked jam cakes. For the longest time, he was afraid of fish."

It still, somehow, made him want to laugh. Davis had been bright-eyed and mischievous, always slipping away from his nursemaid to find Arthur wherever he was—but when Arthur had tried to teach him to catch trout in the river, the little boy had sobbed and then thrown them, one by one, back into the water.

"He was only nine when our father sent him to Eton. Younger than most of the boys there. He . . ."

Davis had been terrified. Their mother might have put a stop to it, had she still lived. But she had been dead a year already, and their father's cool authority had held sway then.

"He cried," Arthur said, "when our father loaded him into the carriage. Said he'd be good—he wouldn't tease the lambs any longer. I think he'd gotten it into his head that he was being sent away for something he'd done wrong. That was the worst sin he could think of, I expect. Teasing the lambs."

Lydia turned into him, her head beneath his chin. Her sweet-warm scent filled his lungs.

He locked both arms around her. "I wanted to go with him, but the earl wouldn't have it. He told me there was no sense in paying for me to go as well, when Davis had all the potential, and I . . ." He paused. Swallowed. "I was too young and foolish to oppose him then."

"No," she murmured. "Arthur. You were a child, and he was your father. You cannot blame yourself."

She'd abandoned her glass of brandy on the ground, and he nudged it away from the cot with the tip of his shoe. "Perhaps not. But I could have done more. When our father died, I thought things would be different between us." He'd hoped it would be so, with the cause of so much of their rivalry laid to rest. "I thought Davis would come back to Strathrannoch."

He'd wanted too much. He'd pressed Davis to return from London, where he'd lived with friends in the year since he'd finished at Eton. When Davis had demurred, he'd pushed harder. He could still remember how he'd felt, his pen pressed to paper as he'd looked around at his office, the shelves emptied of the books he'd sold to keep Davis at school. He'd loved Davis and envied him for so long that he could no longer see his way clear.

"I failed to bring him home. I charged him with neglecting

Strathrannoch, and in my guilt and shame, I only pushed him further away. I'd had years to observe the changes in him—to watch as our father—" He broke off, not certain how to say it.

Not certain he *wanted* to say it. Not to her. Perhaps it was foolish—she was here with him now, was she not? She had chosen to be with him, in the end.

But still and all, he did not want to tell her that the earl had always preferred Davis.

"He pitted you against each other?" she asked softly.

"Aye. You could say that."

But there hadn't been much of a competition, not really. Arthur had lost before he'd even begun.

He pressed his cheek to her hair. "I think . . . ah, God. I think part of me has never stopped seeing that little boy in him. Wanting to be good. Wanting to stay by my side. When he came to Strathrannoch Castle this year, it took no work on his part to persuade me that he was there to stay. I wanted to believe it."

"That's not a fault in you—never a fault. You love him. That doesn't just go away because you've been hurt."

"Aye," he murmured, "perhaps that's so."

So many things he'd thought he'd buried—deep in the past, alongside all his childish hurts—had begun to rise in him since Lydia had come to Strathrannoch Castle. A wish, sweet and painful, for a family of his own. A desire to be chosen for himself.

He could not find the words for what he wanted to say to her, to this woman who would be his wife. He did not know how to tell her that he wanted more than her hand in her marriage. More than her body.

He wanted her heart—her love—their future together. He wanted everything.

But perhaps—perhaps she knew, even without his saying it.

She had come, had she not? She was here, and he was not alone, and he had not even needed to ask.

"Thank you," he said. He found the delicate bones of her wrists and traced his thumbs along them. He felt a fierce and urgent gratitude as he held her, rising as sudden as desire inside him. "Thank you for everything."

"Oh," she murmured. Her hands turned over, so that he might press their palms together and interlink their fingers. "It was not me. It was Selina who arranged it all."

He gripped her hands in his. "'Twas all you, Lydia. You brought us to Haddon Grange. You got us into Kilbride House. You collected Davis's letters and papers, and you brought us to the person who could help figure everything out. And you—"

He swallowed against the hot unsteady feeling at the back of his throat. "And you're here. I'm—very glad that you're here."

She turned into him and tipped her face up. Kissing her, he found, was as urgent as his next breath. More.

She was warm and brandy-sharp. Her mouth—God, he never stopped thinking about her mouth, never stopped wanting it beneath his. He tasted the soft plump curve of her lower lip, traced his tongue along the arched top. She made a tiny sound in the back of her throat—a needing sound—and leaned into him, pressing her breasts against the thin fabric of his shirt.

He stroked up her waist, cupping one breast. She twisted into his hand, and he felt the taut point of her nipple through her dress. He teased it delicately with his thumb and forefinger, and she made another sound, louder.

Need tightened his belly and stiffened his cock, but he ignored the demands of his body. He nudged her legs to the front of the cot, bringing her feet flat to the ground. And then he went to his knees in front of her.

He almost did not know what he wanted. He wanted her—the desire to feel her body on his again was almost unbearable—but even more than that, he wanted to make her understand. He wanted to show her that he did not take her for granted. That her pleasure meant more to him than his own.

He wanted her to know she had not made a mistake in agreeing to marry him.

He wanted to believe that himself.

He looked up into her face. God, he loved the look of her from this vantage—the flush in her cheeks, the shadows cast by those rose-copper lashes. He loved the way her legs splayed apart to accommodate his shoulders as he knelt between her thighs.

He pushed her frock up. She wore neither petticoats nor stockings, only the thin dark blue fabric of her dress and her simple white chemise. Beneath her skirts she was all heat and softness, all bared skin. He brought his mouth to the inside of her thigh. "Can I?"

"Yes. Please."

Her voice was almost ragged. That unsteady rasp worked upon him—blurred his mind, unfocused him from his purpose—and he tried to recall himself.

It was difficult to think clearly. Everything about her aroused him—the hitch in her breathing, the tiny lift of her hips as his mouth trailed closer to her sex.

He found the crease of her pelvis and ran the tip of his finger along the shallow line, then traced the path with his tongue.

She whimpered. Her knees tightened on his shoulders, and her hips moved restlessly. He put his mouth to her sex and licked up, tasting her arousal, finding the tight bead of her clitoris with the tip of his tongue.

Jesus, she was so wet already. The knowledge that she wanted him rippled through him, flooding his body with an urgent, mindless heat.

He wanted to stand and lock her legs around his waist—Christ, he wanted to be inside her again. But he wanted to pleasure her more. He wanted her to come so hard she couldn't see, and then he wanted to make her come again.

He worked her clitoris with his tongue and ran his first two fingers through her wetness. She made another wordless sound. Her hips rose erratically toward where his hand met her flesh, as though her body felt the same driving need for completion that his did.

He eased back. "Tell me," he murmured. "Tell me what you want."

"I—I don't—Arthur, *please.*"

Her thighs were trembling. He rubbed one palm soothingly along her leg. With his other hand, he pressed two fingers just inside her. He felt her body squeeze down, drawing him in.

"You want to come, my love?"

"Yes—Arthur—don't stop."

God. He loved when she said his name. He loved to hear her, ragged and panting and on the edge. He loved knowing that he could stoke this flame in her, that his mouth, his hands, his body could give rise to the desperate need in hers.

He pushed his fingers all the way inside her.

"I will never have enough of this," he said. "Of you." He slipped his free hand to the soft slope of her belly, and she groaned, low and loud, as he brought his mouth again to her sex, as he worked her harder with fingers and tongue.

One of her hands came to his hair, grasping for purchase. Her hips bucked, desperate, and he pressed his palm against her abdomen to hold her in place. She gave a sobbing cry as he did so, at the way his fingers curled up, and then he felt the powerful rhythmic contractions of her body and tasted her release on his tongue.

She was wordless in her pleasure, all breath and heat, and as soon as she stopped clenching around him, he stood. His hands went to the buttons of her dress, unfastening them in a shaking rush, pulling her bodice down to reveal the pale bounty of her breasts.

The cot was too damned small. He caught her to him, spreading her legs to straddle his hips, and brought both of them down to the ground.

She gasped a little as she shifted in his lap, her knees pressed to his sides. There was still a fine trembling in her body that redoubled when he brought his mouth to one nipple. The groan on her lips was unsteady.

He flicked his lips across the taut peak, and she rocked against him. She reached for the fastenings of his trousers, but he would not let her. He locked his hand over hers and dragged their joined fingers beneath her skirts.

"I'm—" she gasped. "I can't—"

"Aye, you can." He teased her nipples with his mouth, with his free hand, watching them flush in the dim room. "There's no rush. Let me touch you a while."

She whimpered and clutched at his wrist.

He brought her up again slowly, a gentle suction at her breasts and careful rhythm between her legs. He was easy with her—patient—fighting back the clawing need that rose in him at the sight of her nipples wet from his mouth, at the clamp of her thighs around his hips. He brought her hand to her sex and urged her in soft earthy words to touch herself.

Her head tipped back, her throat exposed and her breasts arching forward. He wanted his mouth everywhere on her skin, wanted to taste every part of her. Jesus, he wanted to lick the perspiration that had beaded between her breasts, and then he wanted to slide his cock along that slick valley.

She started to tremble again as their fingers moved together, his inside her body and hers at her clitoris. Satisfaction licked along his skin. Yes, God yes, he wanted her to come again. He wanted—he wanted—

"Say my name," he said hoarsely.

"Arthur," she murmured.

The sound of his name on her lips felt almost like a release in itself—a physical pleasure, a throb of need.

He pulled his fingers from her body and she made a wordless sound of protest. Her lashes fluttered open, her eyes all dazed dark blue as she found his face.

"Say it again," he ordered.

"Arthur."

He thrust his fingers into her and heard a groan, a gasp, hers, his—he did not know. Her voice was a tactile thing, a pulse of bliss that tightened his bollocks as her fingers moved in time with his own. He felt almost uneasy at the pleasure engendered by his name in her mouth.

He had wanted to show her—wanted to prove to her that he could please her, that he could master his own need and attend to hers, again and again, until she was limp and boneless.

But his desire for her body was nothing to his need for her heart. That need had risen impossibly sharp, impossibly fast. He did not know how to control it. He could not.

Her lashes had fallen again, touching her cheeks.

"Open your eyes," he demanded. "Look at me."

She wrenched her eyes open. Her lips were parted; her hair was still wet from the rain.

"Come for me again," he said.

For me. Those were the words that he couldn't say alone, the words that clawed at his chest.

He wanted to satisfy her—God, he did, he loved the way she flushed and fractured—but it was not all for her. He wanted to bind her to him with pleasure, wanted her to know that he could shatter her again and again—wanted her never to need anything else but this. But him.

He felt unstrung, undone with desire, shamed by his selfishness and desperate for the feeling of her culmination.

"I want you with me," she said, her voice jagged. "Together this time. Please, Arthur."

He would never tell her no. He would give her anything she wanted, no matter the cost.

He wrenched his trousers open and then cupped her buttocks in his hands, lifting her. "Put your hands on me." His voice shook. "Take me in."

She did. Her fingers were heady, mind-numbing in their pleasure, and when he eased her down onto his cock, the single, slow, euphoric glide nearly brought him off.

She pressed her head against his shoulder, her soft breasts crushed against his chest. Her fingers tangled in his shirtfront, and her thighs began to tremble. He lifted her, pulled her closer and rocked up into her, small deep movements that took him, shaking, almost to the point of his own release.

She cried out at the moment of her crisis, and the word on her lips was his name.

I love you, he thought as he withdrew, as he spilled himself with a desperate gasp in the cradle of her thighs. *Always.*

But he kept the words inside him, alive in his heart, as fragile and endless as a flame.

Chapter 25

I am built for you, Lydia Hope-Wallace. My body and my heart were formed for the loving of you.

—*from the unsent papers of Arthur Baird*

She needed to go home, Lydia reflected as she sipped at her tea. But she did not want to.

Arthur had remained awake for the rest of the night, watching the back alley out the window from the desk chair, while she had curled up in the cot. Once the dawn had broken, she'd forced him with threats and various erotic bribes to exchange their positions and rest awhile. Tea had appeared as if by magic, and a tray of breakfast comestibles more than sufficient for her and Arthur together. Selina's work, Lydia had no doubt—the woman had probably known of Lydia's return to Belvoir's before Arthur had.

It was midmorning, and Arthur had just now risen and gone to perform what ablutions he could at the washstand Selina kept in an adjoining room. He was rumpled—they both were—and his whiskers had made a significant reappearance. She liked the whiskers, liked the way they drew her fingers to his face. He was more touchable whilst bearded—more plausibly hers.

She kept her eyes focused on the alley, lit now by the watery light of the morning post-downpour. She listened with half an ear to the noisy bustle of the street outside, the clacking of wheels and shouting of hawkers with their wares.

Arthur was uneasy; she could tell it. Though he'd held her for a long time in his arms before he'd gone from the room, she could sense a faint tension in him. She tried to tell herself that his distress was due to his worries over his brother—not to their impending marriage. She tried to tell herself that once they found Davis and Jasper, everything was going to be all right.

She was not a woman accustomed to optimism. But she believed in Arthur, his patience and his gravity and his tenderness. And she believed—more now than she ever had—in herself as well.

The clamor from outside seemed somehow to increase, though she could not discern what was happening on Regent Street—her only view was of the back alley. She came to her feet anyway, curious, and then Arthur returned through the adjoining door.

His shirt was open at the front and his neck gleamed with water. She watched, mesmerized, as a droplet beaded up and rolled down his throat.

She wanted to follow it with her tongue. She wanted—

The door to the office rattled. "Lydia? Arthur? Are you in there?"

It was Georgiana's voice. Lydia exchanged a surprised glance with Arthur, and he crossed to open the door before she could.

On the other side of the threshold, Georgiana stood, her hands full of papers and her usually pristine ringlets sweaty and tangled beneath her bonnet.

She came into the room and dropped the papers on the desk before yanking the bonnet off her head with a sound of relief. "Goodness. I had to walk the last ten streets. Traffic's stopped all over because of the parade."

The parade—yes, that explained the noise in the street, now that she thought of it. Lydia had read of Wellington's welcome-home parade in the papers the previous day, when she'd scoured Theo's office for news from the month she'd been away. It was going to take her several dedicated days to catch up on the various political intrigues she had missed. When she moved to Scotland, she was going to have to bribe Ned extravagantly to keep her informed.

Georgiana nudged the papers on the desk closer toward Lydia. "These are for you, from Selina. I was already over there this morning—she's collected everything she has on your brother, French agents, and the Home Office." Amusement threaded Georgiana's crisp voice. "After a clerk shut the door in her face yesterday on King Charles Street, I believe she's transferred her loyalties from the British government to you personally, Lydia."

Lydia seated herself at the desk and began to sort through the papers, trying to contain the grin that wanted to break out on her face. The very idea of Selina attempting to manage the Home Office and then being roundly rejected was . . .

Well, she pitied the Home Secretary, to be certain.

"Where does Selina mean to go next?" she inquired absently, flipping through the papers. They were not terribly enlightening— dates upon which Jasper had received correspondence at Belvoir's, annotations on the Home Office's crackdown on Bonapartists, real and imaginary.

"I believe she means to travel on to the Duggleby town house to visit Iris. Though even Selina cannot redirect Wellington's parade, so she may find herself run to ground until the bridge clears."

Lydia froze, one leaf of Selina's heavy writing paper still clamped between thumb and forefinger.

Georgiana's words—the notes before her—Davis's letters. The fragments spun, a thousand bits of colored confetti, and then resolved themselves into a picture in her mind.

Wellington.

Bonapartists.

The bridge.

"I know where he is," she whispered. "Davis. And the rifle scope."

Her eyes flew to Arthur's face. He'd taken a step toward her and then frozen, his hands locked on the back of a spindled chair, his knuckles gone white. "Where?"

"The parade." Her voice shook. "I saw the route in the papers yesterday. It goes across London Bridge and directly in front of St. Saviour's Church."

Arthur looked taken aback. "You think Davis is in the parade?"

"No." Oh God—she wished she was wrong, she *wanted* to be wrong. But she did not think she was. "I believe he's at St. Saviour's now. I think he means to fire into the parade."

Arthur's face had paled, but he did not contradict her, did not demand she explain her thinking. Only . . . "Why?" he said hoarsely. "Why would he do such a thing?"

"You said you overheard the Thibodeaux mention a duke, did you not? Now that the occupation of France has ended, the Duke of Wellington has returned to England. The parade is in his honor, meant to welcome him home. He'll be at the end of the parade, in full military dress and on display in an open box." She looked up and met Arthur's gaze, now trained intensely upon her. "Ever since the assassination attempt upon him in Paris in February, Wellington's gone nowhere without armed guards. But if Davis has the rifle scope, it does not matter if Wellington's guarded by half the Bow Street patrol. He'll be defenseless."

"Why would Davis want to use the rifle scope against Wellington?"

Her throat felt tight. She ought to have seen it sooner. With everything she knew of Davis—with the appearance of the Thibodeaux—with all her political knowledge, knotted into a thousand interlocking webs in her head—she ought to have predicted this.

"The first letters we ever exchanged discussed the participation of Scottish troops in the Napoleonic Wars. Davis said Wellington and his men lured the Scots with false promises, then unfairly compensated them for their efforts. He—"

She twisted her fingers together in front of her. "He never mentioned anything like this. But there is a substantial contingent of Bonapartists who have been exiled from France—the ones who organized the assassination attempt on Wellington in February. It's possible the Thibodeaux were a part of that group. And it's possible they brought Davis over onto their side."

Arthur's eyes were fixed on her face, his expression tight with suppressed emotion.

He believed her. That fact settled somewhere in her chest, even as anxiety clogged her throat. He trusted her without question.

Then his lashes came down as he turned and made for the door. "I'll go to the church. I have to try to stop him if I can."

Lydia found she was already on her feet. "I'll go with you."

He turned back to her and took a step in her direction. Another.

His eyes, rings of blue and green and gold, locked with hers. "No. No, Lydia. I need you to stay here. Wait for Jasper."

She shook her head in helpless negation. Her eyes burned; she could not see him clearly. "You can't go alone. You'll be defenseless. It might not just be Davis—it could be him and the Thibodeaux together. You—"

"I cannot let him do this, my love." His soft voice stilled her frantic words, and her heart clenched at the sound. "If there's any chance I can prevent him before it's too late, I have to try."

Of course he would think so. Not just to avoid an assassination, but to stop his brother. To save Davis, if he could, from doing something unforgivable.

I wanted to believe him, Arthur had said. *Part of me has never stopped seeing that little boy in him.*

Fear clutched at her throat, throbbing in her ears. *Don't*, she wanted to say. *Don't go, don't leave, I love you. Stay.*

But she could not ask that of him. Not now, not in this moment.

Georgiana had crossed to them, and now she reached into her reticule and removed a small pearl-handled pistol. She pressed it into Arthur's hands. "Take this. I'll run back to Selina's—we'll go to the Home Office together and tell them Lydia's suppositions." Her face was set and uncompromising. "We will make them listen this time."

Arthur's burn-flecked hand closed around the modest weapon, and Lydia's stomach turned over.

"If Lydia is right about this," Georgiana said, "there's still time. Wellington is meant to be at the end of the parade, not the front. You have an hour—perhaps more—to search the church and stop your brother."

He nodded, wordless gratitude writ plain on his face.

And then he turned back to Lydia. He reached out and

caught her around the waist with his free hand, drawing her hard up against his chest.

He kissed her. He kissed her like it was the last time he would ever have his mouth on hers, like he could breathe his stubbornness and determination into her body. He kissed her like his lips were a promise and his heartbeat a vow.

She kissed him back the same way.

When they broke apart, his hand cupped her cheek—once, gently—before falling away. "I'll be back for you," he said. "I'll be right back."

"Hurry," she whispered, and then the door closed, and he was gone.

It was some long moments before she looked down at the desk and realized he had not taken the pistol.

He had had only that single armament, that lone defense. And he had left it for her.

• • •

It took Arthur nearly the full hour to make it to St. Saviour's. The duchess's man at Belvoir's—either accustomed to misadventure or terrified by Arthur's general air of ferocious intensity—had not asked questions. He'd produced a hack with a sharp-eyed driver as if from nowhere, and Arthur had, quickly and urgently, communicated his desperation to get to St. Saviour's Church.

The driver had passed his thumb across his mustache, considered the congestion on the roads, and then hauled Arthur up front alongside him. And then he'd taken off.

Arthur had spent the journey staring at his ancient pocket watch and grinding his teeth. When they could make out the church in the distance, Arthur had leapt down and taken the rest of the street at a dead run.

The entrance to the church was obscured by scaffolding, but there were no workmen about, only milling pedestrians: street vendors, women carrying market baskets, children bundled against the cold and seated on their parents' shoulders. The parade was nearing its end, though Arthur could not yet see Wellington's carriage—it was still too far back to be visible.

But he knew—he knew all too well—that with the rifle scope, the distance would not matter.

He ducked behind the scaffolding and tested the church's front door, which seemed barred from the inside. He tried to force it open, but it resisted his efforts, so he continued on to the transept, shielded by shrubbery. Several yards down, he located a broken window, half hidden by a pile of refuse and building materials.

He forced his way inside. The metal frame scraped against his shoulder, but he ignored it.

Inside the church, the windows were set in ashlar—a cool, airy stone dressing that was marred by crumbling mortar. The remains of pews were heaped in piles near signs of active restoration: bricks and lime, ladders and trowels. Parts of the roof had collapsed, and the late-afternoon sun made bars of light along the stone floor.

He headed toward the tower at the center of the building, from which the transepts radiated. As he made his way up the dark, windowless stairway, his boot caught the edge of a rotted piece of wood paneling, which came away from the wall.

Jesus. He needed to find Davis before the whole tower came down around them

He hesitated a moment, then closed his fingers around the spongy wooden plank. A pitiful weapon, perhaps, but better than nothing.

And yet his mind recoiled at the thought. Could he truly use a weapon—any weapon—against his brother?

It felt impossible. But he would do what he must if it was the only way to stop Davis.

Arthur shifted the plank in his grip and moved more quickly up the narrow stairs, his lungs working, his heart racing in his chest. From exertion. And from fear of what awaited him.

At the top of the stairs, he found a single, tiny door. Beyond that door was the roof of the tower, the narrow crenellations he had seen from the ground—and Davis, if Lydia's suppositions were correct.

The door wasn't locked. He grasped the handle, eased the door open, and was briefly dazzled by the brilliant November sun and the crystalline blue of the sky.

When his vision cleared, he saw Davis, the butt of a rifle at his shoulder and the barrel pointed directly at Arthur's chest.

Beside him was Jasper Hope-Wallace.

Everyone froze: Davis with the rifle, Arthur with his plank, and Jasper with his hand on the pistol at his waist.

And then Davis lowered his weapon. "Arthur?" he said disbelievingly. "What the devil are you doing here?"

Jasper leapt into motion, pushing Davis aside and moving to the threshold where Arthur stood. "Have you come alone? Damn it, was there anyone else down there?"

Arthur felt blood pounding in his ears, his whole body tense, the muscles of his forearm knotted where he held the plank. "I'm alone. Hope-Wallace, what is this? Why are you with *him*?"

Davis was looking blankly from Jasper to Arthur and back again. "You know each other?"

"Yes," said Jasper grimly, "but your brother is meant to be in Scotland right now." He finished his perusal of what lay beyond the threshold and turned back to Davis, who was still standing between the stone crenellations, the rifle dangling from his hand. "The parade's nearly over. I don't think they're coming, Baird."

"Who's not coming?" Arthur demanded.

At the same moment, Davis said, "How in Christ's name do you two know each other?"

Jasper shoved the door closed with a bang. "I met Lord Strathrannoch when I was at Kilbride House. And why the hell he is not in Scotland where I specifically told him to remain, I cannot fathom."

All of Davis's attention was fixed on Arthur. He was blinking erratically, like a mechanical toy out of proper order. "You were at Kilbride House? Why?"

"I was looking for you, goddamn it! Did you think I would let you take off with the rifle scope and not try to track you down? I couldn't—I couldn't allow you to . . ." Arthur's gaze flicked to the rifle in Davis's hands, but the scope he'd designed was nowhere to be seen.

Jasper turned to Arthur, tipping his chin back so they were eye to eye. "Your brother stole your rifle telescope on my orders. He did not intend to use it."

"On your orders?" Arthur said. "Davis works for *you*?"

Davis was staring at them both, his jaw working, his face tense. He looked agonized, his green eyes blazing in the sun.

"Yes," Jasper said. "Davis has been working for me—for the Home Office—for nearly half a decade."

Arthur's mind reeled. Five years—over the last five years, Davis had seemed to abandon everything he'd once believed in. He'd ingratiated himself with the Scottish aristocracy he'd once despised. He'd supported—he'd *pretended* to support the Clearances.

All of it had been a lie.

"For eighteen months," Jasper went on, "we've been tracking a group of Bonapartists who mean to assassinate the Duke of Wellington. We stopped their first attempt in Paris on the strength of your brother's intelligence, but Davis learned that they meant to try again upon Wellington's return to London. This goddamned rifle scope was meant to convince them to trust Davis. It was meant to be the bait that lured them into the open."

Davis worked for the Home Office. Davis was not part of an assassination plot. He was working to stop one.

His brother had not intended to hurt anyone.

Relief was a detonation in Arthur's chest, an explosion so fast and consuming that he felt light-headed. "Bait?" he said hoarsely. "All of this was . . ."

"A trap," said Jasper. "A trap we've spent months cultivating." He slammed his hand against the stone crenellations, a quick powerful burst of frustration. "And it has not worked."

Davis was shaking his head, his black curls falling over his brow. "How did you know where to find us?" he asked Arthur.

"We found your papers in the boardinghouse in Haddon Grange, and Lydia figured out where you would be. We thought—we all assumed you meant to fire into the parade."

Jesus. Arthur felt a confused welter of emotions tangled in his chest. Guilt that he had believed Davis part of the assassination plot; relief that it was not so. Outrage, still, at the way that Davis had deceived Lydia.

And yet—had the deception of Lydia been part of the Home Office's plan as well—part of Davis's intelligence gathering?

I'm sorry, Davis had written to her, a letter he had never sent. *I don't know how to tell you.*

Davis, meanwhile, looked as though he had taken a blow to

the head. "Lydia? My Lydia? She knew about the rifle scope? She believed that it—that I—"

"Enough," Jasper said. His voice now contained neither the rich tones of Joseph Eagermont nor the frustrated affection of an older brother. He was clipped, fully in command. "We need to go. They're not coming."

"Whom do you mean?" Arthur asked. "Whom did you think to find here? The Thibodeaux?"

The silence that greeted his words was so complete that Arthur could pick out the individual sounds of the parade below: horseshoes striking the ground, a shout, the hoarse cry of a gull.

"What do you know of the Thibodeaux?" asked Jasper carefully.

"We know they're after Joseph Eagermont, the spy they uncovered in Kilbride House. We came to London together to warn you—we tried to contact you through Belvoir's Library." Anger met guilt and frustrated relief in him, rising to a boil. "For God's sake, if the two of you had only told us what was happening—do you realize the danger that you put Lydia in? She might have been targeted because of her connection to you—to *both* of you—and she had no idea of the risk."

Jasper's face had gone a sickly shade of white. "I told Lydia—I *told* her to go back to Strathrannoch Castle with you."

"She was worried for you," Arthur said. "If you supposed she would read your note and remain quietly at home when she believed you to be in danger, then you do not know Lydia as well as you think."

"Arthur." Davis's voice had a strange calm tone to it, an evenness that raised the hairs on the back of Arthur's neck. "Where is Lydia now?"

"She's at the library," he said, "waiting for her thrice-damned brother to show up so she can tell him about the French agents after him—the agents that the two of you already know about! The duchess left your signal in the office window yesterday and Lydia has been waiting there ever since."

"The book?" Jasper asked. "The red book?"

"Aye."

Davis lifted the rifle in one quick movement. Jasper flung open the door to the stairwell. "We have to go," Jasper snapped, vaulting easily through the small opening. "We have to go *right now*."

"Why? What the devil—"

Davis threw himself after Jasper, his dark head disappearing after Jasper's fair one. "The Thibodeaux know about the signal," he said. "They'll know how to find her."

Chapter 26

. . . she felt all over courage . . .

—*from Lydia's private copy of* PERSUASION

"Wait," Lydia said again. "A moment longer."

Georgiana stood anxiously at the door by which Arthur had left a quarter of an hour ago. She wanted to be gone—to take the news of Lydia's revelation to Selina and the Home Office.

But Lydia did not want her to go, not yet, not until she had something tangible to show the Home Office. Without Jasper, all they had were Lydia's insights, and she feared that, once again, speculation would not be enough.

She knew she could put together something that would convince them. Between Selina's notes and Davis's papers, there had to be a way.

If only her cursed fingers would stop shaking so! She blew out a frustrated breath.

"I think this might work," she said finally. She dipped her quill, making a quick annotation on one of Selina's records and circling a parallel in Davis's hand. "Take these and the drawing of St. Saviour's that Iris excavated. And the parade route in the papers. I think it might be enough."

Georgiana nodded and crossed the room to gather Lydia's documents. As she did, she passed by the window that overlooked the back alley. She paused, arrested, her face turned to the glass.

Lydia could see Georgiana's reflection in the pane, her expression frozen in shock and recognition.

"Lydia," she said evenly, "there is someone in the alley."

Lydia hurled herself across the room to peer out the window as well. Her heart leapt for a moment—perhaps it was Jasper, come with reinforcements from the Home Office—perhaps Arthur would not need to face Davis alone.

But it was not Jasper in the alley. It was a couple—a woman in a maroon walking dress and a portly man, balding under his beaver hat.

Claudine and Didier Thibodeaux.

A dozen thoughts crowded her mind, her emotions knotting, her breath catching in her chest.

If the Thibodeaux were here, that meant they were not with Arthur at St. Saviour's. It meant, perhaps, that Arthur was safe—or at least, as safe as he might be.

But—the Thibodeaux were here? How had they known to come to Belvoir's?

She wondered dizzily if perhaps they had been working *with* Jasper and not against him. Perhaps she had been wrong; perhaps they were not Bonapartists.

And then, from the window, she saw Didier Thibodeaux withdraw an iron bar from his coat and begin to prise open the back door. Within his jacket, she recognized the glittering metallic flash of a firearm.

No. They were not Jasper's allies.

Her heart started to beat again, double time, crashing painfully against her rib cage.

"We have to leave," Georgiana said, her voice still calm and even. "Right now. Down the stairs and out the front entrance—we'll blend into the parade-goers outside. They'll never see us."

Yes. Georgiana was right. The streets were crowded with people, with horses and carts and pedestrians decked with flowers. If they ran now, the Thibodeaux would not find them.

But if they ran—if Belvoir's was empty when the Thibodeaux made their way inside—what would the couple do next?

Her brain flicked through the possibilities like engravings in a book. The Thibodeaux—the empty office—St. Saviour's and the tower. Arthur.

She moistened her lips and forced the words past the thickness in her throat. "You . . . you go."

Georgiana turned sharply from the window, where they could see Didier Thibodeaux still striving at the door. "What do you mean?"

Lydia's mouth felt dry, her fingers numb. "If no one's here, they'll realize something's wrong."

"Let them realize! We will not be here to face the consequences."

"But where will they go from here?" She tried to swallow and could not quite manage it. "They might go to St. Saviour's. They might find Arthur there. But if I remain here, I can keep them distracted. You and Selina can send reinforcements to capture them and—and Arthur will be safe."

Even as she said the words, she could hear her plan for the mad impulse it was.

She could run with Georgiana. She *ought* to run. That was the safer choice by far.

But she could not do it. She had to try to protect Arthur—there was no possible course of action other than that. She would never run—*never*—if running meant putting the man she loved at risk.

She had thought of herself for so many years as a wallflower—as someone who hid from the sight of others, who kept herself in shadow. And perhaps, in some ways, that was true. But that was not all she was.

She had stood beside her friends when scandal had broken over them. She had written her pamphlets despite the risk. She had, in her own quiet way, worked to make the world a better place.

She knew when the risk was worth the potential for disaster. And protecting Arthur was worth any sacrifice she might make.

She could stop the Thibodeaux. She knew she could.

"Lydia." Georgiana's voice cracked on the word, and Lydia met her friend's agonized gaze. "I cannot abandon you."

"You must." Didier had pried open the back door partway; there was a splintering sound audible even through the window. "Selina's footman is downstairs—he'll try to stop the Thibodeaux if he realizes what's happening. Go downstairs, take the footman, and run to the Stanhope residence. Tell Selina to send the Home Office. I'll keep the Thibodeaux busy here."

"I can't leave you behind!"

Lydia reached out and gripped Georgiana's hand. "I need you to do this. Until the Thibodeaux are caught and the rifle scope destroyed, we will never be safe. We cannot let them go free if we have the chance to stop them. And I—I cannot let them go after Arthur, not if there's something I can do to prevent it."

"Curse you," Georgiana said. But she moved to the door, her skirts in her hands and her face ferocious. "I'll be back with the cavalry. Don't forget about the bloody pistol—and don't you dare let them shoot first, or I'll come back and kill you myself."

"I promise." Her voice trembled, just a little, and she could not bring herself to mind.

Georgiana gave her one last blistering look, and then she ducked out the door, pulling it closed behind her without a word.

Lydia took a single shaky breath. Then she made herself walk briskly over to Selina's desk and sit down behind it. The front of the enormous desk went all the way to the ground. They would not be able to see the lower half of her body—not unless they dragged her out of her chair.

She reached out and picked up the pearl-handled pistol from where Arthur had left it. It felt small and solid in her clammy palms. Her fingers slipped across the metal bore as she slid it into her lap and tucked it into the folds of her skirts.

She was still sitting there, her hands locked on the gun and the gun wrapped in her dress, when the door burst open.

•   •   •

The horse's flanks bunched beneath Arthur's thighs and he tried—it took powerful physical effort—not to push the beast into a gallop.

Jasper had commandeered the mounts of three uniformed men straight out of the parade with a low-voiced whisper and a few choice names. The young soldier on the bay had practically flung his reins at Jasper in a burst of fervent subordination.

Once they were mounted, Jasper had led them alongside the parade route, picking their way through the maze of pedestrians and bellowing orders when they seemed to be slowing. Arthur wanted to give his horse its head, but there was no use—they were going as fast as they could. It felt like a crawl.

Lydia. All he could think about was Lydia, and the fact that the Thibodeaux knew where she was.

"How do they know?" he asked Davis at his side. His voice was tight and rough, and his hands felt clumsy on the reins. "How do they know about your signal?"

Davis hesitated a moment before replying. His horse was a large bony chestnut, tall enough that Davis's head was level with Arthur's own. "'Twas in a letter that I passed along to the Thibodeaux from Hope-Wallace. I could tell they were growing suspicious—I had to prove my loyalty somehow. But I cleared it with Hope-Wallace before I gave it to them, damn it!"

"And none of you thought to inform the duchess?"

Davis swore blisteringly. "No one from the Home Office was meant to use the library for communication again. There's no reason that book should have been in the window."

"Well it was. And now Lydia is there, bloody *defenseless*, because the pair of you had to keep your goddamned secrets!"

There was a long pause before Davis spoke again, and when he did, his voice was raw. "Was she well? The last time you saw her. Was she all right?"

Somehow Arthur felt he had not stopped seeing her. Her face was always before him—pale and tense as she told him to hurry, soft with sleep as she lay on the cot. Flushed and smiling at him in endless moments, the light playing in the curves and dips of her mouth, lingering on the shape of her happiness.

"Aye," he said, "she was all right."

"She knows, then? That—that I was the one who wrote the letters?"

"Aye." The horse wanted to run; Arthur could feel it. He let up on the reins and squeezed his knees, just enough for his gray to push its nose ahead of Davis's mount and press closer to Jasper's.

They were over the bridge; the roads were clearing.

They could get to her in time. He would make it so.

"I'm sorry," Davis said.

Arthur turned his head to look at his brother: dusty and familiar and somehow edged with despair, his body a line of tension atop the chestnut horse. Davis was not looking at him, only staring straight ahead.

"For what?"

"I'm sorry I stole the scope. I never meant for you to be involved. I never meant any of this."

"I don't care about the goddamned scope," he said, and found to his surprise that he meant it. He understood why Davis had done it. He knew Davis's intentions had been good. "But I don't understand why you could not tell me the truth. If I'd known—"

"You would not have believed me."

"Of course I would have—"

Davis turned sharply, his eyes bright and vehement. "Would you? If I'd told you I needed the scope but I could not tell you why? If I said I'd been lying to you—to everyone—for nigh on half a decade but I could not explain any of it?"

Arthur's chest felt tight, and he had to look away as Jasper ahead of them angled his horse down an alley and picked up speed.

Would he have trusted Davis? He would have wanted to. But his beliefs about Davis had been informed by a lifetime of rivalry, by five years of lies. What he thought of his brother—and of himself—had been twisted up into a wrong shape and had long ago calcified.

What would it have taken to break away from that old familiar shell? What would have been required to shatter it?

"I don't know," he answered honestly. "I don't know what I would have thought. But I can tell you truly now that I understand why you acted as you did when it comes to the rifle scope. But why"—his jaw went tight, and he had to force himself to get the words out—"why did you lie to Lydia?"

Davis shook his head. "I don't understand how any of this happened. She was never meant to be involved. She was meant to be at home, safe and unaware of all of this. I . . ." He hesitated. "I was going to tell her. When all of this was over, the French agents captured, I was going to tell her the truth."

"I don't understand why you lied to her in the first place."

"I never intended for it to go this far. I thought to gather some intelligence—I did not even know her identity at first! 'Twas half a year of passing information to the Home Office before I learned she was Hope-Wallace's sister. And then—Christ, by then the lie had gone on so long I did not know how to extricate myself and still—and still—"

"Still what?"

Davis's horse pressed forward, its head outstripping Arthur's mount. "Still keep her!"

The words lodged somewhere between Arthur's ribs, a hot heavy weight.

It had not been one-sided, then. They had had feelings for one another, Lydia and Davis. That much had not been a deception on Davis's part.

Davis was not a traitor. Lydia had believed in him, and she had not been wrong.

All those letters—all that correspondence—Davis and Lydia had been aligned in truth, not just in pretense. Davis *had* been the man Lydia had come to Scotland for. Arthur had been wrong.

"What would have been left if I told her the truth?" Davis said harshly. "How could she forgive me once she knew I'd deceived her?"

"Davis—"

His own gray horse had nudged forward again, but Davis pressed his knees into his chestnut's flank and shoved ahead. "No, goddamn it. I wanted her to choose me—to want *me*—and all along she believed that I was you. Do you know what that was like?"

"Of course I do." His horse rocked into a canter. They were coming past Jasper, squeezing together through the narrow alley.

"Strathrannoch," Jasper snapped, but Arthur waved him back. "I recognize the streets. I know the way."

Davis's feet in their stirrups jostled Arthur's own. Davis's voice dropped, a clear imitation of the old earl. *"You're all surface, boy, no substance*—that's what he used to tell me. You were the steady one, the one he trusted with the estate, with the tenants. I was good for nothing so much as dinner parties. Even with Lydia, 'twas your name—your ever-honorable bloody words—that won her over."

Arthur almost could not make sense of his brother's words. *He* had been the one his father had trusted?

Davis had been the favored son. Davis had been the one their father had made much of—the one he'd sent to Eton, the one he'd taken to meet his friends. The earl had told Arthur—again and again, with his words and his actions—that Davis was the son he valued more, the one who ought to have been his heir.

But—the realization was slow and sweeping, crashing like a wave through his understanding of their past.

Their father had sought to foster rivalry between them. Their father had told Arthur time and again that he was less worthy than his brother.

But what had he told Davis?

Arthur had assumed that when they were alone together, the earl had praised Davis, the same way he'd always done in Arthur's hearing.

But he did not know that, not really. He had not heard what their father said in private. *All surface*, Davis had said, *no substance*. He could hear it in their father's voice—the way the earl would have said the words and laughed.

Arthur had not seen it. It took him hard and suddenly—how many things about his brother he had failed to see.

He had been wrong about Davis. He had *wronged* Davis. And he had not—he had not protected him from their father's influence. Had not even known that his brother needed his protection.

His voice came out unsteady. "Wait. Hold a moment."

His brother was leaning over his horse's mane now, pushing ahead. "I didn't need him. Or you or Strathrannoch. I made my own way."

The resentment on Davis's face was as familiar to Arthur as the shape of his own hands. He knew it in every bone and sinew; it colored so many memories.

But not all of them. He could look at his brother's dark head, bent over his mount, and see the boy who'd thrown the trout, one by one, back into the river.

And then Davis looked up. His knuckles had gone white on the reins. "But oh—Christ, Arthur. This time I cannot do it alone. We have to get to her in time, and I need—I—" His voice cracked, his words stumbling to a halt unfinished.

But he did not need to finish. Arthur knew what he meant.

"Aye," he said. His own voice was hoarse, barely audible over the sound of his gray's hooves on the street.

He knew precisely how hard it was to ask for help when you

did not believe that you deserved it. When you did not think it would be freely given.

Anger, fear, regret—none of that mattered now. Nothing mattered except making sure that Lydia was safe.

"We're almost there," he said roughly.

Davis did not look at him when he spoke. "I can't let her be hurt because of me."

"It's all right," Arthur told his brother. "We're going to make it in time. I swear it."

Chapter 27

To my dear br— J—

> *—fragment of a note left at Belvoir's,*
> *ink-smeared, illegible*

Lydia was starting to suspect that Claudine Thibodeaux did not have a weapon on her person.

If she'd had one, Lydia was fairly certain Claudine would have pulled it out and fired the third time Lydia knocked over the inkwell.

Unfortunately, Didier's pistol was still trained on Lydia's chest and had been since the moment the Thibodeaux had come through the door. They'd been expecting Jasper in the office, but they had not been disappointed to find her instead. In the confusion, it had become clear to Lydia that though they still did not know Jasper's true name, they had uncovered the fact that he was her brother from the note he'd left in her chamber at Kilbride House.

Lyd, he'd written, *I've been called back to London. I'll break the news of your marriage to Mother. Stay here in Scotland with Strathrannoch.*

They knew Jasper was her brother—and they knew he was a spy.

The larger revelation to Lydia, though, was the fact that Davis had not been working with the Thibodeaux, as she'd believed, but rather for the Home Office alongside Jasper.

Traitre, Claudine had called him. Traitor.

Lydia's first reaction had been a relief so potent it nearly knocked her from her chair. Arthur—Arthur was going to be so happy. His rifle scope would not be used for violence. His brother—his beloved baby brother—had not intended to hurt anyone.

But her relief had been short-lived. She'd been mistaken about the Thibodeaux's plans—they all had. Once the Thibodeaux had worked out Davis and Jasper's association from the letters in her chamber, they had altered their scheme.

Now, it seemed, they meant to mount an attack on the Home Office itself. And they thought to use Lydia as bait.

His pistol pointed at her chest, Didier had informed Lydia in no uncertain terms that she was to write to Jasper at the Home Office and tell him to come and find her at Belvoir's. They meant to lure him here and then—

Well. They had not said precisely, but Lydia did not think it boded well for Jasper.

She'd dithered and dallied, allowed her voice to tremble pitifully. For once, the tears that came easily to her eyes felt not like a vulnerability but a strength.

Let them think her helpless. Let them believe she was not a threat. She held Georgiana's pearl-handled pistol tight against her thighs.

Eventually they'd proven averse to further distraction, and so she'd progressed to writing the note that they'd demanded. She'd spelled every third word wrong on purpose, but either Didier was scarcely literate in English or he thought that she was, because he had not mentioned it.

"How would you like for me to sign it?" she asked desperately.

"In whatever fashion allows you to finish this goddamned letter in as few words as possible." Didier's patience seemed stretched to its limit.

"Well, generally I sign notes to him, *Your loving sister*, but as this one will be arriving at his place of work, I wonder if that's not entirely appropriate—"

There was a solid crash on the door to the office, a noisy splintering of wood.

Didier whirled. Claudine produced a pistol of her own and aimed it at Lydia from across the room.

The lock held. The door stayed closed.

"Lydia!"

It was Arthur's voice, rough and familiar. Relief flooded her—gratitude—love—and fear too. Fear most of all.

Arthur was at the door, the wood a fragile barrier against a weapon.

"Get back!" she shouted. "Get away from the door! It's the Thibodeaux—they each have a pistol—they—"

Claudine lifted her gun. Lydia shrieked and threw herself beneath the desk just in time for the sound of an explosion.

Oh God. Oh no. Oh God.

She couldn't see anything. The front of the desk touched the ground—she was boxed in on three sides by thick wooden panels. Damn it, who had been shot? What had happened?

She had to know. She picked up the gun from where she had dropped it on the rug and crawled toward the side of the desk. Didier Thibodeaux's hat lay on its side on the ground.

When she'd gone far enough to make out the contours of the room, she froze. The door had burst inward, the sound drowned out by the explosion of gunfire. She could see Didier's back, his arms bracing his pistol. Beyond him, she could see Jasper and—she could not make out any more figures in the sliver of room that was visible to her. But Arthur—she knew she had heard Arthur's voice.

Her ears rang, and the scent of gunpowder was acrid in her nose and eyes. There was plaster dust in the air.

The gunshot. Where had it gone? She craned her neck to try to see. It was difficult to tell from her vantage on the floor, but it seemed likely that Claudine had fired into the wall behind the desk.

She cautiously wiggled her fingers and toes, then put her free hand—the one not brandishing a pistol—to her face.

No blood. Everything seemed in working order. She was fairly certain she had not been shot.

"Gentlemen," said Didier, "there is no need to act in haste."

He was not facing her. She did not know if he had seen her. Her fingers tightened on her weapon.

Could she shoot him, if she needed to? But oh God—what if she missed? What if the bullet ricocheted and hit someone else?

There was a muffled sound, a suggestion of motion that Lydia could not see.

"Stop," Didier said sharply. "Do not come any closer, Strathrannoch, or I will shoot you where you stand."

"You're down to one gun," Arthur said. "You're outnumbered. If you use your gun on me, the others will have free rein to shoot you and your wife both."

"Yes," Didier said, "but you will still be dead. Do not underestimate the satisfaction that would give me."

"How satisfied do you think you'll feel if you are six feet underground, Thibodeaux?" This was Jasper's voice, she knew—but she scarcely recognized her rakish, laughing brother in those icy words.

"If you shoot Strathrannoch," Jasper went on, "I will kill you myself. I rather think they'll give me a medal."

"Well," Didier said, "it appears we are at an impasse then."

His broad shoulders flexed beneath his jacket. His gun—he was lining his pistol up to take a shot.

Now, Lydia thought. *Now is the time you act.*

She leapt to her feet.

Everyone in the room whirled toward her. Every eye was on her—Arthur's beloved face taut and pale; Jasper's lips parting on a shout; Didier's pistol trained, once again, on her own body.

She was sick with terror. She could barely feel the gun in her fingers.

But she could do this.

She held the gun out shakily, allowing it to dangle loose in her hand. "Let them go," she gasped. "Please, Jasper. Don't do this. Don't let this become a firefight. Just . . . let them go."

"Lydia," her brother rasped. He held his pistol almost casually in front of him, but nothing about the lines of his body suggested ease.

Oh God. She might be wrong. This might be a mistake. But she thought—she was almost certain . . .

"Please," she said. She looked at Jasper, trying to show him with the force of her expression that she meant what she said. "I need you to do this."

He looked back. His blond hair was damp with perspiration; his mouth a grim line.

Trust me, she tried to tell him. *I need you to believe in me.*

And, slowly, Jasper stepped aside, leaving the threshold open for the Thibodeaux to walk through. The door hung crazily at an angle, the frame half-shattered.

Gratitude blossomed inside her, even as Jasper's grim expression went grimmer. Cautiously, she deposited the pistol on the desk in front of her. "Go," she said, shifting her gaze to Didier. "They're letting you go. This is the best chance you'll have to get away safely. Take it and run."

Didier's eyes flicked across the room, from Claudine and Jasper to Arthur and the remaining figure—a lean, dark-haired man who had to be Davis Baird.

Ever so slowly, Didier pivoted, his back to the open door and his gun trained on Lydia. He jerked his head toward Claudine. "You first," he said in French. "Take the stairs. I will be right behind you."

Claudine, her face contorted with fury, did as she was bade.

The dark-haired man—Davis—had begun to ease himself in Lydia's direction. The tip of Didier's pistol shifted from Lydia to Davis and back again. "What do you think you are doing, Baird?"

"Standing," Davis said. His accent was identical to Arthur's, though his voice was lighter, a smooth tenor. He took another step, putting his body between Lydia and Didier's firearm. "I'm not in your path, Thibodeaux. The door is right behind you."

Didier nodded once, his gun still fixed chest-high. And then he stepped backward through the threshold and moved cautiously to the stairs.

"Shut the door," Lydia choked out.

Arthur was the closest. He shoved the broken door back against the shattered frame and held it fast with his body.

She could not tear her eyes from his face. He was still haggard, his hazel eyes dark with fear and locked upon her. She wanted to throw herself at him; she wanted to beg him to come away from the place where the Thibodeaux had gone. She wanted to drag him underneath the desk, wrap herself in his safe, solid body, and never move again.

"Lydia," said Jasper, "what in God's name—"

"Go to the window," she whispered, still staring at Arthur. "Look outside."

There was a shout, a gunshot, the sound of clamor. She pulled her gaze from Arthur and turned to Jasper as he crossed the room in two long strides.

He looked out the window and his mouth came open in shock. "What the devil—"

Tears of relief were spilling from Lydia's eyes, hot and cleansing. "I told Georgiana to bring reinforcements. I heard sounds in the alley a few minutes before the three of you came exploding through the door. I thought—I hoped—I believed Georgiana and the Home Office would be here. I did not think the Thibodeaux would get away."

But she had not known. She had not been certain.

And Jasper had trusted her anyway.

"It's them," Jasper said. "My agents. They've captured the Thibodeaux." His voice had lost the sharp air of command. His shoulders had softened, his whole body seeming to let go of some indefinable attitude of tension and responsibility. His hand, as he lowered his gun, was trembling slightly. "It's over. It's over, Lyddie."

She sat down hard in the desk chair. There was plaster dust all over it—the hole in the wall was not so far above where her head had been in the seconds before she dove under the desk.

And to her surprise, the man who could only be Davis Baird

fell to his knees in front of her. He reached out and clutched her hands in his.

She stared at him in utter consternation.

He was certainly Arthur's brother—there was no doubt of that. His hair was darker, and he was built on a smaller scale, his body lean and compact—but the curls were Arthur's, and the cheekbones, and the arched curve of his mouth.

"Lydia," he said hoarsely. "I'm so sorry."

She blinked down at him. There was a tiny raw scrape across his cheek. Her dark blue dress was smeared across the knees with plaster dust. Their hands were locked together in her lap.

Six weeks ago—or else a thousand years—she had imagined that the first time she met the man with whom she'd corresponded since 1815, they would simply recognize each other and fall into the habit of conversation built by three years of letters.

And somehow, her imagination had been right.

She recognized him. She *knew* him, Davis Baird. He had deceived her, had used her for information—but he had not meant to hurt her. He'd wanted to tell her the truth and had been prevented from doing so by forces beyond his own will or desire. She could forgive him for the secrets he'd kept, just as she could forgive her own brother.

"It's all right," she said. "Davis. It's all right."

"It's not." He looked up. His face was pale and fixed intently on hers, his green eyes fierce and encompassing. "I know I have no right to ask this of you," he murmured, "but—will you marry me?"

There was a very long silence.

Her brain refused to parse the words he'd said. It seemed distantly possible that she'd forgotten how to speak English. Perhaps the gunfire at close proximity had broken something inside her ears.

"I—beg your pardon?" she choked out.

He stared up at her, his expression tender and hopeful. "Make me the happiest man in the world," he said earnestly. "Marry me, Lydia Hope-Wallace."

There was a long frozen moment in which she tried to think what she could possibly say to such a thing.

Then she lifted her eyes to where Arthur stood bracing the door.

But he was not at the door any longer. The threshold was empty, the door swinging slowly and crookedly on its broken hinge. She could see the long hall, the wooden stairs—the corridor silent and still as a grave.

Arthur was gone.

Chapter 28

I see now that I should have spoken. I waited too long. With my silence, I let you think that I did not love you, when love for you was the marrow of my bones. If there is one thing I regret above all others, it is that. That I let you believe, even for one instant, that you were less than everything to me.

—from the unsent papers of Arthur Baird

He had wasted a fortune in paper, Arthur reflected as he stared blearily about the downstairs drawing room at Strathrannoch Castle.

He'd started the first letter to her within hours of buying his fare on the mail coach. He'd been surrounded by letters—had watched the mailbags fill and empty and fill again as the post was delivered—and he'd thought, *Yes. Write to her. Tell her how you feel.*

He'd started to write on a fragment of an envelope dropped by a grandmother in the seat beside him, which seemed to him an unfortunate metaphor for the state of his suit. What a prize for the woman he loved beyond measure: a torn piece of paper, used and discarded by a stranger.

But he'd taken up the scrap and put his pencil to it right there in the coach, desperate to find the words to tell her—everything. The declaration that had frozen, time and again, upon his tongue. The words he did not know if she would welcome or spurn.

He wanted, foolishly, for her to have letters from him. Real letters—not his own words in Davis's hand. Nothing but the truth of his heart, plain and painful and unvarnished.

He tried to summon forth the words—again and again he tried, scribbled apologies and confessions and avowals.

But everything came out wrong. With each mile the mail coach put between them, his sense of apprehension grew. He'd thought—

Oh God, he'd thought he was doing the right thing. Leaving her there. Removing the impediment of his presence.

But as the carriage took him farther and farther in the direction of his home, every revolution of the wheels felt wrong. He'd wanted to give her the gift of time and freedom, had wanted her to have the chance to know her own mind—to sort out whether or not Davis *was* the better match for her.

But that was not the whole of his motivation. He could admit that to himself now.

When he'd heard her soft words of forgiveness, heard Davis's heartfelt proposal, the only thought in his mind had been to flee. He had not wanted to know what her response would be. He'd seen her cheeks grow pink—with embarrassment? With pleasure? He had been afraid to find out.

She was loyal beyond belief. He knew she would not want to throw him over, not when she'd given him her word. He'd been terrified that when she looked up and met his eyes, her face would be written with nothing so much as horrified regret.

And he—

God forgive him, some part of him had wanted to protect his little brother from pain. He couldn't separate out his tangled emotions—his regret over their past, his years of resentment. Somehow, he had not wanted Davis to be hurt—even though the very thought of losing Lydia made him feel scorched inside, hollowed-out and desperately alone.

So he'd fled.

But it seemed to him now, as he tried to find the words to write, that what he'd meant as a noble gesture—pulling away, freeing her from obligation—was more cowardice than generosity. He'd left her there without a single word—and he could not sort out how to ask her forgiveness, not when he was still five hundred miles away.

As he dipped his pen again, the door to the drawing room came open. He looked up, blinking at the figure silhouetted against the rectangle of light.

What *time* was it? He had arrived at the castle at twilight and had gone straight to the drawing room to try to finish—begin?—*finish* the letter of explanation and apology he meant to send to Lydia. He had not thought so very many hours had passed, but the amount of light pouring in through the threshold suggested otherwise.

He glanced at the room's moth-eaten drapes, which were, he supposed, limned with wintry sunlight. Was it *midday*? Of the *next* day?

And then he looked back at Bertie, who still stood framed dramatically in the doorway.

"Yes," he said, "come in."

Bertie crossed to the desk and seated himself. "I did not realize I required permission."

Arthur pressed the heel of his hand to one eye, behind which a headache had gathered several days earlier. "You don't. Of course you don't. This is your home as much as it is mine."

Bertie glanced down at the papers spread haphazardly across the desk, written and cross-written, the words scratched out and started again.

I have made many mistakes in my life born of fear or desperation or the desire for safety . . .

You stagger me . . .

I should never have let you go . . .

Arthur dropped his hand, intending to sweep the inchoate mass into a pile, then gave up on the notion and let his fingers splay open across the ink-spattered words.

"Strathrannoch," Bertie said bluntly, "what the devil is going on?"

Arthur's hand closed into a fist and then loosened again. "I scarcely know where to begin. I—"

"When did you return?" Bertie's voice was curt, almost distant. Arthur felt uneasiness curl inside him at the sound.

"Last night. I've been here in the drawing room. I wanted to . . . finish something I'd started. I—"

"And you did not think to let me know that you had arrived?"

He had. Of course he had. Only he'd been half-paralyzed, desperate to finish his letter to Lydia and afraid—still afraid—to finally put his feelings into words.

But he had forgotten, somehow, in all the turmoil of his anguish and his desires, that he was still Strathrannoch, and that he could not abandon the people who relied upon him. He had been gone from Strathrannoch for nearly a month. He ought to have thought about something other than himself.

"I'm sorry, Bertie. I did not realize how long I had been in this room." The words sounded inadequate to his own ears, unconvincing. He stared at the papers spread out beneath his hand. "I'd meant to come to you today. This morning. I know I should have found you immediately—I don't doubt there's much to speak of about the estate and the tenants after my absence." There would be papers to sign and seal, small disasters to resolve. He'd missed Polly Murray's wedding—he would need to make up for that. "I ought not have shirked my responsibilities to you or to Strathrannoch."

"Arthur."

He looked up, startled. Even after a decade, Bertie rarely called him by his Christian name.

Bertie had taken off his spectacles and begun polishing them with quiet aggression. "What have I done to convince you that my first reaction would be not to welcome you home, but to reproach you for your failures?"

Arthur said nothing in response to the other man's words—could think of no possible answer. He felt arrested, somehow, his thoughts unable to keep up with the sudden painful acceleration of his heartbeat.

He could not quite seem to make sense of himself. Bertie rarely criticized him, and certainly never for lack of care to the estate.

And yet that had been his first thought. Bertie was here, and upset, and the only thing that Arthur could conceive of was that he was failing, again, as Strathrannoch. That he was not enough. That he would never be enough.

"I suppose I thought so because it is your position," he said finally. It was an answer—and, somehow, underneath, it was a question he could not find the courage to ask. In the corners of his own foolish lonely heart, it was the same question he had not been able to ask Lydia. "That's why you are here, you and Huw—for Strathrannoch. For the earldom."

Is it? Is that the only reason you are here?

If you had the freedom to go anywhere, choose anything—would you still remain?

"Is that all it is, then?" Bertie's voice was clipped, but his tone could not hide the hurt in his words, and Arthur felt their impact in his chest. "We are your employees and nothing else?"

"No. Of course not. Not to me. But I hired you—I pay your wages. I understand that I should not . . . that I cannot expect more from you."

Bertie laid one hand flat against the desk, covering the papers with his deft slender fingers. "Expect more."

"I—I don't know—"

"Expect more," Bertie repeated. "You deserve to expect more. Damn it, Huw and I deserve better than this!"

Arthur pushed back in his chair, away from the words, and looked blindly down at the desk.

Huw and Bertie deserved better. Better than Strathrannoch. Better than him. He had known it was true for a long time now.

Grief seized him, and he tried to push it back, tried not to let Bertie see. If they wanted to go—

He would not force them to stay on with him out of guilt or obligation. Or because they realized how much he needed them.

"If there's something I can do," he said hoarsely and then broke off. Jesus. He was tired from the trip on the mail coach, that was all. That was the reason his eyes burned.

He tried again. "If there is some alteration to your positions I can provide, I will do so. I would like—for you to be happy." His voice had cracked on the words, and he wanted to say, *Anything. Don't go.*

But he could not say that.

"If you have decided to move on"—his voice was thick, and it was so hard, sometimes, to do the right thing—"I will of course provide a character."

Bertie fixed him with a keen-eyed glare. "Listen to me, Arthur Baird, and listen well, for I do not intend to repeat myself. We do not want to leave Strathrannoch. Not even when you are being very foolish, as you are right now."

The words took hold inside him, a relief like the quenching of white-hot steel.

They did not want to go. They did not.

"I'm sorry," he got out. "I've—"

"I am not finished."

He closed his mouth.

"Despite what you seem to believe," Bertie went on sharply, "we are not here only for the estate. We are here for *you*, and you are more than the title. You are more than the earldom. You may have been the heir to a blackguard, but despite his best efforts, you are not one yourself."

Arthur took a breath, his lungs working in a chest gone tight.

He had spent so much of his life trying not to seek out approval. Telling himself he did not need affirmation or loyalty or love. But the words from this man—who had been more of a father to him than his own—came to him with the gentle devastation of a fresh-sharpened blade.

It was impossible to lie to himself now. He needed the words. He needed to hear it.

Bertie's voice had softened, but his next words still landed with the force of a blow. "Your father may have believed that a man is made by tearing down others, but he was wrong. His hardness was not strength. It was brittleness. It was fragility."

"I know," Arthur said shakily. "I have learned that from—from the two of you."

From Bertie and Huw he had learned the kind of manhood that he believed in: gentle and steadfast, loving and loyal. They were the pattern upon which he had tried to mold himself, the kind of person he wanted to become.

Arthur watched the black ink grow blurred on the papers in front of him. He tried to steady his voice before he spoke. "I did not mean to let you down. I am sorry that I've made you feel as though you were no more than employees to me. You've always been more than that. From the very first."

"Then stop acting as though you do not have a family," Bertie murmured. "Because you do."

Bertie's words pressed down upon him, scoring themselves along his skin. What had he told Bertie, all those weeks ago, when Lydia had first come to Strathrannoch Castle?

That he did not need love or family. That he did not want those things.

Because he had been afraid. Because wanting was dangerous.

Because he had wanted more from his father—and from Davis—and been hurt. Because it was easier to pretend that loneliness was contentment. That safety was indistinguishable from fear.

And yet all this time he had not been alone. He *had* a family. He had Bertie—and Huw—and Fern and Rupert, and he loved them, and *how* had he gotten so turned around as to deny what they meant to him?

How had he come to be here, surrounded by helpless words and afraid to tell the truth to the people he loved?

He looked up, into Bertie's open face. There was safety there, and care, and the steadfast devotion of family. He had been a fool to try to pretend he did not want those things.

"I need help," he choked out. "Please. I've—I'm trying to fix things, but I've bollocksed it all up, and I don't know what to do."

Bertie's gaze fell to the papers on the desk and then he looked up, pressed his hands together, and nodded. "Of course," he said calmly. "Tell me what's happened."

The words were so familiar—so bloody reassuring—that Arthur had to look down very hard at the desk for a moment or two before he could compose himself enough to speak.

"Lydia," he managed. "I left her in London. Davis—he wasn't the villain we'd thought, Bertie. None of it was true. And he wanted her too, had wanted her all along. I thought it would be better for her if she had the freedom to make her choice."

His voice wobbled on the words. He felt the sheer idiocy of his actions yawning before him like a great cliff, off of which he had leapt without a second thought.

"Oh, fuck," he said hoarsely. "I shouldn't have left. I know I shouldn't have. Only I was so goddamned afraid to ask her . . ."

"Ask her what?"

"To ask her to choose me."

He did not know how he would survive if she said no.

Bertie was regarding him from across the desk, his face gone unreadable. When he spoke, he almost seemed not to have heard Arthur's incoherent confession. "Did I ever tell you why Huw and I left London all those years ago?"

Arthur hesitated, uncertain. "You said 'twas easier for the two of you to be together somewhere far from the city."

Bertie inclined his head. "Yes, that's so. We left the place of my birth—the place where we met—because the father of one of our friends accused us of having led his son into iniquity and threatened to press charges against us for our relationship with each other."

Arthur gritted his teeth. He knew—of course he knew—that things had never been easy for Bertie and Huw, but he hated how helpless he was in the face of it.

"We lost our community," Bertie went on, "when we left London. Other men and women who loved as we did. Jamaican immigrants whose voices recalled to me my own parents. It was a great loss, a terrible loss—it took years for us to find a new home and begin to rebuild."

He paused a moment, nostalgia and grief twined in the gentle planes of his face. And then he fixed his gaze upon Arthur. "But even that loss, great as it was, was worth it so that we need not be parted. I would have given up anything to remain with him. Even the world."

The words were slow and featherlight, and they landed in Arthur's heart and made themselves at home there.

He knew what Bertie meant, knew it like he knew the color of Lydia's hair and the texture of her laugh.

There was nothing he would not do to remain at her side. There was no sacrifice he would forbear to make. Even if what he had to give up was every shred of protection he had built around his heart—every piece of armor put into place over a lifetime.

The softness of recollection had fallen entirely from Bertie's face as he looked at Arthur. "I had always imagined that when you fell in love, it would be the same for you."

"It is," Arthur said hoarsely. "It is that way for me."

Bertie reached out and, in one quick movement, gathered the papers on the desk into a pile. "Do you know," he said briskly, "where Huw is?"

Arthur leaned back, bewildered by the question. "I assumed he was here with you."

Bertie shook his head, tapping the papers into a stack. "He's on his way to London. We had word—well, my dear boy, we had word of Miss Hope-Wallace's impending wedding in London.

I must confess, we assumed it was to you. I was terribly sorry I had to stay with the estate and could not be there."

The words came to Arthur as if from a very great distance. "A wedding?" His stomach performed a slow, swooping revolution. "*Lydia's* wedding?"

"Mm." Bertie tipped his head at the papers. "You might want to finish your letter to her. Or"—he broke off, Arthur having leapt to his feet so quickly that his chair clattered to the ground—"you might consider speaking to her in person."

"When?" Arthur managed.

Lydia's wedding. To Davis? It must be. The sight of his brother on his knees, Lydia's hands clutched in his, was as clear in his mind as if seconds had passed and not days.

Every corpuscle of his being revolted against the thought. He could not let it happen, not without speaking to her first. He had to try.

Christ! He had not told her how he felt before he ran from London. What if she had turned to Davis because she thought that he, Arthur, had abandoned her?

You did abandon her, you spectacular fool, some part of his brain was shouting. But he could scarcely hear it over the crashing rhythm of his heart.

"A few days hence," Bertie said with maddening calm. "I suspect you'll have time, if you go quickly."

Arthur found himself halfway across the room. He had forgotten to right the chair. He turned back—dizzy, dazed—and Bertie was there, pressing the stack of blotched papers into his hands.

"What would you risk for love, my dear boy?" Bertie murmured. "Your pride? Your heart?"

Everything.

He was not certain he had even said the word aloud. But Bertie nodded as if he had heard.

And quite before he knew what was happening, Arthur was on Luath's back, riding hard for Dunkeld and the mail coach.

And from there—bloody fucking *hell*—on to London, to try to break up a wedding.

Chapter 29

Please forgive me. I love you. Let me set things right.

—from the papers of Arthur Baird

Mrs. Hope-Wallace, as usual, had responded to disappointment with millinery.

"What do you think of this one, my darling?" She held up a stiffened silk bonnet, which she had trimmed entirely around the front, sides, and top with shiny grapes of a magenta decidedly not found in nature.

She really *must* be concerned, Lydia reflected. Normally she had excellent taste in hats.

Lydia tucked her legs farther beneath her on the settee and held her teacup between her palms. "Lovely, Mother."

Georgiana, across the sitting room, gave a scoff so vehement that Bacon, who had scarcely left her side since their reunion, clambered off her lap in a huff.

Mrs. Hope-Wallace turned her gaze on Georgiana. "I beg your pardon?"

Georgiana gave her a rather wooden smile. "A tickle in my

throat, Mrs. Hope-Wallace. It's—ah—lovely. That is the only word I can think of."

Mrs. Hope-Wallace threw the bonnet down in disgust and leapt to her feet. Several discarded plumes fell from her skirts to the ground, as though she had begun slowly and decorously molting.

"This is ridiculous," she declared. She began to circumnavigate the room with the general air of an outraged pigeon.

Lydia set her teacup down. "Mother."

Huw Trefor, who had mostly spent the last day or two hiding from Lydia's mother, peered out from a wingback chair, half-concealed behind a book on hoof diseases he had discovered in the Hope-Wallace library. At the sight of Mrs. Hope-Wallace's small form striding toward him—a coronet of roses bristling with outrage on the top of her head—he ducked back behind the tome. Lydia admired his equanimity.

"How much longer does he expect us to wait upon him?" Mrs. Hope-Wallace demanded. She extended one delicate finger and nudged Huw's book aside.

"Mother," Lydia said again. Her voice was still quiet but her tone this time was firmer.

There was a part of her, even now, that wanted to make herself small. Perhaps there always would be. She would never be the model of social ease that Georgiana was, at home in any circumstance. She would never command a room like Selina.

But her own voice—soft and sometimes wobbly as it was— was enough.

She was trying very hard, despite everything, to believe that that was so. She was trying to share in Huw's steady calm.

"Ah," Huw said, "I am afraid I haven't a precise timetable for his return, but I assure you, if you'll only be patient—"

Mrs. Hope-Wallace spun on her heel. "Be patient!" She threw up her hands, and one of the roses succumbed to the power of her emotions and toppled off her head. "Be patient! When that—that—*nincompoop* returns to my household, I shall show him where to put his patience—"

There was a sudden, vociferous, and very familiar clamor in the hall. Something crashed—from the sound of it, something made of porcelain. Muffled shouting was followed by the thud of bone meeting flesh.

Lydia leapt to her feet.

"Over my—dead—body!" That was Ned, who'd quite lost his head this last week. "I—will—murder—you—first—"

Something else smashed. This time it sounded like furniture.

Arthur burst through the door.

Lydia's hand, which had been tangled in her skirts, flew up to her mouth to hold in an indelicate sound of alarm.

His curls were standing on end. He had a brilliant red contusion across one cheekbone, and nearly two weeks' growth of beard. His jacket had come off one arm, and Ned was clinging wild-eyed to the dangling fabric like a dog on a leash.

Arthur shook off Ned and crossed the room to Lydia in three long strides. "Lydia!" His hands rose as if to pull her into his arms, then dropped helplessly to his sides. He searched her face. His left eye was rapidly swelling closed. "Am I too late? Oh Christ, please tell me I'm not too late."

She paused to consider the question, her heart in her throat.

"No," she managed finally. "No, you're not too late."

He made a wordless, torn-off sound. Instead of dragging her to him, he only touched the side of her face with the tips of his fingers, gentle and searching and afraid. "Lydia," he said hoarsely.

Mrs. Hope-Wallace, whose remaining roses were now hanging drunkenly off the side of her head, interposed herself between them, jabbing one small finger into Arthur's broad chest. "You," she snapped. "How dare you?"

"I'm sorry—" he began, looking rather desperately between Lydia and her mother, but Mrs. Hope-Wallace cut him off.

"I should hope so! Why, if Mr. Trefor here had not assured us that you were called away on emergency business, I would have thought you had abandoned my daughter after one of the most terrifying experiences of her life!" She pursed her lips, glaring up at Arthur. "To leave your wife for so long with no word of when you would return! I am gravely disappointed in you, Strathrannoch. You may call me Mrs. Hope-Wallace until further notice."

Arthur looked as though he had been struck in the head. His bewildered gaze sought out Huw, still in the corner in the wingback chair. "Huw said—" His eyes, a thousand shades of blue and green and gold, came back to Lydia's face. "You're not—"

"Mother," Lydia said. "Ned. Everyone. Perhaps Lord Strathrannoch and I could have a few moments alone."

And to her great surprise, without a word of argument, everyone filed out the door, even Sir Francis Bacon. Huw, as he passed, gave her upper arm a comforting squeeze and murmured something under his breath to Arthur that sounded rather like *Grovel*.

But perhaps she had not heard correctly.

Before the door had even closed behind her family, Arthur had her hands in his. "Lydia," he said again, as if her name were the only word he knew, the only thing that was certain in a madly spinning world.

Her heart made a slow and dizzy swoop in her chest. She had hoped—oh God, how she had hoped.

He squeezed her hands, worrying his thumb across her fingers.

"I'm sorry. Oh God, I'm so sorry I left. It was a mistake, I knew as soon as I went that it was a mistake—only I did not—I could not—"

He looked down at their joined hands, her pale fingers in his larger ones. "Bertie told me you were getting married. He said that Huw had come down to London for your wedding. You're . . . not married?"

She stared up into his face in frank astonishment. "He told you *what*? Huw came to London days ago to return Georgiana's dog, not for my—" A sudden hot anger boiled up in her, and she yanked her hands out of Arthur's grasp. "My *wedding*? You came racing back in a dither because you thought I was marrying your *brother*?"

She whirled and stalked away, her pulse skipping and her cheeks growing hot with outrage.

Arthur chased after her, spinning her back to face him. "You told Davis no? You turned him down?"

"Of course I turned him down! I was under the impression that I was marrying *you*!"

Arthur caught her shoulders and held, as if he did not know whether to draw her to him or push her away. "But you wanted him first. I thought—when you knew that he was not a traitor— when you learned that his intentions had been good—"

"You thought I would flit from your bed to his, is that it? You thought I would have whichever Baird brother I was in closest proximity to?" She jerked up her chin, furious for once at the difference in their heights. She would have liked to tower over him in righteous anger. She would have liked at this particular juncture not to feel the desire—still, always—to lean into his strength.

"No!" he said, and now he did drag her closer, burying his face in her hair and enclosing her in his arms. "No. Oh God, Lydia,

I've not had a rational thought in days. Weeks. Possibly since the first moment I saw you at Strathrannoch."

She tried to hold herself stiffly in his embrace, but it was no good. He smelled of soap and sweat and burnt honey, and he was Arthur, and he was here. She tucked her cheek against his chest, and felt his whole body shudder with relief.

She knew him—had known he would not abandon her. But oh God, every part of him was solid and warm, and she was glad—so *glad*—he was here.

"Huw told my mother that you had been called away on business," she said, "but I knew better, of course. He told me to give you time. He told me not to judge you too harshly for running away. He said you'd be back." She pressed her face harder into him, into the thin linen of his shirtfront and the sturdy muscle of his chest. All the tears that she had suppressed the last nine days overflowed silently, dampening his shirt. "I trusted you. I did. But I could not help—feeling afraid—"

"Oh Christ," he groaned. His hands traced her shoulder blades, the back of her neck, tangled in her hair. "Lydia. I do not deserve you. I'm sorry. I love you. I'm so goddamned sorry I left."

She pulled back from his chest and looked up into his battered and lovely face. "Why did you do it? Surely you cannot have thought—after what passed between us—that I—"

He gave a strangled croak that might have been a laugh. "My love. My beloved. I've been trying to find the words to tell you for days now. Bertie must have grown tired of my folly and decided to prod me along."

He broke off and untangled his fingers from her hair to rifle through the pocket of his dangling jacket. He unearthed a remarkable assortment of papers—torn notes, a bit of newspaper, one extremely large folded-up sheet of foolscap—all covered in pencil and blotched ink.

"I've been trying to write to you." He pressed the papers into her hands. "If you'll only look. Oh God, Lydia, I've never been easy with words this way."

She looked down at the papers in her hands.

You are the summer and the winter, the spring and the fall . . .

My body and my heart were formed for the loving of you . . .

If there is one thing I regret above all others, it is that. That I let you believe, even for one instant, that you were less than everything to me . . .

"What is this?" she asked.

"An apology," Arthur said hoarsely. "A vow." His fingers found her face again, one thumb brushing her cheek, the line of her jaw. "I love you. I have loved you for so long. My brave and brilliant Lydia. My heart. My home."

His thumb brushed across her lips, first the upper and then the lower. She trembled.

"Your smile is my light," he murmured. "Your laugh is my shelter. If you'll"—he hesitated, then steeled himself, looking for all the world like a man facing the gallows—"if you'll allow it, Lydia Hope-Wallace, I will spend the rest of my life trying to be worthy of you. I will never leave you again. I will stand at your side when you need a partner and I will shield you when you need a place to rest. Hell, I'll move to London every Season and vote my seat in the Lords, if you want me to—only—"

He broke off. He pushed his fingers into her hair, a soft pressure against her scalp, a knotted plea. "Only say you'll have me. Only say you'll let me try to make things right. Please."

She looked up at him, tousled and bruised and uncertain. She put one hand to his chest and felt the beat of his heart—rapid, but steady. Undeniable. Hers.

"Yes," she said. "I love you, too."

And then she curled her fingers in his damp disheveled shirt and dragged him down to her mouth.

"Oh Christ," he groaned against her lips. "Oh fuck. Lydia."

And then he was kissing her, frantic and hungry and probably too rough for the state of his bruises. She gasped, and he made a desperate sound into her open mouth, kissing her harder, pulling her tighter. His hands were everywhere—her hair, her back, beneath the leg she'd somehow wrapped around him.

He picked her up and carried her until her back pressed against the wainscoted wall. A small and breathless laugh escaped her, and he pressed his forehead against hers. "I love that sound. I was so afraid I would never hear it again."

She let his letters slip to the carpet and then she wound her fingers into his hair. "I am still vexed with you, you know." She squeezed her legs around his waist to emphasize the gravity of her words, and he groaned—a different sound this time, rougher, raspier—and rocked against her.

Her head grew slightly muddled. Perhaps she had chosen the wrong way to underscore her point.

"I know," he muttered, his mouth finding her neck. "I'm glad. Be angry with me. I should like to spend the next decade making atonement." He took her earlobe between his teeth and bit down. She whimpered, and his hands tightened around her hips, holding her in place while he sucked and nibbled at her skin.

She tipped her head to the side and let him.

"What do you want?" he murmured. "What can I give to you, my love? I have about a hundred rambling letters. I have a castle, if you'd like it, though I fear it has numerous windows that need replacing and very little furniture. I have sixteen zebras." His voice was lower on the next words, almost inaudible, but she heard him anyway. "I have a family who loves you a great deal."

She reached up and caught his face in her palms, moving him back so that she could look into his eyes. "I regret to inform you, Arthur Baird, that I do not want for anything except"—her voice caught at the sight of him, so hopeful, so precious to her—"except the man I love. He's been notably absent of late."

"Never again," he vowed, and then he bent his head and brought his mouth back to hers.

Some minutes passed, in which Lydia was sensible of very little beyond Arthur and his hands and his whispers of *Hush, my love,* and then *The hell with it, let your brothers kill me, I'll die jubilant.*

She was still breathless and panting when he lifted his head. "Lydia, will you—" He broke off. His eyes were blue with yearning, gold with devotion, green with hope.

"Ask," she said. "Arthur. You can ask me anything."

His thumb made small distracting circles against her waist. "Will you say it again?"

Her lips curved up as she looked at him. Love wasn't a cautiously unfurling petal in her chest this time, but a garden, a profusion of glorious tangled blossoms.

"Which part?" she asked.

"Any of it. All of it."

"I want you," she said. "I choose you. I love you without end, without hesitation, and I will say it to you every day for the rest of our lives, if you'd like me to."

"Oh God," he said hoarsely, "I should like that very much."

"I will, then," she said. "I promise."

Chapter 30

Today is the twenty-second of November in the year of our Lord eighteen hundred and eighteen. Yesterday in front of several witnesses, I vowed to love you reverently, discreetly, advisedly, and soberly. And this morning, for you alone, I vow this: I will love you indiscreetly and unadvisedly, fearlessly and without reservation, with all my body and all my heart, today and tomorrow and until the end of time.

—from the papers of the Countess of Strathrannoch,
left upon her husband's pillow

Arthur's mouth was warm against Lydia's ear, a soft and humid caress. "Close your eyes."

"I—" Her voice was a squeak. She tried to modulate it. "I cannot!"

"Aye, you can." His arm slipped steadily around her waist. "Close your eyes, love of mine."

His hand was large and solid on her hip, and she found herself rather mesmerized by the sight. "I—I can't do it."

He hummed into her ear, a deep vibration that was almost a

laugh. "I could blindfold you. Would you like that, Lady Strath-rannoch?"

"I—I—" Oh, she'd gone shivery all over, heat rising to her skin. He could—she thought she might—

She blinked rather rapidly, recalling herself, then whirled and stuck her finger into his chest. "No! We are in the middle of a public street, and the road is made of stones that I suspect have lain here since the fifteenth century. I will not close my eyes and stumble about like I've spent the morning tippling—"

"Do you not think I would catch you, my love?"

She disregarded that with an additional poke of her finger into his delicious left pectoral muscle, directly above his heart. "And I certainly will not permit you to cover my eyes in broad daylight where anyone could see."

Now he did laugh, and the sound rippled through her, a steady tide of pleasure and affection. "But later perhaps? In the privacy of our room?"

She shifted her finger up slowly, coming to rest in the notch of his collarbone. With a sigh, she savored the feel of his warm bare skin. "I shall consider it."

He laughed again, and caught her wrist, and pressed a kiss to the tip of her index finger. "I'll hold you to that. Come then, Lady Strathrannoch. Let me take you to your wedding present. 'Tis on your own head if you're not surprised."

After their reunion at the Hope-Wallace residence, they had lost no little time in making for Scotland. Lydia did not, under any circumstances, mean to inform her mother and brothers that she and Arthur were not already wed. She had spent enough nights without him in her bedchamber—she had no desire to prolong that particular separation.

A journey to Gretna Green would have been shorter, for the purposes of a most expedient Scottish wedding. But Arthur had fixed upon the notion of returning to the coaching inn along the Great North Road where they had stayed after his escape from the Thibodeaux's carriage. She'd been surprised by his insistence—she'd supposed he would want to put the entire escapade behind them, now that the Thibodeaux were to be tried for their crimes and Davis had disentangled himself from the Home Office.

Davis had written Arthur a letter, passed on through Jasper's hands.

I know you'd wish for me to come back with you to Strathrannoch, Davis had said, *but I must learn to make my own way. I've taken a post in Upper Canada, at a timber company. But I will write to you, Arthur. I swear it.*

Arthur had been quiet for a time, then folded the letter and placed it in his coat pocket. He'd looked—not so wounded as she might have feared. Conflicted, perhaps, but at peace with Davis's decision.

His mouth had tipped up at the corners when they'd arrived back at the familiar inn on their way home to Strathrannoch. Inside she'd found a rather smug-looking Selina and her husband, as well as Georgiana and Sir Francis Bacon.

They'd arranged it all—Arthur and Selina and Georgiana together. He'd wanted her friends to be there to witness their vows.

The thought seemed to glow inside her, a bit of starlight captured somewhere in the vicinity of her heart. They'd pledged their troth right there in the public room and then retired to their bedchamber promptly and at a most indecent hour of the afternoon.

The next morning, Arthur had informed her—looking nearly as pleased as when he'd removed her shift in their bedchamber the day before—that he had a gift for her, in honor of their wedding. He'd needed to take her to it down the street, a fact which struck her as slightly alarming.

He brought her, in the end, to a milner at the edge of town. The man—a round-faced fellow of perhaps twenty—came tumbling out of his house, face alight.

"You're back!" he said happily. "And with your lady wife too! Ah, good. You'll be here to take her home with you, then?"

"Aye," said Arthur. A smile had made itself at home on his mouth, and Lydia wanted quite desperately to kiss him there. "We'll be taking her back to Strathrannoch with us."

She stared up at him in bemusement. "Taking whom with us?"

"Come, Lady Strathrannoch," he said in answer. "Let's see your gift."

He led her around to the back of the milner's cottage, whereupon she discovered a small stable yard that housed two dusty chestnuts, a sturdy gray, and—

Her mouth dropped open. Her gaze flew up to Arthur's face. "My horse!"

He was grinning quite in earnest now. "Aye. I knew you'd not wanted to part with her."

Lydia dashed toward the stocky roan, Arthur close behind her. She devoted a moment to pats and kisses, and then turned back to him. "How did you manage it? I thought never to see her again after you sold her."

He wound his fingers in the horse's red-brown mane. "As to that—well, in truth, I never sold her. I left her here, in this lad's keeping. Told him, ah"—at this he looked a trifle embarrassed, his throat going pink—"that the mare belonged to my wife, the Countess of Strathrannoch, and to treat her as such."

"I don't understand." The mare lipped at Lydia's hair, and Lydia stroked her nose. "You came back with money—enough for the mail coach and more besides. How did you manage it?"

His mouth tilted, his smile just the faintest bit lopsided. "I sold something else instead. Something that mattered to me far less than your mare did to you."

"What was it?"

He brushed her cheek with the tips of his fingers. "My father's signet ring."

Her mouth dropped open

Still smiling crookedly, he tapped her lower lip with one finger. "Dinna fash. I made a wee mold of the thing ages ago. I don't need the ring to mark my letters with the Strathrannoch seal. 'Twas sentiment, I suppose, that I kept it for as long as I did."

She managed to recover herself, and she captured his hand with her own, pressing it to her cheek. "Arthur—you did not need to do that. You could have sold the horse."

"Aye," he said, and he sobered a bit as he looked down at her, at his palm cupping her face. "I did not need to do it. But I suppose—well. It took me no little time to have this revelation, I know. But I suppose that was the first time I began to understand that I did not need to hold on to him any longer. To the lies of his that I'd let myself believe."

His fingers moved a bit beneath hers, his thumb coasting along her cheekbone and then her lower lip. "That was the first time I said it aloud, you see. That I wanted you to be my wife. That I wanted to make a family with you. I had not let myself believe, until then, that it could be possible."

Her vision had blurred, and when she blinked, two hot tears came loose and ran heedless down her cheeks. "I love you," she said. "Every day. Always. For the rest of my life."

He bent his head and brought his mouth very close to hers. "I'll hold you to that as well."

Epilogue

Dear Lydia,

You're asleep right now with the baby on your chest, and I cannot bear to wake you. I—hell, I ought to sleep as well. We've an hour at most until Maisie's up again, only I—

I wanted to tell you that I love you. There is nothing in the world so fair as you, asleep, with our daughter in your arms.

I love you today and tomorrow and into the hereafter. My heart beats for you—and for Maisie now, too.

February 1821

Dear Arthur,

I've given Maisie over to Bertie for the afternoon—I love Bertie. Did you know I love Bertie? Have we considered naming the next baby Albert? I think it rather charming. Albertina is also acceptable.

Oh! I've just spotted you out the window. Davis is perched on the pitch of the Widow Campbell's roof and you are directing from the ground.

There is some part of me that cannot regret the blizzard, you know. We will be repairing for months, I suspect, but—it brought Davis back to us. To you. I know how you've missed him.

I cannot see your face, my love, but I can tell that you are smiling. Have I told you how much I love your smile?

July 1821

Dear Lydia,

You'll be glad to hear that I've delivered your next three pamphlets to your duchess at Belvoir's directly. I expect the Seditious Meetings Act to be repealed promptly upon your orders (and will say as much in the Lords tomorrow). Your brothers are well and intend to descend en masse at Christmas, I fear.

Bleeding hell, I miss you. If you've had that baby before I return, please know that I'm never leaving your side again, no matter how urgent the Act of Parliament.

The very sun seems dimmer without you. I wake each morning from dreams of you—and yet I cannot regret the dawn, because I'm one day closer to holding you again. I miss you. I love you. I'll be home soon.

July 1821

Dear Arthur,

I am pleased to inform you that I have been delivered of a son. Due to your absence and inability to protest, I have named him Arthur.

I love you. He has red hair.

July 1821

Dear Arthur,

　I did not know the mail coach could travel so quickly!

　You appear to have fallen asleep sitting up and are unconcerned about what Maisie has put in your beard. I believe it is lemon curd, but I am not confident in this assessment.

　Thank you for coming home. I love you. It was difficult to walk around whilst missing half my heart, you know.

　By the by, you fell asleep before I could share my suspicion that your brother is courting the Widow Campbell. She threw an egg at his head. I think this will be good for him.

September 1824

Dear Lydia,

　For all you've told me you and Maisie are off picking elderberries, I can see her from our bedroom window, up on your roan. I imagine you let her ride on ahead of you. I suspect your heart is near to bursting with pride in our girl. I know mine is.

　Art is stacking parrot feathers on Jamie's wee bald head, so I assure you, things are well in hand, and I've plenty of time to write you a lengthy missive.

　I love you, dear heart. I'd never dreamed to be this happy.

February 1825

Dear Arthur,

　Did you know Huw has rescued something called a hartebeest? Do you know what that is?

　I love you and all this raucous and extraordinary life.

December 1825

Dear Lydia,

I am sorry to inform you that I saw Davis emerging from the Widow Campbell's house just before dawn, when I went down to check on the antelope calf. As it is still 1825, I win our wager. Prepare to stand and deliver this evening in our bedchamber. (Standing is not strictly required.)

February 1826

Dear Arthur,

How do you feel about a fourth small Baird as part of Davis and Elspeth's wedding party?

This question is rhetorical. I suspect this newest one will be joining us by Michaelmas.

September 1826

Dear Lydia,

It's been half a decade, and I am still very, very sorry that I missed Art's birth. That was—

You are—

Good Christ. You are, as ever, the bravest woman in the entire world. You are the very breath in my lungs, Lydia Baird. You are my heart.

I wish I could find the words to tell you the shape and breadth of my esteem for you. You are my wife, my own, my dearest love. The most gifted writer, the cleverest planner, the center of our family.

None of this—not the village, not the castle, not Davis and Elspeth, not our own wild bunch—would be here and whole without you.

Everything I am I owe to you, and everything I have is yours. In all my life, the greatest thing I will ever do is this: wake each day and love you down to the depths of my soul.

The baby's stirring. If I can settle him and let you rest a moment, your head upon my shoulder, I'll count my life worthwhile.

Author's Note

Perhaps surprisingly, quite a lot of the events of this novel are drawn from historical reality!

In February 1818, a plot to kill the Duke of Wellington in Paris was foiled after a Scottish aristocrat, Lord Charles Kinnaird, informed Wellington's staff that he had been approached by exiled Bonapartists who had attempted to secure his cooperation in the assassination attempt. The exiled Bonapartists were never convicted.

In November 1818, the occupation of France ended, and Wellington returned to England, where he was greeted with a military parade. St. Saviour's Church was indeed under renovation in 1818—it's now known as Southwark Cathedral. There was not, so far as I know, a plot to assassinate Wellington at the parade.

The rifle scope that Arthur invents is also based in fact. The first attempts to build and patent a telescopic rifle sight began in the late eighteenth century. Early designs proved impractical, and the technology was not perfected until the 1830s.

The letter that Arthur writes about the Highland Clearances is a lightly edited version of a real newspaper account from 1819.

The Clearances, and the attendant removal of thousands of people from their ancestral land in the name of technological innovation, were a major topic of British political debate in the early nineteenth century.

The excerpt from Lydia's letter to Davis in Chapter 7 is borrowed from Maria Edgeworth's 1834 novel *Helen*. The titles of Lydia's pamphlets are taken from works by Mary Astell (1706) and Judith Sargent Murray (1790), as well as the parliamentary speeches of radical Scottish MP Joseph Hume (1828).

The animals that Huw rescues from various menageries are—remarkably—all drawn from the itemized list of creatures held by the thirteenth Earl of Derby. Derby's home menagerie in northwest England included over fifteen hundred animals in the midnineteenth century. There were even more surprising animals on the list, which I did not include out of fear that the facts would be too preposterous to be believed.

Acknowledgments

And so we come to the end of Book 2! Second books are notoriously difficult to write, but this one somehow spilled easily onto the page?

No, just kidding, I have an entire other novel's worth of discarded scenes, and the fact that this is a coherent narrative is due to the support and enthusiasm of many wonderful people. Honestly, the only scene that didn't change from the first draft is the one with the zebras.

Thus, my first thanks have to go to the early readers of this book, most of whom read entirely unrecognizable versions in which Lydia and Arthur commit crimes all over Scotland. Marianne Marston, Kate Lane, Leigh Donnelly, Bella Barnes, Jane Maguire, Jenna McKinley, and Colleen Kelly—thank you, thank you, thank you. Colleen especially—thank you for putting "lol" a hundred times, helping me find the best parts of the story, and also for giving the book its working title (*Pumpkin Spice Earl*).

Immense thanks to BookEnds Literary and especially to my agent, Jessica Alvarez, who is an absolute rock and has been a force of calm, practical positivity in the whirlwind of bringing my historical romances into the world. Look at all these books?! Who would have predicted it?!

I am deeply grateful to everyone at St. Martin's Press who's worked on the books and championed my historical romance novels and novellas. My editor, Christina Lopez, is a gem, and I am enormously grateful for her enthusiasm and thoughtful editorial guidance. (I honestly did not think I would ever meet someone quicker with emails than Jessica?? The two of you are more precious than gold, honestly.) I also want to thank my former editor Lisa Bonvissuto, who helped shape Lydia and Arthur's story into what it is today. I'm so grateful to have gotten to work with you!

Thank you also to art director Olga Grlic, illustrator Petra Braun (seriously, this cover is so far beyond my wildest dreams!), as well as my fantastic marketing and publicity team, including Kejana Ayala and Angela Tabor. Thank you to copy editor Martha Cipolla, production editor Laurie Henderson, and managing editor Chrisinda Lynch. Thank you also to my sensitivity readers, including Kat Lewis and Alexia (@bookishends), for your thoughtful guidance.

Thank you to the librarians and booksellers who have championed the Belvoir's books, with an extra sob of hysterical gratitude to Blue Cypress Books in New Orleans, particularly my love Jodi Laidlaw. You make everything special.

Special shout-out to SF2.0 and the dream team (Myah Ariel, Naina Kumar, Laura Piper Lee, Ellie Palmer, and Jill Tew) for all the earl puns, even though we only got to stick two on the cover. *A Whole New Earl* still has legs, I think.

Thank you to my dearest friend Felicity Niven, without whom this would be a much lonelier and less fun career. Thank you to the authors who have generously read and blurbed the Belvoir's novels and the Halifax novellas, talked up the books on social media, been in conversation with me at events, etc., etc. Romance is a lovely and kind community, and I am so grateful to be here.

Thank you to my family, especially the little Vastis, my raucous and hilarious darlings.

Thank you to Matt, for everything. You are the most joyful part of my life. (And now you really can't ever live down missing the birth of our son, because I have committed it to fiction!)

Finally, thank you to everyone who's read, reviewed, shared, preordered, made art about, and otherwise supported these gleeful, sexy, earnest books of mine. Thank you for loving my characters and for making it possible for me to continue to write the stories of my heart. I can't wait to share Georgiana and Cat with you very soon!

About the Author

Scarlet Raven Photography

Alexandra Vasti is a British literature professor who has loved historical romance since age eleven. After finishing her PhD at Columbia University in New York City, she moved to New Orleans, where she lives with her very large and noisy family. Her books, including the Halifax Hellions series and her debut novel, *Ne'er Duke Well,* have been featured in *The New York Times, Entertainment Weekly,* and elsewhere. For sneak peeks and exclusive bonus content in the world of *Earl Crush,* sign up for Alex's newsletter at alexandravasti.com.